LOVE AND OTHER ENCHANTMENTS

"Masha Zur Glozman's novel draws us into two worlds that seem, at first glance, radically different from one another: contemporary, pleasure-seeking Tel Aviv and the world of the thirteenth-century Crusades. The novel's most impressive achievement is the way it exposes the deep similarity between human relationships in any era. The thirteenth-century knight is not so different from the protagonist living in the twenty-first century: both long to extract from life all that can be extracted—from sweets to loves."

—Israeli Ministry of Culture Debut Novel Prize, 2020

LOVE AND OTHER ENCHANTMENTS

A TIME-CROSSED TALE

MASHA ZUR-GLOZMAN

Originally translated by Joanna Chen and Zoe Jordan

UNION SQUARE & CO.

NEW YORK

Union Square & Co.
Hachette Book Group
1290 Avenue of the Americas, New York, NY 10104
unionsquareandco.com
@unionsqandco

Originally published as *Lehasbia et ha-drakon* (*Satisfying the Dragon*) in Hebrew by Yedioth Books, Rishon LeZion, Israel, in 2019.

First U.S. Edition: July 2026

Union Square & Co. is an imprint of Grand Central Publishing, a division of Hachette Book Group, Inc. The Union Square & Co. name and logo are registered trademarks of Hachette Book Group, Inc.

The publisher is not responsible for websites (or their content) that are not owned by the publisher.

Contact your local bookseller or special.markets@hbgusa.com regarding special discounts for bulk purchases.

Print book interior design by Rich Hazelton

Library of Congress Control Number is available upon request.

ISBNs: 978-1-4549-6147-5 (paperback), 978-1-4549-6148-2 (ebook)

Printed in Canada
MRQ-L

10 9 8 7 6 5 4 3 2 1

Dedicated to all the loves:
jarred, spoiled, smoked, preserved,
brined, and frozen—and most of all,
to the one that still simmers on the stove.

Atlit (Château Pèlerin), Kingdom of Jerusalem
c. 1240 CE

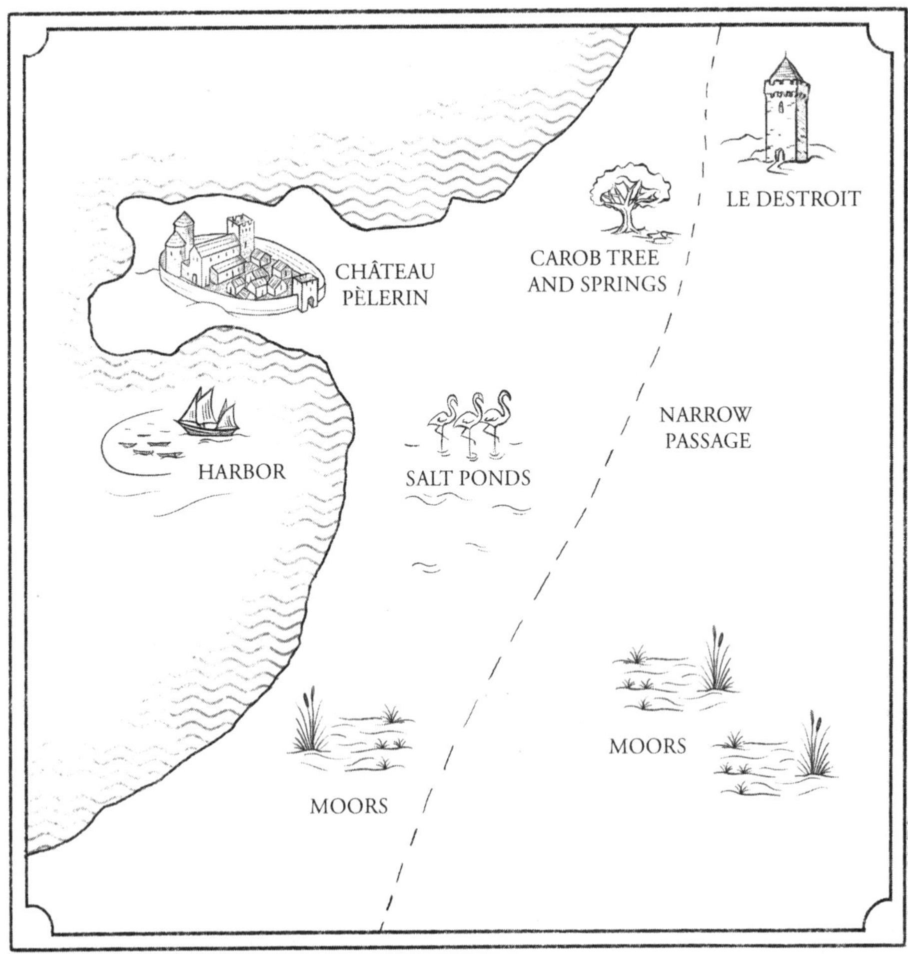

Atlit, Israel

Present day

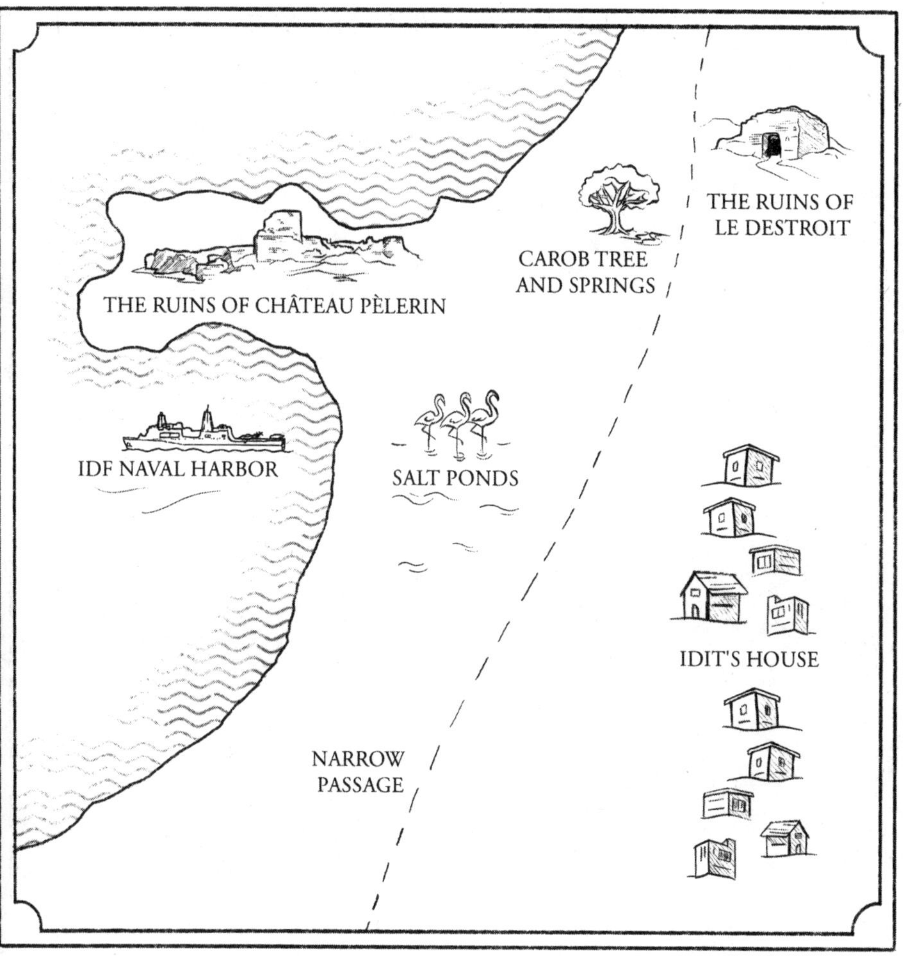

CHAPTER 1

I sprinkled salt over the salad and looked up at the horizon to the sun as it rolled toward the sea. I had become accustomed to high-rises, other people's windows, air conditioners, antennae, solar water heaters, and cranes. The sight of a clean, unfettered skyline blurred by smudges of water and the sun's glare was mesmerizing to me.

I'd had plenty of opportunities to contemplate the sea—on vacation, during random hours of recreation, on occasional trips to the beaches of Tel Aviv. But I was captivated by this now-permanent backdrop to my daily routine. When the glare burst through the window behind my head in the bathroom mirror—wavy brown hair, foxlike face, green eyes—suddenly, a blue horizon stretched between my curls and the mirror frame like a pet sprawling in the background of a portrait.

I reveled in the fusion of this fresh view into our daily routine, which did not change much with our move from Tel Aviv to Atlit. Halimi was a creature of habit—something that always surprises people familiar only with his proclivity for clubbing. He usually wakes up very early in the morning, gets out of bed a few seconds after opening his eyes, and powers up with strong black coffee and two Camel cigarettes. His brutal morning cough heralds the start of my day.

After Halimi recovers from his hacking fit, he goes out to buy fresh bread rolls. The rolls are just an excuse. A morning stroll in the fresh air is something he's been doing since his early teens, whatever the weather—be it the August sun already beating down at eight in the morning or a torrent of December rain, though he hates rain more than cats do. Even during his long years of partying, he always insisted on leaving the club in the early hours of the morning. "I love hearing the birds wake up," he'd say. Usually, he said this to the girl who happened to be with him at the time, as he offered to treat her to breakfast in some dive.

It was like that with us too. We met in the spring at one of those birthday parties that begins on a Friday afternoon and, depending on human chemistry and the quality of alcohol and drugs and hors d'oeuvres, lasts through Saturday morning. There's always someone playing guitar, and someone else holding court with earnest emotion. The older the crowd, the greater the number of couples with young children in tow, trying in vain to relive their carefree years but facing the fact that they are now grumpy parents trying to control toddlers who clearly skipped their afternoon naps.

I arrived at this particular birthday party with Ronen, my boyfriend at the time, a morose character and a childhood friend of Eran, whose birthday it was. None of my own crowd was there, aside from Eran and his wife, Hila. Here and there flashed familiar faces—from the café, the neighborhood, dinner at Eran and Hila's, from Facebook.

Ronen was a mistake from the beginning. He was the silent type, which attracted me at first since he was the polar opposite of the man I'd dated before him. Meanwhile, I'd become totally sick of his silences. For some time, I'd been debating the least stressful way of breaking up with him. We argued constantly, including right before we left for the party.

We were in my bedroom. He wanted me to wear a leather miniskirt, but his very insistence made me go for a long skirt and high-necked shirt instead. "You look like a nun," he'd said with distaste, and from that moment on we didn't have a civil word to say to each other. Shortly after arriving at Eran and Hila's palatial rooftop, we went our separate ways. Ronen wrapped himself in silence like a cloak, nursing a bottle of beer and drinking from it in small, annoying sips. I went off to chat with Hila while Ronen lay down on one of the swanky daybeds as though dead, his dark tea-shade sunglasses deterring any eye contact.

While I was chatting with Hila, I noticed Halimi giving me looks from the lounger he was sprawled across, his long limbs stretched out every which way. Back then I didn't know he was blind as a bat and, for some insane reason, avoided eyeglasses and contact lenses. The look I interpreted as bold was, in fact, a result of the fact that his world was a blur beyond a radius of three feet.

I knew who Halimi was. There had been a bit of an uproar when he was appointed chief editor of a popular women's magazine; rumor had it he was a womanizer. He had a long nose, a wide forehead, and a pointed chin, while his lips were narrow and his cheeks sunken—by no means your classic heartthrob, but I'd seen women of all ages lose their cool in his presence. I often worked in a corner of the café where he hung out in the mornings, and more than once I looked up from my old laptop to see a woman throw her head back in laughter at something Halimi had said.

Halimi, for his part, couldn't see me clearly while I chatted with Hila, but he had a radar that he'd perfected through years of trial and error. He noticed the way I held myself ("It seemed so graceful to me, the way you moved your head and hands," he told me later) and could tell immediately that I was checking him out. He didn't see himself as a womanizer, but more like an old-fashioned, intrepid explorer. He was a true Casanova in his love for women—he didn't have specific tastes or fixed preferences. He could get turned on by women much younger than him, older than him, thin ones, thick ones, neurotic or stoic, impetuous or inhibited, flirty or hard to get. Crying didn't inhibit him; sometimes it even turned him on. He frequently got involved with women whose lives were already bursting at the seams—a husband, kids, a career. In short, any woman who crossed paths with him and who aroused the slightest spark of interest became uncharted territory on his life's map of conquests.

All that I understood much later.

Hila, perceptive as ever, immediately noticed the looks we were giving each other. "Do you know him?" she asked, waving Halimi over with a smile.

He smiled back and gestured with his hands, "Come over *here*."

"Wait," Hila motioned to him, her thumb and forefinger pressed together.

"Just in passing," I said. "Sometimes I see him at the café."

"Okay, well, if you want a hookup, he's your man." Hila loathed Ronen but was fond of me. She knew our relationship was on the rocks and clearly wasn't shy about introducing me to someone else. It always amused me, and this time I felt an almost physical urge to dive into an adventure, as insignificant as it might be, just to bug Ronen.

"He likes to fill the role of"—Hila's eyes wandered, as if she were trying to capture the precise phrase—"momentary fantasy." She gave me a salacious look and added, "He's also got a weakness for women who are already taken." She told me of Halimi's talent for dipping into women's lives, making them feel hot and wanted. When he was done, Halimi would disappear in a cloud of debris, sometimes trying to make amends by running a flattering story about them in the magazine or signing off on a reference for a lucrative job. She rattled off a list of names borne on the wings of Tel Aviv gossip, and I restrained myself from asking her if her name was also on that list.

Halimi kept staring at us, holding a cigarette in one hand and a glass of whiskey in the other. I was almost positive he knew what we were talking about, and I felt my cheeks burn.

"I need a cigarette," I said suddenly. Hila pulled out a pouch of rolling tobacco for me, but I shook my head. "A real cigarette," I said. I flashed her a smile and walked over to Halimi.

Halimi straightened up, feigning surprise. "Can I borrow a cigarette?" I asked, my heart pounding a little faster than usual. He vaguely recognized me, telling me later that he'd noticed the "cute lady" buried in her laptop at the café most days. Sometimes we nodded to each other, and once I asked him for a light. He claimed to remember this because he'd noticed my green eyes—but somehow, he had never hit on me before.

"Borrow?" he smirked, scratching his cheek. "Sure, you can borrow one. But only if you return it with interest." His speech was nasal, but there was something captivating about it. He elongated certain vowels with a pronounced sluggishness, and it was obvious he had a fetish for words. "They're Camels," he warned me, pulling out a crumpled pack from the pocket of his skinny jeans.

"My favorite," I said.

The sun had already set, and the golden patches that mottled the fortress of Atlit dissipated into shadows. I added olive oil to the salad, removed slices of toast from the toaster, and went out into the yard. Lily, hair pale and unkempt, cheeks flushed, sat on the blue plastic swing we'd tied to one of the boughs of the big Persian lilac tree. Her legs hung between the safety bars, and she swayed backward and forward in the light breeze. Halimi sat by her side on a chair he'd dragged over from the deck and fiddled with his phone.

"Dinner's ready," I said quietly. Halimi jumped, startled, and his guilty smile immediately hardened my jaw. *Son of a bitch*, I said to myself, careful not to reveal my annoyance. Halimi assumed a serious expression, which was a novelty. I ignored him and went over to Lily.

I picked her up off the swing and embraced her warm little body. The evening breeze turned cool, making me shiver in my shirt.

"Mommy," Lily said, trying to grab my eyelashes. "Why do you have eyes?"

I smiled at her and said, "That's quite a question."

Halimi slipped his phone into his pocket. "Diti, quit being so suspicious, it's nonsense." He walked over and hugged me from behind.

"Life is mostly nonsense," I answered, my body unyielding. "It's just that I thought you might lay off your nonsense for a couple of weeks out of respect for our new life." I spat out the words *new life* in a mocking tone.

Halimi moved away and took a deep breath—the kind meant to convey patience but that actually conveyed a complete lack of it. I wanted to cry. All the afternoon tenderness, the sunset, and the tingling memories, all of it dissolved in the evening chill. "Idit, don't act like an idiot," Halimi said, in an icier tone than he probably intended, which depressed me even more. I knew what he was up to, and he knew I knew. He didn't bother apologizing or try to make it up to me; he assumed a combat position. We'd had this "you make the rules" and "but you didn't exactly follow them" conversation a thousand times. A thousand times I swore to myself that I'd play his game, and a thousand times I realized that there were no winners in this game.

CHAPTER 2

And may I ask the fair maiden's name?" Halimi asked me, openly flirting as he lit my cigarette. "Idit. Rozhevsky," I said, exhaling smoke.

"Hmm, Rozhevsky," he repeated after me. "What's that, Russian?"

"Daughter of," I answered with a smile.

"I dig the Russians," he said playfully. I wondered if he presumed I knew who he was.

"And the lord's name?" I courted him back.

"Saul Halimi," he said, looking me in the eyes. "But everyone calls me Halimi."

I'd always been good at predicting what the future might hold. I used to go to interviews, for example, imagining the intimacy I might develop with the dictionaries stacked behind the editor's desk or the hallway leading to the restrooms. Now I imagined the two of us making out in a hammock, and I'd already nicknamed him "Lim-Lim." I almost said it out loud just to shock him but stopped myself. "Did you want to say something?" he asked. It was mesmerizing how he projected the idea that he already knew what I was thinking. With a stab of guilt, I peered at Ronen, still reclined on the daybed with his tea shades on the end of his nose, a few feet from us. Probably snoring.

"Boyfriend?" Halimi asked with interest, following my gaze. "Something like that," I answered uneasily, then recalled Hila's words. I looked at Halimi again—swarthy, laid-back, with large, strong hands. *I really do want to get properly fucked*, I thought and turned my entire body toward him.

We ate dinner quietly. Lily filled the silence with her own demands. "I want yogurt, not cheese!" she yelled when she saw the carton of soft cheese, something she'd requested only seconds earlier. I usually tried not to give in to her sporadic tyranny, but this time I acquiesced, switching the soft cheese for yogurt.

"Mommy, wear a dress now," Lily said.

I sighed and said, "Why?"

"Because you look nice in a dress," Lily and Halimi said together. Although this little dialogue had taken place dozens of times, Lily was startled that Halimi knew what she was going to say. "Funny Daddy!" she giggled and then repeated in an imperious tone, "Mommy, wear a dress now."

"Because you look nice in a dress," Halimi repeated.

After a bath and a bedtime story and a good-night kiss, Halimi switched off the light in Lily's room and came into the living room. I was already curled up on the couch. There was a half-smoked joint on the table, and I was half-heartedly searching for something to watch on Netflix. Halimi didn't like weed; he was mostly into chemicals and alcohol, but he always bought me the purest medical cannabis he could find. Naturally, he had the best connections.

"Still moody?" he asked in his soft nasal voice. He smelled of clean laundry and Lily's soap. It was difficult to be angry with such a devoted father who'd just finished the long and arduous process of putting Lily to bed while I had rolled a joint and smoked it peacefully on the balcony, straining to hear the sound of the waves from the shore. It was much easier to give in to him, to snuggle up to his chest and let him stroke my arm.

"I hate getting mad about these things," I said, imagining the slut he'd probably texted earlier. I figured she was a production assistant with full lips and big tits, perhaps the one who'd arranged the meeting with the reality TV show star he'd interviewed the week before. It didn't surprise me but made me somewhat wistful how the slender wedding ring on his finger made him even more attractive to those vibrant young women whom he charmed with his knowledge and generosity. "I hate you getting mad about those things too," he agreed, and I smiled despite myself.

There was no point in arguing. Our conversations on the subject went nowhere—every time I thought we'd reached an understanding, I realized I was delusional. Whenever it looked like I was going to break up with him, he would threaten to kill himself and embark on a self-destructive rampage. It always ended with the two of us breaking down in tears, hiccupping pledges of love to each other.

Two months after we first hooked up, he began pestering me to have a kid. "Have my baby" became the catchphrase of our first year together. "Put the kettle on?" I'd text him on my way home. "Only if you'll have my baby," he'd text back. At first I thought he was just saying it, but he pushed the topic even when we were fucking, deadly serious. "I'm going to put a baby in you," he would whisper while penetrating me deeper and deeper, pinning my hands above my head. Whenever I recalled this, I was faintly embarrassed, but it made me come every time.

Back at the party, a long shadow obscured Halimi's face, while I laughed at his story about a dangerous liaison with a reindeer in the snowy reaches of Lapland. I looked up and saw Ronen standing over me. The tea shades were now resting on his forehead, there were pretzel crumbs on his trimmed beard, and his eyes were even narrower than usual.

"Having fun?" he asked, his voice venomous.

"Totally!" I said and opened my eyes wide in his direction. *Ugh*, I thought with revulsion, *how could I have slept with this creep?*

Halimi looked him over with interest.

"Right, I'm out of here," Ronen said, expecting me to follow.

"Bye then," I said. "We'll catch up later," I added, so as not to seem like a complete asshole. Ronen raised his eyebrows, threw a virulent glance in Halimi's direction, and walked off. Relieved, I watched him walk away.

"So, he's your boyfriend?" Halimi asked, removing an invisible crumb from a lock of my hair.

"Was my boyfriend, I guess," I said.

"Seems like a nice guy," Halimi said lazily.

"Don't be a jerk," I said.

We fell silent and watched Ronen go. When he paused to say goodbye to Eran, they both cast glances in my direction. Eran looked a bit spooked, but Hila, who was standing next to him, raised her glass in our direction.

"What a sweetheart," Halimi said.

"Totally," I agreed and then added, "A good fuck too?"

Halimi choked on his drink. "What, she told you?"

"Actually, no, but I guessed as much," I beamed. Halimi smiled back, revealing small, overcrowded teeth. He surveyed me with renewed appreciation.

"So was she?" I asked again.

"Was she what? A good fuck?" Halimi repeated my question. I shrugged my shoulders and took a drag of my cigarette.

"And why would you want to know?" he quizzed me.

I exhaled smoke slowly. "You can never tell," I replied. "Maybe I want to sleep with her?" He laughed and stood up. "I'll bring drinks, and then I'll tell you everything you want to know. Whiskey?"

"I don't really drink," I admitted, one hand dipping into my bag for the little joint I always had ready at parties.

"Today, you do," Halimi determined and blinked once in my direction, like an owl.

"You've got nerve," I said.

"Damn straight," Halimi agreed. "Whiskey?"

"Vodka," I replied. "And something nice to wash it down with."

He liked that.

"'Vodka and something nice to wash it down with,'" he repeated. "Did you walk straight out of a Russian novel?"

"Perhaps," I said.

"'Vodka,'" Halimi repeated again, as if to himself, and moved in the direction of the drinks.

I got out of the uncomfortable chair I'd been sitting on and dragged a sun lounger over. I flopped onto it with a sense of liberation. I checked out all the couples who were gathering up their overheated children, barking orders at each other, and dedicated myself entirely to the pleasure of being free. I thought with gratification of the novel I'd finished translating a few days before, meaning I was free for the next two weeks. I looked at Halimi chatting with Eran and whispering something to Hila—who erupted in howls of laughter that disturbed a raven on a nearby antenna. I wondered how wanton I'd feel if I slept with him that very night.

The movie finished. I tried to reach the remote to turn it off, but Halimi's head had cemented my arm to the couch, and I had to squirm my way out from under him. He lay on his side, his nose thrust into the embroidered cushions. I stopped the movie as the credits began rolling and switched off the TV. A distant noise made me look up, then silence resumed.

New sounds, I told myself. *I need to get used to those too.* It takes time to differentiate among the different barks of the neighborhood dogs, the habitual gurgling in the pipes, the rumbling that sounds like footsteps but is simply the generator adjusting itself.

Halimi's cell phone vibrated. He usually kept it close to his person, and I preferred not to snoop too much. More than once, I'd come across text messages that sickened me and made me hate him. This time, in a rush of adrenaline, I reached for the phone, ready and waiting to hate him, to accuse him of being a complete bastard. I imagined the two of us fighting, me scratching and kicking, him slapping and shaking me. Not that anything like that had ever happened.

"Saul, call when you can" was the WhatsApp message in French. His mom. I put the phone on the table and hugged Halimi from behind. A few hours later, we dragged ourselves, exhausted, off to bed.

In the morning, after stashing fresh rolls in the bread bin, Halimi sat down beside me on the bed. He stroked my head, and I opened drowsy eyes, my hand searching for his. "How was it with Liloosh?" I mumbled. Lily was still undergoing a period of adjustment at her new preschool, and I was grateful to Halimi for not stressing over her predictable morning tears when he parted from her in the preschool yard. "Awesome, she barely cried," Halimi answered, pleased with himself. "There's a kid there who cries much more than Lily," he added. He leaned forward and planted a gentle kiss on my nose. He continued kissing me, traversing my mouth, then my neck, his hands gathering up all my warm flesh.

"Are you trying to take advantage of me?" I asked, tingling a little at his touch.

"Absolutely," Halimi replied. He spread my legs with his knee.

"I'm not in the mood to fool around. Let's just fuck, okay?"

"No problem at all," Halimi said, and I flipped over onto my belly.

Later, he announced that his mom was arriving from France in a couple of days. Predictably, this filled me with both happiness and anxiety. My relationship with Simone Halimi was suffused with affection and mutual interests, but there was something else. She'd immigrated to Israel from France alone, about forty-five years ago—a young widow, pregnant, with two small children. She got by thanks to an extensive network of family connections and sheer willpower. She worked for years as a secretary in one of the government offices, steadily working her way up to the most senior position.

She had returned to Paris ten and a half years ago, completed her graduate studies, and continued on to a PhD, specializing in medieval illuminated manuscripts. She married Richard, a Frenchman who was both loaded and highly cultured. Together, they led an exceptionally enviable life. She would send photos of herself and Richard via WhatsApp—hanging out in an Alpine chalet or gallivanting around a millinery shop. She was going to celebrate her seventieth birthday next year, but anyone looking at her from behind would dramatically underestimate her age. From the front, the years of struggle were plain to see, but her face projected beauty and fortitude. Her thick hair was white and hung over her shoulders with a vintage hair clip. The first time I saw her, I knew that this was how I wanted to age. I also knew I didn't stand a chance.

Halimi adored Simone. He worshipped her, and she accepted his adoration with magnanimity and love. Whenever she came to Israel, he picked her up from the airport, whatever the weather or time of day. He made a point of bringing a flower to present to her in the arrival hall. Sometimes it withered a little before reaching her ladyship, but the thought was what counted, and Simone always inhaled the scent of the flower with joy. With a mother-in-law like that, it didn't matter how much affection or how many mutual interests we shared. I always felt like the dirt the flower was plucked from.

"Let's get the hell out of here," Halimi said. Eran and Hila had enough money to rent a spacious apartment with a massive roof on a quiet street in the city center, not to mention classy catering and expensive drinks for a thirty-second birthday party. Halimi and I were among the last to leave, and now we were obstructing the cleaning crew that had invaded the roof—clearing tables, folding chairs, disposing of leftover food, and scrubbing down surfaces. We took leave of our friends and went out into the quiet gloaming of Tel Aviv on a Friday evening.

Here and there, traditional Sabbath melodies wafted through the air. It always amused me to hear them in the mostly secular metropolis, but it also soothed me. A few sparrows fluttered between power lines and ficus trees. Bicycles whizzed by, pedaled by hipsters, young families, delivery boys.

The vodka was rushing through my blood, and I was afraid I was going to throw up or pass out. "Wait up a minute," I said and sat down on a low stone wall.

"Are you okay?" Halimi asked.

"I told you I don't drink," I replied.

"What kind of a Russian are you?" Halimi retorted. "You should keep on drinking so you'll feel better." I laughed, which encouraged him to continue. "I'll tell you what: We'll go get something to eat. I went to an excellent Japanese place yesterday—do you like Japanese food?"

I thought about it for a moment.

"I love it, but I don't think sushi is going to do me any good right now," I said. "I'd rather take a nap."

Halimi scrutinized me. "Come to my place," he finally said. "I give you my word, I won't take advantage of you." I rolled my eyes at him but couldn't suppress a smile. "Not right away, in any case," he added.

"So, what *will* you do with me?" I asked. "Do you live far from here?"

"I'd be happy just to watch you nap," Halimi said. "And I live right here, just around the corner."

Later, he said he found me sweet. I had laughed when he tried to flatter me, while my eyes said, "Give me a break" and my hand pushed him away. I had looked him right in the eyes with what he called "polite audacity" and answered his penetrating questions honestly ("It aroused tenderness in me," he said, the implication being that it aroused him sexually). It clearly turned him on that I made my living as a translator, that I spoke four languages and could read and write in another four—two of them dead. He said he couldn't quite figure me out and hoped I would continue to remain a mystery for a while longer.

It was difficult to explain why, but I trusted him completely. It appeared he had no hidden agenda. He was seducing me with my consent. I felt comfortable with him, something I hadn't felt with any other man for a very long time. I didn't allow myself to be swept away by this feeling but followed him up to his apartment anyway. The thought of my lonely little bedroom in a shared apartment was slightly depressing; I was also curious to see where he lived.

It was your typical bachelor pad, with sharp angles and lots of empty space. Here and there were crates yet to be unpacked, even though he'd been living there for a year and a half. Still, there were two bookshelves full of books, a massive and impressive collection of LPs, and a few posters of old movies on the walls (I only recognized Stanley Kubrick's *Lolita*).

"Make yourself at home," Halimi said, and I kicked off my shoes and deliberated rolling a joint or just collapsing onto the couch. Halimi went into the kitchen, and I heard him filling the kettle with water. I decided to roll a joint.

I heard him peeing, which made me horny. I wondered if the length of his nose said anything about the length of his penis and idly speculated that I'd probably find out soon. When he came back, I noticed he didn't sit down on the couch next to me but settled into a small armchair close by. He clearly didn't want to put any pressure on me. He fished out another Camel and shook his finger *no* when I offered him a hit of the joint.

"I don't like how it makes me feel," he said. I shrugged my shoulders and took a couple more hits. Suddenly, I felt lonely, a bit superfluous.

"Music!" Halimi exclaimed as if he'd just solved a riddle. He turned to his computer. "Chill or mind-blowing?" he asked.

"Chill, chill," I said. My mind was already blown.

In the middle of the night, I awoke to the sound of Simone and Halimi entering the house and then the quiet hum of their conversation in French and Hebrew. I heard the door to Lily's bedroom opening, soft steps, and then the door closing. Simone murmured superlatives, and I hoped she liked the way I'd arranged the house. It had originally belonged to Richard's family—he'd inherited the land from an elderly uncle some years earlier, although the family wasn't Jewish. At the time, I had not understood exactly what the story was, and then I forgot all about it. When the last tenants left, Richard didn't have time or feel compelled to rent out the place again, so it stood empty for two years. We decided to move there after our last crisis, the one that almost finished us completely. We left Tel Aviv and the parties, the friends, the all-night kiosks, cafés and clubs, bike paths, and construction sites, in an attempt (for the last time, I promised myself) at a fresh start.

I'd always regarded myself as a person with good taste and hated to think I was ever sucking up to Simone, but when I'd arranged a bouquet of orange peonies the day before in the blue jug she'd given me, I'd hoped she would appreciate the color combination. Halimi was indifferent about anything to do with décor, but he was always happy to go along with my collecting schemes, whether it was an old couch I came across and wanted to reupholster or a beautiful old laboratory cabinet I found abandoned in a schoolyard. In our house in Atlit—a spacious two-story single-family home that looked from the outside like all the other houses in the neighborhood—I finally managed to create the ambiance I'd always wanted with textiles, carpets, and seating areas. I meticulously considered the look of each wall with appropriate pictures and light fixtures. Now, I was consumed by the idea that Simone might find it excessive.

I went back to sleep, knowing that Halimi and Simone had much to discuss, and even if they didn't, I was happy to give them a few hours of privacy. I never knew how much Simone knew of her son's bad habits and to what extent he shared our ups and downs with her. Either way, I figured she had probably worked it out for herself.

When I finally got up at 10:00 a.m., the house was quiet. "Where are you?" I texted Halimi. "We're down at the beach with my mom," he wrote back. *So, he didn't send Lily to preschool today*, I thought with a twinge of annoyance. She needed to get used to the new routine. But the thought of the three of them on the beach made me feel a certain tranquility. "Don't be a bitch," I said out loud. I made coffee and sat on the balcony. "Great. Buy eggs and cottage cheese if you get the chance," I texted back.

An hour later, I heard their voices approaching and the key turning in the lock. I glanced around the house, checking that there were no dirty socks littering the couch. When they entered the living room, Lily raced over to me, eager to show me the treasures from the beach. "Shells!" she squealed. I laughed and turned to Halimi and Simone. "Look what we found," said Halimi. He pulled out a weird-looking copper coin.

"*Bonjour, ma petite chouchou,*" Simone said to me and hugged me warmly. Everyone in the Halimi family spoke French mixed with Hebrew, a mishmash I easily adopted. I surrendered to Simone's hug, sensing there was more to it than just happiness at seeing me again. I was now positive that Halimi had told her about his ex-coworker and ex-lover, Nina, and the chaos her presence left in our lives. I didn't care. On the contrary, I hoped Simone had scolded him, and I wondered whether she'd had anything to do with Halimi's proposition two months ago that we move to the Atlit house.

"Let's take a look," I said, curious. Halimi took a bottle of vinegar and a rag and began polishing the coin.

"I think it might be a dinar from Crusader times," Simone said.

"Crusaders? You think?!" I asked with increased interest. I leaned over Halimi's shoulder. The coin was small and tarnished, not quite round, its surface embossed with something I couldn't decipher. "Do you think it's worth anything?" Halimi asked his mom in French. "We'll see," she replied.

"I wanna coin too!" Lily shouted.

"Ask nicely," Halimi said.

Lily glared at him and then acquiesced: "I wanna coin too, please."

He gave her a ten-agorot coin out of his pocket. She played with it for a few minutes and then tucked it into my purse, which was hanging off a chair.

"Keep it safe for me," she said. "And don't spend it!" she added in the tone of a kindergarten teacher.

Simone and I made dinner while Halimi played with Lily. He hoisted her onto his shoulders and tickled her until she laughed so hard, she almost choked. Roaring, she raised her plastic sword, and they dueled. His cell phone rested on the table in the living room, and I noticed that he hardly glanced at it. I wondered if this was a calculated move on his part—so like him—but decided not to go there. Simone was a great cook, naturally, and we got on well with me as sous chef. Later, I tucked Lily into bed, read her *The Runaway Bunny* twice, and fell asleep beside her.

Halimi woke me, and we sat with Simone for a while over a bottle of port she'd brought especially for me. She told us about a new paper she was writing about the illumination workshops in the Crusader city of Acre. She also described her last trip abroad with Richard—a tour of Crusader castles in Cyprus. Halimi told her about our new exurban life, the cashiers in the supermarket and the local postman, Lily's preschool teachers, and the different sand in Atlit.

Later, in bed, Halimi whispered, "I've got an awesome idea."

"Go on," I whispered back.

"Let's leave Liloosh with my mom for the weekend, and we'll do mushrooms," he said, nuzzling up to me under the blanket. "We haven't tripped for way too long."

"Hmmm . . ." I responded, dubious, but kind of into it. "Where will we get them? And where will we go?"

"Dan's been growing them for a while now. I thought we could hang out at the Le Destroit ruins." He looked up at me. "It'll be a real journey. What do you say?"

* * *

"How are you, darling?" he asked. It took me a moment to figure out where I was. I must have fallen asleep on the couch in Halimi's bachelor pad when he went off to fix me some coffee. Quiet music played in the background—French chansons with Cuban touches and a sophisticated rhythm, the divine voice of a young girl—and my maxi skirt had ridden above my knees. "I think I'm okay," I mumbled and began yanking down my skirt, but Halimi stopped me.

"It's incredibly sexy," he said, and passed his fingers over my black pantyhose. He sat next to me on the couch. On the table stood two cups of Turkish coffee and a bag of white sugar with a teaspoon stuck in it. "Not exactly tea with the queen," Halimi said playfully.

I sat up. "I can suspend my lady-in-waiting mode for a few minutes," I answered him. I stirred a spoonful of sugar into the coffee.

"Do you always talk like this?" he asked, his smile broadening, his hand traveling a little above my knee and under the skirt. "Or is it just for me?"

"Wow, you're good," I said, eyeing his fingers on my leg. The hand paused. "What do you mean?" Halimi asked.

"Look," I began, stammering a little but determined to be honest. "I've heard all the gossip about you." I smiled broadly to make it clear I wasn't judging. "I've seen you in action, okay? You charm women just for the fun of it," I continued. He took a deep breath to respond, but I pushed on. "And I'm into it . . ." I looked down and then up again. Halimi narrowed his eyes, unsure. "In other words, you're welcome to keep going."

Halimi pulled me to his chest and stroked my hair.

"Really? You like that?" he asked, amused.

"Yes," I said quietly.

I prepared myself for an embarrassing, clumsy first round of sex, but our bodies matched perfectly. I'm on the petite side, and he's broad-chested with powerful arms, but he didn't feel heavy as he leaned into me. He wasn't in a hurry, nor did he draw things out for too long. I liked his salty taste; after a few dry months with sleepy Ronen, I gave it my all—fingers, nails, lips, and tongue. I went down on him and even let him go down on me, and I came like that and then came again when he was inside me. I fell asleep, my head on his chest, while he stroked the length of my back up and down, up and down.

Halimi told me later how he'd stayed awake to watch me sleep and tried not to get too excited ("Not that it helped, *au contraire*," he'd added in that pervy tone of his). "So you're not just sweet, funny, educated, and intelligent," he wrote me on WhatsApp as I slept beside him, "the sex was awesome too." It awakened within him, he told me later, a sudden hope that had died long ago. He enjoyed his conquests, but lately sex had been nothing to write home about. Occasionally, his cock had failed him. "And then you arrived" is what he always said, "like some German porno fantasy from the '70s." Later, I heard him boasting to his closest girlfriend, Zozo, that I was the embodiment of a hot librarian.

It was already close to midnight when I got up to pee, wondering how I could solve the problem of my contact lenses if I stayed the night. When I exited the bathroom, I bumped into Halimi on his way to take a shower, and he dragged me back into the room with him. We climbed over the bathtub's edge, and I stood naked while he adjusted the temperature of the water from the shower nozzle above. I was flustered, overly self-conscious.

I cast a fleeting glance at his hefty body. He reached for me with both hands, and we clung to each other under the flow of water. He soaped himself, then me, with vigorous and purposeful movements that stimulated me more than any foreplay could. We fucked again, holding each other tightly under the hot water. It doesn't always work— something about the water clashes with the fluids of sex, and it can chafe painfully—but this time it did work, loud moans and hands spread out over ceramic tiles made slippery in the clouds of steam.

After he came, Halimi sat on the edge of the bathtub, supporting himself with one hand on the wall, breathing heavily. I lay down in the tub. "At least it's easy to clean up in here," I said. Halimi caught his breath and rinsed off, standing over me and grinning. He leaned over, kissed me hard on my forehead, and left the room.

I sat under the flow of water and lost all sense of time. *What just happened?* I moved my head from side to side, hot water trickling through my hair. My mind wandered between various insignificant recollections—familiar streets from my childhood in Jerusalem, empty talk heard at a party, people from the café, everything random and unrelated. It was a bit like falling asleep, only the same question popped up again and again in my head, unanswered: *What just happened?*

"Hey, Rozhevsky, you okay?"

"I feel like I just died and was reborn a thousand times," I sighed, my eyes shut.

"That bad?" The shower curtain was swept aside, and I looked up blurrily. Halimi was dressed—the same skinny jeans but a different T-shirt—and looked refreshed. He smiled at me, and I returned the smile.

"I'll be out in a minute."

He grinned and left me a clean towel on the edge of the sink. Walking along the hallway, I paused by the living room. "You wouldn't by any chance have a clean pair of panties?" I asked.

He guffawed and raised his head from the computer. He shook his head slowly. "So, maybe dirty ones?" I smiled at him. "Maybe," he chuckled affectionately. "I guess I'm just going to have to wear my tights without panties," I said, puckering my lips. "That's tough," Halimi said, in the tone of someone comforting the bereaved. I winked and went to get dressed in the bedroom. When I came back, I sat down on the couch and took a sip of the coffee I'd left on the table earlier, now cold. "Ugh, you do that too?" Halimi grinned.

"Who else does that?" I asked.

Halimi took a sip of his own cold coffee.

The doorbell rang, and I was spooked. It was already past midnight, and there were hardly any sounds from the street. Halimi went to the door, and it occurred to me that I was in a strange place with a person I barely knew. I imagined him coming back into the living room with his brother, a friend, or another lover. I felt a sharp stab of nausea. But he murmured something at the door and came back with a takeout order. Relief must have been etched on my face, because he burst out laughing. "Who did you think it was? My mom?"

"Something like that," I admitted.

"Pas de problème," Simone said, raising her eyes above the frames of her elegant eyeglasses. "Richard's arriving on Thursday, and I've reserved a room for us at that swanky hotel in Mitzpe Ramon. I wanted to invite you as well, but if you want a bit of time alone together, we'll take the little one."

Halimi and I looked at each other. I was pretty sure Halimi was going to change his mind and persuade me to embark on our little adventure some other time. But he said, "No . . . we've made plans already. Liloosh will have a ton of fun."

"Whatever you like," she said and looked at us both. "Are you going to do drugs?" Halimi burst out laughing, and I widened my nostrils and suppressed a smile.

"Yup, probably," Halimi said. "Why, do you want some too?"

"I thought if you've got hash, it might be nice out in the desert," Simone said blithely.

"Hash," Halimi said. "That's so '60s. Anyway, as you know, that's Diti's department."

"Of course, of course," I said right away. "I don't have hash, but I've got excellent weed."

"Magnifique," Simone said, smiling.

The week passed by pleasantly. April was blessed with balmy days, soft sea breezes, and an affable sun that caressed the skin without beating down too hard. I worked in the mornings, sitting with my old laptop by a table on the balcony, cigarettes and coffee, horizon and sea within reach. Simone and Halimi hung out together, taking walks around the nearby villages and along the beach. Sometimes, Simone sat with me for an hour or two on her iPad, gathering material for her next article. She showed me a medieval manuscript she was researching—a work of art in crimson, gold, and royal blue—written by Jacques de Vitry, Bishop of Acre, at the beginning of the thirteenth century. "What's funny is that he was one of the people who founded the fortress at Atlit, less than a mile from here," Simone said.

I glanced at the ruins of the fortress—always obstructing the skyline. Château Pèlerin was built as a Crusader fortress by the Knights Templar in 1218. I'd wanted to hike there ever since we moved, but it had been closed to visitors for many years, serving as a secret Israeli naval commando base. It drove Halimi insane—he fantasized about sneaking in by way of the sea, either swimming or in a rubber dinghy, but he never managed to convince me we'd get out of there alive. RESTRICTED AREA—TRESPASSERS ENTER AT THEIR OWN RISK announced signs on the fence around the fortress.

Simone actually liked the idea that the fortress still served as a military base. "It's just wonderful," she exclaimed on one of our walks along the beach, when we stopped to look at the ruins beyond the fence, alongside the white, square structures of the military base. "What was good for thirteenth-century Templars is good for a modern army as well." She narrowed her eyes. "Aside from that, I bet everything there is beautifully preserved because there are no visitors. Whatever's left, that is."

Simone and Halimi consulted an antiques specialist, a friend of Simone's, who confirmed that the coin found on the beach was from the Crusader period. He even traced it to the age of Frederick II, the Holy Roman Emperor and disputed King of Jerusalem.

One afternoon, after Halimi and Simone came home from their walk and Simone went off for a nap in the guest room, Halimi handed me a long magenta box.

"What's this?" I asked, surprised, and even a little suspicious. There'd been too many gifts over the years from Halimi to compensate for all the heartache he'd caused. "Open it," he said, leaning against the balcony door.

Inside the box was a thin silver chain through which the coin from the beach had been threaded. It had been polished and shined but was still badly corroded. A small, square cross with widened edges was engraved on one side of the coin, delineated by a circle with a blurred inscription. I couldn't make out the engraving on the other side.

"Limi, it's gorgeous," I murmured, putting on the necklace. Halimi had gauged the length perfectly, and the pendant stuck to my skin, slightly above my cleavage. I expected the ancient metal to be cool to the touch, but the coin was warm.

"Where did you manage to find takeout open at one a.m. on a Friday night?" I asked. Halimi opened a series of identical plastic containers. There were smooth, yellow mashed potatoes alongside roast beef in a dark sauce, fresh coleslaw, garlic bread, and even chocolate brownies. I knew most of the restaurants in Tel Aviv and couldn't think of a single place that offered mashed potatoes and roast beef so late on a Friday night.

"Ah, I know some people," Halimi said, but I could tell he enjoyed how impressed I was. I leaped on the food, which was delicious. Halimi nibbled on a hunk of garlic bread.

I devoured the meat, vegetables, and bread and had a brownie with coffee that Halimi made me. He didn't touch the brownies. "Are you watching your weight?" I asked. His eyes were riveted on me as I licked my lips—his chin resting on the palm of his hand, a contented smile on his face. "Don't really have a sweet tooth," Halimi said, getting up and walking over to the dresser. "Shall we go dancing?"

He produced a small bottle containing some kind of clear liquid, which made me tense. I thought he was about to suggest we shoot up or something.

"Relax, it's G," Halimi said, measuring the liquid into a large glass and then adding Diet Coke.

"What, you mean GHB—that date-rape drug?" I asked anxiously. "I've never tried it."

"Look, it's not a roofie, but it's true that if you mix it with alcohol, it can have lethal effects," Halimi said, sipping from the glass, his face slightly contorted. "That's why you'll stick close to me."

"I dunno . . ." I began, but Halimi smiled and sat down next to me. "What's up? Are you scared I'm going to take advantage?" His hand stroked my thigh through my pantyhose again, and I tingled.

"A little," I said. "God knows what you'll do to me if I'm helpless."

"Look, you don't have to, of course," Halimi began, his long fingers climbing up my shins. "But it's a fun drug, if you follow the rules. Don't you want to fly with me?"

I looked at him and found it all a bit hard to believe—but yeah, I wanted very much to fly with him, and I wanted to fly high.

The G hit us when we got to the gate of the Block around 2:00 a.m. The tall, bald doorman recognized Halimi, nodded at him, and smiled at me good-naturedly. As soon as we entered, Halimi bought two bottles of water and gave me one. "This doesn't leave your hand, you hear me?" he instructed. "If you need to go to the restroom, let me know, and I'll come with you."

I felt as if I were walking a few inches above the ground and my hair was floating around my head, as though I were underwater. My entire body was itching to dance, and for a moment I imagined myself taking my shirt off and dancing topless near the DJ.

Halimi's eyes flashed with a foreign spark. I panicked for a moment, and he sensed it. He gave me a bear hug, the kind of hug friends give each other after a long separation. I looked him up and down, and when our eyes met, I felt sure we'd met in a past life—I saw scenes of us in various strange situations before my eyes. We began dancing. The place was full, but not packed. The DJ was great—the hottest star in the whole cold universe.

I couldn't stop dancing, not even for a moment. From time to time, people approached Halimi, but I couldn't work out what they were saying. Someone cracked a joke, a few of them stared at me; I could not have cared less. Afterward, he pulled me into the lounge, and we sighed contentedly into one of the couches. I drank from the still-chilly bottle of water in my hand. I felt the cold liquid diluting the blood in my veins and stroking my muscles.

"Halimi!" a girl called out—smooth black bob, thick eyeliner, flaming red lipstick. She sat down heavily on a nearby couch. "It's been so long, where have you been?" Halimi cast me a glance, and I reacted with a sheepish smile, eyes wide, feigning innocence. "Really, where did you disappear to?" I said, "I haven't seen you for a long time either."

The girl studied us for a few seconds. "So, were you abroad?"

"Yep, I went to Lapland," Halimi replied, his knee rising and falling to the jumpy rhythm. "What about you?" he asked politely. I guessed the last time they met, he'd been less polite and more sociable, because her face fell and she said, "Fine," and walked off abruptly.

"So, is this how it's going to be?" I asked, moving my lips close to his ear. "A different girl at every stop?"

He laughed and said, "Could be. Is that a problem?"

"Not yet," I said, and it was true. It turned me on, to tell the truth, and I figured that by the time it began to bother me, we'd have already exhausted whatever was between us.

We danced and then did some more G in the bathroom with a friend of Halimi's. The guy seemed distracted, but I felt amazing—the effect was powerful, but not crippling, like being very drunk minus the dizziness, or the urge to throw up, or the lack of control (which is precisely why I didn't like drinking). I still felt this sensation of floating above the ground, like if I stomped my feet hard enough, I might push up into the air and fly away. I smoked cigarettes that burned out a second after I lit them; I danced until I was breathless and my legs shook. Halimi dragged me off to the bathroom again, and I laughed and said, "I don't want any more, I'm good."

He pinned me to the wall of the toilet stall with his body. "We finished everything," he said, "but I wanted to ask you a really important question." His normally meticulous diction was slurred, his voice a few octaves lower than normal.

"What do you want to know?" I giggled, wondering whether I'd violated the G protocol.

"I want to know how wet you are from one to ten," he said, thrusting his hand between my legs. I wasn't wearing panties under my tights, and I trembled at his touch. "Eleven," I said. "But seriously, here? That's gross," I mumbled. "Yes, it is," he agreed, rolling my tights down to my knees and lifting up my skirt. We both came before anyone knocked on the door.

By the time we left the club, the sun was rising. Halimi told me how he loved listening to the birds' dawn chorus. We ate spicy Eritrean injera at a tiny restaurant. Everyone there seemed to know Halimi. With a touch of regret, I said it was probably time for me to head home, but Halimi wouldn't hear of it. So, we stopped off at my place; left a note for my roommate; and packed some clean clothes, a toothbrush, eyeglasses, a packet of daily contact lenses, and a phone charger. Then, we grabbed a taxi and went to his place, where we snuggled under a down blanket. I fell asleep almost immediately and woke up just for a moment, when I heard him coughing in the living room like a dying man.

CHAPTER 3

Richard drove from the airport in a rented car, arriving early Thursday evening. Lily didn't really remember him from the previous summer, but he swiftly won her over. After giving Simone a hug, slapping Halimi on the back, and kissing my hand chivalrously—I responded with a curtsy—he sat down on the rug with Lily in his suit and tie and fancy shoes and showed her how to make fruit from Play-Doh by using plastic molds. Richard whipped out gift after gift—a snow globe with a candy cottage à la the Brothers Grimm, a music box with a twirling ballerina, and a wooden sword. The hilt of the sword was decorated with delicate engravings in silver and green. Lily held it tightly in her fist and refused to let go, even when she went to sleep.

Richard and Simone retired early to the guest room while we tidied up. Then, Halimi went to take a shower. He'd left early that morning to pick up the mushrooms in Tel Aviv. I had expected him back just after noon, assuming he wouldn't pass up the chance to swing by the Minzar or Prince bar. I imagined him extolling the details of his new bourgeois life to random acquaintances ("When you grow up, kids, you'll come to appreciate the difference between life with and without a dishwasher").

At two o'clock, still with no sign of him, I was seething with anger, and by four I had retreated into my usual frosty mood when I can't cope with Halimi. There was no time for cross-examination—I was bringing in the laundry when I heard him come in, and then Simone returned with a huge bouquet of flowers, rye bread, and treats from the deli. Lily was watching *Robin Hood* but kept demanding things ("Chocolate milk!" "In the pink cup!" "Where's my sword?" "Mommy, come sit with me!").

When Halimi went to take a shower, I walked into the bedroom, thinking he would have undressed there. But he must have stripped in the bathroom, so I went in, pretending I needed to pee. He poked his head around the shower curtain. I made a pathetic attempt to smile, and he retreated behind the curtain without saying a word. Without moving off the toilet seat, I reached into the pocket of his pants, which were on top of the laundry basket. I pulled out his phone and dropped it into my pocket. I stood up and flushed the toilet (Halimi said, "Ouch").

Alone in the kitchen with the despised metallic beast, I tapped in his password and began scanning the apps that usually most aroused my suspicion: Facebook, Twitter, WhatsApp, Instagram. I went through his Web history and checked whether he'd installed Tinder or some other dating app and stashed it away in a hidden folder. I went through his call log, his text messages. I tried going through his timeline on Google Maps, but he must have turned off GPS. Apart from that, everything looked innocent. A text message to Dan in the morning and then two phone calls—one to Zozo, his good friend, and another to Simone. A one-minute conversation. He'd probably asked Simone when she was coming home. I checked what time he'd made that call: 12:10 p.m.

"You won't find anything there," Halimi said. I was startled and jumped, and the phone fell from my hands.

"I know you hate it, but it's a bit much to smash it on the floor," Halimi joked. I wasn't in the mood. With shaking hands, I picked it up; unfortunately, it had survived the fall unscathed.

"Diti. What's up?" Halimi asked, still keeping his distance, standing by the fridge. His ridiculously large white bathrobe was wrapped around his big body.

"What's up? You know exactly what's up," I said. "Where were you?"

Halimi took a deep breath. "I was in Tel Aviv," he said purposefully. "I stopped by Dan's place and got us some mushrooms, then I sat in the sun with Zozo for a couple of hours and had a beer, and I praised our life here until Zozo wanted to bury me alive, then I went to the beach and walked along the shore from the northern part of the city to Jaffa and back again."

"Really?" I wanted to cry, but the lump in my throat just hurt in my ears and pricked at my eyes. I saw a hint of a smile and got mad all over again. "But you get why I'm paranoid, right?" My suspicion bloomed in the silence. "Why did you go walking on the beach?" Halimi liked walking, but he hardly ever went to the beach in Tel Aviv, and now he had the entire Atlit seashore at his disposal, and it was so much nicer. *Probably lying again*, I thought. He came nearer, and I felt ready to erupt.

"Diti, you're right, you're so right, relax," Halimi said quietly. Blood pounded in my ears. I imagined myself scooping up Lily in the middle of the night and fleeing by car.

"I totally get your paranoia," Halimi continued, increasingly serious, his voice pleading. "I'm a jerk, I should have texted or called. I'm an asshole, really."

I heard the candor in his voice, and the hard knot in my stomach loosened. He took another step toward me, and I shrank back again. "I swear on my mother's life that I just needed to walk and be alone for a bit. Get off the grid for a few hours. But I'm an idiot. I should have told you."

I believed him. After all, most of the time he didn't exactly lie but rather squirmed or sidestepped or tried to cover his tracks, and my radar was well attuned to signs of adultery. I had good reason to be paranoid, but there was no incriminating evidence, which there always was when my suspicions were justifiable. I took a deep breath and went over to the couch. "Make us tea, you dumb jerk," I told him.

Simone and Richard left early Friday morning. Lily busily packed her giraffe backpack with colored crayons and her *Mr. Happy* book. Richard stowed the sword he'd given her in his duffel bag. Halimi transferred Lily's car seat to the rental.

Lily and I waited on the front porch. We'd left her several times with my parents, and my sister Dina when she came to visit, and even with Simone and Richard in Paris, but we'd always put her to bed, and we were always back by morning. I didn't want to make a big deal of it, but I looked at Lily playing with the zipper of her backpack and couldn't help myself. "You'll have fun," I blurted out and immediately regretted it. Lily looked up at me and smiled. "Have fun," she repeated. "I got colors, you wanna draw?" she continued, yanking out the pack of crayons. I began explaining that she was going away with Simone and Richard any minute. Naturally, there were tears when we parted, and when I kissed Lily's wet cheeks, I had to hold myself back from crying.

"Bye, sweetie," Halimi said, leaning through the window on the other side of the car. "*Au revoir, Maman, au revoir, Richard,*" he added, straightening up as the car reversed out of the driveway.

"She'll be fine, right?" I said.

"Sure," Halimi said, with more confidence than he was probably feeling. "By the time they're out of Atlit, she'll have forgotten you ever existed."

I snorted, and we went inside. The uncanny silence of the house put me at ease. Light shone warm gold through the windows onto the tile floor, the furniture, and Simone's bouquet of flowers—anemones and chrysanthemums. "So, what's on the menu?" I asked Halimi. I rolled myself a cigarette and filled the kettle.

"Whatever you like, Diti," said Halimi. He went over to the computer and put on Nick Cave's *Let Love In*. I smiled at him. "I suggest coffee, then sex, then food and drink while watching whatever show you like, then either a power nap or a real good sleep, and then we'll head out."

"Sounds perfect," I said. "But is it okay to eat before we do mushrooms? I can't remember. The last time was in Amsterdam."

"We'll eat around noon. By the time it begins to take effect, whatever we ate will be long gone," he said amenably.

"Whatever, but forget about sex because I have my period," I announced.

"I'm not worried," Halimi answered, rummaging through the fridge, pulling out soft cheeses, salami, pickled vegetables left over from last night's dinner. He made coffee using the blend he'd bought in Tel Aviv the day before and brought the food out to the balcony.

When the coffee was ready, I poured out two cups and went out to join him. Halimi was sitting there with his phone (I slipped by and glanced in his direction—he was checking his Twitter feed). We ate and drank and smoked. I read for a while, and Halimi messed with his phone. "Come over here, sit in my lap," he suddenly said. We made out for a while and then retreated indoors. I started going down on him, intent on pleasing him.

It really turned me on, but I had a strict no-fucking policy when I had my period, despite Halimi's efforts to persuade me otherwise. During my adolescence, my mom had hammered into me the four hard rules of a menstruating woman: Never sit on cold stone, never let a cold wind enter your panties, never bathe in cold water, and on no account allow a man to penetrate you. When I was young, I thought this was all superstition, but my mom insisted it was a surefire way to avoid cervical cancer. Although I was never totally convinced, I stuck to it. Halimi tried his best to convince me for years but knew exactly how stubborn I was. At the beginning, it turned him on; he thought it was a religious thing. Later, as the years went by, it became a kind of sport, a challenge to get me to "drop the complex," as Halimi called it.

I broke free of Halimi and went to take a shower. I presumed he'd either jerk off or just forget about it, but he followed me into the bathroom. I got into the shower and closed the curtain ("I need to rinse away the blood first," I told him), and Halimi stripped. Then, he got into the shower, rubbed himself up against me, and jerked off.

"To my credit," he said when he was done, "my appetite for you has only increased over the years."

I grinned and sprayed him with water from the showerhead. "I don't know if it's to your credit or mine," I replied. "Is it like that with your lovers as well?"

Halimi's face fell. "Do you really want me to answer that?" he said icily.

"No, not really," I said with comparable coolness. His gaze softened, and he pulled me toward him.

"You're the best sex, seriously," he said.

"So, why do you even do it?" I asked.

"It's not for the sex, babe," he said, folding his wet arms around my soapy body. "It's so I don't rot."

"Whatever," I responded. "Actually, I have great sex with my lovers."

"Ha ha," said Halimi, knitting his eyebrows together. "I'll kill them all."

We watched a few episodes of a British detective show while eating *mujadara* with tahini and tomatoes that Halimi made. He fell asleep in the middle of the third episode, and I began nodding off too. From outside, I heard the sounds of children coming home from school and cars returning from shopping for the weekend. A pigeon settled on the table on the balcony and began pecking at crumbs.

"Limi," I said quietly. "Li-mi," I repeated, extending the syllables.

"Give me five," he mumbled.

I called Simone. They were already at the hotel. Lily had slept all the way there in the car and was now lively and talkative. Simone carried on a conversation with her while she was talking to me, so it was hard to tell whether they were on their way to the swimming pool or on their way back from it. Either way, Halimi was right: Lily was fine.

I got off the couch and stretched. A sense of sweet indolence spread through me. I'd earned it. I stood on the balcony and looked out at the sea. I inhaled the salty air and sipped my now-cold coffee.

I went back inside and saw that Halimi had woken up and was handling the mushrooms with excessive precision, adding and removing bits from a tiny digital scale.

"How much are we taking?" I asked.

"Dan said between two and a half to five grams," Halimi replied, adding a little more.

"So I'll make it five. He said they're pretty mild."

As I locked the front door of the house, I had a nagging feeling I'd forgotten something. We left Halimi's phone at home, taking only my own old phone in Halimi's backpack in case Simone called with something urgent. "Did you bring water?" I asked Halimi, who was already standing on the sidewalk.

"Of course, Diti. Let's get going," he answered, staring northward to the end of the street.

I dropped the house key in my purse and stroked the door handle in an almost involuntary gesture, as if I didn't know when I'd be back. I shook off the feeling and followed Halimi.

Like most times when I left the house, I was aware of the discrepancy between the manicured gardens around me and our own wild backyard with the Persian lilac tree whose foliage reached in every direction. A beautiful red and yellow lantana, whose thorns pricked anyone who came too close, was entangled in the bars of the garden fence; this was the real border between our house and the rest of the world.

A silver Jeep raced toward us. Halimi grimaced. He had a general aversion to vehicles, and he absolutely loathed Jeeps—in his heart of hearts, he was a true Tel Avivian who got around exclusively on bicycle or, when absolutely necessary, by taxi. Since our move to Atlit, we had needed the car more, which aroused his defiance.

As we walked hand in hand, I felt a sense of serenity.

I loved Fridays in Atlit as much as I'd loved them in Tel Aviv, and in Jerusalem before that. The impending quietude, the clatter of pots and pans from the windows of nearby houses, the gradual stillness of the road.

The air was warm, shot through with cool gusts of salty breeze. The smell of fried onions and garlic that wafted through windows grew fainter the farther we walked away from the neighborhood. Halimi's hand tightened around my wrist as we left the paved road and continued onto a dirt track.

The rich, dark taste of the dried mushrooms we had eaten lingered in my mouth. I imagined them migrating down to my stomach, stirring nerves and stimulating synapses in my brain. We kept going, our eyes on the strip of beach to the west, toward the ruined fortress and military base. We also looked northward, in the direction of Le Destroit—an Old French name meaning "Narrow Passage"—and all the construction work in between. I knew that Le Destroit had been built by the Knights Templar in the early twelfth century as a fortified watchtower hewn from living rock—sandstone—to protect coastal travelers; they had then dismantled it once the larger fortress, Château Pèlerin, was complete. But unlike the château, the ruins of Destroit were open to public, offering a romantic and somewhat melancholic gaze to the past.

The sun was dazzling, despite the wide-brimmed hat I wore. I sat down on a rock by the side of the track. "Pass me the water?" I asked. He took the bottle out of his backpack. I heard the faint sound of string instruments coming from far away and a high-pitched singing voice. "Can you hear that?" I asked him. He inclined his head while I drank water in big gulps.

"The birds?" he asked.

"No," I said, "strange music. I can barely hear it myself. Probably hikers with a guitar."

"Stop freaking out, Diti," Halimi said. His pupils were dilated. He was skittish and excited, raring to go. If he'd been alone, Halimi would have walked all the way up the coastal road to Haifa without stopping.

We kept walking without talking. We took deep breaths, and each time I inhaled, the air reverberated in my chest. Everything around me resonated with everything else.

"Wow, this is powerful," I said, panting a little. "It's only just hit me, and I'm already seeing spirals in the bushes."

"Look, look," Halimi said and suddenly grabbed me by the arm. "Look!" I raised my eyes in the direction he was pointing and saw a flock of flamingos descending upon the salt pools, gigantic pink birds whose wide wings I heard flapping before I even understood what was happening.

"Is this real, or am I hallucinating?" Halimi didn't answer and I focused on the flamingos as they landed. How had Halimi noticed them with his terrible vision? I stared at the flamingos for a long time, and in my mind's eye I saw them going up in flames and being reborn out of their ashes.

All at once, I become hyperconscious of my own body and every-thing covering it—linen pants the color of slate and a pale-gray tunic in finer linen. The sun hat protected my eyes and kept my mind inside my head. I knew that if I removed it, the whirlpool in my brain would overflow. I felt beads of sweat appearing on my forehead, my heartbeat reverberating in my veins, the tampon I'd inserted before we left widen-ing inside me, drenched in blood.

The coin hanging on my neck felt hot and pulsing. I placed a hand over it and felt it throbbing in sync with the beat of the flamingos' wings overhead. Now and then, one of them flew above us, raising its tremen-dous wings, and sometimes two or three joined the group—awesome delusions in flaming pink. We stared at them for an indeterminate amount of time—perhaps a few minutes, perhaps an hour.

Halimi was the first to snap out of it.

"Come on," he said, and I pulled myself together. We resumed walking.

We got to the Narrow Passage, the ancient pass that delineated the ruins of Le Destroit from the south, and Halimi helped me scramble down the hillside. I looked with longing at the strip of sea to the west, then began climbing behind Halimi in the direction of the small fortress.

We sat down under one of the carob trees, whose branches afforded us a shady green canopy. The melody of the string instruments sounded closer. From here, it didn't sound like a bunch of hippies singing Donovan or Joan Baez. Maybe "Scarborough Fair." Maybe.

"Can you hear that tune?" I whispered.

"I don't know," Halimi replied. He was lying under the tree, his arms crossed behind his head, his legs stretched out. "I'm going to shut my eyes for a while."

I sat under the tree and took in the surroundings. Birds chirped everywhere; I was conscious of even the slightest movement of a blade of grass. I fanned myself with something I was holding in my hand and then recognized it was a palm branch I had picked up without noticing. The coin on my necklace was still pulsating, and the tampon continued to expand inside me. I wanted to keep on walking. I glanced at Halimi; his chest was rising and falling at a steady pace. It was weird. On hikes together, I was always the one who needed a break, while Halimi preferred to push ahead.

"Limi," I said. He didn't respond.

"Halimi," I said in a louder voice, and a tiny spark of fear ignited within me, and my voice trembled. He was still breathing peacefully. "Saul!"

Halimi opened his eyes instantly. He gave me a big smile. I slapped his face playfully, and he pulled me toward him and said, "What can I say, we're getting old." His smile deepened. He closed his eyes and murmured, "I need to nap a little. When I shut my eyes, I'm having these crazy visuals."

I giggled and kissed him on the forehead. "Fine, I don't know what kind of mushrooms Dan sold you, but it's having the opposite effect on me. I've got to walk some more. Rest up for a few minutes, and I'll wander around."

"Uh-huh," he mumbled. I stood up, taking the backpack with me.

The landscape sprung up in front of my eyes. I understood intuitively how the pink star thistle supported the sandstone, consoling it for the way humans had devoured it in chunks for thousands of years and for the damage that weather and time had inflicted upon it. I got down on my knees and kissed a few flowers.

"Rozhevsky, don't go crazy on me," Halimi said behind me. I turned to look at him, lying under the tree, one eye open.

"I'm fine," I shot back. I needed a moment to remember where we were in time. My lips felt pink and fleshy. I remembered I had a little girl named Lily, who was probably being offered a lavish evening meal at the hotel but was only pecking at food that came in plastic containers, like yogurt, or food that had a distinct shape and color, like the yolk of a boiled egg or a piece of dry bread. It all made me laugh.

My legs carried me abnormally fast, and the music became clearer. There was none of the usual laughing and chattering of picnickers out in nature. The sounds were sharper, like a vibrating echo of the plucking of strings passing through me.

Two voices cantillated, starting and stopping, as if in a rehearsal. Two male voices, half-declaiming, half-singing.

Something in the landscape altered, and my heart pounded in my chest. With every step, the silence thickened, enveloping the entire vicinity. The chirping of birds intensified, as if someone had switched on a gigantic loudspeaker with a tropical jungle soundtrack with whistling, chirping, squeaking, and snorting of insects and birds at full volume, accompanied by other sounds I couldn't identify. The vegetation solidi-fied. The air turned steadily translucent.

Suddenly, I realized I'd left my hat with Halimi; I sensed my con-sciousness leaking out, engulfing my head in vapors. *Nothing like this had ever happened to me*, I imagined telling my sister. I summoned comfort-ing scenes of myself sitting on the balcony with my laptop, cigarettes, and coffee, while Lily watched a movie in the living room.

But the air had a completely different smell to it, as if a giant had trampled on all the surrounding bushes, releasing their fragrance. *I'm going to faint*, I thought.

The soothing scent of hash rose up from one of the nearby trees. Perhaps it really was a bunch of people having a picnic. I decided to go over to them and ask for a hit. As I walked toward the smell, I saw two men. They appeared to be semitransparent, and although I blinked and jerked my head from side to side a few times, they continued to flicker, shaded by a carob tree. *Two hipsters from someplace abroad*, I thought. One of them was a pot-bellied dude with a handsome face and lush brown hair, wearing a suit of . . . velvet? A blue cloak or robe over yellow sleeves and a silvery belt that held the whole getup together. He clutched a weird, misshapen guitar to his body and wore a puffy blue beret on his head, decorated with gold ribbon. There was another guy with him, lounging under the tree, wearing lighter clothes—a yellow silk shirt with a kind of brown hoodie, loose-fitting harem pants in red, and a leather belt from which hung small leather pouches. *Was that a dagger?* His dark hair was gathered in a half-ponytail. He inhaled something from a small receptacle and exhaled a cloud of smoke. Two large dogs stretched out by his side.

I fanned myself with the palm branch again. I was very close to them now, but they still hadn't noticed me. The dogs roused themselves, agitated, and began barking at me. I wasn't afraid; they were also semi-transparent, like holograms. Mushroom logic.

A spring gurgled nearby. I'd never noticed it before on our previous hikes—I wasn't even aware there were springs around Atlit. I made a bee-line for the cool water and drank from it, but it was as if nothing passed my throat. I submerged my head in the water but felt no sensation of dampness or cold. *These mushrooms are too much*, I managed to think before the coin on its chain detached itself from my sweaty chest and fell into the spring. And suddenly, there was an explosion in my head. I was swept into the water as if it were a whirlpool—sucked in, like a crumb going down a drain.

Turns out that breathing underwater is possible. I rose up on a tidal wave and was thrown onto dry land.

CHAPTER 4

In the name of the Holy Mother!" I heard a shocked voice say in oddly accented French. I opened my eyes and saw the two men leaning over me, the velvet-cloaked one with suspicious eyes and the half-ponytailed one looking concerned. The dogs barked wildly. They were no longer translucent.

"A pilgrim maid, clearly parched," Half-ponytail said in a voice full of compassion. "Do you not see she holds a palm branch?" There was a very strange gap between what I heard, a kind of garbled French with a rolling *r*, and the fact that my brain interpreted everything and understood. I sat up.

"What in the name of all saints is she clothed in?" mumbled Velvet Cloak, surveying me as if trying to work out whether I was dangerous or not. Half-ponytail continued to stare at me and said, "I know not. Perchance she has arrived from a foreign land. Silence, Brunette! Cedrique!" The two sight hounds gave one final yelp and settled down.

"Is all well, sirs?" a worried shout carried over the tree's canopy, from the direction of Le Destroit. "Indeed," Half-ponytail shouted back. "Resume your duties."

"Sorry, guys," I said in French, expressing myself with as much clarity as my pounding temples would allow. "I did 'shrooms, and they must have been really powerful. I thought I might smoke some hash with you guys, you know, to chill out."

A tablecloth was spread out on the ground. On it was a bottle of wine, half a loaf of bread, and a hunk of cheese. To one side was a round clay dish with a silver spout, issuing smoke. The dogs gave me a warning glance; they looked as though they were about to pounce. "Perhaps a crust of bread, too, if that's okay with you. That will make me feel better," I said, trying not to stare at the dogs.

The two men looked at each other and shrugged their shoulders.

"Do you comprehend the maiden's words?" Velvet Cloak asked. He returned to his position, guitar or whatever it was in hand. He was still looking at me pointedly—I couldn't determine whether his look was one of lust or suspicion. Probably both.

"I believe so," Half-ponytail said. "She wishes to share our bread. In all likelihood, she is indeed a pilgrim." He pulled his hoodie up.

"A pilgrim wench," Velvet Cloak snorted, strumming on his musical instrument. "Her hair exposed like that of a whore . . ."

"Your Royal Highness!" Half-ponytail admonished.

"If so, methinks she is a fairy," Velvet Cloak said, as if reconciling himself to the situation. Startled, I realized these two lunatics were speaking Old French.

"Your Royal Highness, you think that any beautiful woman who is not your wife is a fairy," Half-ponytail said. Velvet Cloak chortled and shot me another look. Half-ponytail took out a large knife from a scabbard on his belt and sliced the bread. "If you please, my lady."

I giggled and took a chunk of bread. It tasted extraordinary, like biting into congealed porridge.

"Begging your pardon, did she not materialize at our feet from the void? Are her eyes not green like the eyes of Lilith?" Velvet Cloak sang, strumming all the while to accompany his words. *Twang, twang.*

"Excuse my lack of manners, but who are you?" I asked. "French tourists?"

Half-ponytail passed a hand through his handsome beard and said, "I beg your pardon! What did you say? That we hail from France?"

I scrutinized him carefully. He was slender, with long, elegant fingers. His dark hair fell in bangs on the sides of his face. The hoodie he was wearing partially obscured him, but I saw his face was finely chiseled and swarthier than that of his friend, with inquisitive, amber-colored eyes.

"Allow us to introduce ourselves," Half-ponytail said, throwing a glance at Velvet Cloak. "The noble lord to my right is Thibaut IV, Count of Champagne." Velvet Cloak cleared his throat theatrically, and Half-ponytail quickly corrected himself with a smile, "I beg your pardon, Thibaut I, King of Navarre." Thibaut nodded his head slowly as he listened, his chin rising slightly.

"Please meet the good knight Jean Foggia," Thibaut addressed me but did not take his eyes off his companion. The good knight released a snort of laughter, and Thibaut added with emphasis, "That is to say, Jean d'Ibelin, Count of Arsur." A look passed between the two men; I didn't even try to decipher it. Then, they turned toward me expectantly.

I decided to go with the flow. "I'm Idit Rozhevsky-Halimi, Countess of Atlit," I said with a flourish. The "king" put down his guitar and looked at me with interest. By his side was a long sheath bound with leather straps, which likely contained a sword. I could see only the tip of it, studded with precious jewels. Lying close to the "knight" was another sheath, out of which poked a more modest handle, but no less threatening in size; he reached for it with one hand. These guys were real pros.

"Édith?" asked Jean, if that was even his real name. "Countess of which district?"

"What?" I said. I couldn't figure out whether they were high or simply didn't get my accent.

"Excuse me?" Jean repeated.

The three of us burst out laughing. The dogs barked again, but not as wildly as before. Thibaut resumed strumming.

I polished off the chunk of bread. The crust was extremely hard and cut the palate of my mouth a little. Shyly, I offered the crust to the dogs. The brown one approached me cautiously, sniffed my hand and the crust of bread, and finally took it with utmost delicacy between her teeth.

"Gorgeous dog!" I exclaimed. I kept my hand outstretched, and after the dog had swallowed the crust of bread, she sniffed my hand and tilted her head toward me. She came closer and thrust her snout into my shoulder.

"Upon my life," said Jean, "never have I seen that hound go from suspicion to friendliness so swiftly."

I wondered how long it would take Halimi to get here and hoped he was still enjoying beautiful visuals with his eyes shut under the tree.

"Okay, can I have a go with your hookah now?" I asked, my eyes on the clay pot. Velvet Cloak, aka Thibaut of Champagne, seemed perplexed at my words, but Jean, who was much mellower, got my drift perfectly. I took out my water bottle.

"What is that?" Thibaut asked, still strumming.

"It's a water bottle," I said slowly.

I drank half the bottle and held it out to them. Jean handed me the clay bowl and began examining the bottle.

He tapped on the plastic with a fingernail, sniffed the nozzle, and cautiously swallowed some water. The black dog gave a loud yelp. I handed the cap to Jean, and he examined it thoroughly, placing the cap back on the bottle without screwing it in place. I took the bottle and screwed the cap on myself. Jean's mouth hung open slightly. *He's wasted,* I thought to myself, my brain humming like crazy from the mushrooms.

Jean clicked his tongue when he saw that the clay pot was no longer burning. He removed a strange, curved metal object, rubbed it against what looked like a piece of stone, and then brought the whole thing to a bunch of dry weeds, which were kindled by the ensuing spark. A small flame spread through the dry weeds, and Jean took a piece of hash, warmed it in the flame, and dropped it in the pot, using a pair of small tongs. He took a hit and passed it over to me.

"You know your stuff, huh?" I remarked. "Is it some kind of professional cosplay?" Thibaut stopped strumming and frowned. While I took deep hits from the little hookah, he and Jean whispered together; I heard the word *Saracen* several times.

When we moved to Atlit, I'd done a quick background check on its history. I was amazed to discover that the fortress had been one of the Crusaders' most powerful strongholds in the Holy Land. In fact, it was the final bastion from which they sailed their last remaining ships. And I knew that *Saracen* was an ancient European term for a person of Muslim origin. Simone had told us about the period, sharing anecdotes with us from her new research.

Groups of tourists came to Atlit occasionally. They covered all the historic and prehistoric sites and received a crash history course from their tour guides, so it was not out of the ordinary to bump into passersby overflowing with knowledge of the place. That said, I'd never come across such loony tourists, much less ones who acted more at home here than me, looking as though they'd just escaped a period drama.

"How did you get here?" Thibaut asked in a sober tone. "Where are your companions and servants?" His black dog stood at attention beside him, growling.

I encouraged myself not to get spooked. Although Thibaut spoke in a somber tone, when I glanced at Jean, he seemed relaxed, and I could have sworn he was suppressing some kind of private joke. I decided to go with the flow.

"My servant is resting a short way from here," I said. "He was most fatigued by our journey, and I permitted him to sleep under a tree while

I wandered around a little," I added, eying Thibaut defiantly. I wondered what Halimi would think of these two. He'd probably want to interview them for the radio show he'd been hosting.

"Night is falling fast, my lady. Where do you intend to lodge?" Jean asked.

"We live around here," I replied. Jean said nothing, but his eyes narrowed with suspicion for the first time since we'd met. It was a cautionary, even cruel look. I felt a sudden need to apologize, to explain that I wasn't really from these parts at all, but from somewhere much farther away. I panicked. The dog lifted her head from my lap and went to sit beside her master. A spasm in my throat brought up the rich, brown, earthy taste of the mushrooms, and I calmed down. I put a hand to my heart and took deep breaths.

"I'm insanely high," I crooned to myself. Jean rose to his feet in an instant.

"Pray point in the direction of your destination," he asked.

"Okay," I said.

Thibaut raised an eyebrow.

"I beg your pardon?" Jean said. "I do not understand that expression."

"I said, 'Okay.'" I was tired of this game. But Jean behaved with the utmost courtesy and supported my elbow as I got up off the ground. When I lost my balance, he held me by the waist. "Oh-ho," said Thibaut from his spot under the tree.

I'm going to kill Dan, I thought to myself. *That jerk was insane to suggest such a high dose.* Jean scrutinized my pendant. "Why are you bedecked with a copper dinar?" He held the coin between two fingers and examined it carefully. "It looks like the coin I threw into the holy spring a few minutes ago."

"And you asked for a wish and refused to disclose it to me," Thibaut remarked from under the tree. *Twang, twang*, his fingers plucked the strings.

"That is the seal of the house of Ibelin of Beirut," Jean said slowly. He surveyed me up, down, and up again, increasingly warily.

"I found it on the seashore," I fumbled for the right words. The fanaticism of these two history buffs was beginning to feel a little dangerous. I grabbed the coin between my fingers and stared at it.

It looked new.

Engraved on one side of the coin was the same cross with the widened edges, encircled by an inscription. On the other side was a decorative gate of a stone tower. The coin shone. I swallowed hard. "I . . . I . . . I don't understand . . ." My heart began beating wildly, and shapes drifted before my eyes.

"I barely understand a thing she utters." Thibaut looked at me as though he were checking out a new car and then looked at Jean, who was holding me by the elbow. "Take care, my lad, that this fairy does not spirit you away to the otherworld." Jean laughed in response—there was something youthful about his laugh—and he walked me out from under the canopy of the huge tree.

I meant to say something, but I choked instead.

At the site of the small fortress and broken rocks of Le Destroit now stood several single- and two-story buildings. The entire area up to the Carmel Hills was covered in fields and orchards. Here and there were small clusters of stone dwellings, probably hamlets or farms. There was no trace of cars or highways. Suddenly, I realized that one of the strange noises I had heard on the way, and had not managed to decipher, was the snorting of horses—tied to metal rings in stone walls, now grazing on grass. The horses were dressed in fine cloth decorated with noble insignia. The simpler cloth on Jean's horse was checkered yellow and red; the other horse sported a textile embroidered with luminous threads in shades of blue, yellow, and silver—apparently the colors of Thibaut. *Count of Champagne, King of Navarre,* the words whispered in my brain. Spellbound, I turned my attention to the seashore.

Instead of the ruins of the Atlit fortress, with the white structures of the Israeli naval base, there rose a gigantic stone fortification with turrets and towers of the kind found in Italy or Spain. Above some of the turrets hung large pale flags. Close to the fortress, instead of coastal vegetation and salt pools, was a small town surrounded by walls. I heard what sounded like the pealing of church bells. Along the plain that lay between the fortress and the town, and between the range of hills, were orchards and groves, fields and gardens. All the new building sites, the bulldozers, the trucks and the roads, the houses of Atlit, the power lines, the makeshift shacks, and the caravans near the beach had disappeared.

I fell to the ground. It felt as if all the blood had drained from my body. Helpless, I watched a flock of flamingos on the southern edge of the town, preparing for flight.

"I'm going to faint," I whimpered in Hebrew. Jean tensed up and knelt beside me. Brunette padded up to me and thrust her nose into my armpit. I took a long breath and inhaled air redolent with horse droppings, trampled vegetation, and the scent of the sea. My brain contracted, and then, all at once, I threw up. I took another gulp of air and threw up again. From the window of one of the buildings of Le Destroit, a head wearing a strange helmet appeared, looking out at us with concern.

"Are you sure all is well, my lord?" shouted the guard.

Jean glanced at him and shouted back, "All is well, my good man. We came across a pilgrim; she is much parched. Return to your duties. I commend your vigilance." The man did not look convinced.

"As you wish, my lord," and his head disappeared from sight.

Jean led me back to the spring and helped me drink some water and wash my face. "What's going on?" I barely managed to get the words out. "Where's Halimi?"

"Where is who?" Jean asked.

"My . . . my servant," I said. "We must find him." With a glimmer of hope, I began rummaging deliriously through my backpack, looking for my cell phone. I sighed with relief as I fished it out of the bag, but when I switched it on, nothing happened.

"What is that?" Thibaut asked, setting down what I now presumed to be a lute.

"I . . . I can't say," I said weakly.

"She is either a fairy or a *poulain* or a Saracen in disguise," Thibaut proclaimed. "Those kinds always have various sophisticated instruments, not to mention satanic."

I blinked at them several times, came out from under the tree's canopy, and then went back under it. I sat down heavily near the spring and washed my face again.

"Perhaps this is all a dream?" I said out loud. The thought afforded me instant relief. I had simply fallen asleep near Halimi, and those goddamn mushrooms had tripped me out. I should wake up any minute.

"Life is but a dream," Thibaut hummed, strumming on his lute. "A pleasant but fleeting dream . . ." *Twang, twang,* his fingers whipped through the air with a soft, sweet melody.

"My lady, it will be my pleasure to assist you in locating your servant," Jean said, scowling at his friend. "His Royal Highness Thibaut and I are residing at Château Pèlerin. I am sure that the good knights will be happy to offer you shelter for a few nights if you and your servant have lost your way." He spoke slowly to me, as if he thought I was not quite right in the head. *Perhaps I wasn't,* it dawned on me. Perhaps the mushrooms had caused irreversible damage. "Halimi!" I suddenly remembered. "Let's go look for my servant," I told Jean.

"That's the name of a Saracen," Thibaut said, but he was smiling this time.

Twang, twang.

"Why not proceed, your Majesty, and ride to the château?" Jean suggested to Thibaut. "You can announce the arrival of a pilgrim lady who has lost her way, and they will have time to prepare lodgings."

"What impertinence!" Thibaut snarled, adding with surprising affection, "And the wretched brothers will have to atone for your raging impulses with infinite prayers, mortifications, and fasting." He fell silent for a moment and looked at me again. "Périgord will undoubtedly appreciate such a beauteous addition to the gloomy château. Very well, then." He leaped elegantly to his feet. "And since it is you who insisted we set out without squires, it is you who will pack up our chattels. That is what a savage such as yourself deserves."

"Certainly, your Royal Highness," said Jean. The two men grinned at each other, and Thibaut slapped Jean on the back. He packed up his lute in a lavish velvet sheath, secured the loops with practiced speed, and slung it over his shoulder.

"Don't spirit the poor fool away to the otherworld, my lady," he winked at me. "Have mercy upon this lowly creature; he has a wife and offspring."

Thibaut mounted the horse with incredible ease for a person with a body like his—he was tall and solid with a sizable paunch and massive limbs. As he leaped onto the horse, a pungent odor of sweat and moth-eaten clothes was released into the air. His large sword and lute, slung across his back, settled into place as though they were integral parts of his anatomy.

"Adieu!" he cried to us, spurring his horse, who broke into an easy gallop southward. Cedrique ran effortlessly behind them, barking joyfully. I followed them with my eyes until they descended beyond the Narrow Passage, disappearing onto the quarried road. The hoofbeats resounded for several moments. A short while after that, the figure of horse and rider appeared beside the walls of the fortress before being swallowed up inside.

I blinked again and shook my head. I held my breath, eyes closed, and tried to imagine Halimi waking up under the tree. I thought of the silence, the dark green shadows, and how he would begin looking for me. I imagined Simone putting Lily to bed in the hotel in the south. I took a deep breath and opened my eyes.

The fortress still loomed on the horizon, majestic and rock solid. The buildings of Le Destroit were scattered along the sandstone ridge. A seagull squawked overhead as if hurling curses at us. I burst into tears. Brunette came up to me and licked my hand. Jean, who was busy gathering up the leftovers and replacing the utensils in their containers, raised his head.

"We will begin the search for your servant *tout de suite*, my lady. Pray, do not worry."

"I don't know what's happening," I said in a voice that came out in small yelps. "I'm afraid I've flipped out." As soon as I said those words, I tried to swallow them back down my throat. Jean closed the satchel that hung off the saddle and walked over to me. "Come sit with me," he said. He also had a faint odor of sweat about him, but it was pleasant, with a dash of rose water and perhaps lemon. Brunette sprawled at our feet, eyed me for a moment, and then let her head sink down between her outstretched paws.

"I understand your distress, Lady Édith," Jean said in a practical tone. "Let us examine your predicament logically." A neurotic squeal of laughter escaped me, and my face again contorted into weeping. I let my head slump between my knees. "Fine," I said, in the general direction of my thighs. A warm, dry palm stroked my back. I straightened up. Jean smiled at me.

"Let us suppose this is indeed a dream," he said, his eyes merry. "Perchance, it is even a hallucination, but this is no nightmare. Am I mistaken? There are no evil monsters begging to devour you. *Au contraire*—there is someone who is ready and able to defend you." I looked at him doubtfully and turned his words over in my mind.

"That's true. It's a powerful trip, but not necessarily a bad one," I muttered.

"Ah . . . *excusez-moi?* What is powerful, but not bad?" Jean asked.

"The dream," I replied. "You're right. And perhaps I really am a kind of fairy. Perhaps I really did come from another world." He smiled at me. "*Voilà*, you're having an adventure. So am I. And Thibaut of Champagne will have a beauteous new *chanson*. Is that so terrible?"

I shrugged my shoulders, still disturbed.

"But everything is so real . . ." I said, in spite of his words. "And my husband, he came with me, and I don't know where he is now. He may be worried." I bit my lip and looked at Jean, momentarily flustered. He chuckled and said, "So, your servant is, in fact, your husband?"

"Yes," I answered with a nervous laugh. "I don't know why I said that."

Jean nodded and chuckled again. "That is a most precise description of a faithful husband," he said and rose to his feet. He held his hand out, and I stood up. "Shall we search for the good nobleman?" I nodded.

We began walking briskly southward, and I looked around with greater ease. Brunette ran circles around us, panting enthusiastically. My eyes returned constantly to the fortress. I was trying to work out whether there was an emblem on the flags that fluttered there. The thought that this might be a pleasant dream, however overpowering or shocking, calmed me down. I wondered if I might be able to fly, but I decided not to try my luck.

"Is it true, what Thibaut said back there?" I asked. Jean looked at me quizzically but kept walking.

"About your wife and children," I added.

"Indeed," Jean smiled. "I am wedded to Lady Alice, and with the grace of God we have been blessed with two children, Balian and little Jean, and my wife is presently with child."

Brunette barked.

"Hmm," I responded. "You definitely don't look like a married man with kids. Nor do you look like the kind of person who says, 'with the grace of God.'"

Jean roared with laughter. My smile was guarded, wondering what he found so funny. We were already nearing the Narrow Passage, which appeared to be in much better shape than the worn pathway I knew. Jean softly whistled the tune Thibaut had played earlier. Halimi was nowhere to be found.

"This is unreal," I muttered to myself in Hebrew.

Jean looked at me with intense curiosity.

By this time, the sun had sunk down almost as far as the sea. I was appalled to think I might be stuck here for the night. I couldn't entertain the possibility of getting stuck here forever. I felt as if I were doing a connect-the-dot puzzle, half-blinded and held upside down.

"My lady is in distress again," Jean said.

"I don't know how to get home," I said, and tears started running down my cheeks.

"Prithee, tell me how you arrived here," Jean said. The way he spoke reminded me of the tone I used when trying to calm Lily in the middle of a temper tantrum. "Perhaps we might solve this mystery together."

We began retracing our steps, and I cast a final glance at what was supposed to be Atlit but looked more like a swamp. I could almost see the greenish vapors rising up from it. Brunette ran as far as the Narrow Passage and then returned to us.

"Just tell me first," I said, my heart pounding, terrified of the answer. "What's the date today?"

"What do you mean?" Jean wrinkled his brow.

"What year is this?" I asked impatiently.

He gave me a hard stare, a glimmer of suspicion in his eyes. "It is the twelfth year of the reign of Conrad the Second of Jerusalem," Jean said slowly, gauging my reaction. "The last week of April. Yesterday, we commemorated St. George's Day."

"But . . . but . . ." I tried to express myself, but the words shattered in my mouth. "What year is"—and suddenly, it hit me. "How long ago was Jesus born?" I almost shouted. Jean nodded his head thoughtfully and said in a serious tone, "This is the year 1240 after the birth of our Savior."

Every single hair on my body stood up. I felt weak at the knees. I recalled the strange feeling I had had as I locked the door to the house that same morning. The date hammered the unbelievable into my brain.

"Speak, my lady," Jean said. Without threatening or intimidating, he was nonetheless demanding answers. "From whence did you come, and how did you get here?"

"You'll never believe me . . ." I said bitterly.

"Try me," Jean answered.

"Okay, so . . ." I began. "This morning, we sent our daughter to go stay with her grandparents." Jean frowned but said nothing. "We ate, showered, we watched a bit of TV, fell asleep . . ." I saw he was opening his mouth to ask something, but I waved my hand to cut him short. "Never mind. We fell asleep and then woke up. And then we ate magic mushrooms. Do you know what they are?"

"Are you referring to fly mushrooms? Of the fairy circles? The red ones with the white dots?" Jean asked with gravity.

"Something like that, yes."

"Did you eat them on purpose? For the love of God, why?" He looked at me as if I were deranged.

"Sometimes, we like to extend the boundaries of our consciousness," I said with a sense of self-importance. "Like you and your hashish."

"Hashish affords me tranquility and blurs the edges a little," Jean said, still wary. "Those mushrooms drive people mad."

"But this wasn't our first time!" I said defiantly. "And everything was fine. We're not novices."

"I see," Jean said, still patient. "And then what happened?"

"We left the house and . . ." I recalled the feeling I had had as I locked the front door, and I swallowed another lump of erupting anxiety. "We were heading out to the ruins."

"What ruins?" Jean asked.

"In my time, this place is just a ruin, a pile of stones," I said.

"Your time . . . do you believe you came from another time?" Jean asked haltingly.

"I know I did," I said. I heard the stubborn petulance in my voice and almost burst into tears again. Brunette rested her snout on my thigh. "I knew you wouldn't believe me," I added in the steadiest tone I could muster. Jean nodded his head, but his gaze was directed toward the sunset.

"Never mind," I said and continued—more for myself than for Jean. "We walked out of the neighborhood, over there"—I waved toward the south—"and we watched a flock of flamingos landing by the salt pools, and then we crossed the Narrow Passage and, after a while, sat down under one of those trees." And now I pointed north. "Trees that one day will be there," I added, after a moment of reflection. Jean said nothing, just looked out, eyes trained on the direction in which I pointed. "My husband lay down, which was unusual; he even closed his eyes, which was even more unusual, but I decided to keep walking. I heard strange music, like a distant guitar, and voices singing . . ."

I stopped speaking and contemplated it all over again. Was it Thibaut I'd heard playing the lute in my own time? I ran my fingers through my hair and continued. "I began thinking something was up, and then I smelled your hashish. I drew closer and saw you both, but neither of you noticed me. I went to drink from the spring—I'd never seen it before—and then there was a kind of explosion in my brain, and I felt as if I were drowning, and I fell backward. And when I opened my eyes, you were leaning over me."

Jean was speechless. I scratched my forehead and rubbed my nose.

"It's as if I'm describing a dream to a character in that very dream," I said. He chuckled and looked at me appreciatively, as if I'd just said something truly clever. I felt an enormous sense of weakness. If I'd been alone, I would have curled up on the ground and closed my eyes. *Perhaps if I fall asleep, I might wake up in my own time*, I thought. I fantasized about taking a shower, changing my tampon and my sweaty clothes, removing my contacts. I fingered the coin dreamily between my fingers. It was getting chilly, but the coin around my neck remained warm. Almost hot.

"Did you really throw a coin like this into the spring a few minutes before I appeared?" I asked Jean.

He glanced at the coin, then took hold of it, and the necklace pulled tight against my neck; I felt a strange vibration. "*Precisement,*" he replied. "This is a coin from Beirut, minted by my noble father, may his soul rest in peace. I suggest you remove it from your person if you do not want to attract unnecessary attention. Not everyone here is a devoted follower of the house of Ibelin, and a copper dinar is an extraordinary ornament in these parts."

"Are you from Beirut?" I asked in disbelief, removing the necklace and burying it deep in my backpack. "How's that even possible? I thought all the Crusaders were French. Or English. German at most."

I presumed Jean didn't hear what I was saying or didn't understand. He rubbed his face with the back of his hand. "This is all very peculiar." He lifted his head and gazed up at the horizon. "Perchance I smoked too much hashish."

I couldn't resist laughing at this. "I ate too many mushrooms, and you smoked too much hashish, and here we are together, and there are eight hundred years between us."

Jean lifted his head sharply. He was visibly flustered. "Eight hundred years?" he asked, lingering over each word. His eyes were like saucers, and for a moment I thought he believed me.

"I know it's hard to wrap your brain around it, but I've got to prove to you I'm not insane." I opened my purse, regretting that it closed with a button and not a zipper. "I know!" I called out in Hebrew and pulled out a ten-agorot coin that had fallen to the bottom of the purse, along with the dead phone and a handful of receipts and Post-it notes. It was the coin that Lily had asked me to look after.

A coin was something Jean could understand—indisputable proof I was from a different time. The date stamped on it was the Hebrew one, in Hebrew letters. It didn't really help me. Nevertheless, I held the coin out to Jean, who examined it, turning it over and over, shaking his head in disbelief.

"What is the language of this inscription?" he asked, pointing at the golden coin. "Hebrew," I answered, wondering how he would react. But he was clearly an educated man. "The language in which the Jews pray?" he asked, with a smirk. "This really is peculiar. Perhaps you erred and meant that you came from an earlier time?"

"This is a coin of the State of Israel," I said in a loud, clear voice, hoping my serious tone might convince him. "The state established by the Jews in 1948." I sighed. "That will be established," I corrected myself.

"If I were you, my lady, I would not repeat those words in the company of others," Jean said with a restrained smile. "If your purpose is to convince them of your sanity, I imagine you will achieve exactly the opposite effect." He handed the coin back, and I stared at it with the same attention.

"Here, look at this," I said and pointed to the inscription in Latin letters, *ISRAEL*. He took the coin back and examined it again and then looked at me, horrified.

"I beg you, my lady," he said, and for the first time that day, I heard something other than confidence in his voice. "I do not want to believe you are a demon sent to drive me insane. You are too beautiful and refined to have been sent by the devil. Take this cursed object from me and allow me to gather my thoughts." I retrieved the coin and slipped it into my pocket. *He thinks I'm beautiful and refined,* I hummed to myself with a sense of pleasure inappropriate for the occasion.

Despite what he had said earlier, Jean began busying himself with his satchel. He took out the clay hookah, a small pouch from which he removed a lump of hash, and the strange utensil with which he produced a flame. He also took out a leather canteen and drank from it in large gulps.

I waited patiently while Jean lit the hookah and took a few hits. I was taken aback by the intimacy I felt when he held out the hookah and offered me the rest of the hash. We sat there without talking for a few more minutes, and I suppressed the urge to rest my head on his shoulder. We enjoyed the final rays of light before the sun disappeared over the horizon, and then we stood up.

"And so, Lady Édith, your husband is nowhere to be found, and there is no sign of him having been here in the vicinity for the past few hours," Jean said. "Would you ride with me to the château and allow me to assist you further?"

"Yes, please," I said in a whisper. The thought of visiting the mighty fortress aroused my curiosity and even a modicum of excitement; I hoped that if I could rest my head on a pillow, I might wake up where I belonged.

"Okay, just let me freshen up," I said, walking over to the spring to wash my face again. I collected cold water in the palm of my hand and splashed it over my face. I certainly didn't want people from the past to think I was a filthy junkie. I took out the ten-agorot coin again and looked at it. This was the coin Lily had claimed as her own and asked me to keep for her. *My world still exists. I'm not crazy*, I told myself. I hoped Jean wasn't secretly planning on dragging me off to a medieval mental asylum. I took a peek at him. He was leaning over the saddle, murmuring something in the horse's ear. Brunette shifted restlessly.

I took a deep breath and submerged my entire head in the spring. I felt a hard tug, as if someone was yanking me by the hair and dragging me into the spring. My hands shot forward instinctively, to counteract the tremendous pull. My right hand was clenching something that, I realized later, was the ten-agorot coin. I managed to raise my head out of the water for a moment, one hand resting on the muddy floor of the pool, and I caught the expression on Jean's face as it morphed from composure to astonishment. And then I was sucked into the little pool, which was just the right size for my body, as if a magnet were pulling me with unbelievable strength. I heard Brunette barking, and then everything disappeared.

A sense of drowning and then a sharp twist, like I'd dived into an exceptionally narrow pipe, and then my lungs miraculously drew in air.

I was spread-eagled on the ground among low star thistle bushes. I was flailing, kicking at the air, and flinging clods of earth all over the place. My fist was closed tightly over the ten-agorot coin. The spring had vanished. There was a tree close by, but its canopy was sparser and its trunk more slender. Beyond, the Carmel Mountains towered above me, and below, the eastern side of Atlit, the coastal road packed with cars speeding by.

I looked out at the seashore, searching for the enormous fortress I'd gazed upon a few minutes earlier in the company of Jean d'Ibelin, Count of Arsur. My eyes lingered over the ruins and the white polystyrene-like structures of the Israeli naval base. Some distance away, a dog barked, and I could have sworn I heard the whinnying of a horse.

CHAPTER 5

A re you sure you're okay, Diti?" Halimi repeated, his eyes reduced to thin slits. I'd already told him several times that I was fine, that I just needed rest, that Dan deserved a thrashing, and that I would tell him what had happened later. But I sure as hell didn't look fine.

He'd just lit a cigarette, still disturbed by the fact that he'd fallen asleep in the middle of a mushroom trip, when I showed up, exhausted and glassy-eyed in the waning twilight, all but materializing in front of him from the void. I was still holding the ten-agorot coin, and the palm branch was tucked into my pants.

Halimi told me he'd had a wonderful dream: A little after I wandered off, he got up suddenly and walked to the shore at lightning speed, and when he got to the sea, he simply continued walking through it, and the more he walked, the lower the level of the water went, as if the tide were rapidly going out. The sea receded even faster than he was walking, leaving in its wake strips of sand and sandstone that sprang to life like a cartoon, sprouting bushes and trees and weeds, filling up with the buzzing of insects and the sound of distant voices. Finally, he reached an ancient village, and the people there were dressed like cavemen, in rags of leather and fur, and everyone stared at him and gestured strangely. They followed him as he walked to the center of the village, where he saw a circle of small stones, like a miniature Stonehenge, and in the middle of it, a spring was gurgling. He couldn't remember exactly what happened there, but in the end he almost drowned in the spring and was ejected back to the same tree he had fallen asleep under. He awoke, his senses overwhelmed.

Peering at the sky, Halimi noticed that at least two hours had gone by since he had fallen asleep. He'd wondered where I'd disappeared to and whether he should run back to the house or start looking for me. After this, he said, an inner voice told him that I was close by, and he resolved to take it easy. I'd probably gone off somewhere to pee, he thought, and perhaps I'd been here the whole time.

And then I suddenly emerged, just when he had decided to go look for me. I told him I'd had this crazy trip but couldn't talk about it right away. Then, I cried on his shoulder, and laughed, and then whimpered, and finally I drank some water and asked for a cigarette. We smoked in silence, and he watched me as I fiddled with the lighter, flicking it on and off.

"I don't even know how lighters work," I moaned, which must have sounded wacky, striking the metal cog and holding the flame to my face. Halimi chuckled and hugged me. "There are so many things you don't know, my dear, it's a wonder you survived at all," he said, holding me close. We smoked some more; I sipped water.

"Did you speak to your mom? Is everything okay with Lily?" I asked, my eyes still closed. "How could I have spoken to her? You've got the phone," he said.

"You're right," I said tiredly. "Let's head home."

He gave me the key to his apartment the morning of our fifth day together.

When I finally awoke on Saturday morning after our first date, Halimi was working on his laptop and talking on the phone. I waved to him shyly from the hallway, about to stumble into the bathroom, and he gestured to me with one hand to come. I signaled that I was going to brush my teeth, and he waggled his finger dismissively. "Get over here," his lips mouthed the words silently. I walked over. Halimi continued his phone call, and I sat on his knee. He immediately placed one hand on my right breast.

"Look, dude, there's no way we can put it off until next month, he'll go crazy," Halimi said to the person on the other end. "It's not that I mind pissing him off, but I'd also like to see it wrapped up," he said, rubbing his nose against my shoulder.

I planted a kiss on his head and stood up. "I need to pee," I whispered in his free ear. Halimi grabbed my hand and followed me, clutching the phone to his ear. I closed the bathroom door in his face and sat down on the toilet seat with relief. When I came out, he was still standing there, leaning against the wall, his phone call over. "Coffee?" he asked, and when I nodded, he walked over to the tiny kitchen. "I've got nothing to offer you to eat, what a disgrace," he said. "You'll probably hate me now. Maybe I can rustle up some cornflakes. Shit, there's no milk."

When we went back to the living room, I said to Halimi, "Yesterday at the club, when you hugged me, I got the feeling that we'd met before, in another life."

A wide smile spread across his face. "You were Cleopatra, and I was Caesar, right?"

"No, not like that," I said, throwing a cornflake at him. "I know it sounds dumb. It's nothing, only I had these hallucinations—I saw us climbing up some mountain together, and . . ." I tried to re-create the memory like a blurry dream. "Maybe we also sat together on a couch with a blond child. Stuff like that. Kind of silly."

"Not silly at all," Halimi said quietly. He sat down next to me on the couch and embraced me. "It might be difficult to believe, but I'm actually a really romantic guy. I totally believe in love at first sight."

I laughed and gave him a little shove. "Don't make fun of me."

"I'm not," said Halimi in a hurt voice. "I swear to God."

"Okay, okay," I said. I didn't want to ruin the vibe between us. I held out my hand and smiled at him. "So, we met in a previous life."

We drank the rest of our coffee without speaking. I smoked a cigarette, and then he did. Soft Brazilian music played from an Internet radio station on his computer. Halimi hummed along to the music. The chirping of birds replaced the noise of cars from the street below. An episode of *Seinfeld* blared out from the neighbors' window. The Sabbath serenity was absolute; I felt totally at home.

"It's too good to be true, right?" I didn't mean to bring him down, but I sensed an unexpected spark of panic in Halimi's eyes. "No, I didn't mean . . . ," I continued, sipping my coffee carefully. "It feels like something out of time, right?" I didn't wait for a response but pushed on swiftly. "Let's act like tourists—on vacation in Tel Aviv for a few days. What do you say?" I looked up at him.

"I adore you," Halimi said, holding out his arms to me. "Do you want to marry me?"

"Sure," I said. "Now or after breakfast?"

Halimi loved the idea of a vacation and began planning our itinerary with the thoroughness of a seasoned tourist. He began rummaging through email invites he had received to various new restaurant and exhibition openings, suggesting places and quizzing me on my food preferences.

For a few days, we explored Tel Aviv as though we were visiting for the first time. We went to restaurants and movies, walked through gardens, sunbathed at the beach, wandered around streets, and sat on park benches. I smoked whatever I had on me, and he drank whiskey and smoked his Camels. We made love constantly. Halimi was passionate about me to a degree that made me doubt his sincerity, but every time I expressed skepticism at his excessive compliments, he acted hurt. I never made any declarations of love, but I clung to him as though he were mine alone.

I decided to go back to my place five days later. I told him I had stuff to do, which was true—there were still a few adjustments to make to the translation I'd finished, and I had no clean clothes left to wear. When I got out of his shower, Halimi was nowhere to be found. I got dressed, wondering where he was. I texted him, "Where are you?" but he didn't reply. I packed my overnight bag and smoked a cigarette by the window, deliberating whether to write him a note before I left.

As I got off the couch, I heard the apartment door opening. I stood there, a little sheepish, my overnight bag by my side, a smoldering cigarette butt in the ashtray. Halimi pranced into the living room, holding a key between his fingers. "This is for you," he crooned.

"What?" I asked.

"I had a key made for you," he said and pounced on me, tossing my bag aside and pulling me onto the couch.

At about eleven that night, I insisted on going home. "Are you coming back?" he asked me several times. "Of course I am," I told him. He walked me home but didn't come in. He was a little sullen, and as I began climbing the steps, I decided it was ridiculous for five beautiful days to end like this. I walked back down. Halimi was still standing there, like he was waiting for me to enter my apartment before leaving.

"Limi, don't be an idiot," I said softly, embracing him. "I'm just going home for a little, and then I'll come back, if you like."

He held me close and said, "I'm going to kidnap you and never let you go."

I laughed, and he patted me on my ass and said, "*Yalla*, good night, darling."

Before I fell asleep, burrowed under my soft bedsheets, my thoughts wandered to the key he'd given me. The very existence of that key, dropped into my little blue purse as though it were nothing, imbued me with a deep tranquility. I imagined walking home on a rainy day and dropping in to see him, scampering up the steps to his apartment, removing the key from my purse, and letting myself in. I could almost hear the rain coming down as I drifted off, even though I knew it was only water dripping on my windowsill from my upstairs neighbor's AC.

At about eight the next morning, he texted me: "I'm here." I got up, tugged my tank top down, put my glasses on, and went over to the window. He was sitting on the wall with his back to me, a fancy bottle tucked under his arm. Placed on the wall beside him was a bulging plastic bag. I opened the window and gave a low whistle. He turned around, and his face lit up. "Can I come up?" he called. I stared down at him. "What's that, champagne?" I asked, trying to figure out whether he was drunk or not. "Yup, I just bought it," he answered, staring at the bottle in mock surprise. "And I got you fresh bread rolls for breakfast," he added. "So, what do you say?"

My roommate was still asleep, and Halimi acted with overzealous caution, exaggerating every movement. He spoke in a stage whisper even though I talked normally. We went into my room, and he dropped onto the bed right away, extending his legs and leaning back comfortably, as if he'd lived here all his life. He looked at the walls, the bed, surveying the posters and all my knickknacks, casting a curious glance at the pile of clothes discarded on a chair.

"I guess I can't smoke in here. Your roommate and all that," he said.

I pointed at the window. "You can smoke there."

"How did you sleep?" Halimi inquired.

"Pretty good," I answered. He smoked by the window and didn't speak. I got dressed unhurriedly and, after tying my hair back, noticed Halimi looking at me, mesmerized.

"So, what's your routine?" he asked, extinguishing the cigarette on the windowsill and flicking it outside with two fingers.

I grinned. "Shower. Breakfast. Laptop. Sometimes, I go to the library. After that, I usually work at the café. Sometimes, I meet my best friend, Libby. I generally eat lunch at home." I was going to continue, but then he asked, "What do you generally make for lunch?" I went over to him and put my arms around him, sitting on the windowsill. He buried his nose between my breasts, and his voice sounded muffled as he said, "Maybe come live with me?" and I laughed and said, "Maybe."

* * *

As soon as we got home, I took a long shower. First, I removed the soaked tampon and threw it into the trash without wrapping it in toilet paper, which I always did. I was still dazed by what had happened. After steaming my body in scalding hot water, I toweled off and decided not to put in a tampon. I chose a pad instead: I wanted to feel the blood flow unabated.

When I was done in the shower, I skipped dinner, drank a lot of water, and then crawled into bed. I placed the bedraggled palm branch on the dresser and beside it the necklace and Lily's ten-agorot coin. Halimi sat beside me on the bed. He told me he'd spoken to Simone and all was well. While he detailed Lily's antics at dinner, I pretended to fall asleep. I couldn't bear his endless chatter.

After he left the room, I tossed and turned. I was so fatigued, it felt like every cell in my body had melted. I told myself: *It's okay, you're fine, you're home now.* But I couldn't sleep. My thoughts returned to that wild trip I'd had. Was it possible to imagine such things? The skittish snorting of horses, the twang of Thibaut's lute, the pungent smell of trampled grass, and the way Jean whistled to himself as we looked for Halimi . . .

Halimi. Who sat, smoking at his leisure, while I teetered between sanity and insanity, on the edge of an abyss. My legs convulsed and twitched when it dawned on me that I had totally wasted my magical trip looking for Halimi, while he had been taking a nap and having a dumb dream. As always—Halimi did as he pleased, and I went out looking for him like an idiot.

I heard him pacing back and forth on the balcony. I figured he was having difficulty formulating what troubled him. Of course, he'd done mushrooms several times before and knew the effect of psychoactive substances. He'd experienced more and less powerful trips, but he'd never fallen asleep and had never heard of anyone else who'd fallen asleep when the 'shroom trip peaked, or during any other kind of trip. And as for me . . . something had happened to me during my trip, and I didn't want to talk to Halimi about it. He didn't know what to make of it.

In my mind's eye, I saw him stubbing out his umpteenth Camel in the overflowing ashtray on the balcony and forcing himself to unwind. I could hear him thinking: *Diti will be fine, I'll be fine, and next time, we'll be careful and take less. And perhaps we're simply getting too old for this.* I knew that this line of thought, in first-person singular, would have sent shudders through him a few years ago, propelling him into a rampage of unbridled drinking and fucking; now, first-person plural, the thought was consoling.

I heard him go into Lily's bedroom. He gathered up a few scattered toys and lay down on her bed, a kid's bed from IKEA, with decorative metal side rails painted white. He was probably lying diagonally across the mattress, his long legs hanging down; maybe his thoughts were wandering back to when I had materialized in front of him.

I squirmed at how I'd privately blamed him for my bizarre adventure. I also remembered the relief I'd felt when I saw him, when I'd realized it had all been nothing more than a trip—intricate and realistic, but impossible to believe that it could have been anything more than that. Relief surged through me again, and I closed my eyes. The astonished look on Jean's face appeared in front of me, the shock that had petrified him as I was sucked into the spring. A giggle escaped my lips in the darkness.

I continued tossing and turning. Finally, I got up and went quietly down the stairs. The house was drenched in moonlight. I went outside, and even though it was the middle of the night, the yard was lit up, almost as though it were broad daylight. I sat down at the massive wooden trestle table. It took me a while to work out that I wasn't sitting alone at the massive table: Jean d'Ibelin was sitting there, too, his head between his hands.

"You again?" I asked. He lifted his head and smiled at me with barely a glimmer of surprise. It felt natural to me that he was sitting there too.

I allowed myself to reach out for the giant goblet of ale on the table. I drank deeply from it. It had a heavy, sweet taste.

"So, what exactly is happening here?" I asked matter-of-factly. Jean launched into a lengthy reply, but he spoke in numbers and complicated equations, spilling into quantum mechanics and string theory.

"But the most important part is still ahead of us," he concluded, picking up the Ibelin coin that lay on the table. The silver chain shone in the unnatural light. "Pray, do not forget the coin next time you visit." I took the coin, threaded it onto the chain, and hung it around my neck.

"I must take my leave." Jean d'Ibelin got to his feet. "My wife awaits me." I felt a lump in my throat. I made an effort not to cry. "So soon?" I blurted out. "We didn't even have time to . . ." I felt his light, dry touch on my back, the same way he had touched me before, but when I raised my head, he was no longer there. Nor was the trestle table. I sat on Lily's blue plastic swing. I realized I was dreaming because there was no way I could squeeze my adult ass into the narrow swing seat, and this only made me cry harder.

"Diti," I heard a voice whispering in the darkness, and a large, warm hand took hold of me. "Who is it?" I gasped, getting off the dream swing. "It's me, babe," I heard Halimi say. "Did you have a bad dream?"

I lay back in bed, nestled in Halimi's arms. His scent enveloped me with a sense of the familiar; he didn't mind the sweat that drenched my body. I felt sturdier and more substantial like this.

"Sweetheart . . ." I heard the concern in his voice. "Are you sure you're okay?"

"No," I replied.

During the first few months of our relationship, Halimi was enchanted by his ability to fall in love so deeply. He lost all interest in other women—he tested it empirically—and he felt he'd shed ten years: He was strong and vital, his appetite returned, and even his coughing attacks subsided.

He only drank when he went out. He smoked less. He reveled in the opportunity to be the responsible adult, something he had wanted for years, or so he claimed. He made sure I ate well and drank well, that I got enough sleep, that I was comfortable and wanted for nothing.

We spent hours in *tête-à-têtes* and philosophical debates through long nights in which we walked across town, got wasted in various bars (my alcohol tolerance soon grew, filling Halimi with paternal pride), or lay naked on Halimi's bed. One night, he admitted that most of the women he'd been interested in ended up boring him to death in a few weeks, if not in a few hours. "Obviously, I'll end up boring you too," I retorted half-defiantly, quietly acknowledging his words. "If you don't bore me first," I added right away, determined not to be a bore. Halimi laughed and hugged me.

"There's a better chance of me boring you first," he joked and then suddenly turned solemn.

Throughout that time, former lovers continued to show up here and there. Isolated text messages at night, Facebook chats that popped up on his computer screen with an annoying ping, funny GIFs and emojis, telephone calls that Halimi answered before casting an unnecessarily imploring look in my direction. He spoke briefly and coldly, burning all the bridges he'd sustained over the years with his fuck buddies. It made me nervous in a way I couldn't quite explain. I felt empathy toward all the women who had ever thought they were something special to Halimi, and probably some of them had been. But I knew it was also out of fear that one day he might do the same thing to me. "You're cute and sweet and oh so pious," he'd tell me when I suggested he explain that he was in a relationship rather than act like an asshole.

I officially moved in with him about two months after Eran's birthday party, although I was basically already living there. We made each other laugh endlessly, we discovered a mutual love for books and movies, we told each other childhood stories, and we got to know members of our respective families. Nevertheless, I anticipated the inevitable deterioration—it was impossible to believe we'd simply live happily ever after—and I was sure that he envisioned a doomed future too.

Back in those days, Halimi was editor in chief of a women's magazine that branded itself as snarky and sophisticated. It was scandalous that he'd landed the job: The move was considered "the cigarette in the eye of the feminist struggle." I recalled reading incendiary posts on Facebook before I had even known Halimi personally. Women who'd never read the magazine called for boycotts ("I might not be the typical reader of *Free to Be*, but why on earth was . . ."); every media review website was packed with analysis about it. But Halimi enjoyed the uproar, and so did the magazine's circulation. And in truth, he did a great job. The tips on beauty, relationships, and parenting remained, but the routine covers of smoky-eyed, half-naked women looking feistily into the camera disappeared.

The new covers of *Free to Be* were shot by top photographers or adorned with *New Yorker*-style illustrations, heralding in-depth articles and multidisciplinary projects. By the time we became a couple, Halimi had already been editor in chief for two years—he earned a great salary and had hired an all-female staff that included an experienced deputy editor and high-powered content producers. Occasionally, he had to approve material, attend weekly staff meetings, pitch ideas, put in an appearance at some photo shoots, and snag various key figures—from writers and photographers to interviewees—to oversee the feverish closing of an edition before it went to the printers each month. The rest of the time, he was free to hang out, have fun, and mull things over.

He used to say that his work was bullshit—"Pink frothy bubble bath," he called it—compared to what I was doing. Back then, I was translating novels and textbooks from Russian, French, and English into Hebrew, and I got good enough to be able to pick and choose what I did. I'd been attracted to French since childhood, perhaps owing to its status among the Russian aristocracy, about whom I read in the many books that had migrated along with my parents to cover two whole walls of shelves in their Jerusalem apartment. I'd studied advanced French in high school and completed graduate studies in French and Classical Studies. I traveled to France whenever I got the chance. To better appreciate the various layers of meaning in a French text I'd translated, I began a self-directed study of Old and Middle French, particularly the Norman and Provençal dialects. Part of Halimi's charm when we first got together was his French roots, by way of Algeria—still another aperture for French language and culture to permeate our everyday life.

I spent a few years translating second- and third-rate fantasy and sci-fi series, mostly from Russian and English, until one of them unexpectedly became a big hit. Its reviews attributed its success to the translation, wryly claiming it had improved the book. Other, bigger, and more prestigious publishing houses approached me. French translation work began pouring in. At first, I loved immersing myself in the language I adored, and I also enjoyed my rising status, but after a few years, I was bored out of my mind. Literature as such consisted of tiresome sagas of graphomania and self-importance—novels that ambled along behind an egocentric protagonist with dulled senses searching for himself in vain, usually by exploiting weaker people, groveling to more aggressive people, talking the talk and name-dropping.

There was, of course, literature I enjoyed reading and translating, such as the genre-defying novel by a mysterious Russian writer (who never gave interviews to the press, even though he was hugely successful in Europe and Japan) about the owner of a matchstick factory who's visited by prophetic visions. He resolves to set fire to his hometown and is ultimately declared a saint by the church. I later discovered that Halimi was quoting the book to anyone willing to listen months before we met. When he discovered it was me who'd translated it, he almost lost his mind. He saw it as a harbinger of things to come. He would ask me to read it to him in the source language; it made him horny.

Anyway, I finally tired of French novels. I had signed on for a variety of projects—classic YA series, disturbing graphic novels, juicy fantasy trilogies. Occasionally, I was hired by publishing houses and newspapers as a linguistic editor and translator. I never earned enough to be able to squander money, and Halimi charged like a battering ram at this window of opportunity, paying for everything and refusing to consider that we share expenses. He took me abroad twice in our first year together, once to an urban festival in Barcelona, and once on a monthlong hike through Laos and Cambodia. A few months after I moved in with him, he added my name to his bank account. After I'd had quite a few years of proudly supporting myself and saving money, his cheerful benevolence sucked me in like a whirlpool.

Halimi liked sitting beside me while I translated. He would read a book, work on one of his projects, or simply scroll through Facebook. No one could have been happier than Halimi when I conferred with him over a certain word or phrase. I also loved sitting by his side at meetings in cafés he frequented, typing on my laptop and listening to music through headphones. Sometimes, I would switch off the music and listen in on Halimi chatting with colleagues. It always fascinated me how morsels of gossip and snippets of information could turn into an interesting article or photo essay.

When we went to clubs and parties, which we did frequently in those days, we took care of each other—mostly when we got hammered or did too many drugs—but we didn't have any claims on each other. Each of us tended to wander off alone and disappear from the other's sight—but not for very long. We danced together, but not exclusively so, and when we came across each other in a dark corner or hallway, we would hold each other the way we did that very first time—as if we were meeting after years of living apart.

*   *   *

It took me time to open my eyes the next morning. I felt a dull sense of emptiness that rapidly intensified, and after a few seconds, I realized I was ravenous. I imagined slices of bread swimming in butter and the oatmeal I had to make for Lily. Then, I realized Lily wasn't home, and the habitual vigilance faded. I tracked the sun's rays and, in the morning light, envisioned the figures of Jean and Thibaut, the way they'd been sitting when I came across them over the ridge, writing songs and smoking from that clay pot. For a moment, I imagined them in the yard of my old high school, cutting gym class (*twang, twang*, the strings sounded in my head). I got dressed and went to fix myself some coffee.

Halimi was stretched across the couch, buried under the weekend newspapers. He lifted his head when I came in and narrowed his eyes. I turned the kettle on, poked around in the fridge (I pulled out smoked salmon and vegetables, as well as butter), and when I caught sight of Halimi's smiling face, I gave him a wink.

"Cool, cool," Halimi said, leaning back. "You had me a little worried back there. What happened?" I sliced a loaf of bread, considered his question, and finally said, "Something . . . entirely out of the ordinary." I started to say something else but stopped. "Have you eaten? Do you want something to eat?" I asked him. I cut vegetables, arranged the cutlery, and made coffee. Halimi joined me at the table. "Coffee?" I asked.

We ate and drank, chewing hard and gulping deeply. He tried not to say anything but finally gave up and looked me in the face. "Aren't you going to tell me what happened?"

I giggled with embarrassment. "No, it's just . . . just so crazy," I said quickly. "I had a trip that I went back to the Crusader days." Halimi's eyebrows rose in surprise. "I saw the fortress and the village and the swamps and everything," I continued in a rush. "Did you know that mushrooms can do stuff like that?" I asked him. "I thought that only happened with cacti."

Halimi chuckled and repeated, "'cacti.'" But I could tell he was piecing it all together. "I also went back in time in my dream. I think I went to that Neolithic village buried under the sea . . . and the very fact that I fell asleep . . ." He rubbed his forehead.

I asked him to tell me more about his dream—and he tried—but when he began describing the receding tide, he was actually telling me about the people in tattered furs, and when he tried to describe the spring in the middle of the village, he suddenly began wondering aloud about the pitcher a priestess was holding, and how she had poured a brown-red liquid over his head. As I half-listened, my thoughts returned to the sandstone ridge and the buildings I had seen there.

"Anyway, there's still a bit left. Do you want another round of 'shrooms?" Halimi asked in his mischievous voice, which didn't contradict the questions.

"No, no. Not yet," I trembled. "I thought I'd flipped, honestly, it was so . . . real." I stroked the coin that hung around my neck. It had returned to its worn and lackluster state.

We called Simone after that, who said everything was *merveilleux*—Lily was having the time of her life. She was hanging out with Richard while Simone sunbathed and read. She promised they'd be back that evening, but late.

Halimi suggested we take a walk to the sea. I almost turned him down—I'd already found a comfortable position from which to stare at the ceiling and chew things over—but Halimi insisted. "Come on, let's get some fresh air," he said. "I'm going anyway, but it'll be more fun with you." I dragged myself off the couch, stretched extravagantly, and slipped into my flip-flops. Everything suddenly felt so sweet.

When we reached the shore, we sat down and watched the high waves breaking in front of us. The sun burned a few inches above the sea, and I yielded to those final moments of warmth down to the smallest molecule in my body. I sighed in pure delight, and Halimi beamed with pleasure. He smoked his Camels, and I rolled myself a cigarette. We drank a bottle of Coke together.

Everything was so normal. I stared at the little that was left of the fortress, expecting to feel anxious or alarmed, but the ruins were just ruins. Through the fence, I saw a military vehicle driving through the base behind the fortress. Halimi was in a rare, contemplative silence. He stared out at the sea almost bashfully. "I can't get that priestess from the dream out of my head," he said. He never remembered his dreams and never talked about them. But there was more. "She was naked," he continued, furrows deepening across his wide forehead. "I think she was pouring blood over me. I don't know if it was the blood of an animal or a human." He shivered.

"Weird," I said, almost whispering. Halimi's words ignited an array of visuals inside my head: Jean, lighting the clump of dry weeds with a graceful motion; Thibaut, eyes closed, plucking his lute and humming to himself; the curls of smoke rising up from the hamlet. I glanced behind me, but my eyes met only the familiar landscape—salt pools; roads; construction sites that had unearthed white dust, biting into the earth and sandstone; and clusters of middle-class houses in the nearby neighborhood.

I walked into the sea; Halimi finished his cigarette and joined me. We stood there, not talking, his arm resting on my shoulder, my arm curled around his back, the waves breaking against our ankles.

CHAPTER 6

It happened the year after we met. We went out clubbing, as we did most weekends. We drank a lot, and at some stage Halimi disappeared into the dark recesses of the club. I danced for hours with Libby and a bunch of other people who came and went. At some point I went to the bathroom, and it was there that I heard groans coming from one of the stalls. I smiled—remembering that first night with Halimi—and suddenly realized that I recognized his voice.

I froze up, even though I knew that I had been waiting for this moment. I leaned against one of the walls, waiting for them to leave the stall, part of my brain curious to see how he would handle this.

The girl came out first. It was smooth black bob, thick eyeliner, flaming-red lipstick, the one who'd pestered us that first night. I was overcome with revulsion, if only because of the tacky coincidence. The girl went over to the sink; her eyes were bleary, and her makeup smudged. She tugged at her miniskirt and tried to adjust her shirt. She didn't notice me, just washed her face, threw a glance in the direction of the stall, and turned to leave.

"Are you coming?" she asked briskly.

"No." Halimi's voice was low and gravelly. "Give me a minute."

The girl shrugged her shoulders. "As long as your lady friend doesn't catch you, right?" she asked in the same nonchalant tone. There was no response from the stall, and she left.

I heard a rustling from the stall, the click of a lighter, and a faint crackle of friction between flame and cigarette. I heard Halimi inhaling and exhaling. I was dying to smoke a cigarette, too, but he had the pack. The voyeur inside me knew I would never give up the dramatic moment in which Halimi exited the stall and saw me. I could already imagine telling the whole sorry tale to my sister, Dina ("I caught him fucking some girl in the bathroom of the club! Just like in the movies!")

While waiting, my resolve weakened. I began to cry. The cold and rational voice inside my head said, *Honestly—what's the big deal? It's not like you didn't expect it.* But my mind kept digging in—like a tongue probing a cavity—with a clear memory of that morning when he said he'd impregnate me, and I spread my legs wide and lifted my hips even higher and whispered, "Go for it."

I heard a movement and straightened up a little, and Halimi exited the stall. He headed straight for the sink to wash his face and didn't notice me right away. But when he raised his head, he saw me out of the corner of his eye and turned to face me. Horror was etched all over his face. "Oh no," he said.

"Oh no, indeed," I said.

He collapsed onto the filthy floor, his back to the wall, and his eyes welled up with tears. It terrified, even disgusted me a bit. "I'm so drunk. Dumb. And drunk. Dumb," he said, his usual diction dropped. "Will you come home with me just one more time?"

I decided it would be better to spend the night at home and then play it by ear. We said nothing to each other the entire cab ride back. When we entered the apartment, Halimi got down on his knees and clung to my thighs.

"Give me a break, stop it," I said.

"I'll kill myself if you leave me," he begged.

"Don't kill yourself, you piece of shit," I spat back.

Halimi went off to throw up in the bathroom, and I changed my clothes. I sat on the bed for a few minutes, staring into space. I heard him brushing his teeth. I threw on a pair of old sweatpants and went back into the living room. Halimi had fallen asleep on the couch, his mouth slightly open. I sat down in the easy chair, lit a cigarette, and numbly checked my social media feeds. Halimi gave a small snore. I jumped out of the easy chair, alarmed by my revulsion toward him. I took a deep breath, and the moment I began texting Libby, he opened his eyes. It never took him more than a moment to wake up. "Do you hate me?" he asked.

"Not entirely," I answered, for some reason attempting restraint. Halimi sat up, fixed his eyes on me, and rubbed his nose with a shaking hand.

I wanted to get something straight here.

"See," I began, "I don't really care that much if you stick your dick in some other woman's cunt . . ."

"Diti, come on," Halimi protested, and a half-laugh, half-cry escaped my throat.

"Ah, is that too graphic for your delicate soul all of a sudden?"

"You're right," Halimi said submissively. "I'll shut up."

"I don't care that much," I repeated, emphasizing the word *that*. "But why did you have to do it *there*? In the bathroom of the club, where we . . ." I got angry and dropped it. "Never mind, that's not the point. It's just that I always thought if you ever had a fling with anyone else, you'd warn me first. You'd make sure I was ready for it, I don't know, that I didn't need you right then—"

"You're right, you're right," he said, shaking his head. "I'm a total ass."

"It's just that, I don't know . . . ," I continued. "I thought we were in this together. That you wouldn't pull something like this on me."

"Darling," he said, his eyes imploring.

"Stop looking at me like a sad puppy, Halimi, honestly," I flared up again. "It makes me feel like a librarian annoyed at a student for not returning a book on time."

"I'm an ass," he repeated.

He climbed into bed while I brushed my teeth. When I got into bed, he asked if it would be okay to hug me. Disconcerted, I agreed. He repeatedly told me he was a scumbag, a lowlife undeserving of love, that the girl had started making out with him and he had just gotten carried away.

When he said it would never happen again, I pulled away from him. "It'll happen again, I have no doubt about that," I said. There was silence, and Halimi tried to say something but failed. Finally, he spluttered, "So, that's it, you're breaking up with me? Is that it?"

His voice was matter-of-fact, even cold. In the darkness of the bedroom, I heard the ticking of the clock on the wall and Halimi's breaths.

"I'll tell you the truth, Limi," I said after a while. "You know I fell in love with you completely, even though I didn't mean to. I never believed we'd stay together for more than a month. And I don't know if it can work, considering the kinds of things you do."

"Considering," Halimi said quietly and clung to me again. "I'm willing to undergo chemical castration if you'll stay with me," he added, wrapping his long arms tighter around me. "But only after you give me a baby. Even if you leave me after." I laughed, and the fact that he could still make me laugh, even now, suddenly made it all look idiotic and insignificant. While I thought about it some more, I realized he'd fallen asleep.

I woke him up in the middle of the night and said, "What about an open relationship?"

"Give me a break," Halimi mumbled, his arms still around me.

* * *

"So, he doesn't want to know?" my sister said, thoughtfully chewing on a carrot stick she'd cut for Max. Max and his sister, Eva, came in and out of the frame behind Dina as we chatted on Zoom.

"It's not a good sign . . . If he doesn't want to know, it means he doesn't really want to deal with it."

Throughout her adolescence, Dina shocked our parents with outrageous behavior. She became a heroin addict and went to rehab on a farm in Spain. After that, she floated through different countries. Twice she joined mystical-spiritual cults and stormed out of both. In recent years, she'd settled down in Berlin with Georg, an installation artist who initially came off as a psychopath but was actually a very gentle soul.

We maintained a strong bond throughout the years. I was quite close to my parents, too, but it wasn't the same. Natasha and Sergei Rozhevsky were frozen in the time before they moved from Russia to Israel. Old black-and-white photos revealed a wild youth, all-night parties, fancy costumes, guitars. Stories of underground manuscripts and clandestine recordings of Western music circulated among the few friends who also immigrated to Israel. But in Israel, they became moralistic and neurotic, and when they finally settled in, my sister and I had already left home. It was only on weekend visits later, when I was a student, that I began talking to my mom about her youth and her life.

They would come once a month for lunch at a Tel Aviv restaurant, and sometimes Halimi and I would sleep over at their small apartment in Jerusalem. Halimi loved Jerusalem and its wind-blown hills, the stones that turned pink at sunset, the introspective denizens. He particularly loved Natasha and Sergei's warm little den, its walls lined floor to ceiling with books, my dad's old record collection, and the tea and candies served every couple of hours. My parents adored Halimi—he flirted shamelessly with my mom and made her laugh like a teenager. He argued with my dad over politics. They agreed on nothing, but both of them enjoyed the clashes.

I spoke to Dina almost every day—by phone or Messenger, and sometimes we spoke on Zoom. I visited her frequently in Berlin, and whenever it seemed like things were getting out of hand in Israel, I toyed with the idea of moving there. By the time Halimi and I started living together, Dina was already a mom. Dina and Georg—who met at a crazy party one night at Berghain—decided on an open relationship with clear boundaries from the start: one-night stands only, no affairs, complete transparency with each other, and the right to veto. It worked—they stuck to the rules, their love for each other blossomed, and Dina gathered material for a book on how to sustain consensual non-monogamy.

"That's what I understand from him," I answered. "He doesn't want to know, and he doesn't want me to know either." I tried to get Max's attention by making a funny face. Both Halimi and I were in a kind of anxious euphoria at our joint decision to experiment. Negotiations on exactly how we might do it were dragging on.

"I just don't get why this is what you want to formalize . . ." Halimi would say when I broached the subject of "the rules," holding my hand and stroking the engagement ring he gave me with great ceremony one Saturday morning. I smiled but wouldn't drop the subject. In fact, after agonizing over it for a number of weeks, I wasn't sure that I wanted to marry him just because I was in love with him and pregnant with his child. Eventually I decided that yes, it was enough—but I was determined to straighten out the subject of adultery.

"I just want to deal with it," I'd say to him. He would stare at me with characteristic feline pleasure, totally ignoring my words and ensconced in a halo of blind adoration, as if resisting the urge to jump me.

"I mean, it's clear we both have healthy libidos and a tendency to get turned on by others," I would say, trying to catch his wandering attention. "And instead of causing each other pain, I just want to neutralize it, you know? So we can trust each other."

"You're so sweet," Halimi would say, and once, when he was in a cooperative mood, he continued, "but it's human nature to sin, my love. It's got nothing to do with sex or not, with men or women, right? That's the secret, the excitement, the danger. The fact you're doing something forbidden and it's so fun. That's the sin."

"So, you do believe that you and I are going to sin, right?" I said impatiently.

Halimi fell silent and looked at me.

"Yes, Diti, yes," he answered unwillingly.

"So, you're just going to accept the pain we'll cause each other?"

"Look," he said, trying not to smile, "we need to be super discreet." When he saw my face fall, he quickly added, "Without overdoing it, of course."

"I want to know the truth," I said in a voice brimming with seriousness. "And I expect you to give it to me," I added.

"Come on, Diti, honestly . . ." Halimi pleaded. "You want me to report to you every time there's a chance I might fool around with someone whose name I won't even remember an hour later? Why would you want to know?"

I didn't know what to say in response. A cold fury swept over me, but I didn't let it go. I couldn't believe he wasn't willing to accommodate me.

"And maybe it isn't human nature at all, the tendency to 'sin,' the secrecy and the lying, maybe that's unique to you, Saul," I said brusquely.

"Could be," he said icily, and from that moment until we retired for the night, he treated me with cold politeness. He was horribly distant and reacted with one-syllable responses. This was the first time he'd ever treated me like that—and suddenly it hit me that he was capable of totally alienating himself from me.

I cried that night and felt short of breath. I moaned and groaned, and my pregnant belly moaned and groaned along with me. Halimi tried to feign calm, but he was worried. I stopped him when he began dialing the emergency number. I told him between clenched teeth that I was okay and forced myself to relax both my muscles and my nerves. I breathed deeply, in and out; I swallowed again and again; I inhaled and exhaled. He brought me more water than I could drink, placed a damp towel on my forehead, and then simply sat beside me and stroked my hair, and occasionally my arms. It did the trick, and I fell asleep.

In the morning, it was like it never happened. I worked on my laptop in the living room; he returned from his walk through the neighborhood—maybe he'd bought cigarettes. When he came into the living room, he was humming happily to himself and looked around his former bachelor pad, transformed into a warm nest for the coming baby chick. Drapes and lampshades and pictures and framed memories— tickets from a particularly good music festival where I most likely was impregnated, a poem by a Polish writer we both liked, a photo of us in Cambodia, the red-and-gold bedspread I flung across his old couch— everything that rounded and softened the sharp corners and empty surfaces. I saw the pleasure on his face when he entered the apartment, knowing that all this was his now. He leaped on me with declarations of adoration and gestures of love, and I yielded with bursts of laughter. Anything to do with "the rules" made him revert to his impressive passivity, and me to my ideological determination.

"Why can't we live in solidarity with this thing as well? So that it'll be something we are equal partners in?" I attacked him from another angle, focusing on his weakness for social issues.

Halimi sighed. "Because I'm telling you again," he would begin, and I never knew if the look on his face was sad or if he was simply losing patience. "This. Isn't. About. Sex. If you want it that bad, then okay—I'll try letting you know when I'm attracted to someone, and if you give me the green light, I'll go for it and let you know what happens afterward. Yup. So that's an option. I hope. And you, too, okay? If you're attracted, and so on and so forth, I'll give you the green or the red light, and if you really want to, you can tell me all about it, but please spare me the details." He stared at me for a moment after stuttering this out, and we both burst out laughing.

"But it *is* all about sex, right? I don't know why you deny it," I said to him on another occasion, after we'd watched a movie full of unnecessary cruelty about a tormented foursome. "Because it *is* all about sex. The 'secrecy,' the 'excitement,' and the 'danger.' You don't get that same rush flying model airplanes, do you?"

"Not flying model airplanes, no . . ." Halimi chuckled and then thought for a moment. "But I do get it with drugs and alcohol. I know I'm hurting myself when I'm going through a rough patch, but I get a kick out of it." He looked at me seriously, pronouncing each word with precision. "And the very fact I enjoy doing something that hurts me somehow amplifies the enjoyment. It's a cruel, vicious cycle." He sighed theatrically and sank down into the armchair. Then, he gave me one of his catlike smiles.

"I feel like kicking you," I said for the umpteenth time when he repeated this performance. "Okay, I know it's about transgressing and all that, but let me ask you a straight question. What if I come home one evening smelling of aftershave and semen, and my makeup all smudged?" I said quickly, feeling juvenile.

"Smelling of aftershave and semen, and your makeup all smudged?" Halimi laughed.

"Come on, Limi, I want to know how you'd feel. Really."

"But why would you come home smelling of aftershave and semen with your makeup all smudged?" he asked, utterly amused. He was clearly going to use that sentence in our own private lexicon from now on.

"And why would you fuck a dysfunctional hipster in the restroom of a club while I'm dancing just a few feet away?" I asked, feigning innocence. The corners of his mouth drooped, but I didn't let up.

He squirmed, forced himself to focus, and looked me straight in the eyes. "How would I feel? I'd probably want to throw up," he said slowly, "and at the same time, I'd want to fuck you wildly. And maybe cry a bit too," he added, clenching his hand to his forehead.

"And wouldn't you want to ask me who and what it was?"

"I would probably want to, yes."

CHAPTER 7

On Monday morning, Halimi left early for Tel Aviv, long before the snarling traffic, for a staff meeting at the radio station. Lily lay awake in bed, cradling her blankie to her right ear and staring placidly at the ceiling.

I stopped by the bedroom door before entering. "Mommy . . ." she gurgled, her mouth full with the pacifier. I crept into her bed and under the blanket like a thief, and when I reached the warmth of her body, I gathered her into my arms. Lily squirmed, howling, and hit me over the head with her pacifier. "Okay, okay, okay," I said and took hold of her chubby hand. I passed the back of my fingers over the smooth, tender skin of her arm and held her close.

Lily began wriggling to escape my grasp and tried to get out of bed, squashing one of my kidneys and pinching the flesh of my thigh with her foot. Finally, she escaped and went off to pee. I heard her dragging the step stool closer to the toilet so she could climb up and then the sound of her less-than-graceful attempts to place her little tush onto the toilet seat. I fixed coffee for myself and chocolate milk for Lily, and then some oatmeal. We ate it on the balcony, as usual, with cubes of butter and salt.

"There's no rooster in the hotel," Lily declared.

"There isn't?" I said, scrambling to catch her drift.

"No rooster," Lily repeated, counting on me to explain why.

"Does that make you sad?" I asked hopefully. Lily frowned.

"But there is in the little room with the pillows!" she said angrily.

"What kind of a rooster?" I ventured.

"Robinod's rooster!" Lily's voice cracked, and she began whimpering.

"Ah . . ." I sighed with relief. "You couldn't watch *Robin Hood* in Grandma's bedroom at the hotel?"

Lily shook her head dolefully.

"No, I couldn't," she whispered, a tragic note in her voice.

"But he was in the little room with the pillows?" I tried.

"Yes!" Lily crowed, leaping up and bouncing on her chair. "Okay, okay," I smiled at her. "Sit down, so you don't fall over." Lily, who knew all about falling over, settled back into the chair.

"He was in the little room with the pillows," she said, fixing her eyes on me with satisfaction.

"You're such a little Robinod," I told her. I inhaled air into my lungs, one of those deep inhalations that finally releases trapped breath, and everything looked lovely.

Half an hour later, I was sobbing my heart out by the gate of her preschool, grappling with the question that every parent confronts: *Is it possible that I'm a monster, leaving her like this?* Only the stern gaze of the shop owner on the corner stopped me from charging back in and taking Lily home. I strained to hear if Lily's weeping was still audible, but the preschool's morning commotion was a blanket of happy, well-organized mayhem.

I gave in to the urge and texted her teacher—"Hi, it's Idit, Lily's mom. Is she okay?"—and sent it before I had time to rebuke myself. Once home, I made myself another coffee and found a note from Simone on the fridge door, saying that she and Richard had gone for a stroll by the sea. I went out onto the balcony with my laptop, tobacco, and coffee. I tried calling

Dina, but she didn't answer, and after a cigarette and a half, I texted her, "Call me on Zoom, urgent," and went back inside.

"I feel like a monster," I flung the words at my sister as soon as her face appeared on the screen, her hair wild, her ripped T-shirt with the logo of a heavy metal group I didn't recognize. "I dump my daughter at a place that makes her cry, just so I can have time to fuck around all morning."

"Relax, it's fine," Dina laughed easily. "Lily's just a drama queen." She chewed loudly on a chunk of kohlrabi from a ceramic bowl that covered a quarter of the screen.

I resolved to go pick up Lily from preschool once I'd finished my coffee. My cell phone beeped. A text from the teacher. "Everything's good. She calmed down thirty seconds later. Played very nicely with Noam and now doing great in animal hour. I wanted to send you a photo but couldn't find you on WhatsApp." A surge of relief swept through me. I felt dizzy and leaned back into the couch.

"Where were we?" Dina said, swinging Max up with a practiced hand onto her lap and baring one breast.

"The teacher messaged me. Everything's fine." Max suckled happily at her breast, and his hand played distractedly with her hair. "Dinka, it's gross, he's almost four years old," I blurted out.

"Shut up," Dina answered cheerfully.

I settled down on the couch and reached for my coffee. "Listen. You're not going to believe what happened to me over the weekend."

"I'm not going back to that jerk," I sniffled. I lay there like a pregnant whale, on a sun lounger at a café on the Tel Aviv promenade, trying to ignore the raucous music that was playing. Dina, who'd arrived a week earlier, refused to stay at our place ("I want to be my own person, not creep around your apartment on tiptoe," she answered when I protested) and reserved herself a room in a boutique hotel in the Yemenite Quarter. "She's turned into a cold European," I told Mom, enraged, on our weekly phone call. Mom was also miffed that Dina only stayed with them for one night ("Ditka, I don't think Dinka loves us anymore"). Dina preferred to spend her time in Tel Aviv, wandering around at leisure ("Tel Aviv winters are just perfect"), meeting up with old acquaintances, exploring old and new places. She got a new tattoo, a baby Chinese dragon, and had a fling with the Russian tattoo artist.

I was happy to join her earlier in the day for more modest activities. It felt good to exist without Halimi, whose social life continued, irrespective of my advancing pregnancy.

"I can't believe I encouraged him," I sighed, trying to imagine what it might be like raising a child as a single parent. Just the thought gave me arrhythmia.

Our wedding was wonderful. I had prepared myself mentally for something to go wrong—that the dress would rip around my huge belly, that there wouldn't be enough food. But it was a long, relaxed party on the beach, exactly as we planned it, nothing over the top, mountains of good food and alcohol. Friends and family kidded around together, everyone danced and was happy, my mom got quite drunk, Simone reclined on a sun lounger by the shore, Dina and Georg's daughter, Eva, showered us with flowers under the wedding canopy (Georg and the kids had left the day after the wedding, but Dina stayed "to party"). When Halimi said the traditional "If I forget thee, oh Jerusalem" at the wedding ceremony, he looked me in the eye with steadiness and emotion.

"So, what now?" Dina asked. She drank beer from a bottle and smoked a joint.

"This morning, his phone didn't stop beeping when he was in the shower, and I saw it was a Facebook chat with some chick," I said dramatically. I tried unsuccessfully to find a comfortable position to lie in.

"A Facebook chat, so what?"

"They've been sending each other all sorts of songs with hidden meanings, and cute emojis, and they arranged to meet at some café. The same week we got married, for God's sake," I sniffled. It was infuriating to be thrown into the role of betrayed wife, yet again, and in such a ridiculous manner.

"Go ahead, go ahead, all the best studies say it's great when you're about to give birth," Dina said. I took a hit from my sister's joint, watching two old ladies walk along the waterfront. I got the feeling they knew what I was doing and were judging me. "Okay, so they arranged to meet, so what?" Dina continued, blinking at the sun.

"What do you mean, 'so what'? Does it seem normal to you that a guy has an affair with someone five days after getting married and his wife's about to have a baby?" I began coughing wildly.

Halimi was full of tenderness, but his mind was elsewhere. His sexual attraction to me hadn't diminished, but in my ninth month I was pretty inaccessible. It made me shy and a little withdrawn; Halimi made no attempt to draw me out. When he left the house that morning, saying he had a business meeting, I scrutinized him long and hard. *Good-for-nothing stupid liar*, I thought. I had a feeling he understood what my eyes were saying, but he just picked up his keys, grabbed his bicycle, and fled.

"'Normal,'" Dina repeated contemptuously. "If you'd wanted normal, you should have married some tech CEO and bought an apartment in the suburbs."

"I don't get it," I burst out. "Why are you on his side?"

"I'm not on his side," Dina said. She placed a calming hand on my belly. "I just don't want you getting overexcited. Perhaps it is a business meeting. You know how the younger generation communicates these days: It's all smileys and kisses and hearts."

"Younger generation? Right!" I snorted. I sank into deep thought and tried to reconstruct the chat I'd read.

"It wasn't a business meeting," I said with certainty. "And you know I'm cool with one-night stands. But the week we got married! And why doesn't he tell me? Damn it, that's what we agreed on—that if something's going on, we tell each other."

I sighed. I imagined myself giving birth alone, breastfeeding in the dark in a tiny one-room apartment, ugly and cramped, in south Tel Aviv. The joint went straight to my head after months of abstinence, and I felt a panic attack coming on. Dina took my hand and held it to her breast.

"Everything's okay, kitten," she said softly. "Let it go. He's just a jerk who isn't used to serious love. He's got a lot to learn."

A few weeks earlier, Halimi and I had decided against going on a honeymoon in my ninth month—I was nervous enough about giving birth before the wedding—and planned on a long vacation after the baby was born. Dina claimed that if everything went according to plan and I recovered quickly, this would be our best option for the next few years. "Remember, two months after Eva's birth, Georg and I went to the Glastonbury Festival? It was perfect. Two years later, we went back, and it was a nightmare. I spent every minute of the day running after her to make sure she didn't drown in a puddle or accidentally drink MDMA."

"Let's go there!" I said decisively.

"Go where?" Dina asked.

I rolled my eyes at her. "To the café where they're meeting," I said, feeling both pathetic and like a cat ready for the kill at the same time.

"Be my guest. I'm staying here," Dina said. I gave her a withering look but said nothing. In her place, I'm not sure even I would have gone along with what might easily turn into a juicy family scandal for everyone to see. I quickly found a taxi—one of the advantages of my huge belly—and ten minutes later, I was there.

I went inside as unobtrusively as I could, heart beating wildly. They weren't inside, so I walked through to the pretty patio where everyone sat when the weather was nice. I saw Halimi right away, with a skinny, good-looking girl who was laughing at one of his jokes. Halimi's hand reached out to remove a crumb from her hair. I kept going as if possessed, until I was standing in front of Halimi and the girl.

"Oh my God!" the girl blurted as my huge belly blocked her line of vision.

"Diti," Halimi said, alarmed. "Is everything okay?"

"Just wonderful!" I snarled. I reached behind me with one hand and pulled up a chair. I sat down with a thud. Halimi's mouth hung open. He stared at me for a few seconds, and I stared back.

"Idit," Halimi said icily.

"Saul," I replied, matching his tone. He opened his eyes wide and shook his head slowly. I didn't know whether he was berating me or apologizing. He probably didn't know either. His Camels lay on the table. I helped myself to a cigarette and lit it with deep satisfaction. "Idit," Halimi repeated, squirming uncomfortably in his chair.

"Sorry, am I embarrassing you?" I asked, panting heavily. Halimi was quick to assume an expression of amusement. I gaped at him like an open grave.

"Diti, why are you looking at me like that? Chill out," he said, turning serious again. "Please, meet Annabelle." I snickered bitterly and immediately felt embarrassed. "Annabelle's a highly successful artist from Stockholm, here to work on an important project in Netivot."

Halimi mumbled the last few words into his chin as I turned my attention to Annabelle ("She had killer style and a beautiful face," I later described her to Dina. "Thick, fair hair, pale blue eyes, and all that. A face that reminded me of Miss Piggy, but really beautiful. Yup.").

Annabelle looked me in the eyes, and I could imagine a lump gathering in her throat. "Do you think I'm an embarrassment too?" I asked her without even trying to control the tremor in my voice.

"I don't think so," Annabelle's voice shook.

"Diti, Diti, enough," Halimi begged.

In the taxi home, we each looked out of a different window. The streets flashed by slowly, and all the usual things that people did—crossing the street, dragging shopping carts behind them, casually chatting, waiting for a bus—seemed to me superfluous, like some dumb show that kept on going long after the audience had left.

"You told me you wanted us to be free," Halimi said in a flat voice, without turning to face me.

I nodded my head sadly at the window. "But we agreed you'd share, that you'd tell me."

"To share what with you?" Halimi lunged at me. "That I'm attracted to someone? That I flirted with someone? That I got a boner when I imagined her giving me a blowjob? How much detail do you want?" The taxi driver froze in his seat and took a hard look at us in the rearview mirror.

"Idiot! We're newlyweds!" I yelled at him with all the strength my whale-body could muster. "We just got married last week! What the hell is your problem?"

Halimi's eyes locked with mine resolutely. "Perhaps I really am a bit of an ass," he admitted. "But maybe that's part of this whole issue—I feel so free with you that it's kind of become a way to celebrate what we have together. The fact that I'm truly free." I tried to work out if this was even logical, and I caught the driver nodding his head.

"He really played her," I imagined the driver telling his wife later. "And she fell for it," I imagined him adding, knowing there was no way on earth his wife would stand for something like that.

They're clueless, I thought. *They know nothing.*

I woke up with a start on the couch. My hand reached out for my huge belly, and for a moment I panicked at its absence. But Lily was born a long time ago, I remembered with relief, turning over onto my back.

When I told Dina about my mushroom adventures, she took it kind of badly. She was full of concern; all of a sudden, she looked old. She even called Georg and asked me to tell him everything all over again.

Sheepishly, I briefly repeated the trip I'd had, my rusty German making me feel a bit ridiculous. Georg listened patiently, asked a few questions, and nodded his head gravely. "It's okay, it's okay," he reassured my sister, and then he turned his attention to me, his voice full of good intention. "It's part of the whole thing."

It was truly magic, I told myself, recalling the glossy manes of those magnificent horses, in fine fabrics and exquisite embroidery, better dressed than I'd ever been. I was stressed by all that magic at the time, and yes, I freaked out, I only wanted to arrive back home in one piece—but if it were to happen again . . .

CHAPTER 8

Richard and Simone returned home from a walk around two o'clock, rosy-cheeked and energized. They returned five minutes after Halimi, who was delayed in Tel Aviv—as usual. I wasn't worried. I began making lunch while listening to Gregorian chants. The music was a little gloomy, but there was something sublime about it, and although the day had clouded over, I felt light and airy. While humming along with the monks, I made cute panda shapes out of the rice to appeal to Lily. I welcomed Halimi home with a kiss that oozed affection. He was taken aback. It went without saying that he'd already concocted an alibi for his lateness, a crafty mix of truth and lies, but I didn't care. *Let him do what the hell he likes*, I thought as I went to pick up Lily from preschool. That was the whole idea from the beginning.

Lily was easygoing and all smiles as she said goodbye to her teacher. I gave her an orange to eat, and all the way home we talked about flowers and plants and fruit. I had to stop myself from hugging her every three seconds. Although it was only April, daylight saving had lengthened the days, and Lily convinced me to take her to the playground. She bounced from swings to seesaws while I sat on a bench.

My cell phone vibrated in my pocket. A text from Halimi. "Where are you two? We're waiting." I texted him that we were on our way home, and he asked me to buy bread and hard cheese. I replied with a smiley face.

Lily Rozhevsky-Halimi was born by C-section, which incapacitated me for almost a month. The surgery itself was fine, medically speaking. Halimi sat by my side, wearing a white mask that barely covered his long nose. The anesthesiologist was not the most endearing person I had ever met, but he was attentive and efficient. A green curtain separated me from the lower part of my body, around which the medical team gathered, discussing the procedure and arguing over the right way to slice open a watermelon.

Halimi's eyes were focused on me in an attempt to project serenity and confidence—but once in a while, his attention strayed with tense curiosity to the other side of the curtain. I was feeling nauseated, painfully aware of the low but troublesome hum of the medical instruments. It turned into a C-section because Lily was breech, and I was too stressed to consider any other way. Dina told me not to hassle and simply to go for the C-section (of course, she had had both her children in a paddling pool at home, with only Georg and a midwife in the room).

My parents waited outside, biting their fingernails and walking up and down the hallway.

After they pulled the baby out of me, they brought her to me for a moment. I burst into tears, and they swaddled her deftly and handed her over to Halimi. Sometime later, I found myself in the recovery room—I had no idea what was going on outside the room, and I lay there, alone, wondering if I was going to shiver and tremble like that for the rest of my life. During the two hours in the recovery room, the nurse barely paid attention to me. Dina told me stories about friends of hers who got morphine after a C-section, but perhaps in Germany they treat their patients better. After begging and pleading, between fits of uncontrollable shaking, I managed to get liquid ibuprofen. "It's quite normal," the nurse said in an apathetic voice when I called her to me again. "It's the epidural and the pain medication leaving your system," she said. When I weakly asked if I could get something stronger, the nurse shrugged her shoulders and said that ibuprofen was standard.

My father came into the recovery room and said that Halimi was with the baby, that he and my mom had already seen her and she was perfect, and that everything would be fine. He sat by my bedside for a few minutes. But he was horrified at the sight of me, convulsing uncontrollably. He gave me a kiss and left. Then, my mother came in. She held my hand and stroked me for a few minutes in loving silence, then the nurse asked her to leave and added something to the IV.

I was released from the hospital four days later. During that time, I was crammed into a room with another woman (who had just given birth) and her nudnik husband. I promised myself never to have another C-section. I could not lift myself up in bed unaided. I could barely turn from side to side. Everything hurt. I had trouble breastfeeding. Most of the nurses were unbearably efficient and coldhearted.

It took me a while to get used to the fact that this minuscule creature, crumpled and red-faced, was my daughter. At night, I stared at her and tried not to cry. Sometimes, I failed.

Halimi came and went. He tried to make himself useful but mostly looked after the baby. He negotiated with the nurses and did his best to get them to help me breastfeed.

On the third day, my mood improved a little. I got the hang of breastfeeding. The list of possible names for the baby was whittled down to three. The nurses disconnected me from the catheter and the IV. Halimi lay down beside me in the narrow bed and hugged me. The baby slept peacefully in her bassinet. I started to believe it might all work out.

On the way home in a cab, after long days under the neon hospital lights, the reality facing me seemed precarious, like a paper so flimsy, the slightest stress would tear it. The fact that the world continued to exist as always somehow hurt my feelings. Climbing the stairs of our building, Halimi held the car seat with the baby in it, while I gripped the handrail and dragged my sorry ass up to our apartment.

The house was clean and tidy. I drank some cold water and discovered that the fridge was full of my favorite food. Halimi carefully took the baby out of the car seat and laid her in the new cradle by our double bed. He stayed by her side and looked at her, stroking her delicate cheek with one long finger.

I wobbled off to the bathroom to pee. My body was both heavy and skittish.

After a few days away from home, the bathroom smelled different. I felt like a visitor to my own life. The birth was irreversible, an act that couldn't be undone. I was completely enslaved to the needs of a fragile and helpless creature toward whom I didn't feel particularly maternal. I felt only a sense of endless, burdensome responsibility. It was paralyzing.

"Diti, what's going on?" Halimi asked from the other side of the door. "I'll be out in a minute," I said, trying to sound calm. One heartless thought consoled me: the possibility that if I didn't look after that baby properly, someone would simply take her away (or she would die, another voice whispered, terrified at the thought), and I'd go back to being me. I was overcome with both terror at the existence of such a voice inside my brain and utter shame. Fits of weeping that had begun to subside began all over again. "Diti! Idit!" Halimi said from the other side of the door, a note of urgency in his voice. "Please come out."

I pulled myself together and wiped my face on my dress. I was still wearing my baggy pregnancy clothes, and the dress was stained. Someone would have to do laundry, I thought, and another howl escaped me. Every single task seemed insurmountable.

"Come on, Diti. Really." Halimi was beginning to get impatient. I got to my feet with a groan.

"It might look like I'm overreacting," I moaned. "But I swear, I'm having a really hard time." I said it more to myself than Halimi, suppressing panic.

When I finally opened the door, I got so dizzy, he had to hold me up to stop me from collapsing. We grinned, and he helped me into the living room, where he covered me with a blanket.

"Are you hungry? Thirsty?" he asked. "Both," I murmured. "And I have to take a shower," I said, before falling asleep. I don't know how long I slept. When I woke up, I showered and got dressed in a beloved pair of pajamas that didn't fit me while I was pregnant. I ate well and drank large quantities of herbal tea. Halimi walked up and down our apartment with the baby in his arms, humming to her in a low voice. He changed her diaper. I glanced at the clock and saw it was already eight in the evening. As far as I was concerned, it could have been two in the morning.

"Let me hold her for a while," I said to Halimi. He smiled and placed the baby in my arms. She was dressed in a tiny onesie that was too big for her. Halimi dropped into the armchair and closed his eyes.

The baby latched onto my nipple quite easily, and I felt a rush of pleasure as the milk flowed steadily through my breast. I looked at her and tried to decide whether she was Millie, Lily, or Abigail. The latter name seemed too serious a name for such a young creature, and Millie sounded outdated and foreign. The baby opened her eyes, deep blue oceans behind slightly swollen eyelids. "You're Lily," I told her. I looked at Halimi. "Limi," I said, "Let's go with Lily." He nodded his assent, eyes still closed.

When we got back from the playground, Lily looked for Halimi. "Daddy!" she roared as she entered the living room. She rushed over to him. Halimi got down on his knees and gathered her up, falling backward onto the rug and laughing with pleasure. After that, they played swords for twenty minutes—she with the wooden one from Richard, and Halimi with the old plastic one. Lily was on her best behavior at dinner and ate well. Simone asked if she could put her to bed ("*Ma petite*, we won't be seeing you for a few months now"), and Lily agreed with the generosity of an enlightened despot. Halimi offered to clear the table and load the dishwasher, and I went out onto the balcony for a cigarette with Richard.

"So, what do you think of the house? Are you enjoying living here?" Richard asked, smoking his pipe.

"Very much," I answered and sipped the last of my port. "*Merci*, Richard, thank you so much," I said, feeling a little weird at the huge discrepancy between the magnificent gift we'd been given and my modest gratitude. He waved his hand dismissively. "*Rien de rien*," he said, and we smoked in silence for a few minutes. Later, he told me that he had also lived in the house for a few months, right after he inherited it, but was compelled to return to Paris for work. "I so loved living by the sea," he said. I didn't know if he was just putting it on, since he and Simone were endlessly traveling the world. I asked Richard why his Catholic uncle from Toulouse had owned a house in Atlit, of all places, and he gave an indistinct answer about a property that had been handed down from generation to generation for hundreds of years.

Before I had time to interrogate him further, Simone and Halimi joined us. Halimi amused his mother and Richard with a long, complicated story about some scandalous incident at the radio station the week before, and I rested my head on Halimi's lap and began to drift off. I always loved hearing Halimi speak French, even after all our years together. As he spoke, Halimi stroked my back and ass unobtrusively.

I went off to pee and to see if my period was finished, but it wasn't. I knew that after Simone and Richard left, Halimi would want me, and that we'd make out at least until he came. This both turned me on and annoyed me. I put on clean panties, and when I came out of the bathroom, Simone and Richard had already gone off to finish packing.

Halimi stood in the kitchen and made himself a cup of tea. "Do you want some?" he asked. I shook my head and went over to the couch. Halimi leaned against the countertop and sipped his tea noisily, fixing his eyes on me with lust. "I've still got my period," I announced. "Still?" he complained, as if I had control over it. "It's almost over, but not quite," I replied. I started to say something else, but Simone came down the stairs suddenly.

"*C'est tout*, my darlings," she said, dragging a suitcase behind her. Richard, wearing an impeccably tailored suit, appeared with a slightly bigger suitcase. We all embraced. Halimi led them out to the rental car. I went outside to smoke a final cigarette on the balcony. Halimi's cell phone lay beside the ashtray. Out of habit, I picked it up and ran my finger over the screen to unlock it.

That's when I discovered that Halimi had changed his password.

I put the phone back and smoked in silence, leaning against the handrail, my ears picking up the sea's murmurings, or so it seemed to me. The ruins of the fortress of Atlit were dimly illuminated by the lights from the military base and the moon. *Twang, twang*, imaginary fingers plucked imaginary strings.

CHAPTER 9

I'm going to print out the manuscript," I said. I'd been grappling with a French text the entire morning.

Halimi's morning revolved around never-ending phone calls. He hustled and kidded around on the one hand and projected ice-cold, threatening politeness on the other. He strung along potential interviewees, made pointed remarks to subordinates, and laconically agreed with his superiors. I tried to block out the sound of his voice with Chopin in my earbuds.

I couldn't resist escaping to Facebook, permanently open on my laptop, scrolling through the feed as if possessed by a dybbuk. Someone won a prize in Denmark and posted photos from Copenhagen. Someone else shared a complex historical anecdote, funny and enlightening, with a beautiful engraving from the seventeenth century. There were photos from a day spent wandering through Tel Aviv, selfies with friends and dogs on the grass.

Reluctantly, I returned to the French text. My eyes strayed toward the sea. I took out my pouch of tobacco and rolled a cigarette. I placed it beside my laptop and went to get myself a glass of water.

I sat outside, replaced my earbuds, lit the cigarette, and forced myself to focus. My eyes wandered again and again toward the horizon and to Halimi, who was also smoking while he chatted on the phone.

At a certain stage in the conversation, Halimi's body language became particularly feline—he lounged across the wooden chair on the balcony, his smile deepening by degrees. I switched off the music but left the earbuds in, my finger hovering over the wheel of the mouse. I guessed he was talking to a former reality TV star—she gave a first impression of being brainless but was really quite sharp. Halimi had interviewed her a few weeks ago.

Halimi gave me a look when I snapped my laptop shut.

"I can't possibly read on my laptop, my brain's going to explode," I grumbled. He nodded at me, still talking on the phone. It was obvious he wasn't listening.

As I went out into the quiet street, I gained a sense of calm. Instead of jumping into the car and driving to the post office to print the manuscript, my legs took me northward to the sandstone ridge. *What's the big deal?* I thought. *I'll stretch my legs a bit.* No biggie.

It had rained heavily the night before, unusual for the end of April, but by morning, the weather was brighter. The sun shone warmly for a few hours, the air hung thick with mist, and the street was cobbled with shiny puddles. I wanted to find that spring.

I paused and looked back at the houses in the neighborhood, then ahead to the path that led to Le Destroit. It was at least a half-hour walk to get to the Narrow Passage. On Friday, I'd barely noticed the distance I had traveled, but now, when there was lunch to make and Lily to pick up from preschool, I realized it was quite a trek there and back. I turned around and began retracing my steps. When I got back to the neighborhood, I sat in the car and switched on the radio and started the engine. Instead of turning toward the post office, I continued north on the coastal road. *I'll just cruise a little*, I told myself. I stopped the car behind the eastern ridge of the Narrow Passage and got out. I leaned against the car and examined ancient Phoenician letters engraved into the stone. I wondered whether my sneakers would get ruined if I walked through the thick mud.

I started walking, the coin hanging low around my neck. I gritted my teeth and increased my pace. The air grew thick.

I stopped. Rummaging around in my bag, I found Lily's ten-agorot coin. I held it in front of my eyes and examined it. "I've probably lost my mind," I told the coin. I thrust my hand into the pocket of my jacket and cradled the coin in my fist. I climbed up the ruined structure and surprised a couple sitting there, their heads close together, looking out at the sea.

I stood on top of the structure, which was covered with mud. Then, I climbed carefully down and started wandering across the plain. I glanced back at the ruins; the couple was still there, and for a moment I saw the place as it looked so many years ago—a stone building blending into the ridge with narrow slits in its walls, probably for shooting arrows. I closed my eyes, then gritted my teeth and walked toward one of the carob trees, the one I found myself under when I woke from my hallucination. A sizable puddle pooled under the tree trunk. *Goodbye sneakers*, I thought.

I knelt by the puddle, one hand resting on the trunk for support. I bent down until the ancient coin around my neck dangled into the puddle. I lingered like this for a few seconds, eyes closed, not knowing what to expect. *I'm insane*, I thought again.

I straightened up a little, and the coin lifted up out of the water. I opened my eyes and chuckled again, half-disappointed, half-relieved that everything was the same. *Twang, twang.* I heard a faint strumming. My hand slipped off the tree trunk as I started to turn around. I fell precariously, my hand plunging into the puddle, and the coin hit the water again. Boom, an explosion inside my head, and I was sucked into the water.

Sweet water, and then salty. Dizzying currents, and then the billowing of a gigantic wave. Impossible to hold my breath any longer. I'm about to die. A cautious intake of breath because there's nothing to lose. Joy encompasses me. I can breathe underwater.

"Good God in heaven!" Jean d'Ibelin, Count of Arsur, shouted, accompanied by earsplitting barking. I inhaled gratefully, filling my lungs with thirteenth-century air. Different, dense scents invaded my nostrils, both fetid and delightful. I was once again lying on the ground, my legs dangling into the spring. The rest of my body was on dry earth; there was no mud here. Beyond the canopy of the carob tree, which looked much older—its treetop thick with foliage—thin rays of sunshine flickered. I blinked and pulled myself up into a sitting position.

"I don't believe it," I whispered. I looked around. Everything was dry, but much colder. Jean knelt before me on a mat, wide-eyed with astonishment. By his side was his satchel and a small musical instrument that looked like a banjo. He must have been sitting there for quite a while. His beard was shorter and more groomed. His hair was pulled into the same half-ponytail, tied back with a strip of leather. The cowl had fallen away from his head.

In stunned silence, Jean pulled out a ceramic bottle. Brunette stood by his side, barking wildly, and when he held the bottle out to me, she gave a whimper and fixed her gaze on me. I pulled out the cork and sniffed the contents of the bottle. Wine. "Do you have any water?" I asked. Without taking his eyes off me, he reached for his leather water canteen, which lay on the ground. He handed it to me, and I drank from it as if nothing had passed my lips for days. The water tasted faintly musty. I went over to the spring, collected water in my hands, and drank some more.

"How . . . how? What?" Jean stammered. He shook his head from side to side and laughed to himself, as someone unaccustomed to being surprised. Brunette gave a sharp yap.

"It's the coin," I said, realization dawning on me as I held the necklace. The coin looked new. The cross with the widened edges on one side and the tower gate on the other and the inscriptions. I took Lily's ten-agorot coin out of my pocket; it looked like a toy coin.

The right thing to do, I knew, was to hold Lily's coin and immerse my hand in the spring—the coin from my time, or my dimension, whatever that might be. To go back, right now. But I wanted to collect my senses. To calm down.

I knew that if I went through that luminescent explosion again so soon, and that fantastical drowning, my heart might give out.

Jean took the ten-agorot coin, examining both sides. As he handled it, somehow a mysterious odd tingle also pulsed in my lower back, somewhere between my coccyx and up my spine. Brunette came up to me, sniffed the coin, and retreated.

"And what brings you here?" I asked. Might he have been waiting for me all this time? How could he have even known I would try to return?

Jean looked around with a touch of embarrassment. "Well . . ." he said, "this place is beloved to me. When I am a guest at Château Pèlerin and the military tumult of the Templars disturbs my thoughts, I come here to contemplate and pray by this holy spring." He took a deep breath in order to say something else—and then changed his mind. "After all, this is where we met last time," he finally added, as if to reinforce his claim.

"Have three days passed here as well?" I asked, as I rose to my feet.

"'Here as well?'" he repeated, jumping up. We moved out from under the tree's canopy. I breathed in the crisp, faintly salty air and looked around.

My heart pounded, and I almost threw up, this time out of wonderment. I was overwhelmed by the sight of buildings that stretched across the ridge. Then, I turned toward the sea and cast my eyes over the gardens and vineyards that sloped down between the ridge and the sea, delineated by the town walls, close to the gigantic fortress. I felt a kind of strange envy that in my world, this magnificent fortress was an inaccessible ruin.

Jean gazed first at me, then at the horizon, and back again. "You still don't believe I'm from another time," I said. I wouldn't have believed it either, but I remembered his shocked face when I was sucked into the spring last time. "But you saw, right? How I was sucked in back then?" Jean cleared his throat and moved to where his horse was standing, chained to the wall of the building by a large iron ring.

"I saw," he said curtly. He stroked the horse's mane and turned to me. "After you disappeared, I thought perhaps I had lost my wits. Or that you were some kind of a sorceress, sent to confound innocent Christians," he said, furrowing his brow. He seemed serious and distrustful. I pursed my lips in order not to smile. A sorceress. "And where's your friend, the king?" I asked.

"Thibaut?" Jean asked, his eyes still fixed on me warily. "He tarries in the city."

"And where might that be?" I ventured.

"Acre," Jean replied, as if I'd asked the dumbest question ever. His eyes expressed increasing suspicion. He pronounced the name of the city differently from the way it's pronounced in Hebrew.

"Ah, right, Acco," I said with forced lightness.

We fell silent. Jean examined one of the horse's hooves with great attention. Brunette came up to me and licked my hand. I scratched her behind the ears and took deep breaths. "I dreamed about you afterward," I told Jean. He continued tinkering with the hoof.

"I dreamed you owned a brewery, and you were pleased I liked the drink you offered me."

He turned to me abruptly. The horse whinnied with resentment. Jean's eyes opened in terror, and he placed a hand on his heart.

"This is too much . . ." he stammered.

"What's too much?" I asked.

"I . . ." His eyes wandered. "I dreamed of you too. That we were sitting at a trestle table by a very strange-looking building. You wept and drank from my ale."

The clarity of the day was obscured by a passing cloud, and all at once the atmosphere turned ominous. A raven hovered above, screeching hoarsely, its wings flapping with evil intent. My hand tightened around the ten-agorot coin.

"You are pale, my lady," Jean noted apprehensively.

"I don't know what to make of all this," I replied, barely managing to form the words. "Perhaps I should go home." I knelt beside the spring, too weak to stand any longer, and removed the necklace with the Ibelin coin from my neck.

"Wait!" Jean cried out. I looked up at him. He shifted his weight from one foot to the other. "I know not what is happening. Wicked sorcery or utter insanity . . . but here you are." He paused, and I flashed him a crooked smile.

Suddenly, he was smiling too. He patted his horse distractedly and said, "In truth, why should I be so alarmed? I thought of you and dreamed of you, and here you are, like the fairy Thibaut keeps claiming you are. Let us make the most of it."

I enjoyed listening to him talk, with his rolling Old French *r*. I didn't know whether to attribute the fact that I understood him to the passage afforded me by the spring or to my gift for language.

I moved toward him. I wanted to hug him, but it seemed inappropriate. I patted the horse instead, and it gave a loud snort.

The sun reappeared, and the plain appeared green and full of life. Birds chirped all around, and the deep blue sea twinkled in front of us. The last time we met, I wasted the opportunity by stressing out. *I've got to chill*, I told myself.

"Do you know what the time is?" I asked, fishing my cell phone out of my bag and noting, once again, that it wasn't working.

"What do you mean?" Jean asked. He removed two small ceramic cups from his satchel and opened a cloth sack containing nuts and dates. I noticed that he was doing everything in his power to ignore the instrument in my hand.

"The hour today? Twelve? One?" Jean lifted his head and frowned, perplexed, as if I'd asked another ridiculous question. I looked up at the sky. The sun inclined slightly westward, beyond the zenith, and the shadows were short. It was probably about one in the afternoon. For a moment I was bothered by the idea that Halimi might be worried about me. And then I turned to Jean.

"So, have you been waiting for me the whole morning?" I inclined my head in his direction. I wanted him to be that same youthful, mellow person he had been the first time we met.

He looked at me and smiled broadly. "In fact, yes," he admitted. My own smile broadened too. "Truth be told, my lady, I knew not what to expect," Jean confessed. "But I could not stop myself from returning here, as soon as time allowed." I bowed my head in gratitude, and he responded with a chivalrous nod.

"Perhaps we can ride to the sea together?" I asked. The beach looked wild and utterly empty. I wanted to gallop down there right away, but I continued, "And on the way, you can tell me how you've been these past few days."

"How I've been?" Jean asked, scratching his forehead. "What do you mean?"

I sighed, exasperated.

"I mean, what did you do over the past few days, how did you feel?"

Jean raised his eyebrows in mock surprise, but all he said was, "Very well then, do you have a horse for riding nearby?"

I chuckled. A horse for riding.

"In truth," Jean began, narrowing his eyes at me but still smiling, "there are stables here, a little to the south. There are horses there, not exactly for riding, but pack horses for the quarry carts. Yet they are amenable and well-disciplined, and surely the knights will consent if we ask them."

"I . . . ah . . ." I spluttered uncomfortably, "I've never ridden a horse in my life."

Jean turned to me, shocked. "You jest, my lady?"

"In my time . . . I mean, where I come from, we don't ride horses. We have vehicles that move along by themselves." Jean's eyebrows shot up again. I later realized he may not have understood the word *vehicle*, but at the time I added uselessly, "You just have to drive them." I became flustered, anxious he might ask me how things move by themselves, and of course I didn't really know. But Jean seemed preoccupied with other thoughts.

"Come, my lady," he said, patting the horse affectionately on its backside. He went and sat down on the folded mat under the tree. "We shall partake of hashish and talk awhile . . . about . . . how we've been," he said. Our eyes met, and we burst out laughing. "If you do not ride, why do you ask about it?" Jean asked in a teasing way.

"I thought that . . ." I was a little embarrassed. Jean's eyebrows rose. "I thought maybe . . . I don't know if it's done around here . . . I thought we might ride together on your horse." Jean threw his head back and laughed out loud. I breathed a sigh of relief.

"You are most daring, Lady Édith," he said, and I detected a note of admiration in his voice. "You remind me of my sister, Isabelle." He settled down comfortably under the tree, his back supported by the trunk, his legs straight in front of him. I sat down beside him.

"What's so funny?" I answered. "And what's so daring about it? Was it not you who suggested last time that we ride together to the fortress? Would we not have ridden together on the same horse?" I adopted not only the flowery style of his speech but also his peculiar accent.

Jean pondered for a moment.

"There is truth in your words," he reflected. "But it is one thing when a knight offers a lady in distress the use of his horse in her hour of need, and another when that same lady offers the knight an opportunity to ride with her on his horse for the sheer pleasure of it," he concluded with a wink, and I nodded in response.

"And why do you presume I am a lady?" I asked, teasing him back, stretching my legs out in front of me. Jean gaped at my bare shins, peeking out between sneakers and sweatpants.

Jean looked at me blankly for a moment and then said, "It is clear you lack any modesty or reverence for someone in authority, which gives testimony to your superior lineage. This is further manifest in the Frankish dialect you speak. Despite your peculiar accent, the eloquence of your tongue testifies to a superior education. The same is true of your appearance—the color of your skin, the daintiness of your fingers, the perfection of your teeth. Though your bare head and cascading hair is deemed a sign of wantonness in these parts, you clearly take great care of it." His hand rose up for a moment, as if he were about to stroke my hair, but instead he lowered it to run his fingers through Brunette's fur. "In addition to this," he continued, "at our previous rendezvous, you presented yourself as Countess of . . . I believe you gave a variation on a Saracen name."

"Right . . ." I admitted, blushing. "In my time . . . where I come from, there are no counts or countesses. Everyone is the same." As I spoke, I knew I was being imprecise. Jean's curiosity was aroused. I tried to explain the modern system of government, telling him how it resembled the democratic system of the ancient Greek polis. Jean was deeply impressed, less by the miraculous glimpse into the future, or so it seemed to me, and more by the very fact I had knowledge of the Greek polis and its system of government.

"Countess or not," he said, "a woman who knows early Greek sources is surely a lady. No other woman has either the education or the leisure to study such subjects." After a moment, he added, "Nor man, in truth." I nodded my head slowly. We smoked. I looked around, enchanted by the nonchalant dexterity with which he lit a flame—striking a small piece of metal against something dark and stony and feeding the spark with a handful of weeds. "What do you call this?" I asked Jean.

He raised his eyes to me, bending down. "A fire striker," he said, after a brief delay. "And what do you call this?"

I giggled. "We have lighters. It's the same principle, more or less. I think so. But everything is simpler. You just press a button or flick a . . . kind of spark wheel." God forbid he asked me how it actually worked.

"Do you also use flint stone and steel?" Jean inquired.

"Yes! Exactly! I think so," I said. "It just doesn't look so nice," I added as he held out the hookah to me. While I smoked, he created a small bonfire from the pile of weeds.

We then drank wine out of the little ceramic cups. When Jean noticed I was a little lightheaded, he took out a piece of bread wrapped in a handkerchief from the same satchel. The bread was slightly hard, but my dizziness passed after I ate it.

"When I rode away from the spring after your mysterious disappearance, I was stupefied," Jean began. He replaced his cowl and leaned back against the tree trunk. I leaned back as well. Our arms grazed each other as we reached out to take a walnut or a date from the wooden bowl that Jean had placed between us. Brunette sniffed the bowl, withdrew politely, stretched out at our feet, and rested her head on Jean's shins and her tail on mine.

"When I arrived at the fortress, it was already time for the evening meal. I wanted to eat quietly with the other knights in the great hall, but one of the brothers told me to go directly to Périgord's chambers and to dine there with him and Thibaut . . ."

Jean intended to go on, but I interrupted him. "Who's Périgord? Isn't that the truffle district in France?" I asked, taking another sip from the wine. Jean guffawed. "Armand de Périgord, Grand Master of the Order of Solomon's Temple," he said in a vaguely condescending tone.

"Okay. Go on," I told him.

"What is this word that you say so often . . . 'okay' . . . what does it mean?" He tapped me three times on my arm with the date he was holding.

"It means 'fine' or 'very well' in English," I said, amused by this little gesture of his.

"Do you mean the Normans or the Saxons?"

"Forget it," I said. "I'll try to use 'okay' less, okay?"

"Okay," Jean replied. We exchanged sideways looks and inclined our heads a little closer together.

"And so," Jean went back to his story, "I reached Périgord's private chambers, where I was received with much fanfare. 'Where is the fairy you promised, Thibaut?' Périgord shouted. He already reeked of wine. He and Thibaut continued their banter, and it occurred to me that Thibaut, in his depictions, had already transformed you into some imaginary creature. I, however, was still trapped within the web of your very real disappearance, and I did not appreciate their revelry. I said that in all probability, you were some insane *poulain* or a pilgrim who had lost her mind, since it happened that as soon as I looked away, you disappeared, and all I wanted to do was escape the pitch black and return to the safety of the fortress."

"What's a *poulain*?" I asked, praying it wasn't "whore" or something similar. "I heard Thibaut use that word as well."

Jean's face distorted in disgust. "It is an abhorrent word, and I try not to use it," he began, and once again I felt my face grow hot.

"The Frankish descendants of this land and those who mixed with the locals—Greeks, Armenians, Copts, and so on. It could be said that I myself am a *poulain*, since my ancestors arrived here about one hundred and fifty years ago, with our first king, His Holiness Godfrey of Bouillon, whereas my grandmother, Queen Maria Komnene, had been a Greek princess."

I stared at him, and he must have misinterpreted my reaction. "Only those ignoramuses who have recently arrived use that despicable expression," he added. "I beg your forgiveness for using such inappropriate language in the presence of a lady," he concluded on a formal note.

"I'm not from these parts, so no harm done," I said, shrugging my shoulders. "It's awesome that your family has been here for the past hundred and fifty years, and your grandmother was a queen, and all that. My parents arrived here less than forty years ago, without a penny to their name. I'm the first person in the family to be born here."

Jean raised his eyebrows and said, "And where is 'here'? Where were you born, Lady Édith?"

"In Jerusalem," I said.

"Indeed?" he said, his eyes round like saucers. Suddenly, I could imagine him as a kid. "Indeed," I replied boastfully, although I wasn't totally sure why. "I lived in Jerusalem until I was about twenty-five years old."

"I have been but once to Jerusalem," he said, staring out into the distance, "when I made a pilgrimage with my elder brother, Balian, Lord of Beirut. Jerusalem was dilapidated, devoid of a king to maintain order, full of cripples and amputees, scheming Saracens and wretched Jews. I could, however, see the hills upon which our savior preached, and I walked in the way of the cross, and my heart expanded. I will return there one day and do everything in my power to restore Jerusalem to greatness, as in the days of my grandmother the queen." He sounded determined, which surprised me. Talk of his queen grandmother stressed me out for some reason. I said nothing about the wretched Jews. I concentrated on scratching Brunette's ears.

Jean sighed. He surveyed me and my clothes without saying a word, as I rolled a cigarette from the tobacco pouch I'd removed from my bag. I couldn't find a lighter in the bag, so I lit the cigarette in the little bonfire Jean had made. He watched me smoking, distrust written over his face. He demanded an explanation, so I said that where I come from, it's totally acceptable to smoke dried weeds rolled up in paper.

"Paper, and such fine paper!" he said in astonishment, his eyes like saucers again. "Where did you procure such a precious commodity? And you are burning it for no reason!" He was unable to keep his cool.

"In the time and place I come from, paper is taken for granted."

"In all my days, I have never met a lady such as you," Jean marveled, shaking his head slowly. It made me want to nestle up to him. I stroked the back of his hand fleetingly and withdrew it swiftly. I had no idea how to behave with him.

"Okay," I said and clapped a hand to my mouth, giggling. "Sorry. Very well. And so, what happened after that? How does the story continue?" I asked.

"Okay," Jean smiled. "Accordingly, I lay down on my pallet at first watch and fell asleep immediately. I dreamed of you, as I have already relayed. The dream shook me to my very bones, as though it were not a dream at all but a voyage I had taken out of my own body.

"I awoke at break of dawn and was wholly unable to go back to sleep. I felt the urge to attend confession, if only to pour out my heart, but resolved to ponder the matter awhile. Albeit confession is bound by strict confidentiality, but rumors spread swiftly in the fortress—the holy brothers gossip like laundrywomen—and I had no desire for further jokes at my expense." He frowned, and I pressed my shoulder against his, indicating I was on his side.

"Not long after I awoke," Jean went on, "we rode to Acre. Thibaut and I, and a small band of knights. Lady Alice, my wife, sent me a missive some time earlier declaring her wish for me to spend the last Saturday of April at the family residence, and to further tarry for Sunday Mass at our church in Acre. We rode swiftly, and when we arrived in the city, we parted ways. Thibaut continued with the brothers to the Templar palace, and I made my way to the house of my wife's father, Rohard, Master of Haifa. Everyone rejoiced at my arrival, and the Saturday and Day of Resurrection of our Lord I spent in the pleasant warmth of home, at sumptuous meals and prayers for my sinful soul."

I couldn't decide whether he was serious or just fooling around. After his fervent confession about Jerusalem, his Christian locutions appeared more sincere; nonetheless, there was a perceptible note of irony in his words.

"In the company of my family and under the auspices of familiar household practices, your magical disappearance seemed like a hallucination," Jean continued, and I could see he was enjoying the story. "I told myself that such a thing could never happen. The Saracen who bestowed the hashish upon me informed me that partaking of too much might cause delirium, but up until that moment, I thought he was hyperbolizing for no reason, as is the way of the Saracens."

He drank from his ceramic cup, refilled it, and continued.

"Thibaut decided to stay in Acre in order to clarify . . . several issues, but he asked me to return to Château Pèlerin and supervise his men, to ensure they were training as befit them and conducting themselves with humility. Last night I returned with the fatigued Templars, who had practiced abstinence and prayed with devotion for the past two days with their brothers in the city. We reached the area at late dusk and passed close by this very place. I fancied I could see a strange light, skipping and dancing around, precisely at this spot. I wanted to ride over here, but Brother Hugues told me it was surely the will-o'-the-wisp, and that I should continue onward. I listened to the voice of reason, yet anguish rose up within my heart. What if your disappearance was a figment of my imagination and the real you were out there alone, a lady lost at the mercy of wild beasts, helpless and starving? I vowed to return the next morning to examine the area, and here I am." He paused and then added, "I cannot comprehend this."

"Neither can I," I whispered. I tried to imagine him as a contented landlord, sitting in an easy chair by the fire, surrounded by little children and a wife fussing over him. I couldn't really see it.

"Nevertheless, I have told you of my wanderings, of . . . how I've been. It is a fact that I cannot recall the last time I prattled on so," Jean said, with a courteous smile. "And you have yet to relate a single word of what happened to you. Did you find your good husband?"

"I found him, sure," I said absentmindedly. "I thought I'd flipped, too, and afterward I convinced myself that I'd hallucinated while on mushrooms. After that, it was basically a nice weekend, hanging out . . ."

"Hanging out?" Jean said.

"Never mind," I laughed. I peered at the sky again. Was it 3:00 p.m.? Later than that? Out of habit, I glanced at the dead phone. "I ought to be getting back," I said. "They'll be worried about me." Jean nodded sympathetically. "But I'd love to come back," I added quickly. "To meet you again." A smile spread across Jean's face.

"Tomorrow?" he asked. "Midday?"

I wanted to answer immediately, yes, yes, yes, but when I managed to focus for a moment, I remembered that Lily had a checkup and vaccine at the clinic tomorrow. And I had no idea how Halimi would take my disappearance today.

"I can't tomorrow," I said firmly. "I need to take my daughter to the doctor."

"In the name of the Holy Mother, is she ailing?" Jean asked, alarmed.

"No, not in the least," I reassured him. "Where I come from, the doctors check little children every few months, even when they're healthy, just to make sure all is well."

His eyes narrowed further. "And what do they do if all is not well?" he asked after thinking about this for a few seconds.

"It depends on what it is," I said. "If there are problems with eyesight, then the eyes are tested and sometimes . . . little devices are prescribed, which can help. If there are developmental problems, all kinds of exercises are prescribed. Sometimes surgery is needed to correct the problem."

Jean's eyes widened in horror.

"Children are operated on in order to improve them?" he asked, full of dread.

"Not exactly, it sounds bad when you say it like that," I said awkwardly. "Usually these are minor surgeries, done under general anesthetic. They can prevent a lot of suffering and abnormal development in childhood. And they also lightly infect them with diseases, so they won't be severely infected at a later date," I added vaguely. I couldn't be bothered to elaborate. "Forget it," I said after a few seconds. "It's too complicated." His eyebrows rose up again, but he said nothing. I returned the tobacco to the bag and removed the necklace from around my neck.

"Wherefore, tomorrow you are occupied. Would you be so kind as to visit the day after tomorrow?" Jean asked. He removed a pit from one of the dates, stuffed it with a walnut, and handed it to me. I thought about it for a minute.

"Perhaps it would be better to meet in a week's time?" I suggested. "I can't disappear for entire days from my family without getting in touch, not this often."

"What do you mean, 'without getting in touch'? Can you not send a servant to inform the count of whatever is necessary?"

I groaned. "First of all, I don't have servants. Aside from that, I already showed you this," I said, taking the dead phone from my bag. "This is a device that enables two people to speak to each other from far away as though they were sitting side by side. But for some reason, it doesn't work here."

I held the phone out to him, and Brunette snarled savagely. "If you please, my lady, remove that thing from my sight," Jean said, shuddering. "It arouses within me an incomprehensible fear."

I thrust the cell phone back into the bag and chewed on Jean's stuffed date dejectedly. I felt as if I'd revealed to him some shameful characteristic or repulsive physical flaw. Jean shifted his pose and drew closer.

"Do not be discouraged, Lady Édith," Jean said softly and took my hand. "Verily there lies between us a chasm of foreignness, yet I sense a sturdy bridge stretched over it."

I looked up at him and smiled. "No wonder Thibaut chose you as his partner in poetry writing," I lauded him. Jean chuckled, lifted my hand to his lips, and kissed it. I giggled like an idiot.

"If you did not insist you were a wife and mother, I would think you were a shy virgin, my lady," he said. The truth is, I felt something like that, sitting beside him. It was invigorating.

"Next week then," he said, placing his hand on my leg and then removing it with a light caress. "At the same time and in the same place. I know not if my pursuits will distance me from Château Pèlerin in the meanwhile, but I swear to you that wherever I may be, I will make every effort to honor our appointment."

"I will too," I said quietly. Brunette thrust her muzzle into my armpit. "But maybe Sunday's a better day?" I added after some thought. On Sundays, Halimi went to Tel Aviv for editorial meetings and to record his show. "Do you need to pray or something like that on Sundays?"

"As much as I am able, I go to Mass on Sundays," Jean said gravely, "and due to the large number of Templars in Château Pèlerin and their religious fervency, Mass takes place several times a day in the castle's church, and twice in the town church. I can attend the evening Mass. And you? Do you not attend church?"

I began snickering but then sobered up. Aside from the fact that I'm not religious, I thought, was this even the time to reveal to Jean that I was Jewish, presuming he had not figured it out? I remembered that the Crusaders were not particularly enamored of the Jews. It was hard for me to imagine the relaxed Jean d'Ibelin butchering and pillaging Jewish communities, but I preferred not to tempt fate by telling him now and probably never would. "I pray at home," I mumbled noncommittally.

"Do you have your own chapel?" Jean asked with admiration. "No servants, but with a private *chapelle*," he added. "I would like to visit your earldom someday, my lady."

I really must go, I thought to myself, but it was as if I were glued to the tree, completely aware of his arm now pressing against mine. Just a bit more, and I'd take off. "So, you actually live there, in the fortress?"

Jean guffawed. He, too, looked as if he were glued to the tree, his body leaning toward me. "In the name of all saints, no. I have been accompanying Thibaut since last autumn. From Acre to Ashkelon and then back to the north. For the past few months, he has been leading a pilgrimage for the redemption of the Holy Land and our conquered territories, and now he is exploring"—Jean paused, sizing me up with his gaze—"various possibilities," he continued. "It is of no matter at this time. Inasmuch as Château Pèlerin of the Templars in the Holy Land is large enough to accommodate the troops and their supplies, many of his fighters encamped here, in the meanwhile . . ." He meant to add something else but stopped.

"But we will meet in a week, is that so?" he asked serenely. "We will continue then, yes?"

"Very well," I answered. It was time for me to head back home, and we had not even gone riding together. I would plan things better next week, I promised myself.

I stood up and stretched. In a few minutes, I would be back home with Lily and *Robin Hood*, and Halimi jabbering away on the phone in the background, and then we'd watch a talk show together, and then dinner, a bath for Lily, and then, after she was asleep, a joint and a movie on Netflix . . . it all seemed so indistinct. A terrible thought crossed my mind, that if I stayed there even a moment more—my life not only would appear unrealistic but would utterly lose its materiality.

"So . . . see you next week," I said to Jean, tossing my hair back. *Don't be so gloomy*, I thought to myself. *It'll be nice to go home.*

It was getting chilly. Jean began folding the mat carefully, packing the hookah, the bowl of nuts, the ceramic bottle, and the two small cups in his velvet bag. He hitched the water canteen to his belt, placed his banjo in the shoulder bag, and extinguished the bonfire by scattering soil over it.

"You're so organized," I grinned. He loaded the baggage onto his horse and untied it. Then, he turned to me.

"Next week," he repeated.

"Next week," I confirmed.

"Adieu, my lady," he said and kissed my hand again.

"Adieu, good sir," I bowed back.

He mounted his horse, gave me a wink, and clicked his tongue. The horse turned southward and galloped away with its rider, accompanied by Brunette, running along beside them. I wondered if Jean had purposely avoided seeing me disappear into the spring. I fingered the ten-agorot coin and plunged my head and hands into the water.

CHAPTER 10

The ten-agorot coin worked. Once again, there was a delay after the initial contact of the coin in water, and then a phosphorescent explosion in my head—the sense of being drawn in, a transition through a kind of hollow pipe, and then I was ejected out. I found myself lying on muddy earth, half my body wallowing in a large puddle. I stood up hastily, with a sharp intake of breath, and the air hit my lungs, accompanied by particles of soot and gasoline fumes, and I immediately threw up the bread, dates, and nuts, and a bit of wine. I didn't have any water to wash my mouth with, so I drank from the puddle. The taste was similar to the water in Jean's bottle.

I stumbled back to the car, praying it was still there, and that I really was home and hadn't accidentally landed in the Ottoman period or something.

The car was there, and the humdrum, familiar reality—the bustle of the coastal road with all its smug indifference. The date was correct, the time of day seemed right. I covered my face with my hands and inhaled deeply through my nose, which had begun to drip.

Should I seek help? If I were to tell someone what had happened to me, if I were to insist it was real, no professional in her right mind would hesitate to send me for observation, if not have me committed. No two ways about it.

I sat in the car opposite the rock with the Phoenician engraving and smoked, lowering the volume of the 5:00 p.m. news that had just begun. The heat was on full blast, and I wondered how I was going to explain why my clothes were so muddy to Halimi. Still panting, after I switched on the cell phone in the car, texts began popping up from him: "Where are you?", "Diti?", "Diti, what's going on?", "Diti don't drive me crazy", and a few more. Six missed calls: five from Halimi and one from my mom.

My finger hovered over Libby's number on my phone. It had been ages since we'd seen each other. The last time we met was when I took refuge at her house the previous winter, resolved to divorce Halimi. The affair with Nina was worse than anything that had come before. Despite my appalling crying spells and my nonstop suffering, Halimi kept seeing her.

Nina wasn't just some random chick he met at a party. She was stunning, passionate with purpose, one of the most valued and beloved writers of *Free to Be*. Next to her, I always felt inferior. When I discovered they were having an affair, I thought I would lose my mind.

Libby was adamant. "Find a good attorney who can get you decent alimony, move to a cute apartment, and I'll help you raise Lily," she said repeatedly, fussing as I lay on her couch. She made me tea, covered me up with her best blanket, found us a binge-worthy TV show, and rolled joint after joint.

But Libby never really liked Halimi; after he and I first met, she had told me he had hit on her once at some party, but he was too sleazy for her. She ultimately accepted his existence and even managed to enjoy his company, although it was obvious that my relationship with Halimi came at the expense of my relationship with her. She tried to hide the fact that she was insulted and angry, but when Halimi was around, she acted like he had won a competition and I was the trophy.

But he acted like that around her too.

Libby didn't hate men, but she had been collecting statistics on their emotional intelligence since we were in high school. There had been a few men she had gotten very attached to, but as a rule, she always expected the worst from them. Particularly from someone like Halimi.

A day or two later, when Halimi rang the intercom of Libby's building—I'd lost all sense of time there too—she trotted out every possible cliché ever used in romantic comedies. "You don't deserve her, you piece of shit," she yelled at him from the window while I laughed pathetically. Halimi, standing in the street below, spotted me cowering behind Libby. And then, despite everything, I went down to talk to him.

He told me he had decided to leave *Free to Be* and said that all he wanted was for me to be happy. He showed me a few photos on his smartphone of Lily at preschool that morning. The teachers had taken them to a show, and they were so cute lined up in pairs, holding hands.

Unlike his usual behavior during a crisis, he was neither grief-stricken and remorseful nor cold and surly. He was deadpan, and his hands shook a little. I went home with him.

Since then, Libby deliberately took a back seat. She displayed only superficial interest in our decision to move to Atlit and made several empty promises that she would come visit. It pained me—Libby had been my best friend since high school, and the only one, aside from my sister, whom I could talk to about anything and everything. But she had never been in a relationship for more than a year, or had kids of her own, nor did she believe that Halimi and I really loved each other. She thought we had a sick codependency. That's what she said when I took refuge at her place that last time. And that's what I told myself every time I finished a strained conversation with her, or when I considered calling but decided not to bother.

Libby wouldn't enjoy hearing what happened to me. She probably wouldn't even care. And if she did, she would play the voice of reason and urge me to go into therapy right away. She would launch a campaign and enlist my parents and sister to convince me I needed serious medication. Hospitalization. I trembled all over. My finger wavered over her name until I shoved the phone back in my pocket. Instant relief. I tried to recall the last time I had a secret. I took one long final drag of the cigarette, tossed it out the window, and headed home.

When I parked the car in the street by the house, my heart began pounding in my chest. I would remain calm. *What was the big deal? All I did was go for a walk.*

"You're something else, Idit. Something else." Halimi shook his head in furious disbelief. Lily was eating strawberry yogurt on the other side of the balcony windows, swinging her legs in the high chair. *She's getting too big for that chair*, I thought.

"You're right," I admitted. "I didn't mean to freak you out. It's just I needed to . . . go off-grid for a while."

Halimi reacted as if I'd kicked him in the face.

"You're kidding me, right?" he said with cold rage. "You're like, what, taking revenge on me?"

I stared at him in bewilderment. Then, I remembered how he had disappeared last Thursday and how he had referred to it. I smiled.

"Oh, I know it sounds as if . . ." I said, trying to suppress my smile. "But it's nothing like that. My battery was already low when I left the house, but I really wanted to take a walk and see the flamingos again. Probably the aftereffects of the 'shrooms. I'm sorry I didn't tell you. That dumb phone has the worst battery life ever. I'll take care of it; I'll have it fixed at the lab."

Halimi still looked grim. He stared at me with distrust. He didn't say a word, just smoked his cigarette resentfully.

"Limi," I said softly. He continued smoking, fixated on Lily as she licked her spoon clean. My foot began jiggling all by itself.

"I don't understand why you're making such a big deal out of it," I said, sighing. "If anyone should understand the need to . . . you know, go off-grid, it's you, don't you think?" I made a supreme effort to not let in the slightest tone of sarcasm.

Halimi fell silent for a few seconds and then added, "Have you got a lover? Should I expect aftershave, smudged makeup, and the smell of semen?" There was no trace of humor in his voice. I was furious but got a grip on myself.

"You've got some nerve, acting jealous over literally nothing," I said quietly.

He glared at me for a few seconds. "What do you mean by 'literally nothing'?"

For some reason, this amused me. "Come on, Limi," I said tiredly. "The beautiful Countess of Atlit in wet sweatpants, wowing all the knights. Honestly." The edges of his mouth curved up slightly. I got up from my chair and went over to him.

"It's true I'm a bit . . . scatterbrained," I said meditatively, resting my chin on the soft stubble of his shaven head. "But in my opinion, Dan's mushrooms opened up some weird-ass chakra inside me."

"And what's with all the mud?" he grumbled, scratching at a piece of dried mud stuck to my sweatpants.

"Stupidity," I said lightly. "I wandered around and stared at the flamingos for a few hours, and everything was fine, and just as I was getting back to the car, I slipped and fell in a puddle." Halimi hugged me tightly.

"All right, as long as you're okay. Don't do that to me again, Diti," he said.

I went to take a shower. It looked like my period was over. I sighed with relief. When I came back to the living room, cheeks flushed and hair damp, I stopped for a moment to look at Halimi and Lily, snuggled on the couch together under a checkered blanket, watching *Robin Hood*. The sun had already set, but it wasn't totally dark outside. The TV flickered in the dim light of the living room, and everything felt calm. "Scoot over, make room for me," I said. Halimi, who was half-asleep, smiled and yawned and removed the backrests of the couch. We both fell asleep and woke up as the final song was playing.

"I wanna watch all of it," cried Lily, who loved the entire movie, and even the credits as they rolled up the screen.

I remember my first year of motherhood as a strenuous boot camp that seems like it would never end. Blurry memories of broken nights, the smells of sweat, breast milk, and formula. The buzz and pressure on my breasts from the vile breast pump. Waking up terrified at the sound of crying in the middle of the night. The urine-soaked diapers that went straight into the trash and the diapers with poop in them that had to be wrapped in a plastic bag. Bottle sterilization, bottle sterilization, bottle sterilization. The grandiose preparations every time we left the house and the chance that the slightest disruption could ruin everything.

At some point, I stopped wanting to go out. I preferred moving around the apartment with Lily from one comfortable spot to another. Halimi had enough energy to take Lily outside into the fresh air, and I spent more and more time sitting by the window. I cried a lot, out of frustration, boredom, and isolation.

And then, at night, a new and strange sense of yearning began to germinate. An hour or so after Lily had gone to sleep, when the apartment was relatively tidy, there was a sense that life was almost back on track, that I could watch TV or even read a little.

That was precisely when I got the urge to check on Lily. I just had to know that she was fine. In the darkness of the warm room as she lay sleeping peacefully, I longed for her to wake up.

Knowing that I was eventually going to disturb her, I would creep back to the living room. If we weren't completely spent, Halimi and I would lie on the couch together and review the events of the day. How Lily ate a banana, pointing at the mushy bits, wrinkling her nose in that cute way of hers. How curiously she looked at the toothless woman on the street who thought that Lily was the prettiest thing she'd ever seen. How she realized that the strawberries in the book are the same as the strawberries she eats. Stuff like that. Then, we'd have a good laugh at ourselves, doing exactly what we never expected to do, and say how everyone winds up doing it.

Libby spent a lot of time with us back then. She dropped in almost every day, helping me or Halimi with the cooking, talking to Lily in a squeaky voice, using finger puppets. When the weather cleared up, we would hang out in parks around Tel Aviv. Halimi loved to go out walking with Lily in the baby sling. He often related how he had met some acquaintance who got the shock of their life seeing him like that; sometimes, he took Lily to work. When I went to pick her up, I usually found her in the company of two or three very young, very trendy women lying on the floor and letting Lily crawl all over them and hit them with her rattle until they were called back to their desks.

Shortly after her first birthday, Lily developed a mass of blond, curly hair. She began walking.

Halimi still came home from errands and meetings with a burning desire to hold Lily, toss her in the air, and catch up on her daily exploits. But the amount of time he spent outside the house increased. There were cuts at the magazine, leaving him with only two deputy editors and one content producer. Here and there, he went out "for a drink" with Zozo, returning in the small hours of morning with the strong smell of alcohol on his breath—only partially camouflaged by toothpaste. He would climb into bed with me and cling to my warm, sleepy body.

The other mothers in the park began talking about playgroups. Long sessions of hanging out in the park were replaced by long walks in the stroller, punctuated by random trips to Dizengoff Center. Libby encouraged me to buy new clothes, get my hair cut, put on a touch of makeup, but I would linger in children's stores, resisting the urge to buy some new dress, toy, or book for Lily.

"Don't you think Diti should get out a bit, take a break?" Libby asked Halimi one day when he returned from the open-air market with groceries, after drinking a few beers with one of his photographers. Halimi lowered the shopping bags onto the kitchen table and sat down on the couch. I rested my head on his thigh.

"Definitely," Halimi said, dropping a kiss on the crown of my head. Then, he looked Libby in the eyes and said, "Are you going to babysit?"

I snorted. Libby rolled her eyes. "Don't be so possessive. *You* babysit," she retorted angrily.

"Libby thinks it'll do me good to dance a bit, flirt a bit, let go," I said. Libby didn't smile.

But Halimi agreed with Libby. "There's a few really cool parties coming up this Thursday," he said, stroking my hair, which had fanned out over his knees. "Go, break a few hearts."

Libby's eyebrows rose in surprise, and Halimi nodded at her.

"What about drugs?" I asked, my head still on his thigh. I'd already stopped breastfeeding, and anyway, Lily was down to one bottle per night.

"Don't worry, we'll get you some," Halimi said. "How's Lily? Does she still have a runny nose?"

It was Halimi's turn to put Lily to bed. I wanted to do it myself, to compensate for my disappearance, but Lily insisted on Halimi. My traditional role was making tea and looking for something to watch on TV, but after I'd smoked a joint on the balcony, I just sat there, staring into space.

My attention was divided: One part was pushing me into the kitchen to switch the kettle on and stream Netflix until Halimi finished putting Lily to bed; the other part was reenacting the conversation with Jean under the tree, the warmth of his arm as it brushed against mine, the firmness of the tree trunk against my back, and the feeling of Brunette's muzzle in the palm of my hand. I recalled Jean tapping on my arm with the date. I felt suddenly horny.

With a sense of urgency, I stepped inside and began going through the motions of our evening routine: filling two mugs with jasmine leaves, hot water, and honey; bringing them to the coffee table; collapsing onto the couch; and switching on the tablet Halimi gave me on my last birthday.

Halimi came out of Lily's room, and we went out to smoke a cigarette on the balcony. Halimi stretched out and smoked in silence, his mug of tea in hand. I leaned against the railing and exhaled smoke westward, in the direction of the dimly lit fortress overlooking the seashore. I got goose bumps thinking about the fortress at the height of its glory and my knowledge of how it once looked.

"Get over here," Halimi said. I sat on his knee, my face turned toward him, his rough jeans and zipper rubbing against me. "So, what were you saying about the Countess of Atlit and the knights? It sounded hot," Halimi said, pulling me closer. If it had been up to him, we would have fucked out there on the balcony in full view of any curious neighbor. But not even all the years with Halimi had succeeded in erasing the good girl inside me, and I dragged him to the bedroom.

I was still getting used to the early morning chirping of the birds in Atlit. Sometimes, I dreamed up Tel Aviv noises: the heaving and trumpeting of the garbage trucks at 5:00 a.m., the neighbors yelling at their dogs, a random argument over a parking spot. In Atlit, I sometimes heard the distant clatter of pots and pans and car doors slamming as people set off for work. By 9:00 a.m., there were only birds left.

I stirred under the bedsheets, lay there for a few more seconds, and when I felt myself drifting back to sleep, I got up. Halimi had already taken Lily to preschool and was now in the living room, talking on the phone. By the time I'd finished breakfast, I found myself gazing out lazily at the horizon and seashore.

Somewhere in the background, Halimi continued his phone calls, pacing around the living room. Finally, he came outside for a smoke.

"What did you do to me last night, you little pervert?" he winked at me. I pulled myself together and smiled at him. "What did you do to *me*?" I retorted. It had been a long time since we'd had such good sex.

"Should we thank the flamingos in their salt pools?" he asked.

"Possibly," I said. "Probably."

Halimi didn't respond. He just kept staring at me.

"Maybe you think it's funny," I said cautiously, "but it could just be that my need to get off the grid actually brushed off the mildew. For months now, I've either been at home or running errands. Permanently on assignment. I've forgotten how great it is to let go and just be." Halimi nodded slowly, as if I'd just proven a point he'd been trying to explain.

"It's not exactly the same thing," I said, guessing where his thoughts were headed.

"What isn't exactly the same?" Halimi asked, extinguishing his cigarette.

I glanced at the kitchen clock. "Let's not get into that right now, Limi," I said. "I've got to go to the copy center to print out this French text; otherwise, I'm never going to finish it. Let's talk about it later."

Halimi pushed the ashtray aside. "Okay, my love," he said, his hand already reaching out for his phone. "But this time, come straight back."

"I promise," I said and went off to look for the car keys.

An hour later, I was sitting on the balcony again, gazing at the horizon. "Diti," Halimi said so loudly it made me jump. The pages of the French text, printed and spiral-bound, were flapping in the light breeze.

"What? Sorry," I said mechanically, realizing it was the third or fourth time he'd called my name.

"You've gotten annoying," Halimi said, not at all angry. "Do you want coffee?"

"No thanks," I answered, checking the time. I had to start getting lunch ready, and soon Lily needed to be picked up from preschool. I might have completed the important mission of printing out the manuscript but hadn't so much as glanced at it since I got back. I'd done nothing but stare into space for the past hour, oblivious to the passing time.

"Oh no!" I jumped up suddenly. "Lily has her appointment!" We went to pick her up together and continued straight there. She was due for her last in a round of vaccines. I always struggled with holding Lily firmly enough that she wouldn't squirm when the needle went in, which embarrassed me. I could have sent Halimi on his own—he was very dependable with this kind of thing—but I wanted to be there to hug and kiss Lily when she got the jab and burst out crying. And to prove I wasn't lazy.

Lily did great. To my relief, she was unfazed by the sight of the needle, and by the time she had worked out that it was going to hurt, the whole thing was over.

We went out for ice cream, but the strip mall depressed me, so we grabbed a bunch of napkins and got back into the car and drove to the beach, humming a Beyoncé song playing on the radio.

We parked on the sand, not far from the army base, and walked barefoot to the beach. It was a Tuesday afternoon. During the week, the beach was usually empty, though never completely deserted. We sat on the sand, Lily between Halimi's legs, carefully polishing off her dripping cone.

When she was done, Lily went to play in the waves. Her tights and shirt got soaked, but the weather was warm, so I just undressed her. I lay in the sand, the back of my neck against Halimi's thigh. The fortress ruins rose up in front of me, and for the first time it occurred to me how little I really knew about the place. I wondered whether I might find something online about Jean d'Ibelin or even Thibaut, if I dug deep enough. I also wondered why it had never occurred to me to look him up before. I imagined myself Googling Jean's name and was overcome by laughter.

"What's so funny?" Halimi asked. He was also lying on the sand, his arms folded behind his head.

"I remembered a funny line from that French novel, but it's not that funny out of context," I said dismissively. "It's just nonsense."

"Most of our lives are nonsense," Halimi reflected after a few seconds. I sat up, locating Lily a few feet away, stroking a small dog belonging to a white-haired man. I went to fetch her, and we strolled back to the shore-line, our feet sinking deep in the wet sand.

We sat down by Halimi, Lily cuddled up to me, trembling slightly from the cold. I rubbed her arms and tried to wrap myself around her as best I could. A young couple walked by, and the girl gave us a look that said, "What an adorable family." Lily flashed the girl one of her best smiles and then buried her head in my chest, suddenly shy.

"Are we done here?" Halimi asked. "Lily's getting cold."

CHAPTER 11

The beach was deserted. I was aware only of an insurmountable craving to enter the sea, and I made my way to the water as fast as I could.

I glanced behind as my legs propelled me forward at an inhuman speed toward the water. From east and south of the ridge spread the present-day neighborhoods of Atlit. I could even see our house, which I'd never been able to make out from such a distance before.

The more I focused on the idea that our house was visible from the seashore—with the garden and the Persian lilac—the clearer and clearer the building's details became. For a moment, I even saw our bedroom from the inside, as if I were in bed.

But the spot in the sea continued to call me. I turned back to face the water and discovered that while I had been looking back at the house, my legs had pulled me in, and I was already waist-deep.

I decided to dive deep under the waves. It afforded me instant pleasure. I peered up cautiously as I swam. Here and there were pools of greenish light that broke through the surface above me. With a sense of satisfaction, I allowed myself to drift through the water, like an astronaut in space or a fetus in a womb. Something strange lay ahead, and the nearer I got, the stranger it appeared. Just before I was sucked in, I knew it had been the force of a whirlpool that had attracted me.

I wasn't afraid; I had no expectations, no memories. I wanted nothing else but to let it take me away.

The whirlpool swirled me around in complete harmony with the turning of the Earth around the Sun. This was time. A circular movement of entities around themselves and each other. I laughed. *This is time!* I wanted to shout.

But the moment I opened my mouth to utter this revelation, I was expelled from the water.

"Diti! Diti! Idit!" I heard my name being called. I opened my eyes in our darkened bedroom in Atlit. My heart was pumping like crazy, and I was half-strangled by my hair, wet with perspiration.

"What happened to Mommy?" asked a sleepy voice. It was my daughter. My heart began to quiet. I looked around and saw Halimi leaning over me worriedly. Lily stood near him in her pajamas, the pacifier half-hanging out of her mouth, one hand holding her blankie to her chest.

"Everything's okay," I murmured, "it was just a dream." I had no idea what it was. I remembered diving into the depths, breathing underwater, a ghostly sea, and a whirlpool of time. But now I felt relieved to be back inside my own familiar, naked body, between soft sheets, with Halimi and Lily, who climbed into the double bed, snuggling in between us. I hugged her little body, radiating familiar warmth and love. In the darkness, Halimi looked at me from his side of the bed with concern. He took my hand and placed it on his chest.

"Do you feel this?" he whispered. "Do you feel my heart racing?"

"What happened? Was I talking in my sleep?" I asked in a very low voice.

"You screamed and cried," he said, with a note of fear I'd never heard before. "I couldn't get you to wake up."

"It's okay, sweetie," I whispered again and meant it. Everything was fine, I was at home, I was myself, and everything was normal. I closed my eyes.

By the time I was awake, the house was quiet. Small waves of memory from the dream scattered on the shores of my consciousness. It had been years since I had experienced such a powerful dream. I suddenly remembered what Halimi had said about the priestess from his dream and the dancing around the spring.

I shook my head and got out of bed. Halimi still wasn't back from dropping Lily off at preschool. I ran a bath, placed the showerhead on my belly, and let the water rise.

I lay in the hot water, half-asleep, for a long time. I swayed gently, and the tiny ripples evoked details from the dream.

"Diti?" I heard Halimi calling. I opened my eyes, and he was standing over me, pulling the shower curtain aside. His wide forehead was furrowed.

"Hi, sweetie," I said and raised my arms up to him. "Do you want to join me in here?"

He made one of his funny faces, pursing his lips and raising his eyebrows in surprise, then he sat down on the stool. He began taking his shoes off, without saying a word.

"Good God," I snickered. "You need to change your socks." Halimi laughed, then turned serious. He stripped fastidiously, folded his pants and shirt, flung his underwear and socks into the laundry basket.

He stepped carefully into the bath, and his big body raised the water level. I switched sides and lay in his arms, the warm water rippling gently over us.

"I don't want you to get upset," he said softly, "but I think it might be a good idea for you to speak to a professional. We can go together, if you want."

"Why?" my voice came out in a yowl. "It was just a really powerful dream I had last night."

"It's not just the dream," he said in a conciliatory tone. "You haven't been yourself for a week. I've never seen you like this before. I forbid you to do any more mushrooms."

"You forbid me," I said out loud, and what I really wanted was to get out of the bath, leave him there, head straight to my spring, and jump in headfirst. But I had to be more calculated. And truthfully, I felt a bit sorry for him.

"Limi," I began, trying to make sense of my thoughts. "Maybe I'm acting weird, but I'm not sick. I think I'm just trying to process all kinds of shit in my life in the quiet and tranquility of this place."

He held me close and planted a kiss on my head. Even though he hadn't said it in words, I knew he was thinking of Nina and the pain he had caused me.

"Never mind," I said, suddenly feeling uncomfortable. "That's behind us."

He said nothing but hugged me even closer.

After a few moments, in which I tried several times to start a conversation but faltered, I said, "I think I'm beginning to understand the need to disappear sometimes. It's so liberating to be suddenly alone, like floating in an empty space . . ."

"But it really is stressful," he said, abashed. "I hope you aren't going to start disappearing on a regular basis."

"I thought I might join a yoga class," I said.

"What's that got to do with it?" he exclaimed.

"I need a bit of time to myself, that's all," I said. "I've already checked out a few options. I might try a class next Monday."

"And then come show me some steaming hot poses," he said languidly.

"My pleasure," I said, kissing his hand. "You dirty old man."

*   *   *

I lay on the yoga mat and let the spring sun warm my bones, Lily play-ing beside me. A parrot squawked from the top of the Persian lilac tree. From time to time, I saw it maneuvering through the thick foliage, trig-gering showers of delicate, pale purple flowers. Halimi was inside, but now I saw him walking toward us with the weekend newspapers, which he placed beside me on the mat.

"Do you want me to make room for you?" I asked him, stretching out even more on the mat.

"Wait," he said and went over to Lily. She explained what she was doing with a set of doll furniture in meticulous detail and assigned him the task of bringing some Smurf figurines from her bedroom so she could breathe some life into the display. "And bring me water, please," she yelled in his direction as he walked off.

After a few minutes, Halimi reappeared with a tray, upon which stood Smurfette, Brainy Smurf, Jokey Smurf, and Papa Smurf, alongside two glasses of lemonade and a plate of sesame cookies.

"Mmm, how nice . . ." I murmured as Halimi set the tray down.

"I wanna lemonade too!" Lily shouted and drank half of mine.

In Lily's second year, I went out a lot. She started to go to a nearby day-care, with three other toddlers her age. I regained what Libby called my "humanity." I began translating again, spending hours in neighborhood cafés, meeting friends. I enjoyed buying treats from the local deli and cooking elaborate dishes. Halimi and I no longer collapsed onto the couch at night, and we caught up on several TV series. Once a week or so, I went to a bar or club with Libby. We usually hung out with two gay guys from Libby's office, perfect dancing partners, and occasionally met other girlfriends too.

I added bedtime stories to the lullabies I sang to Lily at night. From age one and a half, I was already reading her stories supposedly written for older kids. She was curious, even when it was clear she didn't really understand. I had a collection of Hans Christian Andersen stories that my parents gave me when I was a kid. I was fascinated by the illustrations long before I was able to appreciate the complexities of the texts themselves. Now, I saw the same erratic details that had attracted me as a child through my daughter's eyes, like Thumbelina's walnut shell and rose-petal bedding, or the silver teapot in which the emperor saw his own reflection, dressed in finery, though he was naked as the day he was born.

It also became scarier to take Lily out, to constantly make sure she wouldn't wander off. Once I lost her in the supermarket, and another time in a clothing store, and both times I almost had a heart attack.

Halimi worked hard. Budget cuts at the magazine continued, and he was forced to spend more time at his desk. The management demanded an increased online presence, which bugged Halimi, who belonged to the old school of print. One brilliant writer, poached from a rival magazine, got Halimi fueled up on the subject of the Mizrahi Jews—he suddenly connected with his Algerian identity and got involved in cultural activist events. As for us, we exchanged daily selfies, either funny or sexy, and that pretty much summed up the romantic side of our relationship.

Throughout Lily's first year, sex between us was rare and mechanical. I was always tired, often on edge, frequently lacking patience. When motherhood stopped being a full-time job, I felt the world opening up to me again. My libido resurfaced—at first shy and hesitant, then bold: In the morning, I would try tempting Halimi back into bed for a few minutes after he dropped Lily off at preschool, sending a text message inviting him back home for a quickie, but he hardly ever took me up on it. I got into the habit of pleasuring myself after they left for preschool.

At night, when I was less horny, Halimi would grope me or pull me toward him in bed; sometimes, we just turned out all the lights in the living room and did it there. For some reason, sex remained mechanical. Halimi was good at knowing where to touch me and how to arouse me, but it somehow rattled me. I felt humiliated, as if I were a microwave oven that just required a basic knowledge of its buttons to be turned on. I used to stare at him, trying to understand what had changed. I still found him attractive, with his relaxed manner and the way he stretched his long limbs, never in a hurry—until suddenly he would disappear all at once and go about his business.

Shortly after Lily's second birthday party, which included her day-care friends, Libby and Zozo, my parents, and Halimi's sister and her family, it suddenly hit me.

"He's stopped looking at me with that adoration in his eyes," I told Dina on Zoom.

"I told you about the terrible twos," Dina said, "and I wasn't just talking about Lily. It's a decisive moment. If you can get through this, it'll all work out."

So, I was horny, and we fucked a lot, but something was missing. It wasn't the orgasms, but something more fundamental that was hard for me to express in words. It took time before Halimi also noticed that something wasn't quite right. It happened one night when I began crying after Halimi came. He freaked out, even got annoyed, and I stuttered something about my microwave analogy. I couldn't bring myself to say it: Halimi no longer adored me.

His male pride was hurt—he was always very pleased with himself when I came hard, even after years of being together. "I don't get it," he complained. "Is it not okay that I know exactly how to make you come? What do you want me to do?"

We tried everything. We watched porn together, but it was tough finding something that turned us both on. He filmed me pleasuring myself, which made him really horny, which turned me on, but after two or three times, it lost its charm. I read him erotic stories out loud, which was effective for a while. He bought me a bunch of sex toys, but mostly we abandoned those for the real thing, which I always preferred.

Occasionally, I would come back from a night out feeling aroused—when someone made a pass at me in a fun way, or when I was still a little drunk, or after I'd fooled around with a guy I barely knew. Halimi loved hearing my silly stories. Usually it turned him on and almost always led to the best sex we had during that time.

One Friday morning, I came back from an awesome party. This really gorgeous guy hit on me, but soon enough it became clear he was dumb as a doornail—which turned me off instantly. He was crushed when I refused to have sex with him, so I agreed to stand with him in the stall while he jerked off. During the act, I felt like someone administering first aid, practical and accommodating and unemotional. He was very nice when he thanked me, with a degree of humility. Surprisingly enough, the whole situation actually turned me on.

The entire way home in the taxi, I thought about waking up Halimi with a blowjob. As I turned the key in the door, I imagined the two of us laughing at that dude. As I entered the house, I heard Halimi snoring. I walked into the bedroom and looked at him for a few seconds; his mouth hung open, and he looked kind of old. I peeked into Lily's bedroom—a tiny room that Halimi had used as a storeroom in his bachelor days—and I heard her deep breathing, punctuated by adorable little wheezes. I went to smoke a bedtime cigarette by the window ledge and looked out as dawn spread slowly over the city.

Often when I sat there like that, on the window ledge, still buzzing from the night's festivities—after drugs and the physical pleasure of hours of dancing, with a horniness that sometimes peaked but often didn't even begin—I would inhale the silent chill of early morning and fill with vitality. Once I texted Libby, as dawn rose over the city: "It's a sense of power that you've vanquished the night, that you don't have to lose consciousness to witness the changing of time." She responded with a smiley emoji with hearts in its eyes.

This only worked at the break of dawn. Later, the energetic, practical light of day would erase those nighttime impressions, blurring what had been, but in those few minutes by the windowsill, I often felt unbelievably happy and lucky that I had at my fingertips both wild pleasure and my beloved, blissful routine.

Perhaps on this specific occasion, I didn't exactly feel that. Maybe I just looked out at the construction sites closing in on the apartment from all sides, the foundations of a new building where there had been jackhammering all week.

Halimi had left his cell phone on the table in the living room. He must have fallen asleep on the couch and dragged himself to bed in the middle of the night. I extinguished the cigarette on the outer wall of the building, and as I went to throw the cigarette butt into the trash, the cell phone flashed. A WhatsApp message. It was kind of a weird hour to be texting. My attention was also drawn to the heart emojis in multiple colors. With the cigarette butt still in the palm of my hand, I picked up the cell phone.

"Monday at Hotel Montefiore ♥ ♥ ♥," sent by Nina Lev-Ari.

The tall and beautiful Nina, the mythological trendspotter, always ahead of the *Free to Be* fashion curve. The brilliant and talented Nina, feminist in all the right ways, whose articles were always the magazine's most popular on social media. My hands began to shake. I felt the blend of vodka and orange juice I'd been drinking all night come up in my throat.

I recalled an incident I hadn't given much thought to at the time: Once, when I dropped by Halimi's office to pick up Lily, who was playing with the secretary at the editorial desk, Nina sat facing Halimi.

Something about their body language aroused my suspicion, which at the time seemed funny. They both appeared relaxed in my presence, and when I asked Halimi if they had something going on, he laughed and said there was zero chance of that. "She's a cold fish," he'd said.

A few months had gone by since that incident. I hadn't even thought about it. It had been a long time since Halimi's last affair. I put it down to his sense of paternal responsibility and general fatigue. Sometime during the past year, he did tell me about two "incidents"—one at a party thrown by the magazine, and the other at a club that had since closed. He used the same phrase for both: "I had a fling with some chick." In both cases, it was a random woman he didn't know or barely knew. He didn't go into details, and I didn't pressure him—I was happy and grateful that he even told me. I wasn't at all jealous. I was reassured that we'd beaten the system. "It works!" I told my sister euphorically, and she nodded wisely.

Libby, as it happens, had told me several times in recent months that she couldn't believe there was no one else. "He would have told me," I stopped her short, faithful to the memory of all those nights in which I'd detailed my own "incidents" in clubs and the sense of joint destiny.

Now, I went into his WhatsApp and scrolled through all the messages between Halimi and Nina. Most of them were pretty tame, but there was one message from about a month earlier that set off alarm bells. It appeared to be a response to previous messages, sent out of the blue in the middle of the day after a few message-less days. "It's not fair to ask things like that," she wrote, followed by two emojis: an eggplant and a peach. It was obvious he'd deleted the rest of the incriminating evidence; this one had simply slipped under Halimi's radar.

As if I were speaking to her that very moment on Zoom, I heard my sister's voice telling me, "Don't jump to conclusions. Maybe it's a business meeting, and because the magazine is picking up the tab, they've decided to indulge themselves at a fancy restaurant. Maybe the message with the eggplant and the peach was in reaction to some remark Halimi made at the office, and they're just kidding around."

Shut the fuck up, I answered my sister, angrily terminating the imaginary call. In my mind's eye, I saw Halimi in his office, fixing Nina with that gaze of utter adoration, the one that used to be fixed on me.

I knew that when Halimi woke up and found his phone, he would realize someone had opened her message. I didn't want him to know I'd read it.

I heard Lily stirring in her bedroom and knew this was my opportunity. I acted completely cold-blooded, calculated. Like a lioness in the savanna, I thought to myself. I went into Lily's room and sat down on her bed. She opened her eyes almost immediately and smiled up at me. She fumbled for her pacifier, which had fallen out during the night. A few minutes later, she was already on the couch, waiting for me to heat her milk and honey.

"Did you play the animal game yesterday?" I asked her. Halimi had a game on his cell phone downloaded especially for Lily, a highly recommended app he'd read about in the "Busy Kids" column of the magazine.

Lily shook her head and grabbed Halimi's cell phone. I turned up the volume on this noisy game, which was very unlike me. A few minutes later, I heard Halimi padding into the kitchen. I poured myself some coffee.

"Good morning," I said. "The Rozhevsky-Halimi household is up early today."

"Did you sleep at all?" he asked foggily. "I'm going to brush my teeth."

"Do you want me to make you a cup of coffee?" I shouted after him.

"Sure," he answered from the hallway.

As we drank our coffee together in the living room, Halimi shot Lily a look. "How long has she been playing that game?" Before I had time to reply, he said, "Come on, Lily, enough already. Give me the phone." She protested, he didn't relent, and I called her to come eat her oatmeal at the kitchen table.

I watched him examining the phone. A few seconds later, he looked up at me with an alarmed expression on his face. I smiled sweetly and said, "Everything okay?"

"Hunky-dory," he answered. "Maybe I should get one of those kiddie tablets for Lily. I'm sick of her hogging my phone."

I felt the blood rushing to my head again. "Watch her for a minute, so she doesn't fling oatmeal all over the floor," I said and went to throw up in the bathroom.

CHAPTER 12

On Monday morning, again I woke up after Halimi had taken Lily to preschool. The night before, he told me the editorial meeting at the radio station had been canceled because of a tax audit. I wouldn't let this stop me. *I'll find some excuse*, I told myself before falling asleep that night.

A few minutes after opening my eyes, I wondered whether I'd be able to cross the spring to Jean d'Ibelin. The days that had passed since our last meeting had blurred the memory into a kind of reverie. I recalled the sight of the Crusader fortress in the last crazy dream I had, beside what must have been the Phoenician port, with modern Atlit in the background. I was sweating a little under the winter blanket, which we had not yet swapped for something lighter because the nights were still chilly.

Twang, twang, the strings reverberated between my ears. I sat up in bed. I fixed my eyes on the closet and wondered what to wear: something not too modest, but definitely not risqué. And something that would be comfortable to wear by the spring. But not too weird if, say, we rode to the fortress.

I chose a woolen dress in red, from way back when I lived in Jerusalem, one of those nostalgic pieces I insisted on keeping rather than tossing into the huge trash bags I donated before we moved. After giving birth, most of my clothes were too small for me, but I was confident I'd get my body back someday. In Atlit, where 24/7 kiosks and restaurant deliveries were not around to tempt me, I had lost a few pounds. I tried the dress on and thanked the powers that be for providing a zipper. A little tight over the chest, but overall nice and comfortable and timeless.

"Wow, look at you," Halimi said, glancing up from his computer as I came in to turn the kettle on. I coughed with embarrassment and wiped my glasses' lenses. "Do you remember this dress?" I asked Halimi, my back to him. "Brrr, it's cold this morning."

"Sure I remember," Halimi said, turning back to the computer screen. He was transcribing an interview with the editor of an important American journal. Sometimes, he was asked to write articles for weekend magazines.

"Listen, I'll probably be back late from Tel Aviv today," I went on, pouring boiling water into a coffee mug.

The clatter of the keyboard stopped. I turned to face him. "Coffee?" I said before taking a sip.

"How come you're going to Tel Aviv?" Halimi asked. He crossed one leg over the other and pulled out a cigarette.

"Don't tell me you're going to smoke inside!" I exclaimed. We weren't particularly strict, but smoking on the balcony was sacrosanct. "I'll air the place out later, you won't smell a thing," Halimi said, lighting his cigarette.

"Come on . . ." he continued as I grabbed a bread roll and began spreading butter on it. "What are you doing in Tel Aviv?"

"Nothing!" I replied, more resentfully than I'd intended. "I told you already, I have to go over the proofs of that children's book." I'd said nothing of the sort, but I figured he only remembered half the things I told him about my schedule or household matters anyway.

"Why do you have to go to Tel Aviv for that?" Halimi persisted, turning back to the computer screen. "Can't they just email you the text?" He knew that since we left Tel Aviv, I'd grown allergic to the place. I hadn't once joined him on a trip there, even though he'd invited me several times.

"Nope, I have to do it with the graphic artist. They want to send it to the printer this week," I said. If the goddamn publishing house functioned properly, this would have been true, I convinced myself.

"Okay, sweetie," Halimi sighed. "Get some decent coffee while you're there, yeah?"

"But you bought some when you went to Dan's, didn't you? There's plenty," I said, my mouth full of bread.

Halimi's phone rang.

"We don't want to run out of coffee," he mumbled and slid his finger over the phone.

I stopped the car behind the rock with the Phoenician inscription. After a particularly nice week of spring weather, the ground was already dry.

At home, I'd changed clothes. "I felt stupid in that dress," I told Halimi when I came out of the shower, already dressed in leggings and a thin, baggy sweater, contact lenses in place. He was speaking on the phone and shot me a quizzical look when he saw me. I put the woolen dress in my backpack. I managed to squeeze back into it while cramped in the tiny car.

This time, there was nobody at the ruins. When I got to the tree, I noticed a small puddle still there, the size of a book. Before submerging the coin in the water, I inhaled deeply, then I dunked the coin around my neck into the water.

Nothing happened, but I was prepared for a delay. A few seconds passed, then a minute, and still nothing happened.

I turned around and came back. I submerged the coin again, in the exact same way as the week before. Nothing happened. My brain came to a dead halt inside my skull and did a little jig around itself.

What's going on? I wondered. It was like I was meant to solve an unspoken riddle. I sighed in exasperation. The red woolen dress was tight. I began pulling at the zipper. There was no one to see me anyway. The zipper got stuck. "Ouch!" I shouted and looked around. My finger had caught in the teeth of the zipper, and a small drop of blood was forming. I sucked my finger, and then I heard it: *twang, twang,* the hidden chords—in my head, or in another time, or in a parallel universe, who the hell knew.

Something gleamed in the puddle. I took my finger out of my mouth and reached out to grab whatever it was that was sparkling, but my fingers failed to grasp it. My body was pulled into the puddle, and a phosphorescent light exploded in my brain.

"Christ the Crucified!" someone shouted, and I blinked under the green canopy of the carob tree, breathing in air redolent of 1240. To my horror, above me was an unsheathed penis attached to a knight in chainmail and a black cloak with a red cross rolled up over his naked loins. I sat up and stared at him, wide-eyed.

"What . . . what . . . what . . ." mumbled the knight, stuffing his dick into his long underwear and clumsily straightening his clothes. Repulsed, I noticed a small, steaming pool of urine on the dry ground, inches away from me.

The knight fell to his knees, closed his eyes, and clapped his hands together.

"*Ave Maria,*" he began muttering. "*Gratia plena, Dominus tecum . . .*"

I froze for a moment, then had a bright idea.

I got to my feet and stood before him, a fortuitous ray of sunlight lighting my brown hair, making it appear golden. I lifted my hand in a gesture of blessing.

"You are pardoned," I said in Hebrew. "Do not fear, my child," I continued in a refined, motherly voice, getting into character. "I will protect you forevermore, wherever you may be."

The knight, or whoever he was, looked up in awe, teeth chattering.

"What is your name, my son?" I asked in French, in the same even tone.

"Geoffroy," the young man stammered. "Geoffroy of Tours."

I placed my hand on his head and recited the most basic Latin blessing I could think of. *"Deus te benedict,"* I mumbled, hoping for the best.

"My lady!" he gasped. "Who are you? How must I address you?"

"I am of the spring," I improvised. "Return to your duties, Geoffroy of Tours. Be courteous and merciful and do not forget thy prayers," I concluded, lowering my arms.

The knight bowed his head and got to his feet. He retreated, walking away from the tree in reverse, still facing me. "Do not bring anyone here and do not approach this site for a full day," I managed to say, in French, before he left. He bowed his head again, mouth still agape, eyes wild, and disappeared among the trees.

Well, that could have gone worse, I thought to myself, *but I handled it well.* I washed my face with the spring water.

It was getting chilly. I leaned against the tree and looked out at the small pool of water that had formed next to it, water from a spring that no longer existed in my own time. Or perhaps it still existed but had turned into a puddle no bigger than a book?

I closed my eyes and inhaled the fragrant air, infused with the scent of burning wood and a faint odor of goat droppings. I knew I wasn't hallucinating or dreaming. The scents were so powerful. I had a sense of triumph and wild strength. My heart slowed, then quickened, realizing that I could carry out this magic passage at will. I looked around more attentively. There was no sign of Jean d'Ibelin. I had no idea what to do here without him. I glanced at my watch, but the hands were stuck, even though I'd checked that it was working back at home. I sat down on a nearby dune and looked out, my mind empty of thought, at the beauty spread across the landscape. Gardens and orchards blossomed in plum and cherry-blossom pink. Olive trees rippled like silvery waves in the sunlight. The blue-green sea crashed into white foam on a strip of shimmering sand, and the flags of the huge fortress fluttered gently in the breeze. A bell pealed, followed by another heavier and slower bell, which echoed across the valley.

My temples began throbbing dully, so I moved back under the shade of the carob tree. I sat by the spring and deliberated whether to go back to my own time, despite the sense of failure. Did I really need Jean d'Ibelin to set out on an adventure? I could just wander around on my own.

I was considering whether I had the courage to venture as far as the town or the fortress when I heard hoofbeats and barking in the distance. Sweat broke out on the palms of my hands. I sat up straight in an effort to look serene and dignified.

A few minutes later, I heard the sound of an easy trot and Jean d'Ibelin's voice through the branches. A few seconds later, Brunette burst through the canopy, a hand moved a sweeping branch aside, and Jean's head peeped in.

"You are here, my lady," he said with gratification. He was still holding the horse's bridle. I sat up even straighter and smiled at him. He winked, and his head disappeared. Through the branches and thick foliage, I spied two horses. Jean tied them through an iron ring to the wall, while Brunette charged me, licking and barking happily.

"You sweet, beautiful creature," I murmured to her in Hebrew as I bent down to hug her. Jean returned, beaming with pleasure at the sight of my enthusiastic reunion with Brunette.

"She likes you very much," he said in wonderment. "She typically reserves such playfulness for my children. She is not given to displays of affection."

He sat down beside me. He was dressed, as usual, in shades of yellow and red. A cotton tunic and silk pants tucked into boots of soft brown leather; a wide leather belt, from which hung various pouches; a long sword; and a bulging shoulder bag. This time, he wore a simple brown hunting hat. He looked something like the early illustrations of Robin Hood. I smiled. He smiled back.

"You are looking particularly spirited today, Lady Édith."

"I am in good health, Sir Jean," I answered, perhaps overenthusiastically.

"I dare not ask how your journey here was . . ."

"Everything's fine, it's just that . . ." I hesitated.

"Pray tell, my lady," Jean said, pausing the unpacking of his bags for a moment.

"One of your guards was here when . . . when I arrived. I suspect he thought I was some kind of a fairy. He began praying and seemed afraid. I acted as if I were an angel dropped out of the sky and forbade him from returning here for the time being," I said with trepidation.

Jean cast a glance behind him, beyond the tree's thick branches, then turned back to me, smiling. "The sergeants are very superstitious, so let us hope his story will sit well with the other legends they tell each other."

I liked the fact that he was so laid-back and confident, lighthearted, and unshakable. My smile broadened, and I said in Latin, "May the Lord God bless you," as I'd said to the poor pissing sergeant.

Jean began removing things from his shoulder bag: a large cloth, which he spread on the ground and upon which he placed a ceramic bottle, a few small apples, a thin sliver of hard cheese, half a loaf of bread, and a handful of sticky dates that he carefully unwrapped from a handkerchief.

"Would you care to restore your spirit with refreshments?" he asked, taking out two small ceramic cups.

"Certainly," I replied. To my surprise, it all felt totally natural to me. "I should like to take you riding today, if it pleases you," Jean said, helping himself to a date. "However, we must fashion something more seemly for you. I took the liberty of bringing you everything an honest woman needs in order to appear in public without giving the impression that"—he stopped himself and smiled at me—"she is of dubious reputation."

"Do you always wander around with women's clothing in your shoulder bag?" I asked, curious to know what he had brought. Jean snorted with laughter.

"Indeed, more than you might envisage," he said. "My wife loves fine garments, and on my voyages I try to procure exquisite fabrics, artfully dyed textiles, or interesting adornments for her." This was the first time, I think, that he had mentioned his wife to me directly. He did this in an offhand way, without avoiding my eyes or apologizing, as if I were his sister.

"You're a great husband, then," I said, helping myself to a hunk of bread.

"I do not think my wife is convinced of that," Jean responded, his eyes twinkling. "But it is of no matter. See for yourself if the garments I borrowed from Thibaut's chest are suitable for you." He removed a beautifully folded parcel from his shoulder bag.

"But . . . but . . ." I stammered. "What do you mean? Do you want me to try them on now? Because, you know . . . someone might pass by." I didn't dare say I was too shy to undress in front of him. Suddenly, I wasn't sure anymore. The mention of his wife had confused me.

"It is rare and infrequent for a person to pass here alone, near the ridge. If, perchance, a band of knights arrives, we will hear them from afar," Jean assured me.

"And what about . . ." I glanced beyond the canopy of branches. "What about that guard?"

"There are two guards who survey the ridge and roads. If they are caught deserting their post for anything besides combat or alerting the inhabitants of the fortress to danger, they will be subject to twenty lashes," Jean declared. "Fear not. Or perhaps my lady is suddenly bashful?"

"I've got my pride, you know," I admitted. "I might be from another time, but yeah, I need privacy to change into those clothes."

"It is not my intention to observe you disrobing," he answered, horrified. "What do you think I am?"

I spluttered indistinctly, and Jean, perturbed, placed the bundle of fabric on the blanket by the tree.

"No need to get angry," I said timidly.

"I have never met such a lady as you in all my days," he muttered and left the canopy. I saw him through the branches, standing with his face to the sea, whistling a tune. I busied myself with the bundle he had left me.

There was a broad, light-colored shift, which I took to be the undergarment, and a loose silk dress in dusty rose. It had a decorative hem and was adorned with exquisite gold embroidery at the neckline and around the cuffs. There was also a long ribbon: a narrow strip of fabric consisting of crisscrosses in pink and yellow. After staring at it stupidly for a while, I figured it was a belt. In addition, there were two pieces of white cotton fabric—one thicker and a little stiffer, the other airier and almost transparent. I guessed they were part of the headwear; I'd need help figuring out how to put them on.

I began to remove my clothes but realized I would never be able to open that damn zipper on my own.

"Sir Jean," I said quietly. The whistling ceased. "I need your help."

He came back in, and I stood there, my back to him, trying to point to the stuck zipper. "You need to pull it down," I told him. "I can't reach it."

"What the devil is this?" he asked.

"We call it a zipper. Great invention, but sometimes it sticks. Just try to pull it down, okay?"

I felt his long, slender fingers take hold of the zipper, but because he had no idea what to do, Jean may as well have had his hands tied behind his back.

"In the name of the Holy Mother, this devilish contraption won't budge," he blurted out after several attempts.

"You need to hold the edges together and then pull gently," I said. Brunette appeared under the canopy, wagging her tail, and sat down next to us. She looked up inquisitively. Finally, Jean succeeded. A sense of relief washed over me. He froze as my naked back was revealed, and I turned around immediately to face him, my hands clasped to my chest. I wasn't even wearing a bra.

I cleared my throat nervously and lowered my eyes to the ground.

"I can't even imagine what you're thinking right now" was the only logical thing to say.

"I must confess, I know not what to think," he replied, attempting to get a grip on himself. We stared at each other for a few seconds.

"If your foreignness were less distinct," he spoke slowly, "and if I had not seen with my own eyes your miraculous appearance and disappearance, I would have presumed you were a repenting whore on a pilgrimage from a distant land."

"Last time we met, you said if I hadn't insisted I was a mother and good wife to my husband, you would have presumed I was a bashful virgin," I reminded him.

"There's nothing like an experienced harlot to make a man believe she's a bashful virgin," he said without thinking, as if he were quoting a famous dictum, and then immediately caught himself. "I beg your pardon, my lady. I did not mean to suggest that you are indeed a . . ."

"No problem," I interrupted him. "I'm neither a harlot nor a virgin; there are a few other shades in between, you know."

"I do not understand what you are," he said, continuing to look me straight in the eyes. "I cannot believe you are a fairy or a succubus. Your talk of a different time, of the future, indeed sounds like the ravings of a woman who has lost her mind." He fell silent. I meant to respond, but he raised one finger authoritatively and continued: "But I see your eyes are clear and your speech eloquent, and thus I try not to think about it too much, so that I will not begin to believe that I myself have lost my mind."

I sighed heavily. "And the zipper? Does that do nothing to convince you that I'm from another time?" I asked in desperation.

"Verily, it is a most wondrous contraption," he said slowly and took a step forward so he could scrutinize the zipper again. Jean started to say something but stopped. He passed his hand over my naked back; I took a deep breath and turned to face him. Jean lowered his head, kissed me on the lips, and took an abrupt step backward.

"Please get dressed, my lady, before I lose my knightly restraint," Jean said, and he walked out from under the canopy before I had time to respond. I removed the red woolen dress—vowing never to wear it again—and slipped the undergarment over my head. It was wonderfully comfortable, caressing my body in a welcome contrast to the tight woolen dress.

The undergarment fit me perfectly. I wriggled into the pink dress with ease and was sorry there was no mirror to see how I looked. I wound the woven belt around my waist and tied it in a big bow at the back.

"I think I'm almost done here," I said softly, and Jean returned. "Most becoming," he said, impressed by my appearance. He came to me, undid the bow I had made in the belt and retied it at the front, to the left side of my waist, leaving the two ends dangling down. "I'm about to lose my own knightly restraint," I murmured as his hands fluttered over my belly and his fingers tugged the material a little over the belt.

He laughed and passed one hand over my head. "And you must herewith cover your beauteous hair, which is unruly and brazen and insults the entire world," he continued. I stared at him with a stupid grin on my face. *Your beauteous hair*, I repeated dreamily to myself. Jean raised an eyebrow and then glanced down at Brunette. I could have sworn she raised an eyebrow too.

"I don't even know where to start," I admitted shyly. "Can you give me a hand?" He shook his head in disbelief but looked at me with kindness in his eyes. He poked around in one of the pouches. "Alas, I do not have a spare thread," he apologized. "Perchance you have another method of gathering your hair?"

I took out a velvet scrunchie from my bag, which I'd left beside the spring, and gathered my hair into a low ponytail.

"What is that thing?" Jean pointed at the scrunchie.

"A scrunchie," I said lethargically.

"Give it to me," he said, and as I removed it from my hair, I noted that the commanding tone in his voice had an immediate effect on me.

"What do you say?" I asked, still holding the scrunchie. "I'm not some serf of yours."

He gestured impatiently, and I relinquished my grasp. He examined the scrunchie thoroughly while I busied myself braiding my hair. A torrent of sexy visions rushed through my head as I watched him stretch the scrunchie and then release it. Finally, he gathered up a clump of Brunette's fur and twisted the scrunchie around it while she barked.

"What. Is. This. Wonderful. Thing?" he asked again, awestruck.

"It's a scrunchie," I repeated. Was it possible that after the plastic bottle, the cell phone, the rolling paper, the zipper, and my steady insistence that I belonged to another time, it was the scrunchie that broke through and convinced him I was from the twenty-first century?

"It's made from elastic and velvet," I added, hoping this might be a better explanation. I picked up the scrunchie, brushed the dust off, and twisted it around the end of my braid.

"Perchance Thibaut was right? You are indeed a fairy?" he asked, his eyes round like saucers.

"I wish," I sighed. "I don't understand it any better than you do. This isn't something I ever believed possible, but I really am from another time. I was born almost eight hundred years from now, and somehow I'm able to travel to your time."

Jean sat down by the spring and washed his face. I thought I heard him reciting a prayer. My Latin was pretty rusty. "So, what should I do with this?" I pointed in the direction of the white cotton bundle. "Do you really not know?" he asked, struggling to erase the disbelief in his voice but resigning himself to the situation. "I really don't know," I answered, puffing my cheeks out.

He drew close to me and took a thin strip of cotton from the bundle. "I would ask if you have a pin, but because I fear further terrifying discoveries, I will use one of my own," he explained and removed two pins, slightly curved and soft to the touch, from one of his pouches. "One more discovery like that, and I might lose my male vigor," he added, winking again.

"God forbid," I muttered.

He wound the strip around my face and under my chin and secured it to my head with the pin. He then secured the tip of my braid with the other pin. He took the thicker piece of fabric and wound it around my head with practiced expertise. Finally, Jean placed a rectangle of the sheer fabric over the entire thing, so that it cascaded down on either side of my face. "Lovely," he declared after surveying his handiwork.

"Do you do this often, putting scarves on strange women's heads?" I asked petulantly. For some reason, I wanted to undermine the self-satisfaction that radiated from him. "I do not," he said congenially, "but

I grew up with a sister who was very fond of me. She allowed me into her chamber at almost all hours of the day when I was a child, and by studying how her maids tended to her needs, I learned many useful things."

"I wish I could see what I look like," I said out loud. Jean scrutinized me, a half-smile on his face, and then his eyes came to rest on my shabby sneakers. Once upon a time, they were black, with thick silver laces that had faded and now looked like dying worms. Although the dress was long, the tips of my sneakers peeked through like two bulldog puppies under a fancy tablecloth.

"Your shoes are a veritable heresy," Jean muttered. "They are unsightly and conspicuous," he added, knitting his brows together. "An oversight on my account. If we chance upon other people, I beg you to make an effort to conceal those under your dress."

"They're really comfortable," I defended my sneakers in a low voice.

"Next time, I will be sure to bring you presentable footwear," he responded, rearranging the blanket on the ground near the spring. Brunette stretched out beside it. *Next time* . . . I suddenly wondered what time it was and remembered my real life. Halimi was probably trying to get a hold of me. If I didn't get in touch with him soon, he'd flip out. I glanced at my wristwatch and remembered it didn't work here.

"What is that piece of jewelry?" Jean asked, his curiosity aroused.

"I'm afraid it will affect your male vigor," I said guardedly.

Jean burst out laughing, and Brunette barked. "Never in my life have I met a lady so quick-witted, Lady Édith, and I have met some of the wittiest ladies in the world," he boasted.

I accepted the compliment with a shrug of my shoulders, hoping I looked graceful, and concluded that wit was apparently not the prime virtue of the ladies Jean had met in his life. I removed my watch and handed it to him.

"What is the meaning of these signs?" he asked, examining the watch from every angle, holding it up close, and then moving it away.

"Those are numbers," I said. "They symbolize the hours of the day." I recalled that in Europe, they used Latin letters until quite late in the century to symbolize numbers.

"Numbers?" A spark of excitement appeared in his eyes. "According to the Saracen system? I read a manuscript on the topic, by a Pisan named Leonardo Bonacci. Sharp as a razor, I met him in Foggia when I was serving the emperor . . . It is indeed similar! Do you know him?"

"I'm not . . ." I began, but Jean was barely listening to me anyway. "What are these needles?" he continued. Brunette wagged her tail vigorously.

"The hands. The needles point to the correct hour," I said in a vaguely patronizing way. "When it works. I think being dunked in the spring and sucked through to another time didn't do it any good."

"May all the saints come to my rescue," Jean muttered again. "Is it truly possible you are from another time?"

I nodded. Jean fell silent.

"If you want—we can try traveling to my time together," I suggested and immediately panicked at the idea.

"I fear I have already tainted my miserable soul by my contact with you. Let us tarry awhile before proceeding to further sins," he finally said.

I sat down on the blanket Jean had spread out by the spring and helped myself to a couple of dates. The dress and the head covering forced my body, particularly my neck, into positions I was unfamiliar with, and now I really felt like the lady Jean took me for. Meanwhile, Jean leaned against the tree, his legs stretched out, one crossed over the other.

"So, where are we off to today?" I finally ventured.

"I know not why, but I long to bring you to my estate, Arsur. Would you care to visit there?"

"Arsur?" I asked, startled. "Is it close by? I thought it was the estate of your forefathers in France or somewhere." Jean looked askance.

"And I thought, my good lady, that you were from these parts. Arsur is situated on the southern coast, only two or three hours away by boat, a pleasant cruise. It was my good mother's estate, may she rest in peace."

Finally, I understood. "Do you mean Arsuf?" I asked.

Jean's eyebrows rose. "The Saracens and the Greek peasants call it by that name, yes."

Jean, Lord of Arsuf. I visited the National Park of Apollonia once, the archeological site of Arsuf. We went there one Saturday with Halimi's sister and her family, and I dawdled by a large arched window that overlooked the sea, where the Crusader ruins stood. A soft breeze whispered in my ears. I broke out in goose bumps.

"Is Arsuf your estate?" I gasped. "So, why don't you live there? And why did you travel to Acre to see your wife?"

"I inherited the estate just four years ago, when my father passed away." He was clearly amused by my avalanche of questions. "For years, the castle stood neglected. My mother left only a skeleton staff there after marrying my father and moving to Beirut. The town thrives, but the fortress is unfit to lodge lords, and it lacks the splendor and comfort that my wife is accustomed to." He paused.

I smiled at him encouragingly, and he continued.

"She loves Acre, where she was raised, and feels at home among the bustle and commotion of the town." I nodded. He became more animated. "I am strengthening the fortifications and repairing the castle at Arsur, in order that in the coming year, we will be able to live there as befits us, lord and lady of the castle. There have not been such goings-on at the castle since the Coeur de Lion took it back from the Saracens."

"The Lionheart? Richard?" I asked and couldn't help but remember the lion in the animated version of *Robin Hood*.

"Is there another Lionheart?" Jean asked with a smile.

"Not that I know of," I said as I popped another date into my mouth.

"The weather is clement, the wind is with us, and I must meet with my seneschal. Would you care to sail there with me, Lady Édith?"

"I think so, yes," I said, turning over his words in my mind. Three hours' sailing there, and three hours back, assuming the wind was with us, as Jean put it.

"What's a seneschal?" I asked.

"My steward," Jean explained. "He is responsible for the upkeep of my estate. He represents me and takes care of all financial and legal issues in my absence." He gathered some herbs and twigs and took out his curved flint and metal contraption.

"Wait," I said triumphantly. "Let me show you what a modern-day fire striker looks like." I rummaged around in my bag and took out a lighter. To my chagrin, there was a cartoon of naked boobs embossed on the side of the lighter, alongside a lewd caption. I hoped Jean wouldn't notice.

"What day is this you mention?" Jean asked.

"Never mind," I said, waving the lighter in front of him. I slowly moved the lighter toward the pile of herbs, to increase the drama. The herbs caught fire as soon as I rolled the metal spark wheel down, igniting the flame. I turned back around, smiling, and saw Jean bending down beside me, his face pale. His eyes were wide, and he looked as if he were about to faint. Brunette scampered around him, yelping.

"May the Lord have mercy upon me," Jean mumbled, making the sign of the cross. I felt somehow abashed and closed my fist over the lighter.

"Give it to me this instant," Jean commanded, his teeth clenched together.

"Good God," I mumbled to myself in Hebrew as I handed over the lighter.

Jean raised his eyes swiftly.

"In what strange tongue do you sometimes speak to yourself?" he asked, staring at me with cold suspicion.

"Hebrew," I whispered, swallowing.

"The tongue in which the Jews pray?" he asked, his head moving faintly from side to side in disbelief.

"Yes, yes, the tongue in which the Jews pray," I replied impatiently. Jean sighed heavily. He resumed his examination of the lighter, holding it up to his nose and sniffing it, trying to work out how to use it. I pointed to the metal roller mechanism. When the flame shot out, Jean recoiled, and Brunette barked. Jean took the lighter and did not relinquish it until he managed to get the hang of it. At first, he released the roller too quickly, and the flame went out. Then, he tried again and was able to sustain a small, steady flame. "Forgive me, my lady," Jean said as he turned to me, distracted, before going over to the spring and washing his face. After doing so, he knelt down and murmured some words in Latin.

"Were you praying?" I asked him shyly when he came back over to me. "Has all your male vigor disappeared?"

"It is highly likely," Jean said weakly, although his eyes twinkled merrily.

"I'm not a devil," I said.

"I know, my lady," Jean replied. "And yet what is happening here is infused with the scent of sulfur." I knew what he meant but made an attempt to brighten things up. "Maybe Brunette's got gas?" I joked, but Jean was not amused. Brunette, on the other hand, seemed to think it was funny.

We sat in silence for a few minutes. I rolled a cigarette and lit it from the little campfire. I didn't dare ask for my lighter back. Jean watched me closely.

"Do you want to try one?" I held out the cigarette.

He took the rolled cigarette from me, scrutinized it, and took a deep drag. From the first moment I saw him, I'd been attracted to Jean, but now I couldn't take my eyes off him. Not just because of his sculpted facial features and his wiry yet muscular body—I was transfixed by his nonchalant, fluid movements. There was youthfulness and strength about him. Brunette rushed around, escaping the smoke, eventually settling a few feet away from us.

"I have never before felt so like the fabled Chinese emperor, inhaling the smoke of indolence produced through the burning of the most attenuated of paper," Jean said, smoking with visible pleasure. He looked so at ease.

"Do you know about China?" I asked. "Has Marco Polo already arrived on the scene?" I added rashly.

"Marco who?"

"Never mind," I sighed. "So, how do you know about China?"

"We live in wondrous times," Jean explained, the edges of his lips curling upward. "Acre is an important station of the ancient Silk Road, and people from all over the world pass through its port. Anyone with the flimsiest of connections with merchants of Venice and Genoa has heard the fables of Chinese emperors so rich, they are worshipped as idols. I often think these are but fables told by merchants to their offspring, to ignite their imaginations. But I have seen several strange and beauteous objects from there." He smiled at me with sudden hope. "Almost like the objects you have presented before me, Lady Édith. Perhaps you are of Chinese descent?"

I laughed out loud.

"They usually have almond-shaped eyes," I said, "and straight black hair. I couldn't look more different."

"I would not change your eyes, as green as emeralds, for any Chinese emperor, Lady Édith," Jean said jovially. It seemed he'd recovered from the shock of my lighter.

"Sir, you are too kind," I answered, enjoying the turn in conversation.

"And now what?" I asked Jean when the cigarette had burned down almost completely. I took the cigarette butt from Jean, dragged on it one last time, stubbed it out with my shoe, and threw it on the fire.

"Are you ready to embark on our journey?" Jean asked, already gathering everything together. "I brought you a woolen surcoat and a thick cloak, so you will not catch your death of cold."

"I'm ready," I chirped enthusiastically, but then felt a stab of guilt and irritating responsibility. "But I think I'm going to have to hop back to my own time to tell my husband I'll be home late and that he won't be able to get in touch with me for a few hours."

"Hop back to your own time . . ." Jean uttered these words slowly. "A combination of words I find hard to believe I understand. And hard to believe you even said. So be it." He shrugged his shoulders and grinned mischievously. "You have managed to bewitch me after all, my lady, despite Thibaut's warnings."

"What about him?" I inquired. "Is he still in Acre?"

Jean didn't answer right away but fixed me with one of his inquisitive looks.

"He tarries in Acre," he finally replied.

"Do you mind waiting a few minutes? I won't be long," I said. The decision to contact Halimi somehow instilled me with confidence.

"Do you think I may also be able to travel to your time if I try?" Jean asked, avoiding my eyes.

I scratched my cheek. I had no idea, although I wanted to prove I was speaking the truth.

"We can try," I said. "But . . ." I thought about the zipper that had nicked me before I time-traveled and the fact I'd been menstruating on my previous visits. Stammering, I explained it was not possible to time-travel without bloodletting.

He took out a large knife and, without so much as pausing, made a small incision on his left arm. "Oh my God," I cried out.

He knelt down on one knee in front of me, and I made a bemused face at Brunette. Jean, however, was deadly serious.

"I hereby swear, by the letting of my own sanctified life secretions, that I pledge allegiance to Lady Édith from . . ." He looked at me questioningly.

"From Atlit," I finished the sentence, accommodating his somber tone.

"To Lady Édith of Atlit," he continued, "to protect her and serve her. As long as her deeds are not the work of the devil and that she not be a hellish creature sent to seduce my soul, may God help me."

I debated whether I was supposed to respond in some way and decided to hold my tongue.

Jean got to his feet.

"Stay here," he told Brunette, who sat down obediently.

Jean held out his hand to me, blood still dripping from his arm. I took a deep breath and grabbed Lily's ten-agorot coin from my bag.

"Here we go," I said and plunged my hand, which Jean held, into the spring.

There was no delay. The whirlpool sucked us up right away, wrenching us from reality. Just one warm and steady hand, holding onto me tightly, reminded me that I had a body, a name, a life. I couldn't hold my breath any longer and inhaled water without choking on it. I was immediately expelled, one hand still entwined in Jean's, the other clutching something small and round and hard.

"Our all-benevolent Father, merciful Holy Spirit, Lord our Savior, Mother of God, Saint Stephen, I beseech ye all," a voice reeled off. I opened my eyes and saw Jean, on all fours on the ground, spluttering and vomiting intermittently. I scrambled to my feet and recognized the ruins of Le Destroit, peeking through the scant canopy of the carob tree. I was back in my own time. We did it.

"It gets easier every time," I noted, half to myself and half to Jean. I was still wearing the clothes Jean had given me. They were quite clean, and not even wet. I fingered the head covering. The transparent, flimsy fabric had been flung to the earth, but apart from that, it was still intact. Jean was still saying his prayers on the ground. "Do you want some water?" I offered. I had a small bottle in the car.

"Where's the spring?" he managed to enunciate.

"There's no spring here, in my time. I hope we'll be able to find our way back to yours," I added as a kind of joke. Poor Jean didn't find it funny at all.

I helped him maneuver into a more comfortable position on his back; I told him to take deep breaths while I brought the bottle from the car. The excitement I felt at having successfully brought him along with me was dampened by Jean's severe reaction. But I remembered the precise moment it dawned on me that I'd time-traveled and what a devastating effect it had on my own body. It was hard to believe that had only been a week and a half ago. As I took the bottle of water from the car, a passing vehicle slowed down, and the driver stared at me in astonishment. I winked at him, all dressed up in my medieval clothes and headgear, as if it were the most natural thing in the world for me to be out like this, and the driver continued on his way.

I ducked back under the sparse canopy of the carob tree and helped Jean sit up and take a few sips of water from the bottle. The color returned to his cheeks, and he even looked around a little. I held my hand out, and we left the safety of the carob tree and ventured out. When he saw the ruins of Le Destroit, he let out a gasp. He surveyed the uniform neighborhoods of Atlit, extending in all directions, at the cars and trucks racing along the coastal road, and finally—when he saw the ruins of the fortress on the seashore, surrounded by the polystyrene-like structures of the Israeli naval base—Jean threw up again.

"I cannot . . . I cannot," he repeated. "What is this atrocity?"

I led him back to the carob tree.

"Why is the air so odorous and heavy?" he gasped. "And everything is so ugly . . . and full of noise."

I felt an irrational desire to defend all this, to justify it, but I knew the timing was wrong.

"Take me back, I beseech you, my lady," Jean begged.

"Hang on for two more minutes," I said. I took the cell phone out of my bag and switched it on with trepidation, because it often gave me trouble. To my great relief, it worked just fine. It was only two in the afternoon, earlier than I thought. There were no unread text messages.

Although Jean had likely thrown up everything he had inside him, he had the desperate look of a person who knew that the slightest provocation would trigger another convulsion. I put the cell phone on speaker and dialed Halimi's number.

"Hi, sweetie," Halimi said. I must have woken him up from a power nap. Jean, sitting next to me, gasped at the sounds emitting from the phone.

"Hi, Limi," I said, my voice gentler than usual.

"What's up? How's the city that never sleeps? Did you get sushi?" Halimi said lazily.

"Yes, sure, everything's great," I said, perturbed that Jean was coughing torturously. He collapsed to the ground, limbs splayed.

"Are you listening?" I said, sitting down beside Jean and stroking his long hair, which fell loosely around his face. Jean's breathing was labored. "My battery's about to die, and things are a bit wild here at the publishing house—they've landed me with a piece of proofreading as well . . ."

I heard Halimi lighting a cigarette.

"Long story short, I'll probably be back late, but don't worry if I don't answer when you call. You know how temperamental my phone can be."

"Okay, Diti," Halimi said. "Thanks for letting me know, my love. Lily and I'll be waiting for you in our pajamas."

I blew him kisses and switched the phone off. I looked at Jean some more. His breathing was still labored.

It was only then I noticed the blood, dripping slowly from his wrist.

"We need to get that bandaged up," I said quietly. "Do you want to rest, and then we'll walk around a little?"

He opened his eyes a chink. "No, not this time, my lady. Prithee, take me back."

I grasped his hand and pulled him toward the book-sized puddle.

CHAPTER 13

In the autumn of Lily's third year, my intensive period of spying began. The *Free to Be* office was in a dilapidated building in one of the neighborhoods of Tel Aviv's Old North. Once every few days I found myself just "dropping by," hoping to catch Halimi and Nina in the act. That didn't happen. I saw her a few times, and my heart pounded so loudly I thought the entire editorial board would hear it, but she was always sitting with the graphic designers, bugging the shit out of them with her obsessiveness.

I browsed through Halimi's phone at every opportunity. This required both tenacity and extreme stealth. When I managed to get my hands on his phone, I would scour WhatsApp, Gmail, Facebook Messenger. Every single text, emoji, or YouTube clip that Halimi and Nina shared sent twinges of physical pain through my body that would then morph into dizzying weakness.

I tracked Halimi on Google Maps and, after determining Nina's home address through mutual friends, understood why he spent so many evenings on Nachmani Street in Tel Aviv. I found myself walking to her neighborhood. It became second nature to check her activity on social media. Whenever there was a correlation between the information I'd milked from Halimi's phone (Google Maps check-in at TaiZu, an upscale Asian restaurant, from 7:40 to 11:20 p.m.) and Nina's posts (an enigmatic and beautiful selfie in the bathroom of the same restaurant within that exact time frame), I felt something akin to how drugs spread through the body. In this case, it was a powerful drug—both exhilarating and depressing, like a shot of sugar, followed by a shot of insulin.

I was honest enough to tell my sister, who said I was addicted to the thrill of stalking Halimi. I disconnected our Zoom call by slamming down the cover of my laptop and didn't speak to Dina for days. After I spent a week refusing to answer her calls, she sent me a long text, apologizing for what she said. She was empathetic and begged me to answer her calls. When she tried the next day, I picked up.

She sat in an oversized sweater, facing the screen. Eva sat beside her, scribbling in a coloring book. My sister gave me her Mother Gaia look and asked me gently how I was feeling.

"The same," I answered, my emotions blunted.

"Nothing changed?" my sister asked.

"What could've changed?" I responded.

Dina sighed and asked what I was going to do about it. I knew she was going to ask, but I didn't have an answer. I couldn't express what I hoped for or expected to happen. Halimi's behavior paralyzed me. He simply acted as if everything were business as usual. Brimming with affection yet distracted at the same time, focused on what he needed but spaced out with everything else. Perhaps more than usual. The fact that he acted like everything was normal, or almost normal, drove me insane. For the first time ever, I began suspecting that my entire life with Halimi was one big lie.

"So, why don't you confront him?" Dina asked. Her hand shot out to steady a cup of water Eva was about to knock over as she dipped her paintbrush into it with dangerous enthusiasm.

Of course I asked myself why, over and over again, I really did. That whole time I refused to speak to Dina, I was forced to admit she had a point. I'd never experienced such masochistic pleasure as the way I felt when I knew Halimi was lying to my face. But that's not why I didn't want to confront him.

It was tough to admit: I was afraid of his manipulations. I knew that if I accused him to his face, if I demanded explanations, he would somehow convince me that there was nothing wrong. And if he had done anything wrong, I would have to forgive him on the spot. I wanted to catch him red-handed, so he would have no choice but to admit that he was the lowest of the low, declare his undying love for me, and dedicate the rest of his life to making it up. I was fantasizing about catching them together when he texted me yet another lame excuse as to why he was running late.

"So, it's business as usual?" Dina asked with distaste.

I didn't answer for a few moments. My sister had already proven, on multiple occasions, that she was capable of analyzing my behavior in highly unflattering terms and that she had no problem sharing her thoughts with me.

"Yup, business as usual," I finally answered. I took a prickly kind of satisfaction in the knowledge that Halimi was clueless. It was a covert competition, in which my sole advantage lay in knowing we were competitors. We both acted normally, more or less, and we were both lying—except that I knew he was lying, whereas he had no idea I was.

We even had sex a few times after that text from Nina. As far as I was concerned, our fucking was desperate and angry, and I think in those moments even Halimi, in a repressed sort of way, sensed that I knew everything; perhaps it even turned him on. All this added an extraordinary edge to our routine performance, and sometimes the sex was truly great. This only made me sadder. Halimi got used to me feeling a bit down after sex, regardless of how good it had been. After a while, he simply accepted it.

"God, that's terrible," Dina said with a mixture of fear and admiration. This stressed me out a bit. Since we were kids—or more accurately, since I was a kid and she was a teenager—it was clear who was the wild one and who was the good girl.

"How much longer are you going to drag this out?" Dina asked with uncharacteristic despondency. Eva had tired of painting and left the room. I wondered how much Hebrew she understood and whether she'd remember snatches of this conversation.

"I don't know . . ." I said. I really didn't know. It's true I fantasized about a confession from Halimi and the grand gestures he'd be forced to make to atone, but I couldn't imagine how we could find our way back to what we had before. My ability to keep going surprised me—to work on grueling translations; joke around with friends in cafés; listen to Libby's woes with her boss and hear about her one-night stands; and read stories to Lily, fix her meals, and find her fun clips on YouTube.

"In my opinion, you ought to confront him. Not for him, for you," Dina said quietly. I saw concern in her eyes; she didn't want to make me mad again.

"You're right," I told her. "Soon."

Back in my own time, I pulled the ancient coin out of my bag and showed Jean how old and tarnished it was. That finished him off completely. His hand lay limply in mine as I submerged the coin in the puddle, and as the whirlpool ejected us into the cold air of the spring of 1240, I was afraid the transition had caused him irreversible damage.

For half an hour he lay there, eyes closed, limbs extended, pale and glistening with cold sweat on the ground near the spring. Brunette welcomed us with an outburst of barking that prompted a guard to come check on us. It was not Geoffroy of Tours.

"Seigneur d'Arsur!" he cried when he saw Jean lying on the ground. He threw me a disdainful look.

"I am the cousin of Lord d'Arsur," I announced stiffly.

"What?" The guard sent his hand to the hilt of his sword.

I repeated my words slowly, trying to mirror Jean's accent.

The guard nodded, his forehead still furrowed with worry. I kept going, hoping that my words at least sounded close to Old French. "I just relayed some disturbing news about our family, and he responded worse than I expected. I am sure that within the hour, he will recover. I will inform you if there is no improvement."

"Where is his squire?" the guard asked. I had no idea who this might be.

"He came alone today," I said cautiously. "The Lady of the Spring will protect him," I added, throwing caution to the wind.

The guard nodded his head slowly, inspecting me with renewed interest and respect. When he saw Brunette standing beside me, wagging her tail as I patted her head, he returned to his post. The dog calmed down and lay beside her master dolefully, placing her head on his chest. She looked at me with what looked like reproach.

"He was the one who wanted to do it," I said self-righteously. If Brunette could have shaken her head disapprovingly, I'm sure she would have. I was still amazed by the ease with which I'd traveled between the two centuries. This was my third time in one day. It was not only as easy as diving into a swimming pool; it also felt physically good, and somehow purifying.

I covered Jean with the cape I found folded on a small rock. While he rested, I rummaged through his bag. I found his wine flask and moistened his lips. With effort, I managed to rip a scrap of material from the red woolen dress and, after washing it with water, tied it around the gash on his wrist.

Then, I sat down beside him and indulged myself by stroking his dark hair. Even disheveled, Jean was incredibly handsome.

When he finally opened his eyes, it was me he looked for. Brunette barked, and Jean reached out with one hand to scratch her behind the ears.

"Are you okay?" I asked, genuinely concerned.

He looked me up and down with what seemed like adoration, which stunned me. I stopped stroking his hair.

"I always thought myself a man of the world," he said quietly, "a man who has seen everything, even the strangest of sights." I nodded with understanding. Jean sat up. A small yelp escaped Brunette, and she buried her nose in his chest.

"At the very least, now you know I'm not deranged," I said.

"You are not deranged," he agreed. "Nor, methinks, are you a spy. I am not, however, sure if you are a fairy or creature of the devil."

I looked at him askance. Was he capable of believing I was some kind of a devil?

"A fairy, perchance," he said with a playful smile. "It all fits—a deserted clearing, a spring, a tree. Édith the Fairy from the Holy Spring of Le Destroit. Who could have known the bedtime stories of an old nursemaid by the fireplace could come true?"

"I'm not a fairy," I said with a tinge of sadness. "I'm from the future."

"It is one and the same," Jean said, gathering my hand to his chest.

Finally, I took the coward's way out and decided to confront Zozo instead of Halimi. When Halimi and I were just starting out, Zozo made me feel somewhat inferior with her refined lesbian chic. Her beautiful face, buzz cut, high-end men's suits, and "don't fuck with me" expression gave the impression that she was a radical feminist who considered every woman who didn't look and act like her a slave to the patriarchy. A few weeks after we became an item, I admitted to Halimi that Zozo intimidated me.

"You're kidding me," Halimi said in disbelief, pulling me toward him. "She adores you," he drawled. "She thinks you're super-smart. If anything, it's Zozo who's intimidated. She thinks you see her as a mindless clubber." As time went by, I discovered that Zozo had no real plans, beside enjoying life—with an emphasis on alcohol and women.

Zozo and Halimi certainly had that in common, I reflected bitterly. That evening, he said he was off to have a quick drink with her. An hour later, Nina posted a photo on Instagram of two glasses of hot cider and a pack of Camel cigarettes, with the caption "a warm evening at home with creatures of dubious reputation." One thing I knew for sure: She didn't smoke Camels.

I called Libby and asked if there was a chance she could come babysit Lily. I lied and said I had to go to an event honoring a distinguished veteran translator and that it would look bad if I didn't show up. "Halimi was supposed to be home tonight, but he got held up at work," I explained.

"That seems to be happening a lot lately," Libby said. I hadn't told her a thing. I knew exactly what she'd say.

"Right," I said in a flat voice. "So, can you come?"

Libby came and hardly said a word to me. She gave me a kiss without looking me in the eye and went straight to the bathroom, where Lily was in the middle of a complicated epic drama with a few rubber ducks and a pirate ship.

"Thanks, Libby-Lou," I said and kissed her on the cheek.

"My pleasure, Dita," she said, still avoiding eye contact.

My feet first took me to Nina's building on Nachmani Street. I wasn't sure which illuminated window was hers, but I knew which apartment she lived in. I imagined the drama that would unfold if I knocked on her door and how pathetic I'd look. I almost collapsed in the middle of the street at the thought. In the end, I took a taxi and climbed the stairs of the block where Zozo lived in Florentin. I'd been there a few times—we occasionally met up at her place before going out for the evening—but I'd never been there alone, without Halimi.

"Idit!" Zozo said, surprised to see me when she opened the door.

"Hi, Zozo," I said in a voice so weak it sounded ridiculous. "Can I come in?"

Zozo gave me a bewildered look that only strengthened my resolve. After a few seconds, she showed me in. "Is everything okay?" she asked, and I could see she was scrambling. She had no moral obligation to me—she had been Halimi's best friend since high school, or the army, I couldn't remember which. All in all, she was a decent person, and I was sure she wouldn't have the faintest idea how to respond. To deny she was an accomplice? Apologize? To tell me to direct all my complaints to Halimi? Or remain loyal to her best friend?

I sat down with a thump on a mattress covered in floral fabric, which served as a couch, and just stared at her without saying anything. Zozo didn't sit down. Her eyes wandered furtively to her phone, which lay on a small table in the living room beside a bottle of beer.

"Can I get you a drink?" she asked, attempting to buy time.

"Got any cyanide?" I made myself laugh.

"Okay, Idit," Zozo said with evident discomfort. "Can I help you with something?"

"I think so," I said slowly. *It's not her fault, it's not her fault,* a rational, compassionate voice repeated inside my head. *She's a piece of shit for covering for him, and she knows it,* a more primitive voice chimed in.

"The thing is," I said, sounding like an anchor on the evening news, "My husband told me he was coming to your place for a drink. And guess what—you're here, but he isn't!"

Zozo swallowed and sat down beside me.

"Is that what he said?" she asked quietly. So, he hadn't updated her, but she was still involved.

"We did say something about it earlier," she said cautiously, "But I guess he got tied up at work."

This filled me with sick joy.

"Let's go together to see if he's still at work," I suggested. "He'd love it! Poor guy, it kills him to work so late," I said, a note of hysteria in my voice.

Zozo stood up, restless and clueless as to how to handle this. She picked up her phone and put it down again. My rational, compassionate voice took over once more. *What did I want from her?* I'd never regarded Zozo as a personal friend, but she was definitely part of the family. She'd been there before me, and she'd likely be there after me as well, I thought glumly.

"If you have any decency at all," I said, exhaustion getting the better of me, "at least don't tell him I was here." I stood up from the low mattress with difficulty.

"Idit," she said, and I could already picture her giving it to Halimi. Every so often they'd have a godawful argument, sever all contact, and then pick up again like nothing happened.

"I guess you want to say I should have known who I was marrying," I said quickly. She stood up and took a step toward me, as if she were about to embrace me. Maybe my eyes conveyed hostility; she stopped dead in her tracks. "That's not what I wanted to say," Zozo said.

"Okay," I said and left.

"Perhaps you can go over to the guard at the lookout and tell him you're feeling better now," I said to Jean, after I arranged a few things on the checkered cloth—cheese and olives from his bag, and leftover bread, honey, and dates. "When you passed out, he heard Brunette's barking and came to see what was going on."

Jean tensed. "Did he not ask after you?"

"I said I was your cousin and that I'd told you of a problem in the family that shook you to the core," I said proudly. I felt I'd demonstrated great agility of thought.

"That you are my cousin?" Jean said admiringly. "How did you think of that?"

"I didn't really think," I answered, very happy to hear his response. "It just came out of my mouth." Jean exchanged glances with Brunette, then looked at me again.

"You are something special, Fairy Édith," he said, rising to his feet.

"He asked about some squire, and I didn't know what to say," I added, imitating the suspicious look of the guard.

Jean smothered a laugh. "Indeed, it is extraordinary that I am riding alone in these parts without my squire. Believe me—my boy, Hugh, is outraged when I ride alone. He is also curious to understand the circumstances in which I decline his services." Jean looked at me for a moment. "But I cannot allow my protégé to be exposed to such a suspicious, mysterious creature as yourself," he winked at me.

He walked off briskly to the observation point and called for the guard. A helmeted head popped up in one of the windows, and a conversation ensued. The head with the helmet disappeared from sight, and Jean strolled back to the spring, pausing along the way to gaze out at the sea. When he ducked under the tree's canopy, he grinned at me like a bridegroom—a goofy, spontaneous smile.

"What happened?" I asked, and my heart fluttered.

"What happened?" he swiftly came over and took me in his arms. "What happened?!" he almost shouted, grabbed me, lifted me into the air, and twirled me around. My headscarf fell to the ground, and my braid tumbled down as Jean lowered me to the ground. He brought his face close to mine, and I could feel his breath on my skin. He said, "There is a magic passage here. It is unbelievable. A miracle." I was sure he was about to kiss me when he said that, but he didn't. My mouth watered, and I was forced to swallow hard, embarrassed.

"Surely it is magic for you too," he said, knitting his brows together. "Or perhaps . . . such passageways like this are common where you come from?"

"Certainly not," I murmured, still very close to him.

"I remember how you reacted when Thibaut and I clapped eyes on you for the first time. You were stunned and lost and spent. It was all new to you," he continued, expecting confirmation.

"That's right," I murmured again. "But now I've traveled through time six or seven times. It really is unbelievable, but . . ." I looked around me. "I just accept it now. And it's getting easier and easier. It's even pleasant," I said in wonderment, mostly to myself.

"Is it even pleasant to be in my company?" he asked, a smile on his lips.

"The passage," I emphasized. "The transition has become easier and more pleasant. To be here . . . to spend time here . . . is like living in a fairy tale . . ." I said, my eyes never leaving Jean's, ashamed of my uneven control of the language.

Jean took my hand and held it to his lips and then pulled me toward the checkered cloth. He produced a large knife and sliced the bread and cheese. We both ate ravenously. In between chewing and swallowing, Jean said, "I have not felt such an uplifting of spirits since I broke through the Lombard siege and reconquered my father's castle in Beirut. Did you sense the same uplifting of spirits when first you returned to your own time, my lady?" I swallowed the lump of cheese in my mouth and admitted that I did not. "But I didn't have anyone to swear to me that what happened was real. I thought I'd hallucinated everything."

"Do not say such things, Lady Édith," he said.

"I guess there will be no trip to Arsuf today. To Arsur, I mean," I said.

Jean sighed. "I fear my strength fails me, and I will not make it there and back in a day. Moreover, it is getting late. It is not safe to bring you back so late at night." He tightened his belt and said, "Why do you insist on calling it Arsuf, like the Greeks and the Saracens?"

"That's what we call it where I come from," I said. "There's a neighborhood there, an upper-class one, and of course the Apollonia National Park. I was there not long ago," I continued. I wondered whether the fortress ruins I saw in the National Park were the same ruins that Jean was now renovating. Perhaps these were ruins from a later period, but the thought I had visited Jean's home without knowing it gave me goose bumps.

"Were you really there? Does it still exist? Eight hundred years from now? By the Good Lord, this is unbelievable. Is my castle still standing?" Jean asked with passion.

"There are ruins . . ." I replied recklessly and immediately regretted it, because his face fell. "They are beautifully preserved!" I added contritely. "I had a very special feeling there, particularly when I stood by a certain window, which was arched and big and faced the sea . . ." I was trying to remedy the situation. It was true. I had lingered for a long time by that window, as the voices of my own family grew fainter and fainter.

"This game is dangerous, *mais oui*?" Jean murmured. His shoulders slumped. "I have a deep urge to know everything, to ask you what has happened in the meanwhile, how the kingdom developed, but . . ." It was now Jean's turn to swallow hard. "Ruins, you say?" He shook his head sadly. "Perhaps it is better not to know."

"In any case, no one lives in castles or fortresses anymore," I said soothingly. "At least not here, in Israel." As I uttered these words, I pictured the residential skyscrapers of Tel Aviv where the wealthy live, with security guards in spacious lobbies and janitors and housekeepers . . . This was not the time to go over the finer points, I decided.

"Israel?" he asked in a whisper. He looked as though he were having another dizzy spell. Jean steadied himself with one hand. "What in hell do you mean?"

I froze with fear. Was now the right time for me to discover that he was a bloodthirsty Crusader and a hater of Jews? I grabbed my bag, groped around inside it for Lily's ten-agorot coin, and held it between my fingers. I edged myself over toward the spring, poised to lunge if necessary.

"I'm a citizen of the State of Israel, the Jewish state," I said in a trembling voice. Jean shook his head in misunderstanding. "The Jewish kingdom," I elucidated.

When I uttered the words "Jewish kingdom," Jean clapped one hand to his mouth and began shaking all over. It took me a few seconds to realize that he was laughing uproariously. I guess the very idea sounded absurd to him. His laughter was so contagious, I couldn't help laughing too.

When the laughter subsided, we dried our eyes and moved toward each other. Jean leaned against the tree trunk, and I nestled in his arms. I looked up, and the leaves on the tree appeared golden in the sun, which was gradually reaching the horizon.

Jean kissed my head and breathed in the scent of my hair. "You have such a sweet perfume about you, Lady Édith. As if you bathed in aromatic oils for two long days." I nestled deeper into his arms and turned to face him.

His lips were as magnetic as the whirlpool in my dream. I held onto them with a kiss. He kissed me back, and we didn't let go.

"Is spouse breach common where you come from?" Jean asked, running his hand over my cheekbones. "Quite common," I answered him, my eyes closed.

CHAPTER 14

I could hardly think straight when I left Zozo's place. As the taxi took me to Nachmani Street, my heart beat so hard, I felt like I might faint. *What are you so afraid of?* I asked myself, even mumbling it under my breath in the taxi.

I closed my eyes and leaned my head against the window. *I'm afraid that I am about to discover that it's all true.* If, up until now, in some firm if forsaken corner of my consciousness I was able to hope that maybe all of this was my own misinterpretation—*he really does work long hours; they see each other every day, so their texting is seasoned with an extensive private lexicon; maybe they flirt a lot but aren't having an affair*—now I was about to find out for certain that this was not the case. I would humiliate him by exposing his lies and, as a result, humiliate myself too—and who knows if we would ever recover.

I paid the driver and got out of the taxi. The windows, which had been lit up earlier, were now dark. I pulled my phone out of my bag and opened all of Nina's profiles. No update since that last one on Instagram, with the "dubious creatures." A WhatsApp notification from Halimi appeared on the screen. "Ditush, I'm home. Letting Libby go."

* * *

I got home earlier than I expected. After returning from the spring, I wandered around on foot for another hour. Dusk seemed to last forever; my legs transported me among the ruins of the Narrow Passage, down the quarried road and back until I was at my car, parked in front of the stone with the Phoenician inscription.

All the while, I felt as though I were under the influence of some intoxicant, but I was calm and light, "like a fairy," I said softly to myself. I picked some flowers and leaves from bushes that I saw on my way. I had no aim or need to be anywhere. I recalled each of Jean's gestures— how he swung me in the air, how he sliced the bread and cheese, how he wrapped his arms around me. I'm sure half the time I was walking, I had a goofy smile on my face. I stopped before the book-sized puddle by the carob tree. It had not dried up yet. I placed my little bouquet of flowers in it, and in the dim light of dusk, a few of the flowers swirled around and sank deep, out of sight.

I leaned against the car, and for the first time in many long months, I felt the absence of a smartphone. I had a physical urge to search for some mention of Jean online, to see if history had recorded anything about him. I got into the car and drove home.

Halimi was surprised that I was home early, but pleased. Lily shouted, "Mama!" from the couch in the living room, and I knelt down in front of her. She ran at me so fast that I nearly fell backward when she slammed into me. "What are you wearing?" I laughed. She was dressed in sea-blue tights dotted with gold stars, a pink tutu, and a black wool vest with glittering black sequins that Simone had given her.

"We were playing Vikings," Lily said and showed me a plastic helmet with horns. "Daddy bought it for me."

We had a nice dinner during which I told them, with total ease, about my journey to Tel Aviv, the stress at the publishing house, and everyone's excellent work, thanks to which we were let go earlier than expected.

Halimi told me that one of the aides at Lily's kindergarten had gone on maternity leave and that the kindergarten WhatsApp group was in an uproar.

Lily said that she wanted to be Egyptian, like a Pharaoh. "Pharaoh was strong, and Moses and the Israelites fled," Lily said with disdain. Halimi and I made a face at each other.

I gave Lily her shower that turned into a bath, at the end of which she persuaded me to join her. Ever since she was really little, since she could sit up on her own, we played a game in which I would pretend to catch her fingers with my feet. It developed and took on a somewhat dark twist over the years and by now had morphed into a whole saga about two sorcerers and a dwarf, with almost no remaining connection to fingers and feet except that we still called it "fingers and feet."

In bed, I read her the Robin Hood book with pictures from the Disney movie, and when she fell asleep, I carried on reading quietly to myself. Suddenly, I wanted to read the original version, or at least one not adapted for children, like the edition with beautiful illustrations that I devoured as a girl and that remained on my parents' bookshelves.

"I thought you were asleep." Halimi's head appeared in the doorway.

"Robin Hood got me," I said, smiling at him.

We sat across from each other in the old Tel Aviv apartment, me on the armchair and him on the couch. I didn't even take off my jacket. I looked around without saying a word and remembered how the apartment looked before I moved in—a dusty, slightly moldy bachelor pad of thrilling intrigue. Now, it was warm and homey, tidy and fresh, and everything was visible and plain to the point of nausea.

"So, Zozo told on me?" I asked finally in a strangled voice.

"You could say that," Halimi replied. He looked tired. There was a bottle of arak on the table next to a glass filled with the milky liquid, mixed with water. "She phoned, worried; called me a pig; and told me that you seemed really upset."

Of course she's more loyal to him, I thought bitterly, *but at least she called him a pig.*

"I suppose you had to cut your cozy evening with Nina short?" I said. "Did you at least get around to finishing your hot cider?"

Halimi looked up inquisitively. "Instagram," I said. He rubbed his nose and shook his head wearily.

"I knew she would get me in trouble," he said. "She can't help herself. She probably wanted you to figure it out." As always when he was drunk, his diction was slurred.

It drove me insane that he pinned this on her. "Get you in trouble," I said scornfully. "What a repulsive way of putting it."

"That's exactly why I didn't tell you," he said, stealing a glimpse at me, then looking back down. "Because I knew you would react like this."

"You are so stupid," I said quietly. "I want to break up. Tomorrow, I'm taking Lily to my parents."

Halimi let out a lengthy sigh. "Ditush, I get that you're really mad. But be reasonable . . ." His eyes darted around, while I didn't take mine off him. "I let off a little steam," he said finally, angrily. "Just like you did at those clubs last year. You want to break up over a little nonsense? And what about Lily?"

Like in some soap opera, at that exact moment, we heard our daughter's voice. "Mama . . ." she called weakly. I shook my head in disbelief, dumbstruck by his nerve, and went to her. She asked for water. Something in her voice was a little off. I gave her a kiss on the forehead. She was burning up. I went to the kitchen to fill her plastic cup with water, and as I passed Halimi in the hall, I said, "She has a fever. I think it's high."

Halimi leaped from the sofa and to the bathroom for the thermometer. As I filled the cup, he took her temperature.

"Thirty-eight point four," he said as I came into the room.

"Get the Advil," I said and sat down beside her.

I stroked my daughter, who sighed and turned over, shaking and shivering. She looked so miserable, and somehow I felt like it was my fault. *What will I do?* I thought over and over. Halimi brought the dose of children's Advil in its measuring cup and administered it with excessive gentleness.

"Let's go to the living room, Ditush," said Halimi.

"Don't call me that," I said. In the living room, Halimi opened an app on his phone and made an appointment with the pediatrician. He had a remarkable ability to sober up at once. "I don't think we need to drag her to the doctor right away," I said. "It's probably a virus. Let's just let her rest."

"Better to book it, who knows how the rest of the night will go," said Halimi. "Worst case, we cancel at the last minute."

He went to make tea, and I rolled myself a joint. It felt as if my brain were on pins and needles. It was hard to admit, but until then, I felt like we had triumphed over all preconceptions. We had an expression—"the librarian who tamed the libertine"—which came up in a variety of situations, and now it was clear that no one had tamed anyone. All of our lengthy wanderings in our first week together came to me while, at the same time, one question was bouncing around my mind nonstop: *How did I attach my life to this snake?*

Halimi set the two cups of tea down on the table in the living room and, uncharacteristically, took a small puff from the joint.

"You realize how insanely shameless it is of you to compare my stupid hookups at nightclubs to your ongoing affair with your colleague, right?" I asked, my almost-tears rising in my throat.

"Why is it so shameless?" Halimi asked icily.

"If I need to explain it to you, you must be even stupider than I thought!" I shouted.

"Shhh . . ." Halimi said with a look of rebuke and gestured with his head toward Lily's bedroom.

"Don't you shush me, you asshole," I said in a lower voice. Halimi clicked his tongue, inhaled, and exhaled impatiently.

"First of all," I said, resisting the desire to smack the teeth out of his head, "I told you about all of my exploits, and you even enjoyed it. It turned you on. And anyway, those were with total strangers who I never saw again. You have been lying to me for months! Months!" I said, my voice growing louder again. "And with *who*? With *Nina*, who's hot as fuck, who you claimed was a cold fish, and there was no chance of anything happening with her! Who you work with! Every day!" I shouted again and felt hot tears starting to slip from my eyes. I felt shame crying like that, out of control and spluttering. A strong woman would have simply kicked him out of the house without any explanation.

Halimi sat beside me and put his arm around me. "Ditush, my love, shhh, enough," he said, trying to calm me down. It did not help. The licorice smell from the arak made me gag. I moved away from him and lit a cigarette with trembling hands.

"I didn't tell you because I knew you'd react like this," he said again. He watched me crying for several long seconds and finally said persuasively, "I'm sorry, sweetheart. Truly. I didn't mean for it to go on this long."

"How could you?!" I asked again in a half scream. "Lie to me night after night?! Leave me with Lily and take that whore out on expensive dates? And all I get are your stupid selfies?!"

"What . . . why do you think I took her out for expensive dates?" He asked, his eyes inadvertently squinting at his damned phone.

"I don't think, I know! I've been spying on you for weeks!" I told him with a taste of crushing defeat. "I know exactly how much time you spent at her place, at fancy restaurants, at new movies, at launches and parties. I know everything!" I blurted *everything* out with great speed, felt sick, and stood up. I nearly said that something actually bothered me much more—the admiring gaze that he had taken from me and given to her. But you can't beg for looks of admiration.

"I'm going to bed," I said. "My head hurts like hell."

He brought me the Advil and a glass of water in bed. I swallowed two pills, took a sip of water, and lay on my stomach. He lay beside me without touching me.

"You are like the scorpion in the fable about the scorpion and the frog," I said to the dark space.

"My poor frog," said Halimi, and I didn't understand if he was mocking me or stupidly hoping to make me laugh.

"What are you smiling about?" asked Halimi. I lay on our sofa in Atlit and stared at the ceiling. He had gone grocery shopping and was putting things away in the refrigerator and pantry.

"No reason," I replied dreamily and got up to help.

The truth was, I had spent all morning thinking about Jean and the day before: how we lay side by side beside the spring, listening to the burbling of the water; how Brunette lay down between us so naturally, her head on Jean's thigh and her tail on my calf.

"Tell me something about yourself," I said, my eyes wide, my head on his shoulder.

"What do you wish to know?" I heard him say, his voice sleepy and slow.

"Where you were born, where you grew up, how you met your wife," I said without thinking. For a moment, I shocked myself—*Why was I bringing his wife into our conversation?*—but he just laughed.

He told me about the place where he grew up—his father's castle in Beirut. When Jean was young, his older brothers served as squires for the nobles of the kingdom. His sister, Isabelle, was devoted and loving, if somewhat outlandish. He almost never saw his father, who was busy with the constant matters of the kingdom. His mother was delicate and generous but sickly and would spend her days in her rooms looking out at the sea, without much involvement in her children's lives. She died when Jean was ten.

He told me of the unique floor tiles in the Beirut castle's main hall, how walking across them felt like stepping on gentle ripples. He told me of the great ceiling, painted to resemble a blue sky with fluffy clouds, of the marble fountain in the center of the main hall. He told me about the peacocks that stalked the courtyards, of the sea visible from the western wing, and the pastoral meadows from the eastern wing. His eyes glimmering, he added that he had sent a request to his brother Balian, the current Lord of Beirut, to send him expert builders to help him restore, with more modest means, his castle at Arsuf.

When he turned twelve, Jean was sent to serve as squire for his uncle Phillip, the regent of Cyprus, in the name of the child king Henry I of Cyprus. It was a wonderful time for him, he said. He reconnected with his brother, who was also serving in the region, trained endlessly in horseback riding and combat, and got up to lots of mischief with his peers. He continued his studies of Latin and Greek, delved into the Holy Scriptures ("as much as a youth can delve into the Holy Scriptures," he admitted), and broadened his general education. When he was knighted at age fifteen, he returned to Beirut. His sister was in a crisis: Their father wanted to marry her to one of the kingdom's noblemen, through which he sought to strengthen his ties. The man was rich, with resources and servants, but he was also an elderly widower. His only daughter was younger than Isabelle by about ten years.

"Isabelle was stubborn and rebellious," Jean told me. "Maybe because she grew up as the only woman among all the men of the family, or because from a young age she managed the castle's enormous household, or maybe because she acquired her education on her own, in my father's large library. Indeed, she spent a short time as a young companion to our cousin Alice, Queen of Cyprus, but it seemed that this only enhanced her independence, and she was sent back to Beirut in disgrace. She did not consent to marry the Count of Haifa. She ran away from the house and became a nun. My father disinherited her, and nobody but me knows of her whereabouts." Jean sighed and then turned to me. Despite my expression of empathy, he smiled. "Ultimately, my father got what he wanted, and that is how we arrive to your third question: I married the sole daughter of that same Count of Haifa, Alice."

"So, it was an arranged marriage?" I asked, curious.

"I fail to understand your meaning," said Jean.

"Did you meet her before you were wed?" I tried.

"Certainly," Jean laughed. "We knew each other well. Her father is one of the most powerful men in Acre, and when my father fought the emperor's men and founded the Acre commune, he was constantly aided by the Count of Haifa. I relayed many messages between them, which is how I got to know Alice. She was always one of the most intriguing of the young women that I met, and her dowry was among the handsomest in the kingdom." Was it possible that I felt a twinge of jealousy? I shook my head, telling myself firmly, *Don't be stupid.*

Jean turned to me and said, with restrained amusement in his voice, "And yourself, Lady Édith? Where were you born and raised? And how did you meet your husband?"

I opened my mouth to answer, but then he said, "Actually, you told me that you are from Jerusalem. Did you leave there long ago?"

"I left after finishing my degree at the university," I said, as if this was small talk on the bus, not a conversation with a man from the thirteenth century. Jean's eyebrows furrowed with incomprehension. "You studied at a university? How? And for what purpose?"

"In my time, universities are an institution for general education, open to all. I studied French, Greek, and Latin. And to what end? Hard to say. But it helps me as a translator."

"What do you mean?" Jean pursued.

"I translate for work." He shook his head in bewilderment, and I explained. "I translate books from French and Russian and English—into Hebrew. And whoever requests these translations pays me money for it."

Jean shook his head and took a long breath in. "In our previous encounter, you said that you don't have any servants, which aroused my curiosity. How is this possible? Who, if anyone, takes care of the household and the children?"

"I have just one daughter," I smiled, "and my house is certainly no palace. Also, my husband does some of the tasks."

"Of course," said Jean. "He must be responsible for maintaining the house and the gardens and the animals, but do you cook and sew? Dust and wash? Launder and clean the dishes? Light the fire in the wood stove in the mornings? Pump water from the well? Educate and look after your daughter? And if so, how do you look so well taken care of and have time to spend all these hours in my company?"

Now, it was my turn to laugh at the onslaught of questions. "I have all kinds of machines that help me, actually. I suppose you could call them servants," I said after some thought.

"What do you mean?" Jean asked in the same tone of eager curiosity I had come to know. He pushed up on his elbows, and Brunette turned over with demonstrable displeasure. I, too, got up on my elbows, and the chemise I was wearing must have exposed too much (the pink silk dress was over by the tree), because Jean ran a finger between my breasts.

"I cannot speak while you fondle me," I said and lay on my back before him.

Jean pulled his hand away and smiled at me.

"Please explain what you mean by that word, my lady, and I will try to conquer my urges," he mumbled and lay back down.

"You and your conquering of urges," I laughed. "So—there's a machine that washes the dishes. I just put the dirty dishes and soap in and press a button, and it washes the dishes by itself. I have a machine that sucks the dust up from the carpets. I have a machine that washes the dirty clothes. I indeed do my own cooking, but there's no need for me to sew because I buy clothes from shops, already made."

"I do not understand what in the devil you are talking about," said Jean and turned to me again. "I pray that one day I will once again dare to cross the magic passage, and you will show me all these miraculous things."

"Say," I said lazily and reached out to stroke his hair. "Do you think the place is called 'Le Destroit' because of our magic passage? That would mean someone else has crossed it."

"That is an interesting question," Jean said thoughtfully. "To the best of my knowledge, our small fortress here received this name as it guards the narrow passage between the Carmel mountains and the sea and the innocent Christians who pass through it from the murderous attacks of the Saracens. But it could be that there is more to it than that . . ." He turned onto his belly, chewing on the stalk of a plant.

"Tell me more about your life," he said, rolling the stalk between his teeth. "And about your . . . those things you have instead of servants." He stroked my hair and pulled me closer to him. "Ma-sheen? Is it Greek?"

"Machines," I laughed with my eyes closed. He moved away from me again and leaned against the tree, attentive in his whole being.

"Listen, it's not so simple," I admitted. "The truth is that I do kind of have help. There is someone who comes every two weeks to dust and clean the house; there is a place where women look after my daughter and keep her entertained together with dozens of other children, every morning until the afternoon. There's no need to take care of horses, because we have chariots that go by themselves; you just have to drive them and fill them with a liquid that makes them move—"

"Like water mills?" Jean sat up again. There was an eagerness in his eyes. "I am just now building one of those by the Jaffa River."

"Not a water mill, no," I said, helplessly. "Maybe a little? I have no idea." I tried to remember car mechanics. "I apologize," I said, ashamed. "I will try to check how it works and tell you the next time."

Jean reached into one of his pouches. He took out my lighter and began to play with it again.

"You are aware that you simply took that from me, yes?" I snapped.

"You are right, my lady," he said, smiling sheepishly. "I was smitten." He handed me the lighter.

"Keep it," I said magnanimously. "I have ten more at home."

Jean whistled in admiration. "I cannot imagine your modus vivendi, my lady," he said. He gathered several weeds and lit them with the lighter. He blew on them, reviving the fire, then added the small, dry branches that he had gathered earlier. Soon, a small fire was burning cheerfully, and he went to his saddle and took a small copper kettle from one of the saddlebags. He filled it with water from the spring and put in herbs that he took out of one of his countless pouches. He resumed playing with the lighter. "Just wonderful," he said to himself. "Is it true that you have many of these? This is an inexpensive item?" He asked.

"Very inexpensive," I said. "And it stops working after a while," I added, in the spirit of full disclosure.

"In that case, would you mind if I were to dissemble the thing?" He asked eagerly. I nodded and even showed him how to pull out the metal wheel. From there, he proceeded on his own.

"So, who pumps the water?" He asked as he took apart the lighter and looked at every component closely. "Someone brings you fresh water every day, lights the fire, and heats the water?"

"We have a system of pipes in the ground," I said. "The water comes from the tap to the kitchen and bathroom, and you can even adjust their temperature from the tap—cold or hot."

"Holy mother of God." He was struggling a little with his undertaking but did not lose patience. "I do not know whether to badger you with questions or leave it at that. I feel as though my head might explode."

"Me too," I mumbled. If all we were going to talk about were the technological innovations since the Middle Ages, it would be an exhausting evening for me. He cast me a glance and ran his hand over my hair.

"It will be dark soon," he said and looked at me woefully. "You should get back to your time before it is too late, and likewise I must return to the Pilgrim Castle before sunset. But if you will permit me, before that, to kiss you again . . ." I rolled onto my back and opened my arms to him.

I replayed my conversation with Jean and everything that came after it again and again in my head while putting away groceries with Halimi. Then, I peeled potatoes for lunch and put them on the grill, sliced vegetables, and roasted a chicken. Halimi lay down to take a nap before picking up Lily from preschool.

Out on the balcony, I lit a cigarette and opened my laptop. Fingers trembling, I typed "Jean d'Ibelin" into Google. I did not expect any results.

As I clicked Google's magnifying glass search icon, spots swam before my eyes. The first link for "Jean d'Ibelin" referred me to French Wikipedia. "Jean d'Ibelin, Lord of Beirut." The second link also led to Wikipedia. As my eyes skipped between the lines of the first entry, I felt like my insides were swirling.

It was a very short entry, about the Lord of Jaffa and Ashkelon and his achievements and titles. This did not sound quite right to me—after all, my Jean was Count of Arsur, but maybe later on in his life he also became the Lord of Jaffa and Ashkelon? I proceeded to the second entry, which was longer and more detailed. "Jean of Ibelin (c. 1179–1236), called the Old Lord of Beirut, was a powerful Crusader noble in the thirteenth century, one of the best-known representatives of the influential

Ibelin family . . . He served as regent and constable of the Kingdom of Jerusalem and the Kingdom of Cyprus . . ."

I speed-read the messy description of Jean's father. The cigarette slipped between my fingers. The entry included a quote mentioning the castle in Beirut, which sounded exactly as Jean had described it. Nothing was written about his family. I clicked on the corresponding entry in English, which immediately displayed the Ibelin coat of arms: a broad red cross against a golden background. I quickly scrolled to the part about his family and there, black against the screen, appeared the name of my Jean, Lord of Arsuf. With a beating heart and a pressing sensation against the inside of my eyes, I clicked on the entry, "Jean d'Ibelin, Lord of Arsuf."

"Working?" asked Halimi from behind me.

I leaped in surprise and turned to him with a smile that might have been overly broad.

"Yes, I need to do a little research for the French book," I said casually.

Halimi lit a cigarette and stood with his back to me, leaning against the railing of the balcony and gazing at the horizon.

I did not leave and take Lily to my parents' place the day after Halimi and I had our big fight about Nina. The doctor diagnosed her with strep throat, and she was very sick for the next four days. My red eyes and exhaustion were probably chalked up to parental concern—disproportionate, if common. Not only did I not leave Halimi; I didn't even have the strength to tell him to get out.

I was afraid to be alone with my worries and Lily's illness. I was so worn out, I barely had the strength to do basic things—eat, shower, make Lily swallow her medicine. Apart from that, the apartment had originally been his. I knew that this was stupid, but I was unable to kick him out of his own home, an apartment that he continued to pay for himself despite my pathetic attempts to contribute to the rent.

"So. Tell me exactly how and when it started," I said suddenly on one of those long days, when Lily had finally fallen asleep after a particularly harsh coughing fit followed by crying. Halimi had ordered delivery from the coffee shop, and we ate in the living room in tense silence. I had no idea if he had told Nina that he'd been caught or what they had agreed between them. I continued to follow her profiles like a woman possessed, and there had been no notable drop in her mood or the remarkable quantity of selfies.

Halimi pushed his plate away with a frown.

"I will never understand your obsession with knowing everything," he said coolly.

Without saying a word, I collected the plates, took them to the kitchen, washed them, and went to the bedroom. I got under the duvet. I knew I needed to look for a proper job. And find a divorce lawyer. And an apartment. I sighed and turned over.

"Ditush," Halimi came into the room and sat down beside me. "I'm sorry, sweetheart. I'll tell you." He stopped and gently pulled the blanket from over my head. "I just don't want to hurt you even more. I promise you that you are the person I love most in this world." He felt around for my hand underneath the duvet. Ambivalent, I released it and let him kiss from my hand up my forearm. He smelled of whiskey.

He lay beside me and told me that at first it was just flirting, like a million other flirtations. When they got a little closer, she told him that she wasn't very interested in sex, because most of the partners she had had in her life had been disappointing, and that she did not want a relationship, because people expected things from her that she did not know how to give. He did not need to tell me that this only further stirred his conquering impulse. *He'd show her a partner who was not disappointing and a relationship with no expectations*, I thought to myself with tears in my throat. Halimi went on and said that all my dalliances had made him feel freer than ever. He told her that we had an open relationship. I couldn't help but snort with disdain.

"In open relationships, people talk about everything, sweetheart," I said but didn't remove my hand from his.

"Well, now I'm telling you everything," Halimi said impatiently. "The question is if you can handle it."

"I want to know," I said stubbornly.

"Mama . . ." The faint voice came from Lily's bed. I rolled my eyes, and both of us even chuckled, like accomplices on death row.

CHAPTER 15

I spent the days that followed frantically reading up on the Ibelin family, the Crusades, and the fortress at Atlit. I researched secretively, wary of Halimi's prying eyes. I was surprised at the extent of my ignorance. I thought that as an educated person, I knew the history of my country, but I had scant knowledge of the Kingdom of Jerusalem, that two-hundred-year-old kingdom that the Crusaders established that, at its peak, extended over parts of today's Lebanon, Syria, Jordan, and Israel. Starting in the late eleventh century, generations of Catholic warriors and nobles, mainly from France, had created a kingdom here, believed and dreamed and built and conquered and wrote, and then destroyed themselves through in-fighting and scattered to the four winds, leaving behind buildings that crumbled over time.

I was obsessed, but I didn't quite know what to concentrate on. I skipped from one topic to another. I looked tirelessly for material about my Jean, but there was little of that to be found. I discovered that his father was indeed one of *the* most powerful people in the kingdom, at the point when it no longer had an acting king. I learned everything I could about the wars between Jean, the Old Lord of Beirut, and Frederick II, the Holy Roman Emperor. With a growing sense of solidarity, I let out a snort of contempt every time I came across mentions of Frederick II's political achievements and educated court.

When we parted ways, Jean had taken back the clothes he had lent me, claiming that he had to return them. He promised that until we next met, he would obtain clothes that I could keep with me or hide by the spring. Now, I was sorry that I had not requested at least the shift, or the headscarves. His scent existed in my head—a hint of lemon and rose water mixed with a light whiff of sweat—but I longed to really smell him.

I discovered, awestruck, as I regularly found myself in those days, that Thibaut of Champagne had also existed; he was the King of Navarre, just as he had said. "The Troubadour," he was called. Feeling faint, I read everything I could find on the crusade that he led between the years 1239 and 1240. I even found a number of modern recordings of some of his songs on YouTube. When I came across the first one, I had the impulse to send it to Jean, before remembering that was impossible. But my discovery was met with overwhelming euphoria—I could not have imagined historical figures whom I had not had the slightest notion of previously, and this, to me, was the triumphant proof that my experiences were not the fruit of madness.

Every day, several times a day, I had to stop myself from going to the Narrow Passage, to go by the spring again and sneak into the citadel, to try to meet Jean earlier than the date we had agreed upon: next Monday.

I wondered if I would be level-headed enough not to tell him everything I now knew about his life—the fact that he would yet become a key figure in the kingdom, the year of his death, the number of children he would have, even the year of his wife's death. I tried to find any possible scrap of information about her, too, but I hardly found a thing.

Whenever Halimi was around, I unglued myself from the Ibelin dynasty and pivoted to my work on the French book. Though I told him that I was doing some kind of research, I had a feeling that he was starting to track my movements more closely. Instead of coming up with lies to explain myself, I preferred to simply hide my new obsession. So, when he was around, I read the French manuscript, writing comments to myself on the printed text and occasionally looking up expressions and concepts with which I was unfamiliar.

"It's really beautiful," I told Halimi one day with a sigh of satisfaction, as I completed another chapter. He looked up affably from his computer. "I wish I could write something like this."

"Mom, come watch Robinod with me," Lily called from the couch. I rolled my eyes and sighed but surrendered. This past week, I was impatient with her and scolded her a lot—when she whined, when she made a fuss over nothing, when she lost things. One afternoon, Halimi was out getting groceries, and I took advantage of the opportunity to read a bit more about the findings in the latest excavation at the fortress in Arsuf. Lily repeatedly demanded my attention, and I shouted at her so loudly that she ran into the bedroom and only agreed to talk to me after I got down on my knees and begged for her forgiveness. Now, I tried to keep my cool and went as far as showing interest in *Robin Hood*, even though I knew it by heart.

I sat beside her on the couch and was calmed by her smell, which always reminded me of burnt sugar, a little like cotton candy. I took her onto my lap and watched the animated movie with renewed curiosity, examining Disney's interpretation of the style of dress and architecture of the Middle Ages with a critical eye. We both heard Halimi parking the car outside and ran to help him with the bags, racing each other for who would get to him first.

"What are you thinking about?" Halimi asked when he found me staring, again, instead of putting away the vegetables.

"I'm thinking how brilliant it was to move to Atlit. I did not expect to be so happy here," I told him, a little emotional.

It was true—when we decided to move, I just wanted to get away from Tel Aviv and the old apartment, from *Free to Be* and everyone connected to the magazine, the cafés and boulevards, and the possibility of running into someone who knew about us and had heard all the gossip. I thought that in the best-case scenario, I might be at peace in Atlit, if gloomy for the rest of my life.

I looked at Halimi—tall and brown and relaxed—with that faint glimmer in his eyes, clearly pleased with my words. He came to kiss me on the head, and again I thought, with some surprise, how much I loved him.

Was it unnatural that I could fall in love with someone else, yearn for him and miss him, and at the same time love my husband with all my heart—the forgetful and chatty and generous and fatherly man that he was?

Lily had gotten over the strep throat, but I still had not taken her to my parents. The intensive week and a half that Halimi and I spent together, worrying over our daughter and taking caring of her, after months of parallel existence, had its impact. As she started to get better and the tension dissipated a little, we resumed doing things together—cooking, watching movies, smoking out the kitchen window—little things that in retrospect I realized we had not done for months.

There were still land mines that we avoided very carefully: I did not dare, for instance, ask him if he had spoken with Nina since that evening, because I was afraid to hear the answer. The immense fire raging in my soul was dwindling, but one must be wary of the hot spots still smoldering here and there. One thing still stuck with me, and once, after I smoked a too-strong joint and felt calm and secure enough to raise the subject, I asked, "That night when you said that Nina probably wanted me to figure it out, what did you mean?" I did not look up at him and continued playing *Candy Crush* on my phone. Just uttering her name made my heart race. *You are addicted to drama*—I heard my sister's cruel words from a month ago in my head.

Halimi did not respond. I looked at him, trying not to appear accusatory. I really did want to understand. "I'm not trying to rub salt in the wound," I added, just as he took a breath to answer. "I want us to be able to talk about this like friends."

Evidently I succeeded in transmitting a sufficiently congenial expression, because Halimi set his cigarette down in the ashtray, sat beside me, and said, "I think she's a bit obsessed with you. She's always curious about you, asks me about things you post on social media. She always wants to know how things *really* are between us." He smiled to himself. "She is unable to believe that I love you as much as I say and that I have no intention of ever leaving you, as long as you want me."

It took me a moment to take in everything he had said—it had never occurred to me that Nina might be as obsessive about me as I had been about her, and I felt compelled to go over all my posts from the last few months and check if I had unintentionally given away things that I wouldn't want her to know. I also considered this new, darker interpretation of everything that she had shared online, possibly with the specific design of getting to me. The idea that they had talked about me and our relationship stirred up conflicting feelings—I was tremendously relieved to hear his declaration of love and tried to imagine how he had sounded when he said it and how she must have felt, but I was also disgusted that he might have used our relationship for some kind of leverage in the dynamic between them.

Only after much consideration did I catch that Halimi had used the present tense.

I drove jubilantly to Le Destroit.

"I'm going to yoga," I told Halimi. I really did sign up for a yoga class in some local, boutique yoga place and had even managed to go once in the week that had passed. It was nice. Halimi, reading the brief for a new Israeli movie, nodded at the computer. "Get salt," he said. "We're almost out."

"It's a long class," I said, taking my bag. Inside it was the printout of a Renault engine illustration, along with complicated explanations in French that I hadn't bothered to read myself. "Three hours, maybe more."

Halimi looked up.

"Whatever's good for you, babe," he said.

"But I'll get the salt, Limush," I added. I came over and kissed him on the head.

When I got out of the car, I fingered the coin around my neck. Then, I took out Lily's coin again—I was very careful not to remind her of its existence—and I looked at it with great concentration. It was warm in the sun, almost too hot, and the birds around chirped as if they had all gone crazy.

There was nobody around when I approached the carob tree. I expected the earth would be entirely dry, but to my surprise, the book-sized puddle was still there. How had it not evaporated over the past week? I did not linger over it long. I accepted the presence of the puddle with the kind of philosophical wholeness that I had adopted in recent weeks. At its edge were some limp flowers, probably from the bouquet that I had left there last week.

I pulled out my pink razor but did not dare to slice my wrist as Jean had. I made a tiny cut in my index finger, waited for the drop, and said aloud, "I drip the holy liquid of life in order to pass through the waters between the worlds and meet Jean d'Ibelin, Count of Arsur." I took the silver necklace from around my neck and wound it around my wrist, then I gripped the Ibelin coin between my thumb and bleeding finger and dipped both fingers into the puddle.

One, two, three, I counted, then surrendered to the phosphorescent explosion.

I lay on the ground, not opening my eyes, clutching the thing that was wound around my hand. I trembled for a while, still recovering. Gradually, I caught my breath. I opened my eyes a slit and was met with the vision of the expansive green carob canopy above me. Dazzling sunlight played between its leaves. I emerged from the tree canopy and sat in silence, looking at the horizon, letting the delicate colors wash away all fear and worry.

Then, I went back under the tree. I did not know if guards were patrolling, and I did not want to overuse the "Lady of the Spring" trick. I wore gray linen clothes—a tunic and harem pants—which I had worn for the mushroom trip with Halimi. It was a little colder in the past, and I was sorry I hadn't brought a shawl or something. I had made no effort to look like someone who could blend in because I had assumed I would wear the clothes Jean would bring.

But where was he? At least half an hour had passed since I arrived, and there was no sign of him.

I began to walk. If he turned up, it would probably be from the fortress, so I walked in that direction. There was a weird feeling in my ears, like they were filled with fluff, like everything I heard passed through some kind of insulation. I swallowed again and again. I drank from the bottle of water I had brought. I squinted in the direction of the beach, trying to see if any knight on horseback was galloping in my direction. The walk lasted for some time, and I was a little tired by the time I reached the beach.

I sat down on the sand, the high wall to my left hiding the town, and looked at the sea. All I could see before me were stormy waves breaking and the lonesome tower on the rock in the sea, a few hundred meters north of the citadel. It seemed to me that I caught sight of some movement. And I could hear muffled sounds beyond the wall—chickens squawking, a hammer or something heavier knocking, sawing of some kind, and people's voices.

The beach was empty and clean. The plantations and salt pools bordered the wall to the south, and the strip of sand continued until it disappeared from sight to the north, into the stormy sea ahead. No barbed wire, no rusty metal signs, no diapers among the bushes, no trailers with their little patches of synthetic grass. I glanced toward the place where the Crusader cemetery was supposed to be. I saw a few dozen tombstones.

I mustered my courage and turned to the gate in the wall. I hoped there was no password. I wondered if I would have to pass through the town. I remembered from literature and movies that people from the Middle Ages did not like foreigners, and for a moment I imagined old, screaming, toothless women rallying everyone against me, and me ending up burned at the stake. I stopped and took Lily's coin from my pocket. I glanced over at the salt pools and the plantations, to the area of Le Destroit, where my spring lay. I took a deep breath and knocked on the gate.

I waited several seconds, which became a minute, and I thought to myself, *Okay, I'll come back some other day*, and then a hatch in the door opened. A pair of suspicious eyes peeked through the lattice.

"*Oui?*" came a coarse voice.

"Greetings to you, sir," I said as politely as possible. "I am seeking Jean d'Ibelin, Count of Arsur. I have reason to believe that he is here at the fortress." I was proud of myself for coming up with "reason to believe" in French.

"Oh?" the voice replied.

"I must see Jean d'Ibelin, Count of Arsur. It is urgent," I repeated as respectfully as I knew how.

"The Pilgrim Castle does not admit women, much less prostitutes," the coarse voice said and slammed the hatch shut.

I stood there shocked. I filled with rage and a strong, slightly hysterical wish to laugh, but I held it in. I reminded myself of how Jean convinced me that I am a lady, with the hands and hair and fine French and all. *I am Monsieur d'Arsur's cousin*, I repeated to myself.

I knocked again, and the moment the hatch opened, I said slowly, in Jean's accent and a lordly tone, which came to me so naturally that I was surprised, "Listen, you leprous dog. Let me in at once; if you will not, you will regret it. Inform Lord Arsur that the Countess of Atlit is here and must see him at once." I glared at him through the lattice.

"Countess who?" the voice said in a hesitant, more courteous tone.

"Tell him that his cousin is here, Lady Édith; he will understand," I answered, sounding self-important.

The hatch shut more politely, and the gate opened with a screech. I entered slowly, and the first thing I saw was the guard, a knight in a helmet, scale armor, and a black mantle with a red cross on it. I managed to keep my expression inscrutable, but I was pumping deep breaths through my tightened jaw.

"Follow me," the guard said without expression through his helmet. He walked along the sea toward the westernmost wall, and I walked several paces after him, taking in the sight of the town: pretty stone houses, one floor or two; several open workshops along the main cobblestoned street, from which a few narrow dirt lanes branched. Plum trees in purple bloom abounded. The houses looked like toys in the shadow of the enormous citadel that towered beyond the western wall. When we arrived there, the guard momentarily joined another guard, standing at the gates. This one looked at me in wonder but nodded in resignation, like a man who has seen it all. "Wait here," my guard said to me.

I stood by the gate and tried not to stand out. A large man crossed the street, startling a flock of chickens, and when he saw me, he stared without stopping. He arrived at what appeared to be a smithy and exchanged a few words with a thick-bearded man working there, and then he sat down on a stool and continued to gawk at me.

I should have brought some sort of scarf or kerchief, I told myself. *I'm so stupid.* My heart began beating wildly, and for the second time it occurred to me that I had made a stupid mistake coming in here. Visions of a medieval madhouse flashed through my mind again, and I almost turned back. Only my fear of the attention that my sudden walking might attract kept me rooted to the spot.

The guard returned and with him another knight, this one in a white mantle with the red cross. They spoke briskly as they approached me. "And how many did he receive?" mumbled my guard. "Fifty lashes," his friend replied. The guard sucked air through his teeth and shook his head, looking pained. "For just one extra glass?" The second knight shook his head and said nothing.

"A message has been sent to Count Arsur," my guard told me. He had removed his helmet in the meantime and appeared more sympathetic. I nodded my head at him with a small smile of gratitude, and his eyes expanded in a strange way. I looked away in embarrassment and leaned my back against the wall. My body was still, but my eyes raced around frantically. I was hit with an abundance of smells—of sheep and of fertilizer, and of freshly split wood, roasted meat, cat urine, and sweet pea. The smell of human waste was stronger here, too, but merged harmoniously with the multitude of other smells. A woman, her head covered with a white wimple, rounded up the chickens that the staring man had scattered before. When she noticed me, her mouth gaped, and she hurried into one of the houses. I tingled with the urge to run away but did not dare move.

I looked at the fortress. Considering its size, it would probably take at least half an hour until the message would reach Jean and he could make it here. I felt a rush of anxiety. *What if he was not here, and this was all a ruse that would end with me being thrown into some dungeon, and no one would ever know what became of me? Or what if Jean's wife arrived, and that's why he isn't coming? Why did I not simply dive back to my own world when I saw that he wasn't coming? Why did I go after him?* My hands began to tremble. The two knights went on talking among themselves. *I'll just go*, I calmed myself. *Don't make drama*, I added and turned toward the eastern wall.

"My lady," the guard stood before me. I froze, my heart pounding. "I apologize from the bottom of my heart for my impertinence earlier. These are overwrought times, but there is no excuse for un-knightly comportment. Please forgive me, and the Good Lord will forgive your sins too." He was large and fair, with straw-colored hair and a slightly stooped back.

"I grant thee my forgiveness," I said with a nobility that I later replayed over and over in my head with great pleasure. "You bear great responsibility. But there is much you do not know about the world around you, and there is a reason why I do not appear as you might expect." I hoped that I had not overdone it again.

"Please forgive me, whole of heart," said the guard, in a begging tone that surprised me.

"Of course, I forgive you, wholeheartedly!" I said, touched, and almost went over to lay a hand on his arm. But something in his eyes stopped me. His friend placed his hand on his shoulder.

"Well, I'll be." A voice was heard from the wall above, accompanied by an outburst of barking. My heart leaped like a helium balloon set free. I looked up and saw Jean d'Ibelin, Count of Arsur, leaning toward us from a nearby tower. I could not see well, but it seemed to me that he was trying to hold back a smile. Brunette must have been at his feet. I heard her barking but could not see her.

"The honorable Lady Édith, in the flesh and on her own at the Pilgrim Castle," Jean nodded.

"You know her, my lord?" the guard asked, chastened.

"Certainly," Jean replied. "Show her here to me."

CHAPTER 16

I tossed and turned all night. It was too hot with the wool blanket, then too cold without it. Halimi snored on his side. The faint hum of a springtime mosquito startled me awake each time I dozed off. Eventually, I got up. The clock in the kitchen showed four in the morning. I poured myself a glass of cold water and went out onto the balcony.

On the table, a package of Camel cigarettes was moist with dew. I took one out but didn't light it. I leaned on the railing. I inhaled the cool, salty air deep into my lungs. I put the cigarette back in its package.

My thoughts came quickly, chasing each other, colliding. Every few moments, I glanced back into the house, as if to be sure it was possible that that same day, I had both lived my regular life, with Lily, who had worn me out in the evening, asking me over and over to join her in the bath, and the French book that I had to finish reading soon, and a supper of scrambled eggs and cottage cheese—and had also ridden an exquisite horse named Éclair with a Crusader nobleman down a rocky ditch, waves breaking from both sides.

When he met me on the other side of the wall, Jean was dressed more beautifully than the previous times. He was outfitted entirely in silk in shades of red and yellow, with a kind of dark velvet vest embroidered with large gold Greek crosses with perpendicular edges and smaller crosses between them, an emblem that I already recognized as the symbol of the Holy Kingdom of Jerusalem. "What's this, did you dress up for my sake?" I said teasingly, after the embarrassed guard led me to him via the tower steps and parted from us, giving me another look of apology.

Jean let out a whoop of laughter, which made his horse stomp nervously on the cobbled ground of the rampart. Brunette barked happily.

"Actually no, my lady, although perhaps I should have." His eyes shone with triumphant cheer. Clearly, it had nothing to do with me, which was a little discouraging.

"We agreed to meet," I said quietly, hoping that I didn't sound like a spoiled child.

"Indeed," said Jean. "At midday." He gave me a puzzled look, then added, "Were you waiting long?"

"A little," I said.

"I was in a very important congress," said Jean, not entirely apologetic—but in a conciliatory tone. "This assembly may dictate the fate of our kingdom and . . . other things." I looked down at the ground. I did not want to make demands of him, but I was a little offended. I couldn't deny it.

"I was going to ride over to meet you as soon as our assembly concluded," said Jean and suddenly held my chin. He turned my head to him, and I saw that he could not control the happiness bubbling up in him. "I could not have imagined that you would simply come here. I presumed that you would wait there until I arrived, like any lady engaging in a rendezvous." His smile grew, and I smiled too. "But you are not like other ladies, are you, Lady Édith?"

"It would seem I am not," I replied, and any remaining irritation disappeared, and also from my face, evidently. My smile spread, and I bowed deeply, holding the hem of my gray tunic.

"I would kiss you," he said suddenly, "if we were not within sight of countless sentries, guards, and other interested parties. I will do so yet in some more private place."

I looked up at him in surprise. He glanced around the walls, the towers, and the citadel looming before us and said, "We must dress you in a more suitable manner before some disaster should befall us."

He leaped up onto his horse and held a hand out to me, which resulted in some fumbling and embarrassment for me and amusement for him, as I tried to climb onto the horse and struggled greatly. Then, I tried to sit in front of him with my legs apart—he shook his head in disbelief and directed me to sit sideways before him, with both of my legs on the horse's left flank. Brunette followed this little farce with barks of encouragement, after which she strode at our side with her head held high.

We left the tower, heading toward the end of the wall, from which a path sloped down the reinforced moat, toward a large gate in the citadel.

The clatter of the horse's hooves on the sandy path were swallowed by the crashing of the waves from both sides. The fortress was getting closer. The open gate looked like a gaping maw, and suddenly I was filled with fear again. *What am I doing here, in the year of our savior 1240?*

"I will introduce you as the Lady Édith from Cilicia, an Armenian noble," Jean directed me matter-of-factly as we got nearer. "I will say that you are a family member from my mother Melisende's side, the daughter of some anonymous cousin of hers. You were on a pilgrimage and on your way to visit my sister at the convent where she lives, and you managed to escape an attack by the Saracens on your entourage, but you lost all of your companions. You behaved strangely on the day that Thibaut and I encountered you on account of sunstroke, but after finding yourself in one of the villages and regaining your strength, you showed me the letter from your father that explained who you are and what is your purpose. Can you remember all that, Lady Édith?"

I nodded. "An Armenian lady, visit to a convent, attack by Saracens, sunstroke, letter of recommendation. Yes." Jean pressed several centimeters closer to me, and with his lips close to my ears, whispered, "Quick-witted little demon."

"So, were you called to come to me in the middle of your important meeting?" I asked Jean in a kind of uncertain apology as we neared the gaping maw of the fortress.

"No," Jean chuckled. "Fortunately, the meeting ended shortly before the messenger appeared. I intended to change my clothes and ride to you, but then, to the great dismay of my servant, he appeared and asked if I knew any 'Lady Édith' who was insolently knocking on the entrance gate to the town of the Pilgrim Castle."

We reached a gate in the wall, over which rose another tower. Yet another Templar knight nodded his head at Jean and moved away from the gate. We entered a vaulted, paved tunnel, in which the horse's footsteps sounded like the ticking of a clock. I shivered. Jean pressed close to me from behind. We left the tunnel into a huge, paved courtyard surrounded by buildings and towers that made up part of the inner wall. After the dimness of the tunnel, the light and the commotion of the yard dazzled me.

Templar knights in black and white with red crosses were everywhere, and other people, too, maybe some of them servants. Here and there, I even saw some girls carrying folded fabrics in their arms or in large woven baskets, evidently doing laundry. I looked around in petrified wonder, but no matter how many times I shook my head, trying to shake off the shock, I was still awestruck.

"Sir," cried a tall young man dressed in red and yellow. He approached us and took the horse's reins. Brunette licked his hand.

Jean leaped down and extended a hand to me.

"Hugh, this is my cousin, Lady Édith. I told you of her," said Jean casually. I closed my eyes as I tried to get down easily like Jean. I landed clumsily but smiled at Hugh.

"My lady," said the youth and bowed. I did not know exactly how I was meant to respond, so I simply nodded with what I hoped was acceptable nobility. He was courteous enough, but I thought I saw a vague hostility in his expression.

"From which side are you cousins, sir?" he asked, stealing a glance at me. I froze, but Jean said, "Mind your manners, Hugh."

"Apologies, sir," Hugh said humbly. He nodded his head at us and pulled Éclair after him. Jean said, "When you have finished with Éclair, bring refreshments to my room."

The youth nodded, "Yes, sir," and turned toward one of the corners of the inner courtyard wall. Jean looked at him getting farther away and then looked back at me. The commotion in the huge yard was overwhelming—I caught a glimpse of a stable, a smithy, a bakery at the far edge, and, judging by the enormous bell on its domed roof, a large church in the middle. Knights, priests, monks, and artisans walked purposefully to and fro. The laundresses—some walking around, and some bent over their work at a kind of fountain—stared at me in shock. One of the knights in black slowed his pace and observed me with a fearful expression. I was not certain that it was not Geoffroy of Tours.

Jean linked his arm with mine and pulled me after him toward one of the covered gateways, Brunette bounding eagerly ahead of us. From there, we passed through a lit portico to a dim stairwell, damp and chilly, until we reached a higher level, a corridor the length of which was lit by several pale torches lining the walls and near several doors. We went into one of the rooms with embroidered tapestries covering the stone walls, long windows with latticed panes, and a huge-looking fireplace in one of the walls; I sank into a chair with a sigh and closed my eyes. I was drenched in cold sweat, and my heart was beating like crazy. My head fell back.

"This cannot be," I muttered in Hebrew, my eyes still closed. I thought I had gotten used to this improbable reality by now, but the short time I had spent in the fortress—surely less than ten minutes had passed since we had come through the gate—totally destabilized me. I felt confused, weak, and terribly slow of thought, like the first time I traveled between the centuries, on the mushroom trip, which suddenly felt very far away. *Hundreds of years away . . .*

"Maybe I should get back . . ." I said in French.

I felt Brunette's wet nose nuzzle into my palm.

I opened my eyes and did not see Jean anywhere in the room. I leaped up in fright and looked around the beautiful, slightly damp room, at the big wooden door and at the walls that the tapestries appeared to have sunken into. A thousand different horrifying scenarios flooded my imagination in the two seconds that passed until Jean pulled back the curtain—and came out from behind it carrying a pile of fabrics.

"Is something the matter, my lady?" He hurried over to me and set his pile down on one of the armchairs, or whatever it was, took my hand, and then turned my face to the light that streamed through the long, narrow window.

"Sit," he said in his lordly tone. "You do not feel well." He supported me as I collapsed into a wide wooden chair with armrests, padded with cushions. I could barely keep my eyes open.

"Where is that stupid boy?" Jean muttered, irate. He was fiddling with the wood stove and brought me a goblet. "Drink," he said, placing the goblet in my hand. "It will give you strength."

I obeyed numbly and sipped a strong wine that made me cough until I nearly choked.

"Water," I finally managed to splutter.

"I will go and seek Hugh," said Jean and turned toward the door.

"Wait," I said. "Don't leave me here alone." Jean returned and knelt beside me.

"Do you want me to bring you back to the spring, Lady Édith?" he said gently, as if he were speaking to a sick child. Brunette rested her head on my thigh.

I reached out for my bag and took out the bottle of water that I had brought with me. I drank and drank, emptying the bottle, took a deep breath, and then said, "Soon. But give me a moment."

I was still unable to fully pull myself together, but I was not willing to give up yet. If I went back now, I would waste a wonderful opportunity—that much was clear to me. *I have to pull it together*, I repeated to myself. *Soon, I will go back to my spring.*

I woke up with a start and a stiffness in my neck and realized that I had fallen asleep on the balcony, sitting on the folding wooden chair with my head drooping. Dawn was rising in the east. A noise made me jump. I peered into the house, which was still dark. As I stretched, intending to go back to bed, Halimi appeared on the threshold of the balcony in a T-shirt and boxers, holding a glass of water. I allowed myself a moment of pleasure at the sight of his long legs as he settled in front of me on a chair on the balcony. He smiled at me, still groggy.

"Couldn't sleep, *ma belle*?" he asked. I did not bother to try to consider if there were some subtext in his question. I simply answered, "Yes."

"Want to talk about it?" Halimi asked, taking a cigarette from its packet.

I shook my head and got up. I went over and sat on him, resting my head against his chest. He was still warm from bed, his smell familiar and dear to me. His arm folded around me, and his hand stroked my back, his other hand still holding the cigarette.

Suddenly, I wanted to ask him how it felt to be in love with both Nina and me at the same time, but I knew that this would spoil the mood. Yet I truly wanted to know. I had no precedent for this expansion of the heart, to be able to cuddle up to the beloved and familiar, while at the same time soaring, borne on this dream of a new, totally irrational love. For the first time since I had discovered their affair, the thought of Nina did not feel like venom spreading through my body.

Halimi was unusually quiet. He had just woken up a few minutes earlier and was not even absorbed in his phone, as he usually was whenever he wasn't doing something else.

"And you, Limush?" I asked from where I was nuzzled into his shoulder. "All good with you?"

Halimi murmured in the affirmative but did not elaborate. The first ray of sun pierced through the sky from the east, and the gray sea in the west turned a light blue.

"I think I'll go back to bed for another hour or so, 'til Lily gets up," I mumbled, still nestled into the crook of his shoulder.

"Good night," said Halimi.

We returned to normal. Lily got better and went back to daycare, where we had decided to continue sending her for another year because the teacher was wonderful. I resumed my translations, which I had neglected during the month when I had been tormentedly surveilling Halimi. Halimi went back to work at the magazine, after the days off that he had taken to be with us when Lily was sick, and made sure to come home at regular hours. Relations between us had become careful, almost polite.

I was unable to ask him if he had broken it off with Nina. I knew that he saw her at the magazine's office—though most of the writers did not actually come in too often, she was a high-handed type, and I knew that she was very involved in the way her articles were published.

"What's your problem?" my sister asked, after several days during which I had not spoken to her.

I did not reply and only shook my head helplessly.

"Do you want me to come?" she asked abruptly.

"No, no," I laughed. That was all I needed, for Dina to be here now, coming to my aid like a knight defending a damsel in distress.

"So, why don't you tell him, in simple words, what you want?" she insisted. Her wild hair was sticking up in every direction.

"Because I don't know exactly what I want, Dina," I said with comparable impatience. I knew what I did not want to be—the punishing wife who forbids her husband from acting on his desires. In my experience, prohibiting something usually just increased the hunger for it—certainly with Halimi.

I also did not exactly want to break up with him: Our lives were entwined, and I loved him terribly despite all of his shortcomings. We still made each other laugh, and even after years together, he was the person I enjoyed talking to most. We were attracted to each other—the sex, even when it was average, was good, and often it was spectacular. I knew that Halimi loved me and needed me and depended on me, and that in his elusive, narcissistic way, he was unable to imagine his life without me.

And Lily was no longer a baby. If we were to break up, that would be the end of our three-way ice cream benders (strawberry for Lily, pistachio for Halimi, and dark chocolate for me) and our cuddling in the mornings, when I would find myself mashed between Lily's foot and Halimi's elbow . . . the end of our watching all the Disney movies ever made, and our trips in nature, and lazy vacations in the sun.

Of course, I did not want him to keep up his affair with Nina. But I was willing to make my peace with it—at least that's what I told myself—if he would just stop lying and hiding it from me. *In a less precarious situation*, I thought, *I would be able to handle an affair with another woman—as long as I knew everything and had control over the frequency of their meetings.*

When I was honest with myself, I knew that what I really longed for was for Halimi to break off the relationship with her without me having to say anything, out of an understanding that above all else, he had to restore my trust in him. But as the one who had pushed for an open relationship, until I saw that message from Nina with the hearts (he had deleted it since then, I checked), I was unable to acknowledge, even to my sister, that I just wanted him to end it. After my vigorous lobbying for free love, having to ask him to stop would be death by humiliation.

"Fine, oh priestess of polyamory," I finally said to Dina, who was exaggeratedly chomping slices of carrot and kohlrabi. Maybe she got her period that morning. "Give me advice, oh wise guru."

"I can't give advice to someone who does not know what she wants," Dina spat, a carrot cracking between her teeth, and some shards flying toward the screen.

"Ew, gross," I laughed.

As soon as the sun had risen and I had gotten back into bed, I heard Lily wake up and put Halimi to work ("Dad, make me hot chocolate! In the pink cup! The pink cup! I don't want the blue one!"). It was earlier than usual for her. By the time I got up, she and Halimi were already out of the house. It was 9:10 in the morning, and I figured that he was probably getting some groceries before coming home. I tried to remember the dream I'd had, like someone trying to chart a path through a sticky spider's web.

Something related to the fortress, the embroidered tapestries on the plastered stone walls, and Thibaut, Jean's friend, was also there, but I couldn't remember exactly.

The young squire placed a crowded tray on one of the little tables, casting not-entirely-pleasant glances at me.

"Why did you delay?" I heard Jean ask sternly.

"Sir, Éclair was skittish," Hugh replied. "I brushed his coat to calm him, and I brought him an apple." Jean nodded his approval, his face still stern, and then instructed the youth to wait on the other side of the door. Hugh nodded and left the room.

"Your young man appears to be rather suspicious of me," I said uncomfortably.

"That may be so, but not for the reasons that might trouble you," said Jean, turning back to the pile of fabrics he had brought. "He is the young cousin of my wife and entered my service only three months back. They are overly close, as he grew up in her father's house, and he evidently suspects the veracity of my story of a distant cousin turning up suddenly out of nowhere. He was resentful and very surprised about my going to the spring without him in the last few weeks. He must be suspicious about the nature of our relationship."

"Hmmm" was all I managed to utter.

"Do you feel a little better, my lady?" Jean asked after I had finished several wonderful apple and raisin pastries and washed down my dessert with a glass of wine mixed with water. I nodded, and he added, "You are reaping the benefits of the important meeting we held here. For the most part, the food produced by the Pilgrim Castle kitchens is ascetic and rationed in a most depressing way."

I laughed and took another swig of the diluted wine. Now that it was not as potent, it was delicious.

"In that case, please change your clothes," said Jean, a light urgency seeping into his words. "The fact that I brought you into the citadel without seeking Périgord's permission is bad enough. If someone should come in here and see you in your strange clothes, with your hair showing and no escort, they would accuse both of us of adultery, apostasy, and God knows what else."

"But . . ." I felt suffocated with panic. "Everyone already saw me when I came in."

"Nonsense." Jean waved his hand dismissively. "A few laundresses and junior knights do not mean a thing. But if the head of the order or some other senior official comes sniffing around, we might get into trouble. Well, come on." He held out the pile to me and gestured with his head toward the curtain through which he had emerged previously. It was a heavy tapestry, a kind of wall carpet that was hard to move. I pushed it with my elbows, as my hands were full of clothes, and entered the bedroom of Jean d'Ibelin.

It was smaller than the sitting room, but more brightly lit. It was a corner room, with long windows in two directions, which looked out at the sea. Now I saw that it faced the southern bay, which was crowded with boats and small ships. There were two or three big ships anchored at some distance. The southern shore was bustling and appeared to be used by the village fishermen.

I sat down on Jean's bed. For several seconds, I restrained myself before putting my head under the blanket and taking a deep breath. The scent of Jean's body filled my nostrils. Brunette, who had come in with me, tilted her head toward me.

"What, do you never sniff someone in his absence?" I asked her in a whisper. Brunette blinked and lay down, her head on her front legs, stretched out ahead.

I took off my clothes and put on the thin slip, soft to the touch, as quickly as possible, and over it a yellow silk dress with wide sleeves.

It was embellished with red embroidery at the neck and wrists. I tied the narrow fabric, also yellow and red, around my waist like Jean had. I gathered my hair into a braid. Very carefully I wrapped the white cloth band around my chin and head and fastened it with pins that had been stuck in it. I wrapped my head with the stiffer cotton fabric and placed the longer, thin strip such that its ends would dangle on both sides of my face.

"How do I look?" I asked Brunette. She blinked in approval.

"Wonderful," said Jean when I came out, scanning me in wonder, until his eyes landed on my feet.

"Ah, the monsters," he said in disgust, referring to my sneakers, and went to another corner of the room. He returned bearing soft leather shoes in light brown, pointy at the toes, very pretty in fact. I would not object to wearing them forever.

He handed me a pair of thick cotton socks, and after putting them on my feet, I looked helplessly at the way they rolled down my shins. He knelt down beside me and tightened each sock with a band of silk underneath each knee and then placed the shoes on my feet and laced them. I stopped breathing.

Then, a knock was heard, and Jean hurried to throw my sneakers behind the tapestry of his bedroom. He made a swift gesture to me with his head, and I hurried to straighten up in the armchair, trying to portray a convincing modest Armenian noblewoman on a pilgrimage.

"Yes?" Jean said aloud.

"Sir," Hugh's head poked inside. His eyes gaped at the sight of me. "His Majesty is here."

"Show him in," said Jean, calmly. He poured wine into two carved wooden goblets.

At the threshold appeared the ample body of Thibaut, Count of Champagne and King of Navarre, wrapped in blue velvet decorated with yellow and silver. Beside him strode his beautiful black dog. Brunette greeted him with a skip, her tail wagging. Behind him walked a young man, dressed in blue and yellow.

"Stay outside with Hugh, Philip," said Thibaut. "Arsur will serve me."

Philip nodded once, allowing his eyes to take me in for a split second, and then disappeared behind the door.

"Oh ho!" Thibaut clapped when he saw me. "So, it was not the invention of the laundresses' feverish imaginations when they were babbling about the green-eyed witch who you dragged away to your private rooms." He snarled contentedly at Jean. "To the Pilgrim Castle, no less. You were always a bold one." He sat grandly down beside me on a luxurious chair padded with many pillows.

"Your Royal Highness," said Jean. "Please, may I introduce my family relation, the Lady Édith. Though in fact, you have already met—but at the time, she was suffering from sunstroke."

"Quit the nonsense, Arsur," said Thibaut and looked at me with a pleased expression. "This is the fairy from the spring, and judging by your increasingly questionable decisions, she has indeed ensorcelled you entirely."

"Since when do you stoop to listening to the laundresses' gossip, your Royal Highness?" Jean asked as he offered Thibaut the carved wooden goblet. He did not dilute his wine with water.

"Your arrogance may be your undoing," Thibaut replied and winked at me, swirling the wine in his goblet and not taking his eyes off me for a moment. "Laundresses know more than anyone about everything, certainly in a place as gloomy and devoid of secrets as the Pilgrim Castle."

Thibaut was plump and haughty, but his eyes were curious and full of life. Now, after I had read about him online and heard the songs he had written and composed, I felt a greater awe in his presence.

"I believe some three weeks have passed since our encounter at the holy spring, my lady," Thibaut said to me. "And it seems you have had an attack of reticence and exaggerated modesty since then."

"Your Royal Highness," I began, lowering my eyes. "I was not myself that day. I was unsettled following an attack by Saracens; parched and with sunstroke, alone, I seem to have permitted myself a degree of inappropriate language. I ask your forgiveness and beg that you not judge my character by my comportment that day." I had gone into character completely and did not dare raise my eyes to Jean.

"Good for you," said Thibaut. "You instructed her perfectly, Arsur. Of course, it would not be difficult for a real fairy to present such a convincing character of a low-spirited pilgrim."

"Did you come for some particular reason, your Royal Highness?" asked Jean, trying to divert his friend's attention.

"Your insolence grows from one moment to the next," said Thibaut, finally turning to look at Jean. "There are countless subjects that I must discuss with you, as you well know. We must discuss the agreement, and the damned orders, and the Genoese cheaters, and the lying Venetians, and the flattering Pisans, and all of our allies who are in such a hurry to change their minds every day."

Jean began to reply, but Thibaut went on, raising his voice ever so slightly. "There is also a vineyard that I wanted to check with you, about a day's ride from here, and yes, I wanted to finish the pastoral that we tried in vain to compose on the day that your fairy appeared. But she seems determined to thwart any collaboration between us," said Thibaut, returning his gaze to me. There was no note of reproach in his voice—in fact, it seemed that he was holding back a laugh.

"I am not determined of anything, your Majesty," I was quick to promise. "Apart from the vow I made to arrive to the place where our Lord suffered and was crucified and resurrected," I added in a voice oozing devotion. All of the materials that I had read on the Crusaders in recent days had, evidently, made an impact on me.

"Certainly, certainly," Thibaut grew serious, the hint of a smile still hiding at the left edge of his mouth. "Lady Alice will certainly be most pleased to hear of the piety of her husband's distant cousin."

Jean sighed and shook his head lightly. I did not know how to react and just nodded my head slightly toward Thibaut.

"Your Highness, please," said Jean, and I heard a pleading tone in his voice. This must not have come easily to him. "My cousin has several important and personal bits of news about our family in Antioch, and I wish to devote some short time to her. After which, I shall join you, and we will discuss all the things that must not be delayed."

"I'll be dashed if you exchange even one word about your imaginary family in Antioch," Thibaut said with a booming laugh. "But far be it from me to stand in the way of youth, springtime, passion . . ." he finished, placing his hand dramatically on his chest.

Jean smiled and nodded his head in gratitude.

"Don't tarry long, young man," said Thibaut in a more serious tone. "The fate of many men depends on what we are able or unable to accomplish."

"I know, your Majesty," Jean bowed his head. Intuitively, I rose from the armchair and bowed deeply.

"I am most grateful to you, your Majesty," I said quietly, my eyes on the floor.

Thibaut growled something and left the room. His black dog got up and followed him.

Hugh's head peeked inside. "Do you need me, sir?" he asked.

"No, Hugh," Jean said, convivial. "Take a little diluted wine and a few pastries and return to the door." The youth thanked Jean, took some pastries, and went back out.

Finally, just the two of us remained. Earlier, when I was changing my clothes in the bedroom, I imagined Jean and I making love on the beautiful bed. Now, I felt that that was not appropriate and, more to the point, dangerous.

"Perhaps we should return to our spring?" I suggested after a short silence.

"It seems that would be the correct thing to do, my lady," Jean said, sighing again. "Somehow, it always feels that the time with you is too short," he added with a hint of melancholy.

"I don't have to go straight home," I said. "We could sit there a little."

Jean smiled broadly and was suddenly full of energy. "Come," he said. "This time, we shall gallop."

By the time we got back to the bustling courtyard, I was completely revived and even a little tipsy—in a very pleasant way—from the wine and pastries I had devoured. The clothes from my time were bundled in a big cloth sack (Jean struggled for a few moments with my sneakers, which stuck out of it). I was already completely in the character of Lady Édith from Cilicia, and I just hoped we wouldn't be intercepted by an Armenian priest who might try to speak to me in his mother tongue. We turned toward the gate, and Jean instructed Hugh to bring Éclair. "Are you certain you do not wish for me to join, sir?" asked Hugh. "Two are better than one."

"Depends on the goal," said Jean jokingly but grew serious when he saw Hugh's frown.

"I do not require your service just now," he said without expression.

"Yes, sir," said Hugh and turned toward the barn with an expression of insult.

Jean clicked and muttered, "What a burden," his gaze following the boy as he walked away. I looked all around the yard. I wanted to walk around, to peek into the church, to see the main hall, to pass by the bakery. But Jean was in a hurry to get out of there, and I knew I did not have much time with him. On our way, we passed an elegantly dressed man, and he stopped before Jean with a look of condescension.

"Young Ibelin," he said and looked at me, licking his lips. He looked about Jean's age, but he was dressed richly in silk and velvet lined with fur, an elaborate hunting cap with a feather on his head, and his mustache and beard looked oiled. A yellow lion was embroidered on the front of his blue velvet tunic.

"De Brienne," said Jean, his jaw tightening.

"This must be the intriguing cousin of yours," said the oily one. Okay, my story really was spreading fast.

"Yes," said Jean, making the gesture of someone intending to continue on his way.

"Strange rumors were spread about her in the castle, Arsur. It is not appropriate to bring her to a holy place like this." He said this in a tone, as if Jean were in on the joke.

"Watch your tongue," said Jean.

"The sergeants are chattering about some 'Lady of the Spring' who materialized at Le Destroit in front of one of the guards," the man chuckled. His breath had the sour smell of baby spit-up. "Thibaut of Navarre is singing of a fairy you met, and the servants are spreading rumors about a shadowy witch who you dragged here earlier. Have you no shame?"

Jean blinked at him once, slowly, as if utterly exhausted, then said, in a formal and customary tone, as if he had already introduced me a thousand times, "De Brienne, this is my cousin, the Lady Édith, daughter of the family Baberon of Cilicia. She is in the midst of a pilgrimage and on her way to visit my sister at a convent near Jerusalem." The oily one bowed his head with respect, his feather almost tickling my nose. "Cousin," Jean went on, "May I introduce you to Count of Jaffa and Ashkelon, Gautier de Brienne, nephew to King Jean of Brienne, may his soul rest in peace, and an important force in our holy army." These were the words that he said, but by the tone in which he said them, it sounded like "Meet the cockiest son of a bitch I know."

I bowed, holding the edge of my dress.

"The pleasure is mine," mumbled the Count of Jaffa and Ashkelon while gripping my hand with his clammy one, kissing it in an almost slimy way—I had to muster my strength not to wipe off his saliva on my skirts.

"Sir," I half-sneezed.

He nodded with a grin to Jean, still limply holding my hand in his damp one. I took my hand back with an additional, sloppy bow.

"Has your uninhibited cousin taken you to the church of the Pilgrim Castle to pray before Saint Euphemia?" the count asked and licked his lips again. I turned my head to Jean, like an obedient cousin.

Jean looked at him in silence and then noticed Hugh standing by the gate with Éclair.

"Another time," he said curtly, taking my arm in his and pulling me after him.

CHAPTER 17

L isten," said Halimi, pouring himself his second black coffee of the morning. I looked up at him from the couch.

I had just returned from Lily's preschool; she no longer cried at drop-off. In fact, she hardly said goodbye to me when I left, skipping toward a little gang of girls and boys. That was a huge relief, but now as I lay on the couch and let myself sink into the memory of Jean lacing my soft leather shoes in the fortress, I felt a twinge of alarm that perhaps Lily might sense something and hold a grudge against me.

"Ditush," said Halimi.

"I'm listening," I replied, giving my head a shake.

"I was asked to write a big piece on that director with the new movie," he said. "To follow him around for a few days, on set and everything."

"Okay, and—?" I replied, indifferent.

"He's filming in Portugal, and they suggested that I go with them." Halimi had been very matter-of-fact these last few days. Though he clung to me at night, crushing me like a drowning man grasping at a life raft, and ambushed me on the way to or from the shower, pulling me after him into the bedroom for urgent, vigorous sex, throughout the day we mostly talked only about necessary things regarding Lily and the household. In the evenings, we watched movies and TV shows, but usually within ten minutes, the two of us were asleep on the couch.

"Portugal?" I repeated. "When? For how long? And they'll pay for all of it? Who suggested it?" I remembered to ask. Since he had finished his role as chief editor of *Free to Be*, Halimi occasionally freelanced, writing articles for various weekend editions and sometimes weeklies and monthlies, too, but he was mainly concentrating on his radio show.

"Next week, for four days. They're covering all expenses. And it was *Free to Be* that suggested it."

My heart skipped a beat.

"What, did she call you?" I asked, more surprised than horrified.

"Not her. Anat, her assistant."

About a month after Lily recovered from strep, we were driving back from a visit to my parents in Jerusalem. It was the end of the weekend, and traffic back into Tel Aviv was completely backed up. Lily fell asleep in the back, and I began to drift off too. Halimi's phone was stationed on its mount between the air vents, since he had used it to check where the traffic jams were worst. Not that it helped.

We had walked around the Nachlaot neighborhood a lot that weekend. The previous afternoon, Lily had stayed in to watch *Aladdin* with my dad while my mom lay down to rest. Halimi and I went to stretch our legs to the tunes of the Sabbath songs coming from the synagogues. The pink light of sunset painted all the houses gold, and clusters of children dressed in white played outside to the lively sounds of clattering dishes in advance of their Sabbath dinners. Halimi and I walked from my parents' house to the center of town and back, making occasional stops on the way to sit a little and smoke a cigarette.

Finally, with great difficulty, I managed to tell Halimi that I could not handle his affair with Nina. That the lies and ongoing betrayal had traumatized me. And that even though I believed in sexual freedom and the possibility of free love, in this particular instance I felt burned. And that without honesty, it could not work. Halimi nodded heavily and pulled me to him again and again, promising me that it was really over. That Nina knew but was having a hard time letting it go. That he could not simply break it off with her ("heartlessly," he quoted me to myself from the start of our relationship), but that both of them knew that it could not go on.

Now, in the car, I leaned my head on the window with a feeling of pleasant fatigue, like I had finished a marathon.

A loud WhatsApp notification sounded, and the whole car was illuminated by the green light of his phone. "Tomorrow at seven but I won't have much time," came a message from Nina across the screen.

"Oh, for God's sake," said Halimi in a panic. I turned automatically to look at Lily. Her head was slumped to the side, deep in sleep. I turned back to the road.

Another message hummed—she had sent something from YouTube. I clicked on the link before Halimi could stop me.

"Born to Die" by Lana Del Rey. I pressed on the link at once. I did not know the song or the clip.

The pretty Lana, nude, in the arms of some tattooed stud against the background of the American flag. Sighing in a grand hall or cathedral. Then, Lana sitting on some kind of throne, with tigers on either side of her, singing of not being heartbroken. Then, Lana running over to the tattooed man, standing in the dark beside his car, and beginning to make out with him passionately.

Halimi recovered from his shock and turned off the device, pulled it off its mount, and threw it into the back seat. I stared at my window.

"Ditush . . ." said Halimi, pleading.

"Shut up," I cried in a whisper. "Just shut up!" I said aloud, but low.

"I don't . . ." he began. Something loosened up on the road, and the cars began to move. He drove the whole way home in silence. I inhaled through blocked nostrils, held back the crying until it hurt in my ears. I desperately wanted a cigarette.

"She's just being annoying," Halimi managed to say when he found parking not too far from the house and killed the engine. I didn't have the energy to try to understand what he was referring to. I got out of the car and said, "Are you taking Lily, or should I?" For a moment, he looked as if he'd been punched in the stomach. Then, he came to his senses, undid Lily's seatbelt, and gathered her into his arms.

I listened to the Lana Del Rey song for days. I analyzed every nuance, toying with new interpretations of the words—Lana singing of feeling intensely alone on a Friday night, of love sometimes being insufficient, and—most disturbingly—of a man who prefers his girls on the edge. I kept racking my brain over the meaning of Lana—covered in blood and unmistakably dead in the arms of her tattooed stud—at the end of the video.

I continued to spy on Nina as if possessed—any time there was a gap of more than two hours between her posts, I would go into distress, refreshing the page like a crazy person, looking for her in responses, in tags, in other people's pictures—from the magazine or from the café where I knew she often sat. I analyzed every post, every tweet, and every picture as if it were meant for me personally. I hated her with a passion.

I also monitored Halimi. Over the years, he had almost entirely disappeared from social networks, even if he continued to surf them to gather information. He always had privacy settings enabled for WhatsApp and Facebook—nobody could know when he was last seen or if he had read their messages. But it was impossible to hide the feature that shows when you are online, and every time I sent him a message, I felt like a maniac, gripped with self-loathing.

In our sad, often silent conversations, I managed to make it clear to him that if he was not absolutely available to me, I would no longer believe that he loved me. He made an effort to respond immediately to even my most prosaic text messages (*we're out of milk, buy Advil, we're at the playground*), as well as the obsessive and despondent ones (*why aren't you answering, where are you, when are you coming home*), with what struck me as increasing impatience. When he did not answer me at once, I would call, enraged. This happened at least three times a day during that period.

This is like the worst kind of drug was my mantra in those days. Only it was in my head, because I was unable to share this dark corner with my sister or with Libby. Each time I humiliated myself, I would be hit with existential depression and nausea, but still I would continue to send endless messages and call furiously, usually to find that he was in the middle of a meeting, or on his way home, or in the bathroom.

Halimi swore on his late father that he had told Nina that they had to stop seeing each other, but he claimed that he could not avoid running into her at work.

"Everybody at the magazine must know about you two," I said one evening when he returned home from work later than usual and poured himself a generous drink with the expression of a victim of circumstance.

"What does that matter?" He answered, mixing the whiskey in his cup. *I see, so everyone knows.*

"It matters that everyone must think I'm a fucking idiot," I snorted.

"Idit, are we or are we not in an open relationship?" Halimi asked coldly. "Don't you hook up with strangers in the middle of the dance floor at the Block, in front of everyone? And come back to our bed with the smell of cum and aftershave? How does that work?" In one sip, he finished what remained of the whiskey and lit a cigarette. He did not appear to expect an answer.

"Good of you to ask, really," I said. "I tried to talk to you about that several times, but you never cooperated." My voice was cold too. I was irritated, because he had a point.

Halimi got up and poured himself another whiskey.

"Pour me one too," I said in a wild voice. I felt like breaking something.

He looked at me in surprise but poured one for me too.

"You never seemed particularly distressed about me hooking up with strangers," I said in a more reasonable voice. "On the contrary, as far as I recall."

"First of all, it did upset me." said Halimi. "Yes, it kind of turned me on," he continued, his anger mounting. "But that doesn't mean that I wasn't jealous and upset. I was just trying to be high-minded about it." I rolled my eyes at him.

It pleased me how irritated he'd gotten, even though I did not for a moment accept this nonsense about pain and jealousy. He had always been amused by my stories, and it had always ended in sex.

"Apart from that, I don't get it." His voice was still cold. "Do you make all the rules? It's all well and good until I do something you don't like?" His voice grew shrill. I was filled with an unbearable disgust.

"I would never do anything behind your back," I spat back. "Certainly not something so involved. And I would never, *ever* continue to do something that might cause you pain," I went on with relative self-control. "And if those one-off nothings hurt you, you should have said something and not acted like it was the sexiest thing in the world," I concluded, drank the whiskey he had poured me in one gulp, got up, and left the house.

"Sure, darlinka, I'd be happy to!" said my mother. She was trying to hide her surprise at my suggestion that I bring Lily over to their place for a few days while Halimi was in Portugal.

"I've wanted to take her for a long time," she added. That was true; in the first two years of Lily's life, almost every time we visited, my mother suggested that I leave Lily with them, but back then, I felt that she was still too little and needed me. Lily was good with them:

She was patient with the Russian that they sometimes spoke to her and even occasionally responded with certain words. She was crazy about my mom's collection of rabbits in every shape and size, from porcelain to horsehair, and my father played hide and seek with superhuman patience and dedication.

But in the last year, we saw my parents very rarely—life had become so busy that we spent time with them primarily over the holidays for a few intense hours, sometimes in the company of other relatives. At our last Passover seder, we slept over at their place on two mattresses in the living room, with Lily on one of the couches. In the morning, she snuck into their double bed, and later I heard her and my mother making breakfast in the kitchen. Suddenly, my heart was a little broken for my parents with grandchildren who lived so far away, in Berlin and Atlit.

"We can meet in the middle," said my father, who joined the call from the phone in their bedroom. "So you won't have to drive so far."

"That's so nice of you, Dad." I was touched.

"What a sweetheart," said Halimi when I told him of the arrangement. "I love your dad." He was meant to fly out to Europe the following week, and both of us were in a particularly good mood. When he carefully suggested that he might extend his stay a little and spend a few days with his brother, Yaakov, who lives in France, I made the necessary display of slight heavy-heartedness but was happy for him and encouraged it.

"Dad, I'm going on a trip!" Lily stood facing Halimi. She was wearing her sparkly Viking outfit again, including a plastic helmet with horns that was a little too big on her. They had just gotten home from visiting the neighbor and her grandson. "And you're going on a trip too. Only Mom isn't," she added and turned toward me, fixing the helmet so she could see me.

"I'll go for walks near the house, Lilushkin," I said, laughing.

*   *   *

Finally, Jean and I were sitting together under the carob tree again. It was like a homecoming. He held a blade of grass between his teeth and sharpened his knife. He sat beside me, the two of us with our bare legs outstretched, leaning against the trunk of the tree. Hugh, whom Jean had decided to bring along following the unpleasant encounter with de Brienne, stood outside the tree's canopy. We spoke quietly.

"So, why did he come?" I finally dared to ask.

"Maybe it was a mistake on my part to bring you into the fortress," Jean said with a degree of discomfort, and at first I did not understand the connection. "I wanted people to see you, so that if you come to Arsur with me, there will be people who already know of your existence. But I did not expect all the gossip and rumors. If I had left the fortress with you alone, in front of all those people, it would have been the end of my reputation as a decent man." Jean cast a worried glance at the place where Hugh stood, stiff as a Buckingham Palace guard.

"And we had to run into the loathsome de Brienne of all people, that stupid, slippery imbecile," Jean muttered sullenly.

"Why do you hate him?" I asked. I had never seen Jean in such a bad mood.

"That fool is one of those responsible for the sad state of our kingdom at present." He stopped himself, looked up at me, and smiled. "But I fear such matters will bore you, my lady."

"Fear not," I said. "I actually find it very interesting."

Jean looked at me for a few more seconds, clearly pleased. Sunlight flickered in his eyes, and I concentrated on them as if hypnotized. Jean laughed and looked away. His gaze caught on Hugh, who still stood as if he had been turned into a pillar of salt.

"Indeed, the kingdom has been in a state of uncertainty for some years now," Jean began in the tone of his storytelling, leaning his head against the trunk and gazing up at the top. At once I saw him telling bedtime stories to one of his children. "In part due to my family's incessant wars with the ridiculous and illegal demands of the emperor's men, as well as the fact that the agreement that the emperor signed ten years ago with the Egyptian sultan is about to expire.

"Egypt and Damascus are locked in dispute, so this is a good respite for our kingdom to gather strength and refresh ourselves and use their rivalry to strengthen our hold on the land. But all of us are up to our necks, drowning in internal conflicts . . . The Genoese are loyal to the barons of the country but despise the Venetians, with whom the Knights Hospitaller and the Temple are allied, and who are also our allies, but quarrel more and more amongst themselves. The kingdom's military cannot exist without the ships and the trade lines of the Italian communes, but they have interests of their own; the orders of knights are the heart of the army, but in their hoarding of resources, they are becoming an entity unto themselves and no longer a tool in the hands of the kingdom," Jean sighed sadly. "Our bishops and priests do their best, but how can they serve properly when they are bombarded by contradictory instructions coming from Rome?" He looked at me. In retrospect, I thought maybe he was checking to see if his words shocked me, but in that moment, I was just listening, trying to follow. I nodded. "We, too, the noblemen of the land, have neglected our duties. Our wealth has dwindled on account of all the wars against the emperor's men, but that is no excuse. If we don't think of the future of our kingdom, who will?"

I nodded with empathy. Jean laughed for some reason and then grew serious again. "Emperor Frederick could have been a wonderful king," he went on, looking back at the treetops. "If only he really governed here himself. But that will never happen. In three years, his son Conrad will come of age and reign in Jerusalem. And if *he* should marry a daughter of the land and produce offspring, then the Holy Kingdom of Jerusalem will shine like a pearl in the crown of Christendom, as it deserves."

I couldn't help but smile, and Jean smiled with me. He poured wine for us both.

"You wanted to tell me why you hate de Brienne so much," I said when his silence grew long.

"Indeed, my lady." He sipped from the wine and continued. "Thibaut arrived last September with a large corps and good intentions. He lingered in Acre longer than he might have—if mostly because he wanted to properly understand the complexity of the kingdom's arrayed forces. At the start of winter, we began to move south, with the aim of strengthening the fortifications of Jaffa and Ashkelon.

"When we camped in Jaffa, two of the barons who came with Thibaut made a fortuitous assault on a caravan of Saracens and returned with a haul of looted treasure. De Brienne was deeply jealous. He pressured some other foreign barons to embark on a hasty and irresponsible attack, fattening their inflated heads with promises of treasure and glory. Bar and Burgundy, Thibaut's longtime rivals, joined forces with Gautier.

"My brother and I tried to dissuade them from the foolish adventure, and Thibaut refused to join his knights in the attack, but de Brienne and his group did not listen. They left Jaffa, where we were camped, in the dead of night, and we went with them so as to try to prevent a crushing defeat. But we failed—many of our best men were killed, and even more were captured, and we were forced to return north in disgrace." He paused and then added in a raspy voice, "The Saracens were full of fighting zeal and gathered their forces, and a month later we lost Jerusalem." He turned his face away.

I could not imagine what that city, my birthplace, meant to him. I was already totally disconnected from it, but its streets and buildings and walls and stairways were building blocks in many of my dreams, and sometimes I even had flashes of it during the day, as if it were branded on my nervous system. Jean took a deep breath and went on. "De Brienne, a fat peacock like him, doesn't even understand where he went wrong. He was raised on the exaggerated legends of his uncle, our poor King Jean de Brienne, who showed so much promise at the start of his reign and was so pitiful at its end." Jean's eyes blurred. "He was the greatest failure of a king in the history of our kingdom, apart from Guy de Lusignan." Here, Jean spat with an expression of disgust, and I jumped a little in surprise. "This overgrown baby, Gautier, thinks that all that is needed to be successful is a strong attack. He does not understand that the attack is just the head of the spear of calculated and meticulous planning, which takes into account all possibilities, resources, and consequences.

"Now, we have a golden opportunity that will not repeat itself," Jean said animatedly, running his hand over his beard. "The internal conflict between Damascus and Egypt could give us an advantage in our diplomatic efforts, and if Thibaut plays his cards right, he may recover many of our possessions, perhaps even control of Jerusalem, and all this without shedding a drop of blood, perhaps.

"But de Brienne continues to drip poison in his ear and in those of the other barons in the council of nobles, instigating fighting and disputes," said Jean with disgust. I almost thought he might spit again. "All he desires is to charge at the head of a company of armored knights with his family's flag flying over him. I pray he will find himself weltering in his own blood." Jean shook his head and turned to me, smiling.

"I must have bored you to death, my lady," he said with a look of self-criticism. "When I should be reading you the poem I wrote for you or kissing your neck," he said, taking up my hand and kissing it lightly.

"It's actually really interesting, but you did not tell me much new information," I said with the raised eyebrows of a know-it-all. "I read everything I could about you and the conflicts between the Ayyubid emirs."

"What do you mean?" Jean asked, shaken, and pulled away from me. "Where did you read that? How?"

"I . . . I . . . read about it in an encyclopedia," I said, embarrassed, frightened by his suspicious eyes. I could not remember when exactly they had started compiling encyclopedias.

"I do not understand what you are saying," said Jean, still tense. His eyes, wandering with concern, landed on the spring. He returned his gaze to me, calmer now. "You're from . . . from the future," he said, as if reassuring himself that everything was all right.

"In my time, there are many books about the history of the kingdom," I tried to explain in a way that would sound reasonable to him. "Quite a lot of books. I read some of them to better understand what was going on here. They describe Thibaut's crusade—"

"Really?" said Jean, a sparkle of pleasure in his eyes, like a child. "Eight hundred years from now, they still remember our deeds of glory?"

"Your name is recalled more than once in the story of the days of the kingdom." That was the truth; here and there, I had managed to find references, if rather laconic, about Jean d'Ibelin, Count of Arsur. I tried not to think about the fact that Jean's near future was in fact my distant past.

"I do not dare ask in what way my name is remembered," said Jean. He shivered. Brunette came back under the canopy of the tree and pressed her nose against his.

"Rightly so," I replied, squirming a little. "I think it's forbidden for me to tell you anything. It could make for terrible problems in the time-space continuum," I added. Jean looked at me as if I had just vomited up a frog.

"Never mind," I sighed and scratched Brunette behind the ears. "Do you know what time it is?" It must have been several hours since I had left the house, but it was hard for me to guess how many. Three, five, or seven? Time passed differently here, without the steady beat of clocks to measure it.

"That is a question that you ask again and again," said Jean, his pretty eyebrows knit together in wonder. "I do not understand your meaning. Do you want to know if it is already the hour for prayer?"

"No, no . . . ," I laughed. "I want to know if I am late getting home. They're waiting for me there," I added sheepishly.

"Why do you not look at the sun?" Jean asked, still looking at me as if at a slow child.

I coughed in embarrassment. Should I tell him about the Industrial Revolution and the structure and importance of hours in the modern day? I decided to put that off until another opportunity. "Never mind," I said. He smiled at me, cupped my face in his hands, and said, "Never mind, really." We kissed for a few moments, but after several seconds, he pulled away from me and gestured with his head to the place where Hugh was stationed, still and inert as a statue, with his back to us.

"Is spouse breach really acceptable in your time?" Jean then asked, with just a tiny dastardly twinkle in his eye. "Does your husband know that you are spending time with another man?" The question seemed to genuinely interest him. I tried to answer him honestly.

"It's much more acceptable but still considered a sin," I said, choosing my words carefully. "And my husband . . . he is no small 'spouse-breacher' himself. But he does not exactly know about this, no. Not just now, anyway." I did not know how Jean would accept my dubious ideas regarding sexual freedom, and I did not wish to put that to the test right now. I went on before he managed to respond. "And does your wife know that you are a spouse-breacher, my lord?" I allowed myself a tiny glimmer of mischief in my expression too.

Jean looked at me for some time without answering, and a smile slowly spread across his face. It seemed to me that he was considering this question for the first time. "I will take your example, my witty lady, and answer as you do: 'Not at this moment,'" he said. I wanted to ask if his wife might be committing adultery herself, perhaps at this precise moment, but I stopped myself. I had the feeling that this would amuse him much less.

I tried to think of an excuse to somehow send that damned Hugh away, but I could not think of anything. I looked up between the branches of the treetop—the sun was already closer to the sea than to the middle of the sky, and I shifted uncomfortably. My thoughts returned to the factory clock.

"I brought you something," I remembered happily and started rummaging in my bag for the Renault car plans I had printed. So as not to wrinkle them, I had put the pages into plastic page protectors. Jean's eyes opened wide when I pulled them out, and he nearly grabbed the plastic from me.

"What is this wondrous thing?" he asked in amazement as he examined the page protector from every angle.

"It's plastic, a kind of material that will only be invented in a few hundred years," I said, amused by the way he put his whole hand into the page protector, pulled it out, and looked with interest at how the thin plastic stuck back to itself. "It is indeed very strong and durable, but it is also the scourge of our time. It does not break down, and it's polluting the whole world."

He was entirely captivated as I showed him how the plastic was also impenetrable to water, dirt, and practically everything else.

He asked if he could keep this "amazing material" and wanted to know all about it. "I can begin to explain, but that is not what I wanted to show you, and I should really get home soon," I said. Reluctantly, he drew his gaze from the page protector and returned it to me. "Do you remember how I told you about our beastless chariots? I brought you sketches of such a chariot," I explained, holding the pages out to him.

Jean took them with what looked to me like holy reverence. "Such fine paper . . ." he muttered and began to flip through the diagrams. I had no idea if he managed to understand anything.

"Did you sketch all this?" Jean whispered and swallowed.

"You think?" I laughed. "I found them in a book and used a copy machine," I simplified things for him.

"Holy Father who art in heaven, have mercy on us," Jean muttered. "I cannot look at this just now." He groaned, tucked the pages into the page protector with determination, folded everything carefully, and placed it in his side bag. Then, he stared for a few seconds into the air with a focused expression.

"Hugh," he said with just the slightest raising of his voice. The squire turned around at once. "Come and pray with us."

This surprised me. Evidently, it surprised Hugh too. He joined us in respectful silence.

"Did you know, Cousin, that the remains of the holy Euphemia were discovered in this very spring by the Bishop of Acre about twenty years ago?" Jean said in a tour guide's voice.

I did not know who the holy Euphemia was, though Jean's oily rival had mentioned her in the fortress courtyard. But I had heard of the Acre bishop, or at least one of them, thanks to Simone Halimi.

"Bishop de Vitry?" I asked in the faint hope of demonstrating some sense of time and space.

Hugh gaped at me, and Jean flared his nostrils, overcome by a smile.

"His Holiness, the Bishop de Vitry, yes," he said patiently. "Please, do not disrespect our saints just because of the negligible differences between the Armenian and Roman churches. We are all God-fearing Christians."

"I apologize," I muttered, downcast. "I did not mean any lack of respect." I was a little annoyed with Jean for complicating things for me theologically.

"Not to worry," Jean said good-spiritedly. "Let us kneel."

The three of us got down on our knees, faces turned to the fortress. Hugh, then Jean, with me beside him. I pursed my lips in an attempt to remain serious.

Jean began to recite some prayer in Latin, and I tried to blend in with a murmur steeped in religious devotion. The two of them closed their eyes, so I did as they did. For a moment, I felt Jean's shoulder press against mine, but when I opened my eyes, he was not close to me—the whole thing unnerved me a bit.

"And now, Cousin," said Jean after the three of us muttered, "Amen," "we shall leave you alone with your reflections in this holy place. Are your companions to come and fetch you?"

I nodded carefully. Jean had high expectations regarding my speed of perception.

"Hugh," Jean turned to the young squire. "Please ride to the guards and ask them, in my name, if there have been any unusual happenings in the area in the last few days. I will join you presently." Hugh nodded, good-naturedly muttered, "Yes, sir," and went at once to untie his horse. It appeared that the prayer had calmed and appeased him.

"He is a very pious young man," Jean said, as if reading my thoughts.

I did not know how to respond. Suddenly, I felt very embarrassed.

"So . . . will we meet next week? Same time and place?" I asked with all the matter-of-factness I could muster.

Jean smiled and pulled me to him.

"The fairy Édith from the Holy Spring," he said into my hair and inhaled me deeply. "Fragrant as springtime, quick of tongue, full of riddles and wondrous objects, the lady of the magical passage."

I practically fainted with longing. I would have given him everything in that moment. But Jean d'Ibelin, Count of Arsur, was calculated as usual. He held my hand and kissed it, looking up at me apologetically. "We will meet again, O gracious lady," he said. "Without prying eyes and gossiping tongues." We parted, and I made for home.

CHAPTER 18

I have to fuck someone to save my marriage. This was repeating in my head as I wandered the streets of Tel Aviv after my fight with Halimi about everyone at the magazine knowing of his affair with Nina. The wind was blowing, lifting leaves and dust into the air. Usually, autumn heralded the return of life to Tel Aviv, but this autumn cooled slowly and would not satisfy my yearning for rain. It had been several hours, but I did not respond to Halimi's phone calls or text messages until he stopped trying. *Let him suffocate with Nina and Lana Del Rey and all of* Free to Be, *where they're probably taking bets on the chances of Halimi and me splitting up.*

Someone to fuck, but who? Who? I had not taken any phone numbers from my little nightclub adventures. I was cold, and I went into a rundown bar on Bograshov. I ordered a shot of vodka and a Coke on the side, then another shot. A group of American men sat at one of the tables inside, noisily drinking beer. I scanned them out of the corner of my eye to assess if there might be a worthy candidate among them to save my marriage. After the second shot, the sight of their overgrown, infantile bodies, the pastel colors of their clothes, their light hair and cheerful noise made me ill. I ordered another shot. I looked the barman over. He had bad teeth and thin hair. He also seemed exhausted and did not look at me when he served the shots. In the corner sat a man probably some twenty years older than me, staring sadly at his big glass of beer.

I took out my phone. I looked through Halimi's messages with apathy: "Ditush, please get back to me," "Ditush, just please don't do anything too stupid." I wondered, with detachment, what he would consider too stupid at this point. I began to scroll through Nina's profiles—until I came across a flattering selfie of her in bed, her thick hair spread luxuriantly over a purple satin pillow with the prominent logo of some textile company that she also bothered to tag. Influence queen.

I went through my contacts. I stopped at our electrician, who was not bad-looking and always flirted with me. I opened WhatsApp and thought about writing him a message. I had no idea what his romantic status was, and I hadn't seen him in more than six months. I went back to my contacts list.

I had nearly reached the end when I got to Ronen, the guy I had abandoned without a hint of remorse in favor of Halimi, back at that roof party thrown by Hila and her ex-husband. Ronen was online. The quiet Ronen, the wannabe hipster whom I dated for maybe three months. I had seen him three or four times since then, and both of us were courteous. We had occasionally liked each other's Facebook posts about various social or political matters. I tried to remember our first dates. He had the dry, measured sense of humor of a fundamentally grumpy person, which captivated me, initially.

I went into his Facebook profile. Sparse, mostly posts of articles from alternative media sources. I went through the few pictures, which were virtually all tags of him at other people's parties. Then, I quickly went to Twitter to read his tweets from recent months. More active than on Facebook, that's for sure, and he even had a few funny tweets, deciphering street signs, that kind of nonsense. I had the feeling that he was single. The vodka made me feel reckless, and I went back to WhatsApp. He was still online. Without pause, I texted, "Hey, what's up?" The message was read within several seconds. Pause. *Ronen is typing . . .*

"Fine." Smiley with glasses emoji. "How are you?"

"Not great," I replied at once. "Want to meet up?"

Ronen is typing . . .

"In bed already," he wrote finally. "It's gross out. Want to come by?"

"Where do you live these days?" I typed quickly. I signaled to the barman that I wanted the bill. A booming laugh came from the group of young Americans. The sad old guy in the corner looked up from his beer with a start.

"Corner of Pinsker and Bograshov," Ronen wrote. I got off the barstool, swaying slightly, and even laughed to myself. "On my way," I messaged.

"Won't you miss me terribly?" Halimi asked. We were lying on the couch, me after a smoke on the balcony and him after bathing Lily and putting her to bed. I didn't feel like watching anything on TV.

"Terribly," I smiled and laid my head on his chest. He was supposed to go in two days, and I tried to look like someone who was not counting the hours. Not that I was suffering his presence—on the contrary. The whole week until he left, in the mornings after Lily went off to preschool, we were swept up into loud sex, and in the evenings, we chatted endlessly and laughed a lot.

I noticed that Halimi and I were enjoying each other with an intensity that could only be compared to our first year together. I did not try to analyze this with him. I simply enjoyed Halimi's brilliant mind, his sharp and sarcastic comments about the things that we saw, that were happening in the world, and the heightened sexual desire, both mine and his.

"Mama, put on a dress," Lily had said earlier at dinner. I did not ask why and just smiled at her. I was in a house dress anyway, but she must have meant her favorite dress, which I only wore on festive occasions: a frock with black velvet on top and a chiffon skirt that I had to model for her at least once every few days.

"We have the most beautiful mama in the world, right, Loosh?" said Halimi. "With or without the dress," he added. I slapped him, and we laughed. Lily was ecstatic over the slap and wanted to slap both of us all evening.

"What do you love to do most?" I asked her in the bath, taking a video on Halimi's smartphone. "To slap!" Lily roared and splashed wildly. I burst out laughing, and Halimi's phone nearly fell into the water. Everything was documented, including my perfect rescue, and in the evening, after Lily fell asleep, we watched it maybe seven times in a row. Halimi sent the video to his mother.

The knowledge that in just a few days, an entire week of solitary independence awaited me—a week in which I would be answerable only to myself, with no schedule but the one I chose, and free to visit Jean and be with him without the pressure to hurry home—filled my heart with pure delight. This was more than just time off: I hadn't been alone for more than a single day in years. The excitement that I would have a whole week to myself also caused me bursts of tenderness and a kind of advance longing for both Lily and Halimi. Every day, we took her straight from preschool to the sea, and we basked in the spring sun and played in the waves for hours.

I told my parents and Halimi that I would be going to a Vipassana retreat so would not be available most of the time, but I would check messages every now and then.

"Vipassana, huh?" Halimi replied, narrowing his eyes in amusement when I told him this. I had just come home from a yoga class. We had meditated in the studio, and I felt so good that nothing could pierce my euphoria. I registered and paid for the workshop on the association's website, so that the charge would appear on the card.

"It'll be good for me to be quiet for a bit, I think," I said and held back an inappropriate giggle.

"With dozens of strangers, definitely," Halimi agreed, also amused.

"It really does sound interesting to me," I said honestly. Did he sense anything? It was impossible to know with Halimi. And I didn't care. He was also in the best mood I had seen him in since the Nina thing blew up. He would look up at me suddenly from his phone or from the book he was reading and smile.

When we were at the beach, which could be pretty stormy this time of year, Halimi ran into the waves and swam out far but still had energy for Lily afterward, spending a long time with her in the shallow water. He built castles with her and took long walks to look for shells and stones and crabs, while I lay on the beach mat, ignoring the ruins of the fortress. When I did focus my gaze there, the walls that once surrounded it rose up in my mind's eye, and the towers appeared in the air, and I could almost hear the voices from the town. I wanted to keep things separate, so I tried not to look for too long. Sometimes, in the distance, I noticed waterfowl flying over and into the salt ponds. Here and there, I spotted a pink flash of a flamingo, one of the last to linger into the summer migration, and I'd shout over to Halimi and Lily, "Look, look!"

"Well?" Ronen asked, in the tone of "What brings you here?" He was in sweatpants and a T-shirt, and it was clear that he really had intended to go to sleep already (*Good God, at ten thirty*, I thought as I entered his sad apartment, which was almost entirely dark, illuminated only by the light of a small lamp in the living room.)

"I thought of you suddenly," I said, clearly embarrassed. I took off my coat but held it on my knees, ready to escape. Ronen did not offer me anything to drink. I was still a little unstable after my shots at the bar. As I walked from Bograshov Street to Ronen's apartment, I had imagined myself telling him, "I am looking to get fucked because I need to save my marriage, are you able to help me?" But now, it did not seem fitting at all.

Ronen no longer had his trendy little beard, but his hair was actually longer, like a teenager whom nobody could force to get a haircut. There was something slightly attractive about him and the relaxed indifference with which he looked at me. I remembered that sex with him was not particularly good. I desperately wanted a cigarette, but it did not look like a smoker's house.

"You have a daughter, no?" he asked suddenly.

"Yes," I replied mechanically. "She's with her dad." People always acted like it was some kind of phenomenon worth investigating, a mom out of the house at night. Usually it didn't bother me, but I thought I heard a moralizing tone.

"So, you came for . . . ?" I knew that he meant to ask clearly if I had come to sleep with him, but evidently he, too, had lost his assertiveness mid-sentence. It made me sad that I was so transparent. Any hint of desire completely disappeared in that moment.

"Yes," I said and got up. "Sorry. And sorry that I was rude to you at that party when we separated."

"Separated," Ronen snorted. "Maybe it would come full circle if we screwed now," he added, looking me up and down, almost expressionless. *Screwed*, I thought to myself. *Ew.*

"But it isn't quite right, is it?" I said, holding my jacket closer. "Right?"

"Not really, no," said Ronen, wrinkling his nose.

CHAPTER 19

I took a deep breath and looked around with satisfaction. The cleaning lady had just left, and five days of immaculate, untarnished orderliness stretched before me—no ashtray overflowing with Camel cigarette butts and cups of black coffee all over the house, no socks and shoes kicked off and left on the floor, no hot chocolate stains on the carpet or little plastic Kinder Egg remnants scattered to distant reaches. It was funny that I took so much pleasure in my spotless home, considering that it was not where I planned to spend my time.

Home . . . I was charmed and amused by my proud sense of ownership regarding the house in Atlit, as if I had built it with my own hands. I loved the balcony like an old friend, and I still explored the charms of the yard with the care and curiosity of a new relationship.

Halimi had left early in the morning the day before, and a few hours later, Lily and I met my parents in Tel Aviv with a well-packed bag and a detailed list of explanations and instructions. We sat at one of the overpriced plastic-chaired restaurants on the beach under a big umbrella, and Lily sat beside us, digging in the sand. My father leisurely drank a beer, and my mother inhaled tomato juice through a straw with great pleasure. I had a cappuccino and thought about the joint I would smoke when I parted from them. I could not help but notice how much wilder the beach was in Atlit, how the sea there looked bluer and cleaner.

"Are you worried, Ditinka?" My father asked me in Russian.

"Actually, I'm not worried at all," I replied in Hebrew. "I trust you guys completely." I went on in Russian. "Lily too," I smiled. "But maybe take her to the zoo or to a show or something," I added. I wasn't worried, but I felt guilty—for handing my daughter over to my parents, who were no longer young, and planning to disappear completely, with no possible way of reaching me.

"What is this *shmipassana* of yours, anyway?" my mother inquired. A few years ago, a question like that would have annoyed me; I would have thought that she was doing it deliberately, pretending that she didn't understand even though I had vaguely explained it to her over the phone. But ever since Lily was born, I had developed a new softness with my mother, almost as if she were my other child.

"Vipassana," I corrected her and laughed. "It's silent meditation."

"Silent?" My father asked with interest but then added, "Why do you have to go somewhere and pay money to be quiet?"

"I will let you know after I do it." I was uncomfortable again, this time on account of the outright lie.

By the time I left Ronen's place at about eleven, I had, unfortunately, sobered up entirely. I considered going back to the depressing bar on Bograshov, but my feet took me to the Minzar bar instead. I did not want to run into any friends or acquaintances, but I did want to be some-place familiar.

My phone vibrated in my pocket. Another message from Halimi. Earlier that evening, I had changed my WhatsApp settings so that no one could see when I was last online or if the message had been read. I had a strong feeling that Halimi had done precisely the opposite.

"Ditush," the message appeared on my home screen. "Please come home, we'll talk about it, we'll fix it."

I ignored him. I knew that I would go home eventually, but I was enjoying this sense of satisfaction too much to give up so soon.

Another message. I looked at it while walking.

"If you don't respond to me in the next ten minutes, I'm calling the police."

Idiot, I thought. *Let him call.*

It had gotten colder, and I was shivering in my thin shirt, so I walked faster. There were lots of people out in the streets, but everyone was walking quickly, trying to take cover from the ugly wind spreading dust and sand. As I neared the Minzar, I recognized a familiar figure sitting alone, her back against a wall.

Maybe my obsessive probing of all of her profiles had burned her image into my brain. I stopped where I was and sat down on some dirty step in the dark, a few meters away. I opened her Instagram profile. The last post was a selfie in the bathroom. Location: the Minzar. Time of upload: twenty minutes earlier. I had not been mistaken.

I went onto her Twitter. "Being stood up gives me more time with the person whose company I enjoy most in the world," posted five minutes earlier. *Only six likes*, I noted with a sense of schadenfreude.

Who had stood her up? Halimi? Could it be that while he was pleading with me to come home, he was actually supposed to be meeting her? Rage coursed through my veins like some acidic, all-consuming poison.

Maybe her date was with someone else, and you're just blowing everything out of proportion. Or maybe she was just tweeting to annoy me or Halimi. I let my suspicion and jealousy run wild, wringing out the pain. But if she hoped that Halimi was going through her newsfeed to decipher the hidden messages, I knew from personal experience that she would be disappointed.

Then again, I thought, staring at her lonesome figure in the distance like a lioness watching its prey, *maybe it's different with her. Maybe he does go through her profiles to figure out what she's thinking and how she spends her time.* I wallowed in this thought like a pig in mud.

I imagined him admiring her at work, and at her place while she prepared cider, and when she took photos of herself and he stayed outside the frame, and when she got dressed after they had sex. My whole body grew weak, and I sank into the cold, dirty stone picturing this, and for a moment I considered just falling asleep there like a homeless person.

Several times I almost managed to get up from the filthy step, each time with a different intention: to pass by her and go inside without a glance in her direction, or to sit beside her and stare intently at her, or to sit across from her and act like I hadn't seen her there. For a moment, I even imagined us having a heart-to-heart conversation, woman to woman. But when I finally managed to get up, I left. Then, I got a call from the police, and I told them that my husband was hysterical and that I was on my way home.

I woke up on my couch in Atlit, and for several seconds longer than usual, I had no idea what time or what day it was and where Halimi and Lily were. Then, I remembered, with a burst of joy that I almost couldn't bear: Halimi was in Portugal—he had messaged me a funny selfie the night before from the hotel, which looked pretty nice (I sent him back a haiku); Lily was with my parents (I'd received a full report from my mother first thing in the morning); and the pantry had enough stovetop coffee for the next six months. I also had excellent weed.

After my parents took Lily, I went from the beach restaurant down to the shore. I sat down facing the waves and smoked a joint. I could still feel Lily's embrace when we parted, and suddenly my eyes filled with tears.

"Mama, you aren't coming with us?" she had asked me, not with surprise—after all, I had explained the arrangement to her several times—but more like someone making sure everything was going according to plan.

"No, sweetheart," I told her and hugged her tight. "You're going with Grandma and Grandpa. You'll have so much fun together, and I'll come get you in a few days."

"Will Daddy come too?" she asked, kicking at the sand with her sandal.

"We'll meet Daddy after," I said, "and he'll bring you presents."

"Daddy'll bring me presents!" Lily informed my mother.

"He's a good father," said my mom and straightened the strap of her purse. "Come, sweetie, we don't want to get stuck in traffic."

Last week, Jean and I had scheduled for the following day. The days were getting muddled for me lately, and I needed to check the calendar every time I tried to remember what day of the week or date of the month it was—but the date I had set with Jean felt like it had a magnetic pull.

Maybe I'll go there now, I thought suddenly as I caught my breath. *What's stopping me, actually?*

I lay on the couch and went back over every detail of my last visit. *Better to stick with the plan*, I told myself, *so I don't find myself in some medieval dungeon.* I shivered until my teeth chattered. *Okay, all right*, I acknowledged to some unknown and invisible entity, *I will not go to Jean today, I will go tomorrow, as we planned.*

I went over to the fridge and took out red caviar, butter, and champagne. I made myself a few slices of bruschetta and ate them while sipping champagne and reading the French manuscript.

The next morning, I shuffled into the bathroom. My face was a little puffy from sleep, and maybe also from the champagne that I drank too much of yesterday. Behind my hair, a sliver of sea glimmered in the window. I got into the shower.

I sat beneath the flow of cold water and considered what to take with me for my time travel today. *Will I sleep there, in the thirteenth century? In Jean's beautiful canopy bed? Should I take a T-shirt to sleep in? Or maybe a more suitable nightdress? Maybe the slip that went under the dress that Jean gave me could work as pajamas? Spare contact lenses? Glasses? A toothbrush? Definitely not a charger. Relax. Stop thinking so much. Breathe. Let go.*

I drank coffee and called my parents. "She's just wonderful," my mother told me in Russian, and in the background, I heard my father bargaining pleasantly with Lily over a candy in exchange for finishing her toast. "I don't understand why we didn't do this sooner," she added. "By the way, have you spoken with Dinka lately?" It was clear to me that my mother was planning to use Lily's stay as a precedent with which to tempt my sister to send her children for an extended vacation in Jerusalem.

"Actually, no," I said. I was also surprised. We had texted in the last few days, but the preparations for Halimi's and Lily's respective trips—along with my endless sinking into musing—did not leave me any spare time or need for the usual idle conversations with Dina.

"Okay, Mom, I have to go," I told her quickly, sending kisses and hugs and forgoing exchanging a few words with Lily so that she would not suddenly miss me terribly. *Bad—bad mother*, I reprimanded myself while packing a bag as I would for Vipassana, minus the change of clothes. I took a few pairs of underwear, just in case.

With great attention to detail, I put on the entire system of dress that Jean had given me on my previous visit to the fortress, including the socks with the ties and the pretty shoes. I carefully put on the complicated head covering in front of the mirror. I photographed my image with my crappy old phone. I looked at the picture on the tiny screen for several seconds: a pixelated ghost image.

I double-checked that my little bag had Lily's ten-agorot coin tucked inside. The Ibelin coin hung around my neck, as always. While I got ready (*On the morrow*, Jean's calm voice echoed in my head. *And don't rush inside the fortress if I should be a little late, my lady.*), I received a text from Halimi.

"Having fun in total silence?"

"On my way," I replied curtly but added a smiley. After all, I was supposed to be on my way to the Arava desert right now, driving toward three days of Vipassana. "And how's it going over there? Rubbing shoulders with the stars? Eating calamari?" I added after a few minutes, theoretically taking advantage of a red light. There was no response. When I went to pee before heading out, my phone rattled. Halimi wrote, "Minimal rubbing. Miss you guys. Have fun my love." I smiled and hugged him tightly in my heart.

About two months ago, the thought of him working on a project for *Free to Be* in Europe, outside my range of monitoring, would have made me lose my mind. I imagined Nina flying especially to oversee the article and misbehave with Halimi. I expected an outburst of hatred to wash over me, but it did not come. I tried again for several minutes. I stared into space and imagined Halimi and Nina meeting in Lisbon. How they would sit and drink Madeira and then go up to his hotel room. She would say she was not actually up to it, and then he would seduce her anyhow. I remained unaffected. If anything, it turned me on a little. I shook my head in disbelief. For a moment, I thought about going to my laptop and rummaging around in Nina's Facebook profile, just to see if I was right—she would definitely post about it if she was in Portugal. I took one step toward the computer and then let it go, and at once felt weightless.

Before leaving, I cast one final look at my clean, pretty house, and suddenly a heretical thought crossed my mind—wouldn't it be even more fun to just lounge around at home for a few days? To lay around smoking pot from morning to night, reading, sleeping until God knows what hour, feasting on smoked salmon and meat dumplings in cream?

Twang, twang. The strings played between my ears as I recalled the first time I saw Jean, lighting a hookah with hashish and sharing a bit of bread with me. I left the house and locked the door.

CHAPTER 20

When I came in, Halimi would not look at me. He stood by the window, smoking, drinking a whiskey. "Haven't you had enough for one evening?" I asked drily when I saw the empty bottle, which had been nearly full when I left the house.

He gritted his teeth.

"Was that enough for you?" he asked, finally looking at me, his eyes cold and venomous.

"Aww, are you feeling a little fragile?" I shot back in a high voice that sounded annoying even to me.

"Idit," Halimi said with meticulous enunciation. "This is not about my feelings. There's a little girl here. You can't just storm off and disappear. I called the police."

I snorted derisively.

"So, when you fuck your colleague and disappear night after night, that's fine for the little girl?" I asked, my voice twisting with sarcasm. "That little girl loves you and misses you, and I'm the one who has to lie to her and tell her that you're running late at work every night." I could feel the back of my throat. I clenched my fists hard to try to stop the tears from coming.

Halimi took one drag on his cigarette and then crushed it into the ashtray.

"I'm going to bed," he said.

Halimi retreated to the bedroom, and I rolled a cigarette and smoked it with trembling hands, sniffling by the window. I took a sip of what was left in the whiskey glass and shuddered. Then, I emptied the ashtray and put the whiskey glass in the sink. I brushed my teeth and hoped with all my heart that Halimi was already asleep. I could not handle hearing his voice.

When I crept into the bedroom, I could tell that he wasn't asleep yet, even though he was lying on his back with his eyes closed. I went over to the closet and, with some effort, took a duvet cover from the top shelf.

"So, am I allowed to ask where you were?" asked Halimi. Still cold, but no longer the ice fields of Antarctica. I stayed standing by the closet, with the duvet cover in my arms. I decided on the less circuitous route.

"I went to Ronen's, if you remember him."

"You went to who?" Halimi sat up straight. Typical of Halimi not to remember the names of my exes. I could list the names of the girls I knew who had had any kind of relationship with Halimi.

"Ronen," I said with fatigue. "The guy I was with before you. Pretzel Crumbs." That was our code name for Ronen, the few times we had referred to him—mainly in our first couple of months together, when faint hints of his pale presence still appeared among my belongings ("What are you doing with this god-awful toothpaste?" "Oh, Pretzel Crumbs left it at my place once.")

"Ew, you went to fuck that worm?"

"Yes," I said wearily.

"And did you get what you wanted?" Halimi asked and turned his back to me.

"It was just the right amount of repulsive," I said and left the room.

In the morning, Lily woke me up, jumping and excited and full of questions as to why I was sleeping in the living room. I told her that Dad snored too loud and that anyway, I wanted some air, which, I demonstrated to her, flowed more freely in the living room. Lily accepted this explanation without further questions. A little later, Halimi came home with a bag of fresh rolls, cottage cheese, and milk.

He didn't look at me and acted normal with Lily—alternately laughing and scolding her. He made her breakfast while I showered, and by the time I finished, they were ready to go, her to daycare and him to the magazine. Lily wrapped her little arms around my neck and planted two kisses on each cheek, and Halimi left the house without uttering a word to me, as if I weren't even there.

When I heard the door slam, I burst into tears. So, that was that—the love between us, the conversations, the explosive laughter, the gut-wrenching sex, the librarian who had tamed the libertine, the lounging around with Lily, the trips and reminiscing, our private lexicon—it was all gone.

I parked the car at the foot of Le Destroit, concerned that if the car stayed too long on the edge of the coastal road, someone would call and have it towed. I hoped that the trucks carrying building materials that parked there all the time wouldn't completely cover it with dust.

I got out of the car, dressed in my medieval lady's attire. I took my big green cotton bag, nice and inconspicuous, I hoped, and at the bottom of it, I buried a bright purple toiletry bag, a large plastic bottle full of cold water, my glasses case, spare contact lenses, and a few other essentials.

I walked over to the carob tree. The little puddle the size of a book was still there. I carefully dipped a finger into the puddle and at once felt a kind of tingling. I took out my razor, made a small cut in my finger, declared my intentions aloud, and held the Ibelin coin between my thumb and bleeding forefinger. I held my cloth bag tightly.

Relax. Stop thinking so much. Breathe. Let go.

I dipped my hand in. *One, two, three.*

The phosphorescent explosion in my head happened in slow motion as I was immersed in water. I was both the ever-burbling spring and also the tree from its top to its roots, and the earth to its unfathomable depths, and the sky and the sun and the moon and the stars. I relaxed, thought of nothing, breathed deep, and let go. I was borne on a huge wave, as big as a wall, and thrown to the ground.

Twang, twang, went the tender strumming of the delicate strings. *Twang, twang, twang.* I blinked toward the broad canopy of the tree. I heard hoofbeats or galloping, but belonging to a creature smaller than a horse, and as soon as I managed to sit upright, Brunette pounced on me, barking and licking.

"My lady, you're here!" I heard Jean's voice. He was sitting with his back against the tree, his lute resting at his side, and with one light step, he reached me and held my hand. The passage became more and more pleasant each time, but the awesome mystery had not diminished. I was indeed here, in the cooler air of 1240, in the shade of a carob tree with a fuller canopy than in my own time, and around us was quiet but for the twittering of birds and hum of insects.

"I did not see how . . . I did not hear you . . ." he mumbled in disbelief. I saw that he was very happy to see me, and I threw my arms around him at once without a word. The scarves fell from my hair.

Jean looked good, his amber eyes shining and his burgundy cotton robe fastened with a bright silver brooch. On his head was the hunting hat from last time, with a small, decorative white feather pinned to it. When I threw my arms around his neck, he leaned in to kiss me. My lips sunk into his soft beard with ravenous passion—afterward, I thought that maybe this had something to do with the stark difference from Halimi's always clean-shaven face. We kissed, gasping and with friction that produced sparks, and Brunette jumped around and barked happily. But my Crusader nobleman, as I had already noted more than once, was a calculated and considerate person, master of his urges. He broke away from me, albeit with some difficulty, and glanced back, past the canopy.

"One of the guards might come at any moment," he said, still a little wild-eyed. "Better to not begin our rendezvous with a disaster."

We both cleared our throats, giggled, and looked more intently at each other. Finally, he shook his head and said in a tone of urgency, "This is great luck, or mercy, that you turned up here now. I nearly despaired. Unfortunately, I cannot stay with you as long as I wish this time."

"Why not?" I asked with evident disappointment.

"I must ride to Acre . . . in fact, I should have departed yesterday, but I could not break my promise to meet you. When you delayed today, I thought to leave you a letter, but I did not know where to hide it."

"But must you leave at once?" I asked, trying to control my reaction.

"Not at once," Jean smiled. "Thibaut is still getting organized. I can sit with you for a while longer."

"And I thought that we would be able to spend more time together than usual," I said in a soft voice, trying very hard not to sound like a spoiled child. "I am on my own for the next four days, free to do as I please."

"What do you mean?" Jean asked in surprise. He patted the sheet of fabric beside the tree, and both of us sat down on it, shoulder to shoulder, hip to hip. "Maybe I should put the head scarf on first?" I asked bashfully. "Just in case one of the guards should come."

Jean reached out and stroked my hair and then wrapped my head with the cotton strip and the two cloths with his gentle, skilled hands. While he was doing this, I told him that my husband had traveled to another country and that my daughter was with my parents in Jerusalem. Jean hummed in response and went on carefully arranging the complicated head covering.

When I was ready, he produced his ceramic hookah and, with a wink, took out the lighter I had given him previously. To my amazement, he had clearly succeeded in putting it back together, and it even worked. He lit the coal. The lighter's flame was smaller than before. "Don't use it carelessly," I warned. "I think it's about to run out." I regretted the absence of the elegant show of friction with the flint rock and the pile of dry herbs.

Jean took a long inhale from the hookah and handed it to me. Then, he examined the lighter's small flame.

"Indeed," he said. "I recall you saying that it is a temporary magic, but you did not tell me the exact duration of the sorcery."

"It's not sorcery, it's technology," I said and took a hit from the hookah. "But it doesn't matter, I'll bring you ten more, if you want. A hundred more," I said smugly.

Jean smiled at me through eyes preoccupied by passing thoughts. He took out what looked like stuffed pastries and a few dirt-encrusted carrots with their leafy tops still attached. "Forgive me, my lady," he said and began to eat the pastry. "I did not yet get around to breaking my fast, and I did not want to start without you for fear of devouring it all by myself." He gestured with his hand to the pastries, and I took one too. It was stuffed with minced meat and maybe raisins, salty and sweet and delicious.

"Well," he said, after taking a sip of wine from a clay bottle. "Four days? In that case, perhaps you might like to accompany Thibaut, myself, and our party on our journey to Acre? I can make sure that you return here in time."

"To Acre with you?" I repeated after him, somewhat confused. "Let me think about that."

Jean smiled and took a carrot, washed the clods of dirt off in the spring, and bit into it. Brunette came over and sat before Jean expectantly.

"Go find yourself a little bird," Jean said to her. Brunette tilted her head and skittered out from under the canopy of the tree. Only now did I notice that beneath his yellowish tunic and his reddish cloak, Jean wore a chain-mail shirt, with a hood of the same material. On the ground beside the lute were leather gloves.

I very much wanted to see Acre in its prime, as the cosmopolitan capital of the Crusader kingdom and an important trading post on the Mediterranean—but the thought that I would have to travel far away from the spring alarmed me. My mind was racing. I was not ready to disappear back to my reality.

"Are there sacred springs in Acre or its surroundings?" I asked.

Jean gave me an inquisitive look and answered with a frown, "I do not know for sure."

"It frightens me to think I will put such distance between me and my passage," I said honestly and felt the disappointment spreading through me.

"I can understand that, Lady Édith. It is wise of you to wish to remain close to the opening to your world," Jean said softly.

We sat in melancholy silence for some time longer.

"You cannot make the trip four days from now?" I asked, heavy-hearted. "Say you are sick, or you have urgent matters to attend to or something . . ."

Jean smiled broadly. "For that, I would have to break every oath that I have ever sworn," he said, in a fatherly tone that I found slightly irritating and that at the same time aroused in me a desire to press my chest against his. "I must act quickly. One of the Hospitaller knights has just returned bearing sensational news that may tip the scales in our struggle. I must meet him urgently, and if he has good news for me, we will sail to Tripoli." I nodded as if I understood something of what he was saying.

I suddenly recalled the Renault diagrams. "Say . . . what about those Renault plans that I brought you? The sketches of the horseless chariot?"

The corners of Jean's mouth drooped, and the excessive smugness fell away. Now, his eyes wandered in embarrassment, eventually coming back to observe me.

"I presume that they have some power and knowledge that I can only dream of," he said longingly. "But I can hardly touch those pages, and looking at them demands extraordinary effort from me. As for understanding their meaning—utterly beyond my grasp."

Maybe I created a tear in the time-space continuum after all, I worried suddenly. Sketches of a Renault car in 1240—what was I thinking? I dipped my hand into the spring and let the fast stream envelop it. I felt better at once. My cell phone doesn't work here, not even my wristwatch, so the spring knows what it's doing. The currents swirling around my fingers produced bubbles that tickled. *Okay, so be it.* I dunked my face into the spring too. At once, I felt the all-embracing knowledge that lay within its eddies and pleased all the senses. I pulled my head out.

"All right," I said to Jean as I wiped my face on the edge of my scarf. "I will ride with you to Acre."

CHAPTER 21

For a while after Halimi called the police on me, we hardly spoke to each other. We were obliged to exchange a few words here and there regarding Lily or the household, but no more than that. He left early in the mornings, taking Lily to daycare on his way to work, and would come home very late, usually after I had gone to sleep.

When the winter rain eventually began, I tried to get used to life as a single mother. I prepared myself for my upcoming divorce proceedings. *All in all*, I told myself, *it's amazing we made it as long as we did.* When Lily asked me where Daddy was, I would tell her, with a lump in my throat, that he was at work. She didn't notice a thing—at least, so it seemed. Not the sadness that enveloped me, or the fact that Halimi was gone from morning to night for days at a time, or that I was cuddling her more than usual. I gave in to her every request—from walking to the park in the gloomy, drizzling afternoon, when no other living soul could be found among the soaking wet slides and jungle gym, to baking every kind of cake or cookie that she could think of, to repeated viewings of *Robin Hood*, *The Jungle Book*, and *Winnie the Pooh*.

I stopped obsessively stalking Nina. I did not check her socials anymore. During the daytime hours while Lily was at daycare, I took care of whatever household tasks needed attention and worked on my translation project in a state of numbness. In bed at night, Halimi and I slept without touching each other. He usually got into bed smelling of arak, with its licorice scent that I particularly loathed. If I was awake, I pretended to be asleep.

One night, he simply did not come home. No message, no nothing. I discovered this in the morning, when Lily crawled into our bed and I saw that the clock was showing eight-thirty. I got up with a sigh, made her breakfast, and got her ready and out the door to daycare. The teacher was surprised to see me since I was usually the one who picked her up in the afternoon, and she was unaccustomed to seeing me in the bright, cheery light of morning.

Lily was excited by this departure from routine. She demanded that we play with her favorite toys, and when I told her that I had to go, her face crumpled. She clung to me and shook her head "no" every time I moved to try to get up. I stayed there for almost an hour, until the children went to the playground, and even then I went with them and sat with the teacher, and we discussed the kids and the cost of living and Tel Aviv's best beaches, until I saw that Lily was entirely preoccupied with command-ing a little group in some complex game that involved the slide and the merry-go-round.

I told her that I was going, she gave me a distracted "Bye," and when I said goodbye to the teacher, she said, "These little ones, they notice every tiny change." I nodded with a smile of "You're so right."

I took a bus to the offices of *Free to Be*. I could have taken a taxi, but I was on an austerity kick, coming to terms with my foreseeable future. *Will I go back to living with roommates? With a child? Do people even do that? But of course Halimi will pay child support, that's how it works, right? On the other hand, he'll probably want shared custody—so what does that mean?* I planned to go online when I got home and clarify some of those details. *Do I know any lawyers?*

The *Free to Be* building was an old two-story building not far from the port, with the magazine's logo on the front. I smoked a cigarette and shivered a little in the cold.

I stubbed out my cigarette and went inside. The ancient security guard nodded to me, and I took the stairs to the second floor; the building's elevator opened directly in front of reception, and I did not feel like making a conspicuous entrance. I walked along the wall and feigned indifference to the deputy editors and their assistants, the producers and graphic designers and secretaries, all women. Here and there was the occasional, unobtrusive man. I hated everyone. I didn't expect anything from them. I did not think that they cared about me, and I loathed them passionately for being witnesses, even unwilling ones, to the circus of my life. That these insignificant people, so self-centered and young—as they appeared to me while I walked to Halimi's office—knew about his affair with Nina before I did.

One of the producers noticed me, waved exaggeratedly, and immediately said something to the woman at her side. She looked up at me, her eyebrows almost at her hairline. The two of them laughed to each other in a nauseating way, and I sped up. I knocked on the door out of habit, and as I was opening it, I heard Halimi bark, "Not now!"

I stood rooted to the spot. Nina jumped off of Halimi's lap.

"Ohmygod," she said.

I looked at the two of them without saying a word. Halimi stared at me in shock for a few moments, and Nina sat on the office chair before him and turned to me with an expectant look. All she was missing was popcorn.

"Ditush!" Halimi suddenly grew animated. "What happened?! Is everything okay with Lily? Where is she?"

"She's at daycare," I told him impassively. "She's fine." I tried very hard not to let any muscles in my face twitch. Lily was all that mattered to him. He probably didn't even remember that he had not come home last night.

"Idit," Halimi said nervously. "You look terrible." (Nina suppressed a snort of laughter.) "Want something to drink?"

"I want a divorce," I annunciated, looking right at Nina.

Nina whistled. "Hear, hear!" she said.

I looked at her without batting an eye, as if she were some inconsequential stranger at a bus stop that I was simply resting my eyes on.

"Neen, don't be mean," Halimi muttered, his eyes cast down.

"Tchhh," Nina snorted and shot him a look of disbelief. He looked plagued by guilt and regret, primarily—I could see clearly—because of Nina's vulgarity. When she did not receive so much as a look, Nina got up and left. *Neen.* He had a pet name for her. A wave of nausea passed through me. I breathed deeply and ordered the nausea away.

"Ditush," said Halimi after Nina slammed the door behind her.

"Don't call me that," I told him in a flat voice. His face crumpled.

"I'm not coming home today," I went on. "That is, to your house," I corrected myself matter-of-factly. "Do whatever you have to do to get Lily from daycare on time. I need to clear my head for a few days, and then I will let you know where I am so we can finalize how to arrange everything."

Halimi looked at me with eyes puffy from drinking and lack of sleep, overflowing with supplication and desire for atonement, but I was unmoved. I wasn't even disgusted. I took a step toward the door.

"Idit, wait," said Halimi.

I stopped.

"You were also at fault, Ditush," he said quickly, his usually careful diction giving way to a tone of urgency. "You did whatever you wanted for months, and then you totally brushed it off when I confessed that I was hurt by all your fuck-filled outings and . . . you left the house and scared me to death and didn't answer me when I was looking for you and . . . you fucked that disgusting guy just to get me back and . . . you laughed at me when I called the police, and you didn't even apologize." I guessed that he had gone over this list in his head a few times. "I didn't do anything to hurt you on purpose. Until then," he added, willing to take some responsibility.

"But you also didn't do anything to stop hurting me, even though you obviously saw that I was hurting, all that time, with you carrying on your affair with . . . *Neen*," I said scornfully.

Halimi sank into his chair. "You're just under the illusion that you know how to love, Saul," I told him mercilessly. "But you really have no idea what love is."

He looked up at me, tired.

"Maybe you can teach me?' he said, with a tiny flicker of Halimi-esque mischievousness, still hoping that he could repair the situation. I admit that something in my soul was stirred, but I was not shaken.

"When you love someone, you want them to be happy," I blurted, the line that had been in my head for the whole past week, the rusty nail in my heart. Halimi's shoulders slumped.

I opened the door and went out into the central space, where everyone looked down at their work and pretended like everything was normal. Nina was nowhere to be seen.

We stood at the junction where the carriage crossing—which stretched all the way from the fortress and emerged from a rock quarry to the point where we stood—met the ancient sea route of well-worn limestone, extending north to south, from Acre to Ashkelon. I sat in front of Jean d'Ibelin on his horse, Éclair, riding sidesaddle with both legs pointing left, out of modesty, per his instructions. It was very uncomfortable. When we had ridden like this previously, his body had served as a kind of support to lean on, and his arms as handles. Now, his body was shifted away from mine, and he instructed me to steady myself on the saddle and sit gracefully while holding onto the saddle's horn. My whole body was tense, trying not to slip and fall. Brunette trotted briskly at our feet, occasionally running ahead to Hugh, seated on a lively looking brown horse.

Several minutes passed until we heard galloping and saw a cloud of dust rising and then, what appeared at first glance to be a small army. There were about fifteen riders, some in varying shades of Ibelin red and yellow, and others decorated with the light blue, silver, and gold of Champagne. There were a few other colors that I did not recognize; maybe they had no meaning. Among them were four Templar knights with lowered helmets and white cloaks with large red crosses on them that widened toward their edges, protected by chain mail from head to toe; their stately horses were armored too. Four members of the party held the reins of additional horses, and a few moments later, a group of loaded mules appeared from behind, some of them ridden by villagers, and some of them roped to their companions.

Several of the villagers were wearing clothes that I recognized as Muslim: cotton djellabas, and their heads wrapped in light-colored cloths. *But how could that be?* I thought. *After all, the Crusaders were the bitter enemies of the Muslims.* I noted to myself to ask Jean about this later.

"Arsur!" called Thibaut as he stopped his beautiful black horse beside us. He was dressed lavishly, his robe so blue that it was almost painful to look at, with silver and gold embroidery sewn into it. He had a thin, golden crown on his head and looked utterly majestic. I was overcome with paralyzing humility. Cedrique and Brunette greeted each other, barking and sniffing. Two more hunting dogs joined them, lowering their heads and wagging their tails.

"Your Majesty," Jean bowed his head in respect.

"The fairy is here again?" he thundered. Behind me, I felt Jean wince slightly, but he dryly replied, "Your Majesty, it is my wish that Cousin Édith ride with us to Acre. I have mementos from my mother that I would like her to pass along to my sister." He and Thibaut looked at each other for several moments. Thibaut winked at me almost imperceptibly, then clapped Jean on the back.

"Certainly!" he declared loudly, and I saw some heads turning to look at him as they spoke among themselves. Thibaut went on in the same tone of proclamation, "Additionally, you found a pleasant way to spend the tedious hours of riding!"

Several of the knights smiled, and some of them returned to their conversations. I shot Jean a look that I hoped expressed both protest and amusement, and he gave me a subtle nod of reassurance.

"Your Royal Highness, you're incorrigible," Jean said, shaking his head at Thibaut with a tone of loving rebuke. Thibaut approached on his horse and took my hand (I was gripping the horn of the saddle tightly in my other hand). He kissed it with great ceremony, his beard and mustache tickling me, and looked up at me with a meaningful wink.

"My lady," he said.

"Your Majesty." I bowed my head humbly and, with the hand that he released, held the end of my dress. I did not dare let go of the saddle.

Jean got down off the horse with a graceful leap (I grabbed the saddle with both hands in response) and approached one of the other horses, a chestnut mare smaller than Éclair, which one of his men was holding. Jean took the reins, and the youth bowed his head enthusiastically.

"Come here, Cousin," he said to me as he brought the horse closer. "This is Rosette, my lovely mare. I brought her along to let her gallop a little and so that I could have a spare horse to alternate with, but she fits you perfectly."

I was wondering how exactly I would dismount from Éclair without completely humiliating myself in front of the group when strong hands gripped me, and only afterward did I understand that Thibaut, astride his horse, had lifted me and handed me to Jean, who caught me and set me down on the ground.

"Good God," I mumbled. *Seriously, so embarrassing. I must have blushed all over.*

Jean gave Thibaut another look of reproach. "Thank you, your Royal Majesty," he said grudgingly.

"My pleasure, my dear boy," Thibaut thundered again, then said in a quieter voice, "Now, present your fair relative to the people."

With the pleasant sensation that I already knew Jean's manner well enough, I could tell that he was flustered by the instruction, but his voice and body language were lighthearted when he said, "Good people, allow me to introduce my cousin from my mother's side, the Lady Édith of Cilicia, daughter of the illustrious Baberon family. She has traveled a great distance in order to make the pilgrimage to all the sacred places in the Kingdom of Jerusalem." The knights nodded their heads, and Jean introduced each one by name, most of which I forgot at once. "Now, if we have concluded with the decorum," said Thibaut a little pointedly, which struck me as unfair since it was he who had commanded Jean to make the introductions, "we shall continue on our way."

Thibaut turned his horse around magnificently and then cried in a booming voice, "Onward, good men! By the grace of God!" He took off along the seaside road to the north, his companions and the Templars breaking into a gallop after him. The group with the mules began to trudge along behind. Cedrique and the other dogs joined the entourage, and Brunette's eyes hung on Jean. He must have somehow signaled to her that she had full freedom of movement, and she ran toward the pack. A few of the knights remained at Jean's side, waiting on their horses.

Jean helped me up to mount Rosette, whispering instructions in my ear at the same time. The mare was calm and good-natured. I felt stupid sitting with both of my legs on one side instead of straddling the horse like a human being. The saddle was designed for male riders, and I had to tense several muscles I didn't know existed so as not to slip off. Jean held Rosette's reins at first, marching her back and forth ("You have to get used to each other") and then gave them to me. I stared at him in horror.

Jean smiled, shook his head, and walked over to Éclair, mounting him with an ease that looked like downright showing off. He began at a fast clip and then picked up the pace, suddenly speeding away. He clearly did not understand or was unable to conceive that I had never ridden a horse on my own. Hugh joined him at once, as did another rider, then two. I remained in my spot, beside two of Jean's other companions, who were clearly embarrassed. Finally, one of them pulled on Rosette's reins, and she began to trot. I gripped the saddle with both hands, trying to remain steady in this senseless position, until the man handed me the reins. Immediately, he and his friend increased their pace and pressed ahead. The mules and their riders looked at me, puzzled, and kept shuffling slowly forward.

The mare trotted at an easy pace, but I knew that any moment, I could fall off and crack my head. I pulled lightly on the reins, and the mare stopped calmly. I saw Jean trot back on his own.

"I told the others to join Thibaut," he said as he neared. "All is well, my lady?"

"Not in the slightest!" I barked. One of the villagers turned around on his mule and at once turned back away from us. "I can't ride like this!" I said more quietly. I did not look up at him.

I don't have to keep going, my spring is right here, I told myself, *and I can always go back.*

"Lady Édith, dear lady!" cried Jean. His voice was full of empathy and compassion, but it seemed as though he was actually holding back laughter. I felt as though I would soon slip from the saddle, and instinctively, I raised my right leg and moved it to the other side so that I was sitting astride the horse. I adjusted my position until I felt stable, and the mare let out a snort that I interpreted as agreement. I resumed breathing. I could feel Rosette better beneath me now, patient but tense.

"Either I will ride like this, or I will go back to the spring," I said, more resolved than threatening. "What do you say?"

Jean smiled broadly and ran his hand along the back of his neck. "Are you able to gallop like that?" he asked, and I nodded without conviction. He took a long breath and made a circle around Rosette with Éclair, pulling the ends of my dress from every side so that they covered the ribbons that fastened the socks to my legs. Jean raised his head, looking around for a moment—it was just the two of us, still several meters from the junction; even the mules had already put some distance between us—and kissed me tenderly. Even in my new position, I nearly succumbed to pleasure and slid off the mare.

He moved away, squinted and scanned me, smiled, and said, "Onward," urging his horse ahead. I stuck my feet lightly into the mare— it came totally naturally; evidently my subconscious had absorbed something from all the movies I'd seen—and Rosette began to walk. After a few meters, I squeezed the horse again, a little harder this time, and she began to trot.

Jean d'Ibelin, Count of Arsur, and I rode alongside each other. The wind blew around me, and I removed the delicate uppermost piece of the head covering and tucked it into my bag so it wouldn't fly away. My butt thumped along wildly, but I felt supreme pleasure at the mastering of this basic skill—riding a horse without falling off. Not a few minutes had passed, and we saw the main group in the distance, with the mules bringing up the rear.

Thibaut waved as we approached, and when we stopped, he scanned me in exaggerated wonder and then gaped at Jean. A few of the younger knights chuckled among themselves. I assumed my most confident, arrogant face befitting a lady.

"What's this?" Thibaut said aloud to Jean, casting glances at the knights and grinning. "Why does your cousin ride like a peasant woman?" A few of his companions chuckled, and Jean's knights frowned. "Should I regret not adding a confessor to our party?" Thibaut added to the cheers of the others.

"This is the riding fashion among the ladies of Cilicia, your Royal Highness," replied Jean, casting an encouraging look at me. "As my cousin is used to this style, she felt ill at ease riding in the manner of our ladies, and I permitted her to ride as she wished." I clenched my jaw so as not to smile at the word *permitted*.

Thibaut muttered something I did not catch, then clicked his tongue at his horse and broke once more into a light gallop. His men continued after him. The Templar knights, careful not to look at me directly through their menacing helmets, joined them. The villagers began walking. Jean's men cocked their heads at him.

"Accompany his Royal Highness, men," Jean said curtly and then turned to one of them and said, "Seigneur Amaury, you will be so kind as to stay within shouting distance. For whatever may be." The man, who bore a faint resemblance to Hugh but, I thought to myself, was older and seemed nicer, nodded.

Jean's men began galloping to catch up with Thibaut's group, and Amaury opened at a swift trot. For the length of the trip, he remained more or less equidistant between us and Thibaut's entourage.

"What could happen?" I asked Jean when we resumed trotting fast and steady. I tried to ask lightly.

"We are in relatively safe territory, Lady Édith," said Jean and looked at me, "but it is not entirely avoidable that the Saracens might attack our group." He said this as one might say, "A rainstorm is not out of the question."

"So, how do they typically attack? Charge with swords? Shoot arrows?" I tried to match his relaxed tone, but I surveyed the surroundings with increasing anxiety.

Jean chuckled. "Don't look so concerned, my lady. You are riding with the most skilled warriors, and what's more, there are four Templar knights riding with us. The chance of danger is very low—we are, after all, in the heart of the kingdom, and its boundaries are well guarded."

He looked totally calm and not like someone who anticipated an attack at any moment.

I concentrated on the physical pleasure of the ride, even if I had the feeling that soon all of my muscles would be sore. I saw Jean smiling broadly at me.

"Is this really, truly your first time riding a horse, Lady Édith?" he asked softly, still incredulous, as if both sympathetic and happy for me at the same time. I nodded, and a laugh bubbled up through me. I looked around—the figures of Thibaut and the rest looked small in the distance, and Seigneur Amaury was in "shouting distance." I blew Jean a coquettish kiss. He chuckled and shook his head, even as he reached out to stroke my arm. Then, he pulled back and brought his eyes back to the road. I sighed and resumed focus on the ride and the remarkable landscape all around us.

We stopped several times along the way: once in order to eat and drink and stretch our bones—Thibaut's men supplied pies, roast chicken, cheese, bread, root vegetables, and fruit; another time because the Templars, who were riding up front most of the time, warned of a convoy in the distance. Thibaut, Jean, and the knights surrounded me, and the Templar knights positioned themselves at the front. It turned out to be a convoy of pilgrims from Normandy on their way from Acre to Jerusalem, three families jostled in oxcarts, themselves accompanied by three Templar knights and a priest. The Templar knights of the two groups whispered among themselves for a few minutes. Then, everyone got down on their knees and prayed together under the direction of the priest, after which the whole group continued on its way. On both stops, I tried as best I could not to stand out and sat modestly to the side, hoping my burning curiosity was not apparent.

I was hypnotized by the beauty along the road. Blue, yellow, pink, and white flowers bloomed all along the desolate limestone hills. I knew most of them, even if I couldn't think of their names, apart from the sea lavender, which I would sometimes pick to put in a vase at home. Now, too, I picked a few flowers for myself at the food stop. The carob and acacia trees, turpentine and olive trees poked out here and there in stands, spreading their shade around them. As we rode past small villages, some residents passed by, returning from the fields and plantations. They always stopped by the side of the road and bowed their heads at the passing convoy.

After what seemed to me like hours of riding—I had entirely lost any sense of time—I could hardly sit straight anymore. I was twisted and sore when, crossing the road, we came upon the sight of a huge bay.

We passed by the ruins of a fortress in Haifa without stopping, and Jean told me that his wife's father was Count of Haifa (he pronounced it "Caiphas") in name only, as he possessed neither the resources nor the will to run a large estate. Moreover, the fortress had been destroyed by Saladin at the end of the previous century and had not been rebuilt.

Acre was visible from the gateway to the Bay of Haifa.

We arrived there after sundown. The feeble light of dusk still dimly illuminated the huge city walls. They were spectacular, surrounding the city all the way to the port. The two iron wings of a large gate in the wall were wide open, with guards standing beside them, and when they saw our entourage, they let us enter immediately.

"A moment before closing!" one of the guards shouted congenially to us. I took in the sights. It was not at all similar to the Acre from my time, with which I was somewhat familiar.

A well-paved path led from the gate to large stone buildings that looked like palaces of several levels, with ornamented windows, porticoes, and turrets, and on the rooftops, flags bearing symbols that I could not make out in the deepening gloom. Beyond them, the domes of farther churches and palaces could be seen, as well as smaller houses closer to the bay, where, in the last light of dusk, the ships anchored there were revealed.

Many people passed us by, and a steady hubbub rose up from the city, as did columns of smoke curling upward, while bells chimed here and there. I felt more exhilarated than when I had passed through the spring this morning, which felt like years ago.

CHAPTER 22

It felt so normal. Jean was driving a little green car, wearing a reddish T-shirt, his dark hair falling across his forehead and short in the back. His face was clean-shaven, and he was wearing sunglasses with red frames. I sat beside him, my legs up on the dashboard. There was a booster seat installed in the back, but no child in it. It was nighttime, and we were driving toward Jerusalem, to my parents. We rolled a joint and listened to some old jazz, and then I woke up.

For some indeterminate length of time, I observed the flickering, unyielding darkness. When I started trying to recollect who I was and where I was supposed to be, it was still quite dark, a bluish gloom over me, and the surrounding walls looked unfamiliar. Strange figures appearing before my eyes made me sit up straight. I looked around and realized that the figures were woven into a tapestry, and then I remembered: I was in one of the rooms at the inn in the Venetian quarter of Acre, and somewhere in this city, not far away, Jean d'Ibelin was reposing in the house of Rohard, Count of Haifa, and the father of Alice, his wife.

I approached the big window. The dawn began to rise, and I could already distinguish the outlines of several buildings. The sea was a gray blanket at the foot of the city. When I had collapsed into bed the night before, my muscles were still sore from the ride, and only the faint light of a lantern lit the room. I could hardly discern where I was. I had just a moment earlier finally understood that Jean and I would not be spending the night together, and out of exhaustion and disappointment, I scarcely glanced out of the window, from which I saw the pitch darkness dotted here and there with faint flickers of light from the windows of nearby houses and ships anchored in the bay.

Now, a pale light began to spread outside. I was cold and shaking in my cotton shift, and my whole body hurt from the previous day's strenuous ride. In a moment's inspiration, I looked under the bed, and with a feeling of victory I found a pot. After peeing, I got back in between the warm, fluffy blankets and closed my eyes. I fell asleep for a while, waking up several times. Every time I dozed off, strange sounds filled my ears, and I awoke in a panic. I wanted to resume my odd dream, which stirred up a sadness and a strange longing, of the modern Jean and me, together in a little green car. I lay looking out the window at the day, which was gradually growing brighter. *Even in the midst of such a wonderful and extraordinary adventure*, I mused wistfully, *I am yearning for some man who does not really exist.*

I sat up in bed and looked around. The room was pleasant and comfortably furnished—the canopied bed was positioned along the inner wall of the room, a woven carpet was spread on the stone floor, and by the window were two wide wooden chairs with armrests, piled with pillows. The fire in the small wood stove was now extinguished, but beside it was a chest with chopped wood and tongs. I didn't know how I was supposed to light the fire. On the walls hung tapestries depicting white birds and peacocks.

I rose and approached the wash basin and the tin jug beside it. I sniffed the water and was surprised to discover that it was not entirely stagnant. I washed my hands and face and smoothed my hair with my fingers, then wove it into a thick braid. I dressed with great care, gathering all of the things that I had cast on the floor before falling asleep. Even without a mirror to observe myself, I felt that I had already acquired a degree of skill. I checked that the door was locked and then rummaged in my cloth bag. I got out my daily contact lenses and put them in. Then, I stared at my dead cell phone for a few moments.

Someone knocked on the door, and I swallowed in fear. I threw my phone back into the depths of the bag and tossed the robe that Jean had left me on top of it before I went to open the door. *It's probably a servant, bringing me breakfast or something.* But at the door stood Thibaut, in a carelessly belted woolen tunic, without a cloak. In place of his usual leather boots, he wore a kind of cloth shoe. His long hair was a little unkempt, and he wore a white cotton cap on his head that made me bite my lip in a desperate attempt to not burst out laughing. Beside Thibaut stood his squire, Philip, neat and polished, but somewhat bleary-eyed.

"Your Royal Highness, Seigneur Philip," I said with a bow when I came to my senses. Thibaut nodded his head at me.

What is the protocol, what is the protocol? I asked myself frantically. *To be silent until he speaks? But he came to my room! And why did he come here?* I envisioned the worst possible scenarios. How could Jean leave me here alone?

"Life is just a dream," Thibaut sang softly, still standing on the threshold. *Could he read my mind?*

"Would you like to come in, your Highness?" I finally said and stepped out of the way. Thibaut grunted a sort of yes, quite kindly, and came inside. I looked at Philip questioningly. "Shall I join you, your Majesty?" Philip asked Thibaut.

"No need," Thibaut replied and approached the window. "Wait for me outside the door." Philip nodded and turned his back to me. I closed the door softly, hoping not to insult him, and turned to face the room.

Thibaut sat on one of the chairs and ran a hand through his hair, which was loose under his funny white hat. He looked around the room, inspecting its length and width.

"Arsur made sure you got the best room. It is second only to the rooms in which I reside," said Thibaut coolly, as if praising his favorite student.

I nodded, still unsure of how to comport myself in his presence.

"But why have they not yet lit the fire for you?" Thibaut was angry. I had no idea what to say.

"Ah, yes," he said, with that friendly, arrogant twinkle of his. "You don't have people—servants—for some reason." I had no idea whether he was just pointing out a fact or whether there was some hidden meaning. My eyes darted around the room and finally landed on the bottle and small clay cups. Here was a comfortable escape from my embarrassment.

"Shall I pour you a cup, your Highness?" I asked softly.

"Certainly," Thibaut said with satisfaction. He called to Philip, who opened the door at once, and instructed him to light the fire. In less than a minute, Philip brought what looked to me to be a small torch and skillfully piled the wood. Soon enough, the fire crackled, and I thanked Thibaut for his consideration. He nodded distractedly, opened his mouth and closed it again, and then drained the cup of wine. It appeared that he wanted to start a conversation but was not sure how to do it. This was clearly out of the ordinary for him—to feel unsure about something.

"Might I be of assistance in some way, your Majesty?" I gambled finally. *What will he do to me anyway, kill me on the spot?*

Thibaut cleared his throat. "I am just asking myself, my lady, if indeed you can help me."

I looked at him with a full willingness to help. The heat that spread from the wood stove through the room relaxed my limbs, which were rigid with cold.

He poured himself another cup of wine and one for me too. I knew that if I drank wine first thing in the morning, after yesterday when I had eaten almost nothing, I would likely faint.

"I am a little weak," I said when his eyes wandered reproachfully from my full glass to my eyes. "I fear I ate almost nothing yesterday." Thibaut clicked his tongue, sighed, and called to Philip again.

"See to it that the lady gets her morning meal," he said. Philip nodded and disappeared. Thibaut sipped from the wine, and I sat in a rigid position, staring helplessly at the door.

"I have written many songs of love," Thibaut said suddenly, which brought me back to life. This confused me completely, and evidently my expression amused him. "You don't believe me, my lady?" he asked with a boastful grin.

"Of course I believe you," I replied at once, and almost added, "I've even heard a few," but I stopped myself in time. Thibaut opened his mouth to say something, but a light knock on the door distracted him. Philip entered, accompanied by a young man who bore a tray with cheese, bread, a little bowl of olive oil, a mound of salt, a bowl of olives, and a cluster of grapes. The youth set the tray down on the table painstakingly, and Philip glanced at Thibaut. He nodded lightly, and without a further word, Philip left with the youth. I tried not to devour the food, but when I saw that Thibaut was wolfing it down with abandon, I started to chew and swallow whatever I could get my hands on.

After we'd spent several minutes eating heartily together, Thibaut leaned back on the armchair. I continued chewing and swallowing, but more elegantly. "I have written many songs about love, and I am a great admirer of women," Thibaut began, still watching me eating. "I always dreamed of meeting a fairy, and I never would have imagined that I would encounter such in the Holy Land, of all places," he went on.

I stopped chewing and swallowing reluctantly. There was no point in protesting. He was there when I passed through the spring the first time and had evidently simply accepted the fact that my presence was enchanted. *What do I do? Start explaining to him that I am from another time?*

"The miraculous and supernatural do not scare me," Thibaut resumed, with a tenderness that began to worry me. He terrified but also intrigued me. Thibaut, Count of Champagne and King of Navarre, had a truly majestic power. The past twenty-four hours had made me feel for him the reverence that was absent from our first meeting. His every nuance held the assurance that his will would be done, and at once. I felt a sliver of attraction to him and pushed it away with all my might.

"Arsur asked that I take care of you during his absence," said Thibaut. I nodded humbly, grateful that he had made sure my room was warmed and food brought to me. "He will surely arrive later today, after he fulfills his duties at home," he added meaningfully. I sipped from the wine and did not dare look at him. I was still irritated and a little insulted by Jean for abandoning me, even though I knew that he had no choice.

"My lady the fairy," said Thibaut, softer still, and I felt weak. "I am a great admirer of women, but I cannot permit you to distract my best knight. Besides, he is married to a good woman and entirely occupied by matters of the kingdom. He asked me to take care of you, but I must take care of him too."

At this point, I had to admit I agreed with him. All of this had suddenly become too complicated and fraught, and I wanted to ask if his Royal Highness might see to my safe passage back to my spring in Atlit, where I would disappear to my world and never disturb them again. But before I could get the words out, Thibaut stood and came over to me, and when I moved to stand, too, he grasped my neck tightly. As I stood, he pressed me against him, and I could feel every appendage of his body through the soft wool.

"I, on the other hand, can give you what you want," Thibaut whispered lustfully. I felt all of my nerve endings light up. He must have washed the night before because he no longer had the musty, damp smell that I had come to associate with him.

"To make love to a fairy—that really would be a fitting adventure for a fine song," Thibaut mumbled and grabbed my behind with his two large hands. "I know what you are; I am familiar with miraculous creatures of your kind," he went on, whispering into my ear and tickling it.

"What am I?" I managed to whisper. I understood that I was under his protection and dependent on his good will, and I was overwhelmed with the feeling that I was cut off from everything I knew. I felt pulled to him against my will and was also filled with disgust for this arrogant king and for myself.

"You are a wild animal disguised as a pious lady," said Thibaut, gently kissing my neck. He looked up, his eyes glued to mine, and he added, "You just want to properly serve a good master, don't you?" In another moment, he would lift my dress and fuck me on the armchair, but his words hit me and made me come to my senses.

"My lord!" I managed to cry. "Your Royal Highness, wait a moment!"

He stopped, but his face was still very close to mine. *What kind of creature am I, really, that all I desire right now is to kiss these arrogant lips?* All the unfulfilled lust for Jean was driving me crazy.

"You are right," I told Thibaut quickly. "Maybe I really am like that. And if it were not for Jean, that is to say, Seigneur Jean, certainly I should be most pleased to . . . serve you," I added, and in that moment, I spoke honestly. "But my soul is truly bound to the soul of your knight, your Royal Highness, and I should not wish to hurt him for any fortune in the world. And I am sure that you would not wish to insult him, sir, your Highness. Please, let me be." I said this with my eyes half-closed, pleading.

"Very nice." Thibaut smiled and stepped back. "Loyal too. Very good."

I collapsed back onto the armchair, trembling.

"Was this a test?" I stuttered in dread and gritted my jaw to keep my teeth from chattering.

"Precisely," said Thibaut and sat back down on the armchair before me, pleased with himself and smug as usual. "If you had not resisted, I should have taken great pleasure in our congress and then abandoned you to the mercy of the judgment of the Bishop of Acre." The insufferable king winked at me. I picked up my cup of wine with trembling hands, then poured some for him. "And you can be sure that there is not much mercy in the judgment of that bloated wineskin," Thibaut added, his cheeriness terrifying. It spurred me to finally speak.

"Your Royal Highness, I believe you are quite right and that I must leave the good Seigneur Jean alone and return to my world at once," I said, still half stuttering as I tried to speak as fast as I could without him stopping me. "I do not wish to inconvenience Count Arsur, but perhaps you might recommend to me the shortest and safest way for me to return to my spring in Atl—in Le Destroit?"

I finished the wine in the clay cup and looked up. Thibaut smiled generously, pleased with my decision.

"I shall ensure your safe sailing passage in the company of a knight or two directly to the Pilgrim Castle. Today, or tomorrow at noon, you will be at your spring, if the wind is good." I sighed with relief. "I thank you from the depths of my heart, your Royal Highness," I said and meant it, but to myself, I added, *you crazy motherfucker.*

CHAPTER 23

I was lounging on Libby's sofa under two fleece blankets, with a cup of tea and an ashtray full of roaches and cigarette butts beside me. Libby sat at the edge of the sofa, stroking my feet every so often. She offered me a hot water bottle, but I told her not to overdo it. There was an episode of some girl show on TV—a generic quartet of rebellious, neurotic, ambitious, and sexy young women in a hyper-stylized urban setting. Libby thought that the best way to lift my spirits would be to plow through all the seasons that I hadn't gotten around to watching, and in a stupor, I immersed myself in their troubles of love and real estate.

My phone flashed. I had turned off the sound, but not the alerts.

"Don't look at that," Libby said. I didn't. I kept staring at the TV screen. The phone kept flashing. I extracted one arm from beneath the blankets and brought the phone closer.

I had three missed calls from Halimi. *Maybe something happened to Lily*, I worried suddenly. I called back. He answered immediately.

"Ditush," Halimi said quietly.

I was quiet before asking, "Is everything all right with Lily?" I knew that it was.

"She's a little congested," he said. "But she's fine, she went to daycare today."

"Okay, thanks," I said, ready to hang up.

"Diti!" he said urgently. "Don't you want to see her? When are you coming home?"

"I want to see her," I said, even though that wasn't exactly true at that exact moment. I missed Lily, but the thought of seeing her in this new status, with Halimi and I no longer a family, made me want to suffocate myself under the fleece blankets.

"Have you thought about the best way to move forward? The separation of powers?" I asked.

"I was thinking of something, Ditush," he said, and my diaphragm contracted. "I thought about a lot of things," he added, "but more than anything, I think we have to talk face-to-face."

"Let him send you the synopsis," said Libby, who heard everything.

"I'm really not up for that now, Halimi," I said. "I'm exhausted." I hung up and covered my head with the blanket.

I chewed my nails in front of the window. Thibaut had brought Philip again and this time sent him to bring another of his companions ("bring the little Burgundy"), an even younger attendant who looked eager to please.

"Go to the Templar fortress and say that you are bringing a message for the master from the King of Navarre." Thibaut removed a ring from one of his fingers and placed it in the messenger's hands. "When you are brought before him, tell him that, with utmost respect, His Majesty wishes to know if it is possible to allocate a small transit ship for his ward, who urgently needs to reach the Pilgrim Castle with a knight or two for escorts, or perhaps she can join some other trip that is already scheduled to leave today or tomorrow? Do not return without an answer. Do you understand?"

The youth nodded eagerly, bowed, and left. Thibaut's eyes hung on Philip, who looked vaguely fatigued.

I wondered what his status was. I could not recall his family name or house from when Jean had introduced him before we departed Le

Destroit. From what I knew about the European aristocracy, the personal servant of a king had to be of high status himself. What depressing humiliation that must be, to be a servant when you are accustomed to being served yourself.

Thibaut invited me to join him in his rooms, chattering lazily on the way. He told me that he could have demanded to be put up in the king's palace in the city, but it was too gloomy for his taste. He had spent a rather dull month there when he had just arrived at Acre. "By the time we assembled a high-caliber group of cooks, laundresses, heads of hunting, musicians, storytellers, and jugglers, it was already time to move on," Thibaut explained to me as we climbed the stone steps to his floor.

I wondered how it was possible that this smug and capricious man could possibly have succeeded—or, perhaps more precisely, would go on to succeed—in obtaining the agreement that promised the Kingdom of Jerusalem the most territory since the First Crusade, and almost without warfare. I liked him even though I was also afraid of him, and I could not wait for Jean to return. I tried not to think too much about Jean himself, with his wife and children, or of myself entangled in this situation. *What do we even do together?* I comforted myself. *We just talk, mostly.* I worried that Thibaut's young man would come back and inform me that I could leave before I had the chance to say goodbye to Jean.

The suite that had been allotted to Thibaut was truly regal. There were three enormous rooms with high ceilings: In the innermost chamber was a huge four-poster bed; and in the other two rooms, one of which opened onto a beautiful balcony, were broad armchairs with red velvet cushions, upholstered benches embroidered in gold thread, and tapestries in muted colors on the walls. Sacks and trunks that had been unloaded from the mules the night before filled the corners. Thibaut's knights sat around and spoke among themselves. Thibaut disappeared into the bedroom and returned a few minutes later, dressed in his blue-and-silver velvet attire, his coronet placed firmly on his head.

He sat down on one of the benches and took up his lute, and his knights gathered around him. Cedrique rose from his bed by the window and sat at Thibaut's feet.

One of his companions held a flute, and another a kind of small tambourine. They joined Thibaut in playing and singing.

"Mercy, my lady," Thibaut began to sing and smiled at me, accompanying himself on the lute. His deep, resonant voice echoed through the large, high-ceilinged stone room, and suddenly I recognized the song from my YouTube expeditions. It was the song that I had felt compelled to send Jean a little while back.

> *Mercy, my lady, grant me reply,*
> *By holy God, I beg you, say:*
> *When death takes you—and sooner I—*
> *What shall of Love become that day?*
> *Your grace and wisdom shine so bright,*
> *I love you more than words confess.*
> *Without our hearts to give her light,*
> *I fear that Love will perish, yes.*

One of Thibaut's youngest accompanists stood beside him and, to the laughter of the rest of the men, broke into a voice that was meant to sound like a woman:

> *By God, Thibaut, Love will not fade,*
> *Not for your death, nor yet for mine.*
> *You mean, perchance, to jest with me,*
> *For plump you seem, in health and fine.*

> *Though death will come, as come it must,*
> *Love does not vanish, nor decay.*
> *It mourns when lovers turn to dust,*
> *Yet keeps its throne in hearts alway.*

The knight sang well in a high, feminine voice, and they continued their melodic, philosophical conversation for several more verses. The knights chuckled and elbowed each other at the start, laughing out loud when the singing knight mentioned Thibaut's plump figure. By the end of the song, some shed a tear, clapped their hands, and stomped their feet. Thibaut and his entourage went on singing—of setting off on the crusade, of brave knights now singing with the angels after dying bravely in battle, of heartless and beautiful ladies, of seductive shepherd girls. I sank into a dreamy daze, enveloped in their singing voices.

I woke up from my half-sleep, and only now did my mind make sense of the words that I had been hearing over and over for some time. "Bless Jean d'Ibelin, the daring Count Arsur," Thibaut's voice sang as he strummed a doleful melody on the lute.

> *The youngest son of Beirut's lord,*
> *A knight of valor, well adored.*
> *He bent before his cousin fair,*
> *Enchanted from the otherworld.*

Thibaut's companions accompanied him on drums and flute, adding a rhythmic and humorous touch to Thibaut's gentle strumming. I sat up straight in my chair, embarrassed, and looked around. Thibaut continued his narrative description of Jean, and I realized that he was making up the words in real time, and that he did so with considerable talent. His eyes were fixed affectionately on the other side of the room, and when I looked over, I saw Jean in the threshold, long-limbed and relaxed and smiling at Thibaut. Beside him, stiff as a broomstick, stood Hugh.

When Thibaut strummed the final chord, everybody clapped, myself included.

"You show me great kindness, your Majesty," said Jean. "There is no greater honor than to serve as a subject for your singing." He sounded like a little brother acknowledging the elder's authority, and Thibaut growled with satisfaction.

Cedrique barked as if to confirm, and everyone burst out laughing. Thibaut patted the handsome dog on the head with pride. Jean bade good morning to each of Thibaut's knights and then sat down beside me. Hugh joined the others.

"How did you pass the night, my lady?" Jean asked quietly. He moved his hand closer to mine, as if wanting to hold it, and then lightly shook his head and placed both his hands on his knees.

"I slept like a log," I said. "But I woke up very early and was unable to fall back asleep," I added, mostly to explain how it happened that I was dozing off in a room full of people. I wanted to tell him about the dream of the little green car, but the moment was not right.

"How did you sleep, my lord?" I asked instead of telling him about the dream.

"I did not sleep much," said Jean. When he saw the embarrassment on my face, he hurried to add, "I had a great deal of work to attend to."

I began to say something and then realized that it was not appropriate, and I tried to say something else, but this was not suitable either. I was disheartened by the formality between us.

Thibaut continued to strum and sing, and his people continued to sing and play along. Every now and then came an outburst of laughter.

"Let's go out to the balcony," said Jean, so we did.

Beneath the climbing grapevine, he asked again how I was doing. This time I told him—without too much detail—about Thibaut's visit and his offer to sail me back to Atlit today or tomorrow. Jean's face fell, but he nodded.

"The Lady Alice, my wife, was very curious to meet you," he said with a half-apologetic smile.

Good God. I cast a glance into the room in the hopes that the young Burgundy had already returned from the Master of the Templars.

"I told her that you are very shy and humble, and that all you want is to see the holy places and to visit my sister at her convent," said Jean, his gaze directed at the harbor. "But she claimed that she could not forgo a meeting with one of my relations that she had never heard of. I fear that we may have gotten somewhat enmeshed, my dear Lady Édith." He spoke as if this were amusing to him. It did not amuse me, but it touched my heart that he called me "my dear."

I could now see the city spread out before us. It was not as dense, noisy, and dirty as I had imagined every large, bustling Levantine city to be. Most of it was built of stone, there were broad passages, and now I could also see the many stone domes and colorful flags. The city had a quiet splendor, full of self-worth. Sea birds screeched and flew over the ships in the bay, and sailboats of all shapes and sizes were moored in the small harbor.

"What a gorgeous city," I said, just to say something.

Jean snorted.

"You don't think so?"

"Indeed, from the heights of the luxurious rooms in the Venetian inn, it really is beautiful," Jean agreed. "But when you are near the ports and the craftsmen's neighborhoods, the stench is strong, and the density is high," he said with disdain. "I am waiting impatiently for the moment when my castle's construction is complete, and I can look out at the sea without thinking about all the waste that is thrown into it every day."

"Arsur!" Thibaut's voice called from inside the room. "Come here!"

Jean apologized to me and went inside. I remained standing on the balcony, my hands resting on the stone railing between the ornamental clay pots. I continued to look out at the city, my head empty of thoughts. Jean returned.

"My lady," he said, "the king asked that I collect an illuminated manuscript ordered some months ago from the scriptorium of the Holy Cross. I thought this might be a good opportunity to have a nice trip with you and speak privately."

"In the stinking, dense city?" I asked mockingly. Jean chuckled. Now, when he was less troubled and anxious, he was as attractive to me as ever. He had also evidently bathed the night before, or this morning, because a sweet, lemony scent came off him in waves; his hair was neatly gathered under his velvet beret; his handsome brown beard was brushed; and he wore his red-gold clothes without the chainmail and leather gloves. I wondered if there were any chance at all that I could pull him into the fluffy bed in my room downstairs.

"I might have exaggerated a little," Jean said good-naturedly. "There are some very nice parts."

We parted from Thibaut—who waved goodbye to us without pausing his singing—and we went down to my room, where I took the cape that Jean loaned me to keep me warm the day before. Hugh remained in Thibaut's rooms to wait for us and to run and summon us in case the king's messenger should return from the Templars with an urgent message.

As we descended the stone steps to the entrance level of the inn, the description of which was not at all suitable to its dimensions or its elegant grandeur, I felt a kind of elation once again. *What do I care about anything? I don't care at all*, I hummed to myself as the entrance hall was revealed before me, its floor colorful with mosaics depicting a large ship at sea and golden portraits of saints on the walls.

A servant standing by the large wooden door bowed to us. We walked out into the street.

I was surprised that it was paved with stones—I had always imagined the cities of the Middle Ages as paths of mud, rotting wood, and sewage. We walked through the streets hand in hand, crossing plazas with fountains, decorated with beds of blooming flowers and covered stalls crammed with wares: fruits, vegetables, fabrics, copper tools, wooden tools, iron tools, leather products, spices, icons, and all kinds of devices whose purpose I did not recognize. The streets were full of noblemen in velvet and silk, merchants from different and strange lands, clerics in black and brown woolen clothes, and harried servants running from one task to the next.

The city stunned me with its beauty; with its paved streets and broad wooden steps wound through churches, monasteries, and palaces; and with sprawling plazas dotted with trees and benches. When did they get around to building all this? How long had they even been here? I tried to calculate—I got to something like a hundred and fifty years. *Don't gape*, I kept having to remind myself. Here and there, passersby nodded to Jean, and he responded with a head gesture of his own. It did not seem that he was trying to hide the fact that he and I had close relations.

"Tell me, my lady, did Thibaut coerce you in some manner to return to the Pilgrim Castle?" Jean asked without looking at me.

"Just a little," I replied apprehensively. I did not want to lie to him, but I also did not want to reveal the fact that for several seconds, I had desired Thibaut. It was bizarre and mortifying, and I hoped to forget about it as soon as possible.

"I am familiar with my royal friend and know that his ways are sometimes . . . a little extreme," he said, glancing at me. "But usually his intentions are good."

I smiled and said, "This time, too, his intentions were good," and I added honestly, "and he loves you and relies on you."

Jean nodded, his smile spread, and his face brightened again.

"I would have liked to spend undisturbed time with you, perhaps in some remote cabin in the middle of the forest," I smiled at him and pressed his arm against mine even harder, hoping to change the subject. "But this whole journey is too much for me, and I worry that it is for you too. I am an unnecessary burden under these circumstances."

"You articulate it beautifully, my l—" He stopped himself and cleared his throat. "My lady." I squeezed his arm again.

"I will not permit you to sail alone with just ill-tempered Templar knights," Jean said resolutely. "You are correct that the present journey is too busy and full. I am angry with myself for inviting you along without proper consideration. I simply did not want to waste the opportunity to spend more time with you than a few cramped hours," he said and stopped. I stood facing him.

"If Thibaut had not been in such a hurry, I would sail back with you in one of the smaller Ibelin ships. There are three anchored here in Acre just now, and at least one of them will sail south today or tomorrow to Arsur, and then on to Jaffa and to Ashkelon. I could have easily arranged a stop for us at the Pilgrim Castle." He sighed and went on. "But it would be disrespectful to forgo Thibaut's gesture in seeking a place for you on one of the Templar sailings today or tomorrow, and so, in the name of the Holy Mother—I will join you and escort you safely to your spring, my lady, my dear lady," he said and stole a glance around. I knew what he wanted, because I wanted the exact same thing. But Jean just sighed and then looked away. "We're almost there," he said in a more matter-of-fact tone and increased his pace.

On the way to the scriptorium of the Cathedral of the Holy Cross, I saw what he meant when he spoke of the stench and the overcrowding. The craftsmen's neighborhoods were cramped and crowded. Clinging smells mingled with soot and sweat. We passed through streets of butchers, tanners, and leather workers, where hides in various stages of processing hung and attracted flies. All manner of cloudy liquids streamed through small ditches where thick foam accumulated. The stench was horrible. I held my nose and hoped I would not throw up.

Then, we left the dense neighborhoods and arrived at a broad, beautiful part of town, crowned with lofty buildings with round towers overlooking the sea, crenellated turrets, and columned porticoes. A huge plaza, home to enormous plane trees, centered on a cathedral so big that I could barely see around it.

"Seigneur Jean," I said quietly, standing before it for a few minutes as I tried to imagine the Acre of my time and where such an impressive cathedral might be. "I dreamed about you this morning, as if you lived in my time." Jean, who was waiting, patient and relaxed as I surveyed the cathedral, turned to me as if bitten by a snake.

"The same dream, again?" he nearly shouted, and two flower peddlers looked at him with interest.

"You too?" I whispered breathlessly.

"We were in a tiny, cramped carriage, and I was holding its wheel," Jean murmured. "You were sitting beside me, and we were borne speedily by some invisible force that was yet natural and self-evident!" He leaned on me to steady himself. "I woke from the dream at the break of dawn and could not return to sleep. Then, I became distracted by my own matters and forgot about it entirely. Did you dream something similar?"

"It was evening, and the stars were twinkling in the sky, and we were passing hashish between us and listening to beautiful music," I said. The cathedral blurred before my eyes. Jean's hand closed around mine. "Come, let's go inside," I heard him say through gritted teeth. He began to walk and pulled me after him. He dropped my hand at the door. I followed after him to one of the prayer benches, and we both knelt down together. Jean murmured something from the depths of his heart, and I pretended to pray. When he crossed himself, I crossed myself too. Then, we rose, and Jean led me through a side corridor before knocking on a big wooden door.

The door was opened by a very young man, and when Jean introduced himself, he left the door open and disappeared inside. Jean took my hand and kissed it hastily, then abandoned it quickly. An older man approached the door. He wore a brown woolen robe belted with a simple string, his hair was cropped, and he wore a black cap on the crown of his head.

"Young Master Ibelin," said the monk or priest, whatever he was, and then corrected himself, "That is, dear Seigneur Arsur." Jean smiled and patted the monk on the back affectionately. "Dearest Father Jerome," he said in turn, "does the Good Lord shine his light upon you?"

"Indeed, we enjoy his marvelous grace," replied Father Jerome and motioned to us to follow him into another narrow corridor. "In the winter, two young and very promising apprentices came to us. One specializes in penmanship, and the other is a natural talent at painting the works of God and his miracles." We walked after him into his study; a large escritoire stood in the middle of the room, and next to it were shelves full of manuscripts and scrolls of parchment. Light from the large window lit up the dust in the room. Jean introduced me as his cousin. Then, he explained that he had come to collect the manuscript that King Navarre had commissioned.

"We had hoped that the king might come to collect it himself," said Father Jerome in a tone of insult, then tried to play it down by nodding. "Many of the monks worked on the manuscript for days and nights so that it would be ready in time for his Royal Highness."

"Of course," said Jean in a conciliatory tone. "And he did intend to do so, but his many obligations prevent him. He longs to see the result of your glorious work in his precious free moments." I recalled the figure of Thibaut, singing and playing the lute while occasionally popping grapes into his mouth, and I looked down at the floor.

"I understand, my lord, of course. I will take you inside," said Father Jerome respectfully.

He led us into a large, chilly hall that smelled strongly of glue. Lanterns hung from the ceiling and illuminated pale circles of light on wooden tables where monks and apprentices worked, some copying texts, and others embellishing them with illustrations and flourishes. Men were busy straightening scrolls of parchment, drying paper pages, and sewing and gluing and binding the prepared pages.

I observed one of the monks at work as if hypnotized; he was immersed in painting complex embellishments in gold, crimson, and blue. *I have to tell Simone about all of this*, I thought excitedly. *This is exactly her subject of research, the workshop of manuscripts in Acre.* I tried to engrave every detail into my memory.

Then, at once, I felt the impossibility of my situation. *Of course, I cannot tell Simone anything.* My thoughts raced. *But what if she has some connection to all of this? Maybe she is actually responsible for my being here right now? She's the one who filled my head with stories about the Crusaders and their kingdoms. And Halimi was with her when he found that coin from the house of Ibelin, with which I was able to travel through the space of time . . .*

The solid boundaries between things began to dissolve, and the black spots reappeared before my eyes. The royal blue and the rich crimson on the pages, the puddles of pale light from the hanging lanterns, the quiet commotion and the smell of glue—the entire scriptorium swirled around me within itself, and I lost my balance.

CHAPTER 24

The intercom buzzed frantically, and Libby went to check what was going on with the delivery guy for the Thai food we'd ordered. It was Halimi. Libby furiously replaced the handset of the intercom and went back to the window.

"What do you want, asshole?!" she shouted.

"Libby!" I heard him shout from below. "Enough with the drama! Where's Idit?"

"You don't deserve to kiss her feet!" Libby shouted. I pulled myself from the couch and stood behind her. "Libby," I said quietly, "calm down."

"I will not calm down!" Libby flared. "This jerk is coming to harass you at *my* house?!"

"Idit!" Halimi shouted.

"Repugnant playboy scum!" Libby shouted at him from the window.

I started to laugh. Libby looked at me, wide-eyed.

"Dita, are you okay?" she asked in disbelief.

I did not reply. This shouting at the building was so stupid. Libby raised her hands in the air and shook her head in despair.

"Idit! I'm not leaving until you come down here and talk to me!" Halimi shouted. A few heads were already looking curiously from the nearby windows. I stopped laughing and silently put my shoes on. Libby sat on the couch. I took the elevator down with Libby's fleece blanket wrapped around me.

It was noon. Halimi was unshaven, and he asked if he could hug me. I said no. He asked if I wanted to see pictures from the trip with the daycare, and I nodded. When I saw Lily with the other kids, the tears began to flow.

"Ditush," said Halimi. "My Diti," he added.

I did not even try to speak.

"I decided to leave *Free to Be*," said Halimi and put an arm around my shoulder after all. "Ditush, my love, I am so, so sorry." His voice trembled. I looked at him in surprise.

"What? You decided to leave?" I finally spoke. "Where did that come from? And how do you plan to make a living?"

"I can't ask her to leave," said Halimi, his voice still trembling a little. "And if we keep on working together, it will just be the same vicious cycle again and again."

I sniffled.

"And as for money, it'll be fine," Halimi went on. "I've had enough with the makeup and skincare tips as it is."

I looked at him. He looked at me.

"I know I acted like total shit, Ditush," Halimi continued. "But you and Lily . . . you are the most important part of my life. The rest is just distraction. The only thing that I care about is that you're happy. And I have another idea . . ." he began. But now I was really crying, and when he pulled me to him, I did not resist.

"Please, Ditush," he said after a few moments. "Please, come home. I promise you—on my mother's life—that we'll start a new life. We can leave Tel Aviv if you want. We'll establish the new state of Rozhevsky-Halimistan. Please. Last chance."

I kept crying, but I knew that now there was also some relief in it. I had no longer expected him to try to win me back, and I certainly had not expected him to give up his coveted job for a chance to mend our relationship.

He waited downstairs while I packed up my minimal belongings. Libby was so enraged, she could hardly speak. "You are making a terrible mistake" was all she said when I thanked her for her concern. She shook me off when I hugged her.

"My lady!" A voice cried in my ear. "Lady Édith!" I strained to open my eyelids, which felt as though they'd been stuck together with glue. There was a pungent vinegar smell, and I moved my head to get away from it. This action tripped a switch in my brain, and I opened my eyes.

Leaning over me were Jean, Father Jerome, and a shape that took me a few moments to realize was a nun. She was holding a bowl up close to my nose, and I almost vomited from the smell. I straightened up, dodging the bowl.

"What happened?" I asked. The three stared at me in puzzlement. I realized I had asked in Hebrew and tried again in French.

"You fainted, my lady," said Father Jerome. I looked around. I was in a small, windowless room, on a straw mattress. The nun served me a goblet of wine and some bread.

"You must regain your strength, my lady," said the nun. I took the bread gratefully. *How much wine do these people drink, and at every chance?* I thought wearily and took a tiny sip out of politeness. I also gnawed on the bread, which did indeed restore my strength.

"I don't know why I fainted," I said to Jean, who was still sitting on his heels before me, his brow furrowed with worry. This was almost correct. I remembered golden and crimson letters, outlined in blue . . . again I saw black spots before my eyes and quickly closed them.

"We have to take you somewhere where you can rest and recover as quickly as possible," said Jean. Someone came to summon Father Jerome, and he asked our forgiveness and stepped out. The nun told Jean to call her if he needed further help with me, and then she left too.

"I'm sorry," I muttered with eyes closed. I kept seeing my spring before my eyes, as if it were calling to me to return.

"Any news from Thibaut?" I asked and opened my eyes.

"Not yet," said Jean. "And maybe that is for the best. Today's sailing is probably already full, and anyway, it is better you not take another journey in your current state." Jean sat down on the floor and leaned his back against the wall.

"Perhaps we will go back to the inn?" I asked.

"Certainly, we will return to the inn," said Jean. "But I think it's better if you do not go on foot."

"What options do I have?" I wondered. The walk to the cathedral had been pleasant, but I was not up to the march all the way back on foot just now.

"I can go to the house of Rohard," said Jean, looking troubled, "and take one of our horses for you. The house is very close, and I will not be gone long."

"Okay," I said weakly. Jean took my hand and kissed it.

"I am sorry, my dear lady," he said. "I will return as fast as possible." I gripped his hand with my other hand, put it to my mouth, and kissed it wholeheartedly. He nodded with a tired smile and left.

Lily was thrilled to see me when she got back from daycare, which raised my sad spirits somewhat. The long conversation with Halimi, which began the moment we got home and went on until Lily joined us, made it clear to me that he was totally serious, and that he had, in fact, already submitted his resignation. I was encouraged by this. If he had done this before he even knew if I would agree to get back together with him, he must still feel obligated to repair the damage he had caused.

When Lily got home, there was a kind of normalcy that I had not felt in the house for weeks now. She was in a euphoric state, which made me think that maybe she had sensed that something was off these past few weeks after all ("These little ones, they notice every tiny change"). She spoke fast and loud, jumped on me and Halimi, and when she noticed him hugging me as I chopped vegetables for dinner, she leaped from her chair where she sat before the television and joined in the hug.

That evening, Halimi brought up the idea of us moving to Atlit for the first time.

"I really want a fresh start," he said. "And I think that it's the perfect place for it. For Lily too. A big house with a yard, the sea close by." As soon as he felt secure that I was back home, the playful twinkle returned to Halimi's eyes. It made me smile while putting me on alert at the same time. I didn't want him to feel *too* secure.

"I don't know," I said. "I have to think about it."

A move to Atlit? To be that far away from Tel Aviv? There was something very appealing about the idea, but also kind of frightening. To leave the city and live in a more rural place, like a respectable, bourgeois couple? Would it last? Or would I find myself a forsaken housewife, waiting in vain for her husband to return? I knew that in terms of my work, there was no real difference if I were in Tel Aviv, in Atlit, or in British Columbia, but it was hard to believe that Halimi could find work that wouldn't require him to commute to the city every day.

"Let's first see how things turn out in terms of your work," I said. Halimi nodded, and we drank tea and kept talking, smoking out the window that looked over a construction site that had developed at a rapid pace.

* * *

Evidently, I had fallen asleep on the straw mattress while looking at the ceiling reinforced with wooden beams. I awoke to the sounds of people talking, which got nearer to the door of the room where I lay. A familiar man's voice and an unfamiliar woman's voice.

Jean opened the door and shot me a glance that I was unable to decipher. Behind him appeared a beautiful, well-appointed woman in a green silk dress hemmed in gold, and her head covered not with the white cloth coverings that I had grown accustomed to seeing on most of the thirteenth-century women but in a turban of light blue silk. She had huge, honey-colored, catlike eyes, and she entered the room looking relaxed. She was pregnant, and her small, protruding belly was flattered by the medieval fashions.

"Cousin Édith," said Jean, "meet the Lady Alice, my wife."

I swallowed and sat up straight.

"There's no need to get up," said Lady Alice with a noble hand gesture. "My husband told me that you felt unwell, and I scolded him for leaving you in"—she scanned the room with disgust—"in this cold, dark place, instead of bringing you to the family home, as he ought."

"I am most pleased to make your acquaintance, Lady Alice," I said in a weak voice and hoped that I had said everything correctly.

"As am I, my dear," said Alice. "I also scolded Master Jean for putting you up in that musty inn instead of bringing you to us. But your cousin has his mysterious considerations, and I do not presume to get to the bottom of his mind." She said this in a tone that seemed to pronounce that in fact she did presume to get to the bottom of his mind but kept her opinions to herself.

"It was not musty, my lady. I was most comfortable, and I would not have wished to bother you," I managed to say.

"It is not a bother at all," said Alice melodiously. "You will entertain me in my loneliness. My good father has been in Sidon for months, while my husband is constantly running errands for Champagne."

Jean coughed in embarrassment. "My lady," he said sparingly.

"Sorry, King Navarre," Alice added with undisguised mockery. Jean sighed.

"In any case, dear Cousin, I do not know to what you have grown accustomed," Alice said without hurry, "but I am not willing to hear of accommodation in an inn. Tonight, you will sleep at our house. Master Jean informed me that tomorrow, he will accompany you by ship to the Pilgrim Castle, and there is no need for you to exhaust yourself fighting off fleas all night. The sea here is not always easygoing, and you must be strong for your journey."

I started itching as soon as she mentioned the fleas.

There was no point in resisting Alice's offer, and for the first time since I had met Jean, he appeared lost. I was angry at myself that I had complicated things for him like this. I should have been satisfied with our fleeting encounters by the spring, that was obvious now, and the many icons that looked at me from the walls made me feel that the present entanglement was punishment for my sins.

Outside the room, Alice's woman was waiting, and as we left the room, she gave me a murderous expression. We left the cathedral. Jean carried the ornate manuscript for Thibaut in an elegant wooden box— the life of Jesus and some parables—and Alice put her arm in mine. Her young woman walked a few steps behind us, carrying a basket. I had never been in such an extreme state of mental anguish. I held myself back from shaking off Alice's arm, running to the Venetian inn, and begging Thibaut to give me a horse to ride back to Atlit.

We crossed one street and then a plaza and stopped before a big house. It was surrounded by trees that produced a dappled play of light and shadow on its walls. Alice's woman caught up, walked ahead of us, and hurried to open the door. She stopped at the threshold and bowed before Jean, who entered first, and then to Alice. She looked at me as I entered with not so much as a nod and with a distinct expression of revulsion. Alice hit the maid's head.

"Marie!" She scolded her. "What is the meaning of this behavior? Bow to our cousin at once."

Marie, who evidently was not surprised by the blow, executed an exaggeratedly over-the-top bow, which earned her another smack on the head. We continued into the house.

"We shall sit in the solarium," Alice said to Marie. "Have the cook prepare refreshments." The girl nodded and slipped into a passageway.

"Get me a different woman, my lord," Alice practically spat as the three of us entered a big, bright room. It was not as large as Thibault's rooms at the inn, but no less splendid. There were tapestries on the walls, upholstered sitting corners and embroidered cushions, and a densely woven rug on the stone floor. A fire burned in the big fireplace despite the spring day, and beyond the windows was the sea, golden in the sunlight. I remained standing. From somewhere came the sound of footsteps, and Brunette burst through the door and started barking and jumping on me happily. I stood frozen and just patted her awkwardly on the head.

"The dog knows Cousin Édith well, I see," Alice said thornily. Jean held Brunette's leather collar and said that he would return at once, after securing the precious manuscript safely in his office, and Alice instructed me to sit down. Then, she rang a small copper bell.

Marie's face appeared at the door. "Where are the refreshments?" asked Alice.

"I shall bring them at once, my lady." Marie bowed, cast another angry look at me, and headed toward the door.

"Marie," Alice's voice rose.

The servant turned back.

"After you bring the refreshments, get out of this house," Alice said without batting an eye. The servant's mouth gaped wide.

"My lady," she said in a chirpy voice that made me sorry for her.

"On second thought," said Alice, and the servant's face brightened with hope. "Tell the cook to send someone else and get out of here at once." The servant bowed quickly, and as she closed the door, I could hear her burst into tears.

"I will not tolerate a lack of respect," Alice mumbled. This woman frightened me to the point of paralysis. I had never felt so helpless, and I didn't know how I would regain control over my fate.

Alice stood at one of the windows, her back to me, and, with a slow, wavelike motion, began to remove her silk turban. Two braids fell over her shoulders. She slowly unraveled each of them, and her hair was completely free; it was long and smooth, honey-colored like her eyes. I watched her, hypnotized. She turned back to the room and looked at me. Lazily, but without taking her eyes off me, she took a white cotton cap from a nearby chest, set it upon her head, and tied it loosely under her chin.

Then, she sat across from me in one of the armchairs and gathered her legs under her. With her hair loose and the childish white cap on, she looked like a teenage girl. A gorgeous girl, who examined me unhurriedly, narrowing her enormous eyes at me. She took up a small wooden stick in her hands, around which wound a cloud of light wool. Skillfully, without looking at what she was doing, she rolled the stick between her hands and fingers, and the cloud began to transform into yarn. *So, this is what a spindle looks like.*

"And so, Cousin," she said, emphasizing the word *cousin*.

"Lady Alice," I said. I had nothing to add. I longed for Jean's presence and dreaded the moment he would return.

There was a light knock at the door, and into the room came a servant smaller than Marie, balancing a large copper tray with evident inexperience. The tray held a glass bottle with diluted wine, three glasses, slices of cheese, cuts of cold meat, pieces of bread, and clay bowls filled with nuts, dates, and dried figs. The little servant sighed with relief when the tray was securely set down on the nearby table. She then bowed to her mistress and to me and disappeared after a nod of approval from Alice.

"Have something," said Alice. "You will need your strength." I picked up a dried fig and began to gnaw on it reluctantly. In light of Alice's industrious hands, I felt even more superfluous and worthless than I thought possible.

"I had never heard of any relatives from Lady Melisende's side," said Alice. "Does Isabelle even know of your existence?"

I answered, trembling, praying sincerely for the help of any of the saints: "I maintained contact with her since childhood through correspondence, my lady. There is nothing that I want more than to visit her at the convent." Lady Melisende, whose name I knew from Wikipedia, was Jean's late mother. Isabelle was Jean's dispossessed sister, who had taken her vows as a nun.

Alice nodded slowly. She opened her mouth, and then came another knock at the door.

"In the name of the Holy Mother," Alice sighed. "Yes?"

Into the room came a plump villager with an ample bosom cosseted in a brown woolen dress and over it a kind of white cotton short-sleeved dress, carrying a little baby wrapped in a red woven blanket. A small boy peeped out from behind her, casting shy glances at Alice and me.

"Lady Alice, Little Jean is coughing. Shall I summon Avraham Ben Simon?" She had a strange pronunciation, with whistling letters.

"Who?" Alice asked angrily.

"The Jewish healer, my lady," replied the villager, whom I assumed to be the wet nurse.

Alice inhaled impatiently, her nostrils flaring, and gave the matter some ten seconds of thought.

"Consult with the master; he is in his study," she said finally. The wet nurse bowed and turned to leave the room.

"One moment," said Alice. The wet nurse stopped.

"Balian," Alice said in a soft voice and set the spindle down in her lap. "Come give your mother a kiss." The little boy released the back of the wet nurse and approached his mother with reverence. He took her hand and kissed it, then stood straight. He was maybe three years old.

"What a handsome boy," said Alice and patted his head. "How he looks like his father. Right, Cousin Édith?" She turned her huge, honey eyes to me.

I nodded weakly. He really did resemble Jean.

"Are you behaving yourself, Little Balian?" Alice turned back to her son. He nodded vigorously, and his eyes looked askance at the refreshments on the table.

"Good for you," said Alice. "Take a few fruits for yourself and go back to Katerina." The boy smiled broadly, which made him look even more like Jean. He took a few dried apricots and left with the nanny. I swallowed hard, and it hurt. Alice waited several seconds after the door closed and turned back to me, taking up the spindle again.

"In that case," said Alice, drawing out the syllables, "you wish to visit Isabelle at that godforsaken convent where she stuck herself. So, why did you travel to Acre if your route is meant to lead you to the desert?"

I took time chewing the piece of fig that I had in my mouth and finally answered, "Cousin Jean said that he had letters that he wanted to pass along to her before I left." I had no other choice. This was the only excuse that I had heard Jean offer for my evidently incomprehensible joining of the royal journey to Acre. I hadn't the faintest idea, of course, if this is what Jean had told his wife.

"Yes, that's exactly what Cousin Jean said," said Alice, almost amused. Sweat broke out in my armpits. I was just about to feign a fainting spell to break out of this situation when Jean entered. Maybe he had been meditating, or the devil knows what, because he looked relaxed and calm and smiled at both of us congenially.

"What a warm, homey sight," he said, turning his eyes to Alice. "My beloved wife and my dear cousin, taking their rest together." It sounded as if he really meant it. I held back from letting out a snort, but Alice grinned with her whole mouth.

"Don't exaggerate, Cousin," she said, emphasizing the word *cousin* mockingly again, but she did not look angry. And he smiled and said, "And you, do not scare away our guest, my lady. She is weak as it is."

Good Lord, I thought and set the second fig that I'd begun eating down on the table, *what kind of twisted game have I been caught up in?* "My cousin, my lady," I said in a cutting tone and stood up. "I thank you for your warm hospitality. I feel that I am stronger and would like to go back to my room in the inn and stop bothering you with my presence."

Alice burst out laughing. "Too late," she said. "My husband's scandalous behavior has set all the tongues in town running wild with gossip. Not long ago, rumors came from the Pilgrim Castle of a most strange, green-eyed cousin, who might actually be a witch, or perhaps a fairy, and now there is no way out but to pretend to everyone that you are indeed a cousin." She bit her lips and then tilted her head to the side. "I never saw a fairy before, nor a witch, and I never expected to have the opportunity to assess my master's taste in women," she added in her unbroken, unhurried pronunciation, as if none of this really concerned her at all.

Jean rolled his eyes. "Lady Alice likes to err on the side of illusions and invent strange stories for herself, Cousin," he said, as if filling me in on a known flaw. "This is the result of an overly sharp mind that does not find its outlet in the dreary management of the household."

There was silence for several seconds.

"Well, then," I finally said, stuttering, "well, then, good for you both, and wonderful; I ask your forgiveness." Alice chuckled, and a look of sympathy came to Jean's face. *Let me not wake up until Jean takes me to my spring already instead of humiliating me before his wife.* I began to concentrate on this while Jean and Alice discussed how Jean must present the manuscript to Thibaut, when a quick knock sounded.

It was Hugh, and again Alice donned a kind of motherly countenance. She made sure that he ate and drank properly and that he was being duly hosted—as she remarked—at the king's court, and only then did she permit him to say what he had come to say.

"My lord," Hugh said looking toward Jean. "His Royal Highness, in his grace, sent me to inform you that there will be a sailing to the Pilgrim Castle leaving today after all. The grand master decided to move up his sailing and will take to the sea just as soon as Lady Édith comes aboard, sir. They said that the wind is perfect. I did not find you at the cathedral, my lord, and it took me some time to realize that you had come home, so I imagine you had better make haste."

"Thank you, Hugh," said Jean. "Go bring the wooden chest from the table in my office and come back here." Hugh nodded, bowed from the doorway, and disappeared.

"Out by the skin of your teeth," said Alice and smiled at me. "Go in peace and never return to Acre, do you understand?"

"I will never return, my lady," I said humbly and meant it. Later, I was angry at myself for being such a doormat, but in that moment, I felt awe and respect for her. She was a true and unapologetic lady, a ruler of her own world.

CHAPTER 25

From the moment that we left the house of Rohard, Lord of Haifa, until we boarded the boat that whisked us from the harbor to the grand master of the Knights Templar's ship, everything moved quickly. It took me time to get over the shock of meeting Alice and the sense that I had seen a side of Jean that I had not dared imagine. Jean, Hugh, and I rode to the Venetian inn, and Brunette ran along beside us. At the inn, we presented ourselves before Thibaut. He and his knights were practicing fencing in the large inner courtyard, surrounded by columns, and we had to interrupt him to say goodbye.

Jean showed Thibaut the carved wooden box containing the illuminated manuscript.

"Thank you, my boy," said Thibaut and wiped the sweat from his forehead. He sent one of his knights to take the box upstairs to his rooms for safe storage, then turned back to us.

"I trust, my lady," he said, twirling his long mustache between his fingertips, "that you will not kidnap Arsur." He smiled paternally at Jean and added, looking back at me, "You know that if you drag him into oblivion, I will track you like a bloodhound—even into the Otherworld."

I nodded and smiled at him like I would an old friend. I could not refrain from imagining Thibaut passing through the spring and suddenly materializing in the twenty-first century, shouting and expecting full service from everyone. This made my smile broader, but I replied appropriately.

"I would not steal such an asset from the Holy Kingdom of Jerusalem," I said. "And I wish, your Majesty, that your journey be successful and bear sweet fruit."

Thibaut's stern look softened, and he took my hand and brought it to his lips. Astonishment crossed Jean's face.

"I am most pleased to have made your acquaintance, my lady," said Thibaut after kissing the back of my hand with surprising delicacy. "Under different circumstances . . ." He did not finish the sentence, rapped Jean on the shoulder without looking at him, and turned back to his knights, who continued to spar in pairs. He raised his sword and cried, "Bar, come on! Show me a fighting spirit!"

We went down to the harbor. There, we parted from Hugh, who expressed faint indignation, but Jean told him in a fatherly way that he trusted him to care properly for the Lady Alice. Hugh relented and straightened up, bowed to both of us, and left. We boarded the boat, which took us to the little ship that was anchored in the bay, whose crew appeared to be bustling with final preparations for the sailing.

Brunette, who came with us, appeared familiar with the process and stayed calm even when the sailors threw down a kind of basket that Jean placed her in and that lifted her aboard. We climbed up a rope ladder. Jean turned to greet a large, impressive man, similar to Thibaut in his arrogant expression, his hair, and his mighty mustache, but somehow rougher in appearance—even though he wore bright white silk Templar robes, densely embroidered with a red cross.

"Your Excellency de Périgord," said Jean, bowing his head. "In the name of the King of Navarre and in my own name, I thank you for granting us a place on your voyage."

"There is no need for such formality, dear Arsur," said de Périgord, who patted Jean's back with familiarity. "I would not miss an opportunity to snatch a glimpse of the famed Fairy of the Spring for all the fortune in the world!" He cried and laughed a crude laugh. I took a deep breath.

"Soon," Jean whispered to me, as de Périgord turned to answer one of the men. "In just a few hours, we will be at Le Destroit."

"Anchors aweigh!" someone shouted, and general pandemonium prevailed. The sails were hoisted, and the ship set off. De Périgord came back to us after consulting with a deckhand and scanned me with a distinctly un-puritanical expression.

"She looks pretty solid for a fairy," he said critically.

"Allow me to introduce to you Lady Édith of Cilicia, my cousin," said Jean drily, resuming his uneasy formality.

"Enchanted, my lady," de Périgord muttered and lost interest. He excused himself, saying that he had several letters to answer. "Duties never end!" he cried as he descended to the cabins below deck.

For weeks, I could not decide about the move to Atlit, and the ball was clearly in my court. At every opportunity, Halimi reiterated that what mattered most to him was that I should be happy. At whatever cost. For a city boy like him, who had breathed the soot of the streets all his life, who needed to be able to buy a pack of Camels at any hour of the night, and who had an ingrained, patronizing compassion for provincial life, this was no small price.

"I know you've lost faith in me, Ditush," he said one evening when we were weighing all the considerations regarding a potential move, again. "And I know that it will take time until that faith is restored. But I swear to you—the only thing that I want is for you to be happy." He said this so many times that the words were beginning to lose their meaning.

He left the magazine two weeks after he announced his resignation and ran around the house most of the day trying to be useful (he fixed a few things that had been neglected in recent months and made food every day while I worked on translating a science fiction book for young adults). I expected him to get on my nerves, but it was fun. We had not spent so much time together since Lily was born.

In the mornings, after he took her to daycare, he would prepare an elaborate breakfast and gently wake me up. Toward noon, he would tempt me into watching some episode or two of a funny series, and the times that I really laughed aloud, he glowed. As a special project, he began to prepare cocktails at home ("I am preparing myself for the role of a fifties housewife," he would say while measuring the exact number of milligrams of the various ingredients, wearing a red apron with white polka dots), to the point where I was tipsy for most of the day.

Slowly and steadily, he got me excited about the idea of starting a new life. There was something stimulating about the buds of thought of a new home somewhere else, somewhere completely different. We went to the house in Atlit twice—once just he and I, and then again with Lily, who was madly enthusiastic—which further tipped the scales.

The house had a bit of a weird feel to it—it had not been lived in for two years, and it was as though the walls themselves missed holding life within them. It was partially furnished, covered with plastic sheets to protect against dust, and when I started to envision where I would put this couch and that table, I was enchanted by the notion of our fresh start.

"We won't have to pay rent for the house, of course," Halimi continued with the advantages and disadvantages. "Richard doesn't make anything off it anyway, and it is his and my mother's gift to us." On that occasion, I tried to find out how it happened that Richard owned such a property; what connection did he have with Atlit? After all, he had enough money to buy an apartment in Jerusalem or Tel Aviv if he wanted a home in Israel, but the most I managed to get out of Halimi was that Richard had inherited it from some strange uncle and that none of his family knew the exact story.

When I saw on Facebook that Nina had been appointed to replace Halimi as the editor in chief at *Free to Be* and read all of the jubilant comments from the women who had been incensed by Halimi's appointment way back when, I finally decided that we would make the move. Halimi, who between cocktails and breakfasts and Netflix also continued his never-ending phone conversations, managed to land a gig hosting a weekly cultural program on the radio, a two-hour spot in the coveted rush-hour time slot. Since they knew that he would bring in listeners, he was able negotiate a nice salary.

A day later, I told Halimi, "Okay, let's do it." I went and bought a basic cell phone of the ancient kind. I reformatted my smartphone, turned it off, and exiled it to the pile of other devices that might still be of use to someone someday.

To Halimi, I said, "I don't want that thing to consume any more of my time" (he smiled skeptically), but I knew that the real detox was about the way it consumed my soul.

"What, are you deleting Facebook and Twitter and Instagram too?" he asked, as if my renunciation of the smartphone was an anthropological experiment.

"Not deleting it, but I have to sever this immediate connection between social media and the palm of my hand," I replied. When I suggested that he detox for a while, too, he said good-naturedly that maybe he would, after we moved and got settled.

More than anything, I just wanted to stop tracking him. I did not want to check, like a spasm every few minutes, when he was online, or stare at our chat box, relaxing if I saw he was typing and getting upset if I saw he had stopped. I truly wanted to stop reaching anxious hands into his secret drawers. I had no illusions that sooner or later I would feel this compulsion again, but for now, I only wanted to just breathe beside him—in body and in spirit.

We moved in early March, and for a month we were busy adapting to the house and adjusting it to our needs. I moved the furniture around again and again, and the lighting, and the pictures on the walls.

I worked on the balcony. I made friends with the yard. It gave me unexpected pleasure. I grew grounded in my new life and would gaze for long minutes out at the sea, which continually surprised me from different corners of the house and property. I was looking forward to the start of spring and warmer weather, weekday dips in the wild waters, surrounded by the ruins of the mysterious and inaccessible fortress.

After the suffocating mental stress of Acre, I surrendered completely to the serenity of the wind and the sea—the wet, salty scent in the air, the blue expanses, and the stretch of coast to the east that accompanied us from a distance.

Jean and I stood by the wooden railing, watching the ship parting the water for some time before we began talking. Brunette lay on the deck at our feet, her eyes closed in the pleasant sunshine. Although I was calm, I was still preoccupied with the episode in the solarium at the house of Rohard in Acre. Alice had no doubt that I was her husband's lover, that was clear, and the way in which he dismissed it as if she were crazy made me a little uncomfortable. I thought of Nina and the day when I had turned up to Halimi's office and informed him, in her presence, that I wanted a divorce.

I sighed. Jean, who was deep in thoughts of his own, turned to me.

"My lady," he smiled at me, but sadly.

"My lord," I replied with a similar expression.

"I never wanted to cause you such distress. All I wanted was to spend a little time together." He looked back at the water. "I love my wife very much, and I did not want to upset her either. I do not know how the Good Lord created hearts capable of such extreme contradictions. He must have been putting me to the test, and I failed."

I placed a reassuring hand on his shoulder, and he looked back at me gratefully. His telling me without apology that he loved his wife comforted me in an unexpected way.

"You did not fail the test, my lord," I told him gently. "In this complex situation, on account of a lack of forethought, your comportment was knightly and noble. It seems to me that your wife is not really so angry at you."

He smiled at the sea, turned to me, and seemed to want to say something else but stopped himself.

"Speak," I encouraged him. "I do not think that we need hide anything further from each other."

He smiled and nudged my shoulder with his, then grew serious and said, "Mine is a life of journeys, while hers is a sedentary one, at home. She has a strong and lively soul, and the obligation to keep quiet and do nothing arouses in her an anger that is unbecoming of a Christian woman. But I love that anger. It sharpens her tongue, which is keen as it is, and though I have known more than a few women besides her, I always return to her bed like a sailor thrown to shore, and she knows it."

I was quiet, but not because I had nothing to say. I tried to organize my thoughts into words in a way that he could understand. More than anything, at that moment, I felt a kind of solidarity with the Lady Alice, stuck there in the Middle Ages instead of conquering the world. Jean interpreted my silence as discontent.

"I apologize, my lady," he said quietly. "It is not right to let you into our business. You make me feel that I can say anything to you, like a confessor, but of course, that is not the case."

"Do not apologize, Jean," I said, courageously calling him by his first name for the first time, with no *seigneur* or any other formal address. "You do not cause me any discontent. Just gratitude for the fact that you trust me and reveal what is in your heart."

He looked at me, trying to understand if I was sincere or just saying things to please him. Evidently, my expression persuaded him that I was speaking honestly, because he pulled me to him and hugged me. "To hell with everyone," he whispered, demonstratively ignoring any gawking we might draw from the people on board. I hugged him back and closed my eyes.

De Périgord's little ship had a designated spot at the anchorage of the Pilgrim Castle. We disembarked to the platform via wooden stairs that were brought for us, and de Périgord took leave of us while hurling orders in every direction. Jean led me into the yard of the fortress and immediately went to look for a horse that would take us to the spring.

"We can go on foot," I told him. We had been just two or three hours at sea, but my legs longed for solid ground. Jean looked up at the sky. By the angle of the sun, we had another two to three hours of light.

"It would be better if we took a horse," he said curtly. I nodded. He left me to wait with Brunette in the bustling castle yard and went to the stables.

I began to scratch my eye. Something was really irritating it. No matter how much I blinked and teared up, the itching did not stop. I rubbed and rubbed, and suddenly I felt my contact lens fall out. "Shit," I said aloud to Brunette. She looked at me with concern. I looked around with one eye closed. Nobody was paying any particular attention to me, but the yard was full of people. I did not dare try to put a new contact lens in and instead narrowed my good eye in the direction of the stables. Jean was nowhere to be seen. At least the itching stopped.

"Lady Édith of Cilicia," said an oily voice, and I looked up and met the moist gaze of Gautier de Brienne. Brunette let out a low growl.

"Seigneur de Brienne," I said and stood, patting Brunette on the head. He gave a little bow, and I returned the gesture. I opened the other eye, too, so as not to appear crazy, and it was strange to see the world half blurry and half in focus.

"Still in our environs, my lady? And where is that mannerless cousin of yours?" asked de Brienne, emitting that sour-milk smell of his in my direction. He must not have bathed in weeks.

"Not for long, sir," I answered respectfully. "Seigneur Jean is looking for a horse for me so I might continue on my way."

"Well, it seems that there is no better time for you to pray to Saint Euphemia for a successful journey," said de Brienne in his slippery way as he clasped my hand. *What's his deal with this saint?*

I released my hand vigorously and wondered for a moment what was preferable, to answer sharply that my prayers were my own private affair or to respond humbly that I was awaiting my cousin's direction. The timely appearance of Jean, holding the reins of two horses trotting after him obediently, solved my dilemma.

"De Brienne," Jean sighed.

"Young Ibelin," de Brienne replied. "Was the king's mission crowned with success?" It was evident to me that he was bitter that he had not been asked to join.

Jean gave him a stern look. "The business and journeys of the king are his concern, and I will not speak of them in his absence." He did not break eye contact with de Brienne, who eventually shifted his gaze over to the great church. Its stone dome was glowing pink in the dimming light.

"How can it be that your cousin appears again and again at the Pilgrim Castle without paying her respects to our martyred saint?" de Brienne resumed his pestering. "Is she a pilgrim or an apostate in disguise?" Jean looked at me, rolled his eyes and shook his head slowly, then said, as if reconciling himself to his fate, "My cousin asked me to escort her into the Pilgrim Church myself. She is a delicate creature and fearful of strangers and large crowds." De Brienne removed his crimson velvet beret with its peacock feather and cleared the way with an exaggerated gesture. Jean led me into the church and tied the horses to rings installed in the outer wall. Brunette accepted her task of waiting for us there and lay down beside the horses.

"Another delay," I muttered reluctantly, but I still relished, even if I was not proud of it, his calling me a "delicate creature."

The church was large, gloomy, and awe-inspiring. The sunlight that penetrated through the enormous round framed stained glass burned the dark stone floor with panes of color. Many worshippers were bowed in the prayer seats, and others were walking around. Although the big iron doors of the church were open wide, it somehow felt both suffocating and cold inside. I tried to keep both eyes open and saw everything half blurry and half focused, and something inside my head began spinning.

Jean led me inside the length of the corridor until we stood at the edge of a group of people, awaiting their turn to pray before the remains of Euphemia. I did not know what to expect—a desiccated leg? An urn of ashes? A cloth bag supposedly containing her bones?

"Who is this Euphemia anyway?" I whispered to Jean under the auspices of muttering prayers. Jean couldn't help but smile.

"Euphemia was a young virgin in the earliest days of Christianity, the daughter of a senator at Chalcedon," Jean began, and again I envisioned him telling stories to one of his children. This time, I could really visualize the big wood stove in the solarium of the house of Rohard in Acre, and Jean sitting with little Balian. "What is Chalcedon?" I whispered. "By Byzantium," Jean replied and moved up in the line. "Euphemia devoted herself to Christianity and was unwilling to make a sacrifice to Ares, the god of war." I nodded knowingly. Jean smiled a small smile. "The Roman authorities put her through unthinkable torture, but she did not give up her faith. Finally, they threw her into the arena of beasts of prey. A wild bear attacked her and mortally wounded her. When the lions approached her body lying on the ground, the crowd roared, expecting the lions to tear her to pieces, but they did not. They approached her and began to gently lick her wounds, until she almost appeared a girl who had fallen asleep on a spring day, in a meadow." The line continued to progress. From behind the backs of several of those waiting, I saw a woman kneeling and sobbing in front of what appeared to be a rather disturbing statue of a wide-eyed woman with a mane of brown hair.

"The saint's remains were painstakingly preserved for hundreds of years in her church in Chalcedon," Jean resumed telling. "But a few decades ago, in a most strange and unusual coincidence, her head disappeared from among her remains. A priest who opened her coffin in order to replace the fragrant herbs discovered this and was horrified." The sobbing lady crossed herself and vacated her spot.

"When His Holiness the Bishop of Acre, Jacques de Vitry, helped establish the Pilgrim Castle some twenty years ago, he prayed one day beside the spring in Le Destroit," Jean went on. I perked up. "Suddenly, before his eyes, out of the water appeared the head of a woman with wild, vivid hair, and eyes deeper than the sea. His Holiness held the cross over his heart, thinking that it was some kind of demon, but the head began to speak to him. The head told him that it had wandered the length of the sea from Byzantium to the Pilgrim Castle in the Holy Kingdom in order to unite East and West, between the Greek and the Latin Church, and to put an end to the age-old rivalry within the Christian world. When the church of the Pilgrim Castle was built, a magnificent sculpture was constructed in honor of the saint, in which they buried the head from the spring and thus preserved her remains to this day."

"Pshhh," I responded with admiration. This was a good story. *That devil of a fellow de Vitry*, I thought to myself. *Interesting if Simone knows this story.* Our turn came. Jean knelt down, and I hurried to do as he did. He murmured a prayer, and I murmured Latin-sounding gibberish, both of us with our eyes closed. When he finished praying, he pushed me gently with his elbow. I opened my eyes and looked up at the sculpture as he did. In the stands, a choir of monks sang Gregorian chants. I did not understand what I was seeing and blinked each eye alternately, no longer sure. Before me stood a painted wooden statue of a woman. She looked disturbingly real: a brown-skinned woman, her thick brown hair tucked under a gold-embroidered cap, her gown of royal crimson, sleeves of blinding white. The bright colors were in inverse proportion to the general gloom inside the church. Her hands were folded modestly yet her stance radiated a resolute strength. Her piercing eyes seemed to follow you, slicing through your soul to its core. I preferred not to imagine what relics were kept inside that unsettling statue, and assumed the opening must be in the back. Jean stood before the statue and crossed himself again; I mimicked him, my eyes locked on the statue's.

The eyes seemed to meet mine with a vivid gaze, and I grasped Jean's hand impulsively. They stared at me, wise and wild and strong and knowing everything about me. What I recalled in that moment was Halimi's mushroom dream of the ancient stone circle and the priestess dancing at its center. I felt like I was on the verge of a stroke.

"Do not remain any longer," I heard a voice say. The lips of the statue did not move, but its eyes spoke to me. As the Gregorian chanting grew muffled in my ears, a disturbing sound hummed inside my head, and I collapsed into Jean's arms.

I had not actually fainted but simply lost all ability to use so much as a muscle of my body, and even though I could see what was happening around me, everything was blurry. A murky vapor shrouded my eyes and head. Jean carried me to the horses, which were waiting outside, and someone helped him untie one of them and lifted me into his arms. Jean held the reins in one hand, holding me to him with the other, and we galloped away, accompanied by Brunette beside us, running and barking.

The way passed hazily before my eyes, and the mysterious voice in my head continued, accompanied by a growing hum. My body leaned limply against Jean, and I struggled not to lose consciousness completely.

We arrived at the canopy of the big carob tree. A greeting was heard from the guardhouse, and Jean cried back in response. He jumped down from the horse without even bothering to tie him, and took me down too. Being close to the spring strengthened me. With unsteady steps, I staggered toward it.

"Are you feeling better, my lady?" he asked after I noisily gulped water from the trickling spring, as did Brunette. "I am much better," I said with difficulty. "But I must pass through. I cannot stay any longer,"

I said with urgency, the terrible eyes still burning before me and the voice commanding me not to linger any longer repeating in my ears.

I rummaged around in my bag until I found the cloth pouch where I kept my coins. I took out Lily's ten-agorot coin and knelt beside the water. Jean knelt beside me. Brunette sat and looked at us with her tongue lolling and a look of concern.

"I'll come with you," he said, and at the sight of my weak protest, he added, "I have to make sure that you arrive there safely." I had no strength to say anything. I held his one hand, and with the other he produced his knife. He made a small cut in his hand and in mine. Brunette barked one lonely bark. I dipped my hand with the coin in it into the water, and Jean and I tumbled in at once, Brunette's sad howl echoing in my ears.

The pulling sensation almost crushed me completely, as if I were passing through a birth canal—it felt as if a dark sponge were pressing against all the organs of my body as I struggled to squeeze through the narrow passage toward the promise of light and air on the other side. A warm hand grasped mine and reminded me that there was a world and life and time. We were spat out.

The sun had already set, and it was dim beneath the carob canopy. We lay on the dry earth for a few minutes. Then, I stood and went out onto the ridge. In the west were ruins of the fort and the military base, and to the east, cars and trucks were speeding along the highways, and the houses of Atlit were visible. It seemed that I had returned home. I took a deep breath and returned to the carob canopy. Jean was sitting up, but it looked like he was not yet entirely lucid. With his cupped hand, he took a little water from the book-sized puddle and licked it.

I went back out from under the canopy to see if my car was still parked where I'd left it. I returned to my cloth bag beside the spring, took the single contact lens out of my eye, and put on my glasses.

"What is that thing?" Jean recoiled.

"These are glasses," I told him with a smile. "They help me see better." The color had returned to Jean's cheeks, and he asked to examine the glasses. He looked through them and recoiled again, then examined them from every angle.

"There was a Saracen sailor I knew who used magnifying glasses on the end of a long stick, and they helped him see where the land was and other things," he said seriously.

"It's the same principle," I said. I looked around me and could not believe that for the past two days, I had been fainting left and right like some gentle lady in a tight corset. I felt an urgent need to call my parents.

I took out my cell phone, turning it on with a sense of expectation and concern that something terrible may have happened in my absence, or that my lie had been found out and everyone knew that I was not at any Vipassana workshop and were wondering where I had disappeared to.

"It's getting dark already, my lady," said Jean, glancing through the branches out at the darkening sky. I looked up from the tiny screen that had begun to flash at my knight, who had crossed through worlds to make sure that I was okay, and I put the phone aside.

"Indeed it is," I said gently, and an idea popped into my head. "Might I offer you to spend the night at my residence? Nobody will disturb us there, and you can return tomorrow morning." Jean looked as though I had suggested to him that we fly to the moon. "Think about it," I said, letting him digest the idea while I returned to the phone.

There were a few messages from my parents and one from Halimi. My father sent a message that I was unable to open, probably a video of Lily. He seemed unable to grasp that I no longer had a smartphone. There were several messages from my mother, with laconic reports on Lily's mood, eating, and state of cleanliness ("We ate pea soup and Lily took a long bath. Now she's asleep. Asked for something that I didn't understand and eventually found her blankie herself."). Halimi sent me three hearts.

I sighed with satisfaction. I had disappeared from my world for two days, and it continued to function as usual, without any drama. I turned back to Jean. In his colorful silk robes in the spreading gloom, he appeared like some precious gem.

"What do you say to my suggestion, my lord?" I asked, ready for any response. Jean smiled all over and stood up straight.

"After dragging you into the depths of my life, my lady, it seems only fair to follow you into yours," he said. "I will not deny a mix of intense curiosity and petrifying fear. I shall come with you." I picked up my cloth bag, and we began to walk to my car.

Jean was not as physically shaken as he had been the previous time that he passed through the spring. Indeed, he looked in every direction and held my hand very tightly, but his steps were certain. When we got to the car, he stopped and stared at me opening the door, jumped at the light that turned on automatically, and then peered inside through the driver's seat.

"This is the beastless carriage?" he asked, his eyes scanning the rather worn and tattered interior of the car hungrily. "This is so similar to the dream I had just last night, only the carriage was green on the outside."

"Exactly," I said. "You get in on the other side."

"I fear that I do not know how," said Jean, mortified at being so helpless.

I led him to the door on the passenger side and showed him how to open it with the handle. Jean wanted to try it himself, so we spent a few satisfying minutes opening the door and slamming it. Finally, he got in and sat down. He closed the door from the inside and was charmed by the strength of the slam. I buckled my seatbelt and, so as not to waste time, I buckled his too. This was very erotic, of course, to stretch across him to pull the strap, but I continued matter-of-factly and started the car. *Now that we've come this far*, I said to myself, *we might as well get into a soft bed instead of making out like teenagers over the hand brake.*

Hearing the rumble of the engine, Jean grabbed my thigh forcefully. "Don't worry," I said. "We'll get going at once, everything is all right." He nodded. I turned on the headlights, and he whistled with appreciation. When I went in reverse, he blanched. He made it through the short, five-minute drive with gritted teeth, looking out the window with one hand placed over his heart. I was afraid he would throw up.

I stopped the car beside the house and very much hoped that none of my neighbors would pass by and ask nosy questions, but luck was on our side. When I had turned the key in the engine, I recalled again the feeling that I had when I went off on that mushroom trip with Halimi a little more than a month earlier. This time, I felt that I had finally returned, for real.

I had never felt such great relief in my life to return home—like someone swept out to the depths of sea on a rotting log for days with no hope of rescue until suddenly, land appeared on the horizon. The feeling of relief was so great that I had to run and pee. I told Jean to go inside and make himself at home while I slipped into the bathroom. The last time I had peed was in a pot in a tiny cabin in the ship of the master of the Knights Templar. It's amazing that I did not wet myself after the shocking experience with the statue at the church. It already seemed hard to believe that all this had really happened. I quickly flushed the toilet and went out to Jean. The house was quiet, and my heart began to pound.

Jean was walking between the rooms, staring wide-eyed at pictures, and when we went into the kitchen, he carefully picked up one item after another, examining each one. I opened the fridge, and he marveled. I heated a few pieces of bread in the toaster, and he was ecstatic. I boiled water in the electric kettle, and he almost lost his mind.

I tried the best I could to explain how electricity works, but failing after a stuttering attempt, I simply looked up the entry for electricity on Wikipedia on my tablet. While he held the device reverently, I made tea and a few slices of bread with butter, sausage, yellow cheese, and tomato.

"My understanding cannot comprehend these wonders," he said after a few minutes. "And the language here is written in such a way that it is hard for me to make sense of its meaning." He set the device aside.

"It isn't so important," I said, still embarrassed by the fact that I could not explain the workings of electricity in simple terms. "Electricity will only appear seven hundred years after your time."

"Everything that you want to know, you ask this device?" he asked.

"You could say that," I said, smiling.

"And how does the device know?"

"It isn't the device that knows," I laughed. "It's simply a collection of everything that we have come to know." I was not sure that he could understand what I meant, and I started to explain to him the general idea of preserving and disseminating information.

He shook his head slowly and stroked his beard. "No wonder so many people thought you were a fairy or a witch. You really do live in a world of wonders and magic."

"Come eat," I said.

He was amazed by the idea of putting a slice of food on a slice of bread, and he was curious about the tomato. When I told him that a few hundred years after his time, they would discover a huge continent full of delicacies that would change the whole world, he fell silent.

By the time we finished eating, he was exhausted with wonderment. He laid his head down on his hands, set on the table, which was somehow childish and poignant. I stroked his head and told him we would go to sleep soon.

"But there is one other thing that I have to show you," I told him, and he looked up. "The splendor of human civilization and the thing for which it really is worth living in modern times: the home shower."

When I showed him how it worked, his mouth gaped. He played with the hot and cold water in the tap, and I asked him if he preferred to dip in a basin of hot water or stand beneath a gushing cascade of water at the exact temperature that he wanted.

"You may think I am overly insatiable, my lady"—("Never," I squeezed in)—"but I would like to try both."

"Not a problem," I said and adjusted the water to the perfect temperature. I showed him how to switch the tap from the bath nozzle to the showerhead, how to adjust the water so it would suit his exact needs, and I instructed him to undress. He removed his boots, stripped off his red silk tunic and his golden silk pants, and remained in a long cotton tunic with cloth tights. Then, he stopped.

"You have to remove everything," I said.

"In front of you?" he asked, agitated.

"Of course," I said, holding back from laughing. "We are both adults, are we not?" He did not understand the connection between the two things and insisted that he could not remove all his clothes in my presence. "Did you never undress before your wife?" I asked in astonishment.

"Never," he said resolutely. "Of course, I have been with her without the overlayers dozens of times, but to stand naked before a woman and her nakedness . . ." He even shuddered a little. I left in peace. I preferred that he enjoy the experience instead of forcing intimacy on him. While I waited for him to shower, I rolled a joint—more as a relaxing routine than out of any urgency to be stoned. It was strange to see Jean so flustered, devoid of his usual confidence.

I started to wonder if I should pay him a surprise visit but decided to leave him be. I also debated for a moment if I should wait for him to smoke the joint. But maybe it was better he not smoke any, given the culture shock that I had imposed on him. I didn't want him getting paranoid.

I lit the joint. I took a few deep tokes and closed my eyes. I felt a pressing need to digest everything I had done and seen in the past two days. I still had a hard time believing that I had left the house less than forty-eight hours earlier.

"Lady Édith," I heard Jean's voice over the noise of the flowing water. I set down the joint in the ashtray and went into the bathroom.

"Yes?" I asked quietly through the curtain.

"I was pondering something," he said, and his head poked out from behind the curtain, his dark hair wet and shiny. "And I came to the conclusion that I must not respond to your generosity and patience with reservation and alienation." He pulled the curtain aside and stood before me in all of his beautiful nakedness. He was terribly embarrassed but was brave in the face of it.

The air left me at once, and I felt a wave of heat pass through my whole body, in a ripple that ran from my center to my limbs. He laughed at my gaze fixed on him, and I threw off all of my clothes and joined him. We embraced beneath the water and were soon kissing wetly and wildly. I felt pain with the desire that he enter me.

"Let's go to bed," I managed to groan.

"After you," he said hoarsely.

I woke up at the crack of dawn and for a long time looked at Jean, naked, sleeping peacefully. His chest rose and fell, and I reconstructed every detail of our lovemaking throughout the night. How he was surprised when I went down on him and only managed to mutter, "I thought only port whores . . ." and then was silent. How he directed himself to the exact spot that made me come with a cry. How afterward we lay holding each other and kissing until we fell asleep. My lips were still burning a little in the morning from all the kissing.

I heard my phone rattle from the living room and rose quietly to see who it was. It must have been 6:00 a.m., and I suddenly worried that perhaps something was amiss with Lily.

It was a message from Halimi.

"Still silent, detached from the world?"

I replied at once. "Still silent, but will resume speaking soon." Then, I added three hearts.

"How's it going over there?" I added after about a half a minute of staring at the phone. I was surprised I felt no pangs of conscience for letting another man into our bed, not to mention enjoying it so much. *But it isn't at our expense, it's not at the expense of our time together*, I told myself, *it doesn't make me love him any less*. I imagined Halimi down to the most minute details in some hotel room, getting dressed to go out for his morning walk. *And maybe Nina was there too?* Now that I amused myself with this thought for a moment, not only did I not feel a pinch of anger; I might have even hoped it was so, just a little.

"Great. The interview went really well, and at noon I'm off to Paris. I miss you and Lily." I wondered if he was in contact with my parents and realized that he probably was.

"I miss you too," I wrote, even though I had hardly thought of him in the past two days. But last night, when Jean was showering and I smoked the joint, I felt a surprisingly powerful longing for the routine of our life together. For Halimi humming in the kitchen or talking on the phone while chopping vegetables for dinner or building some architecturally illogical structure with Lily on the carpet from her colorful wooden blocks.

"Remind me when you get back," I added.

"Three more days, airhead," Halimi replied along with a smiley.

Then, he added, "I bought Lily something really cool. And something cute for you too." I smiled.

"I get home today," I wrote.

"Take care of yourself, my Ditush," he wrote.

"You too, Limush," I replied and stroked the telephone with a finger.

I went to peek inside the bedroom. Jean had changed positions but was still sleeping deeply. Soon, I would have to wake him. With a heavy heart, I remembered Brunette whimpering beside the spring and assumed that she would wait for her master until he returned, even if it took an eternity.

I made coffee and lit a cigarette on the balcony. The sun was already rising, and the morning was clear and bright. *What kind of a person am I?* I asked myself, without guilt or shame. I recalled my sister's lectures on free love and felt a powerful urge to talk to her. I did not remember when I had even spoken to her last. I assumed that I was not the first person in history who had been able to love both her husband and her lover, but it felt that way. Each of them in a different way, with different depths, but even so. *But in fact, Jean loves me and his wife too*, I thought. *And Halimi also loves me, and Nina, evidently, and she certainly did not stop loving him.* I tried to focus on the protracted painful feeling that I felt from their affair. *Why?* I tried to understand in that moment. *Why did it cause me so much misery?*

The answer floated before my eyes: We are sitting in the living room one afternoon. Lily and Halimi are doing a puzzle on the floor. It must have been at the beginning of their affair, around that day when I told my sister I'd realized that Halimi no longer gave me those admiring looks. The hours he spent at home also seemed to be getting shorter and shorter, and the need to "go out" was growing. His perpetual air of distraction. Of course, all the obvious things—the blatant and persistent lies, that I was the last to know, and how stupid and empty and out of control it made me feel. But what really destroyed me was that their love (*or whatever it was*, I thought spitefully) came at the expense of our love. He sacrificed his attention to me on the altar of his attention to her.

I took a long breath and felt a deep and total calm. I went back to the bedroom and got back in between the sheets. I hugged Jean from behind and took pleasure in the feeling of his body between my arms, pressed against my chest and belly, in sleep. I began to kiss him and teared up.

He turned over, opened his eyes blearily, and a whole range of expressions emerged on his face: happy to see me, a full scan of the room we were in, focus on my face, registering that I was crying.

"Édith," he said quietly.

"Jean," I said, and all of the calm and the universal insight seemed to evaporate.

Jean sat and pulled me to him. He hugged me and stroked my hair without saying a word, without trying to comfort me or ask what happened. Something in my soul's mechanics must have malfunctioned because somehow, maybe out of embarrassment, the crying turned into a kind of snot-filled laugh.

"Stop, I can't," I said as I rocked against his chest. "I'm such a damned cliché."

"Pardon?" said Jean and turned his neck to see my face.

"Forget it," I sniffed. "It doesn't matter."

We stood beneath the carob tree by the tiny puddle—me in my normal clothes, which made Jean laugh ("My lady, you look like a little peasant boy"), and him in his silk suit. I needed to send him through the passage and go back again. Nervously, I fingered the two coins in my pocket, and again I heard the disturbing hum that had accompanied the burning eyes, silently commanding me to return to my world. I was unable to approach the puddle.

"I don't know why," I said trembling, "but I am terribly afraid. I don't dare." I tried to forcibly remind myself of the powerful feeling and the all-encompassing understanding that I had experienced the last few times I went through, but all I managed to bring to mind was the terrible, living eyes staring at me from out of that wooden statue, then the feeling of suction, compression, and the suffocating passage yesterday on the way back to my world.

Jean smiled slyly and pulled out a coin that looked exactly like mine, a coin from the house of Ibelin in Beirut. Suddenly, he furrowed his brow and brought the coin closer to his eyes.

"It looks so ancient and worn," he whispered, swallowing. He rested one hand on the tree trunk. "And yet it is identical to yours. Certainly, it will bring me to the same time."

"But who knows if it will work in the same way? I cannot be responsible for you popping up in some other time or if you were to be sucked into some parallel dimension."

Jean bit his lips and didn't even bother to ask me what a parallel dimension was. He was willing to tarnish his good name for my sake, to quarrel with his wife, to postpone urgent matters of the kingdom—but this was probably already too much.

"I will take you through," I declared.

Once again, we made a small cut in our palms and held our coins. We laced our hands together and dipped them into the book-sized puddle. I looked into his eyes and counted to three.

How could I forget? My whole being screamed with exhilaration. It was an electrifying pleasure, almost painful. The phosphorescent explosion not only was inside my head but also burst from the core of the universe. Our bodies merged together, blended into each other, and it did not matter that our daily lives took place on completely different tracks. Within the whirlpool of the spring, we were one body, but actually we were all the bodies in the world, an endless torrent of living breathing material, separated into individuals only so that it might tell itself a bedtime story.

Happy barking accompanied the lurch of being thrown to the ground. Brunette fell upon Jean, who got up at once and breathlessly stroked and hugged and praised her. Maybe this helped him recover from the existential combustion we had just experienced.

"The guards will soon come to see what is going on," I said in a panic when I heard some voices. Jean, who was clearly relieved to be back in his comprehensible, quiet, green world, stood up.

"I will go reassure them," he proclaimed. "Wait here for me."

"Please," I said.

"Please," he said and kissed my hand. "Stay," he told Brunette. I sat down beside the burbling spring and watched her wistfully, passing my hand through the silky waters. I heard whispers of giggles and sighs in my ears, but I resolutely let go of any fear.

"People call everything that is beyond their grasp 'madness,'" I said aloud to Brunette, then I felt like a truly crazy person. Brunette buried her snout in my shoulder. I stroked and hugged her. *At least I know that I really have touched the sublime*, I told myself, *and now I must distance myself from it and come back down to the ground before I lose my way back.*

Jean returned and sat down beside me. For a few minutes, we did not say anything. We looked at each other, smiling and sighing.

"I must go," I said finally, when I could no longer discern between the smiles and the sighs and the whispers floating up to me like an invisible witness from the spring. "I'm about to completely lose my mind."

Silently, I handed Jean the garb that he had lent me, nicely folded inside a cloth bag. I was afraid that if the clothes remained accessible to me, their shining silk might tempt me back into the other world.

"Will we never meet again?" Jean asked in a voice thick with sadness.

"Let us not make such absolute declarations as 'never,'" I said. Further silence. "Maybe I can come back to visit you here when I recover, if you will still come back to the Pilgrim Castle sometime," I added after some thought. "And if you want, you can leave me a message. A small note in a corked earthenware vessel to be hidden in an agreed-upon location." I looked around and pointed to the spot where the trunk of the tree was wet from the spray of water. "Here, in the ground under this part of the tree, we'll carve a small cross into it."

Jean smiled as if I had suggested something completely useless but took my hand and kissed it with complete focus.

I was not satisfied with this and kissed him on the lips. I felt that I was melting into him, and the whispering inside my head grew stronger. The hum returned.

"Goodbye for now, Jean d'Ibelin, Count of Arsur. May you find blessings at every turn," I said, swallowing my tears.

"Goodbye, Lady Édith, Fairy of the Spring," he said very quietly.

I held out my finger, and he made a cut in it. I squeezed Lily's coin in my fist and plunged it into the spring.

CHAPTER 26

The first thing I did when I got home was call my parents.

"What's this, speaking again?!" my father picked up teasingly.

"The workshop's finished!" I replied, laughing. "How's Lily? Can I talk to her?"

From the moment I was drawn back into the spring and then spat back out into the twenty-first century, I missed her terribly. Even though the plan had been that I would meet my parents in Tel Aviv the following day and collect her from there, I thought of driving to Jerusalem to pick her up that day.

"Hmm, they went out for a walk," said my father. "We'll call you when they get back."

We spoke a little more about how things were with them ("She is such a good, sweet girl, even your mother says so"), how things were with me ("It was an extraordinary experience, and disorienting, but I'm happy to be home"), about some news story of which I had no knowledge, and the weather forecast for the coming days.

I made myself tea and drank it in long, slow sips and walked around the house. Traces of Jean still lingered, the memory of him thrilled by the accuracy of the family "portraits" (as in the photos of the three of us on the corkboard beside my computer), putting his hand inside the fridge and taking it out, frolicking before me in the shower. I did not want to think about him so much.

It had been sublime, and now it was time to let go. I got into the shower, and for almost an hour I let the images run through my mind, nonjudgmentally, unafraid, as though I were watching an adventure movie inside my head.

When I finally got out of the shower, I saw a missed call from my mother. I called her back, still wrapped in a towel, and spoke to her and then Lily. I was touched by how much my mother was enjoying their time together. She told me about the walk they took through the Mahane Yehuda market, how the vendors at every stall gave Lily some kind of treat because she charmed everyone, and I surged with maternal pride.

"Mama, Nana Tasha doesn't like Robinod," Lily reported to me first. This was her nickname for her grandmother, Natasha, to distinguish from Nana Simone.

"I like Robinod fine!" I heard my mother object in the background. "But not the Disney movie."

"I'll meet you in Tel Aviv tomorrow and take you home," I told her. "I really miss you."

"What?" said Lily, and I didn't know if she was talking to me or she was distracted by one of my parents.

"I missed you a lot," I said again.

"You kissed me a lot??!" Lily asked cheerfully.

"I missed you!" I said loudly and clearly.

"She's kissing the telephone," my mother said in the background.

I sent kisses into the receiver, too, and we said goodbye until tomorrow.

After clicking through several Netflix series, none of which aroused particular interest, I decided to take advantage of my last free day. Instead of indulging in thoughts of Jean and Halimi and of the transient nature of love, I took the printed pages of the French manuscript, determined at least to finish reading the text today.

I made myself an omelet with vegetables, and in the meantime, I thought about what I would make for dinner to celebrate the reunion of my family. I planned to surprise Halimi and meet him at the airport together with Lily.

I went out onto the balcony with a cup of tea and allowed myself a leisurely midday joint. It was very warm, almost too hot, and I thought wistfully of how the fleeting spring would soon be over, and summer, in all of its sweltering intensity, would be upon us.

I went out for a short walk to get some fresh air and move my muscles. I meant to buy flowers and some basic staples to stock the fridge, but my feet took me over the sandstone ridge of their own accord and to the Narrow Passage that the Crusaders called Le Destroit.

But I did not walk to my spring—or puddle. I realized that I did not want to sit and ponder melancholically under the carob tree, deliberating whether or not to jump in. For a while, I stared at what looked to me from afar like flamingoes over the salt pools.

When I got inside, I set the grocery bags down on the table, took a deep breath, and sat on the sofa. For almost an hour, I did nothing. I did not think about anything. I did not even doze off. I just stared at our house and allowed myself to savor the moment.

Then, I tidied the minor mess that had managed to take hold since the cleaner had been here several days earlier. I wallowed in the sheets, which still bore a trace of Jean's scent, in a kind of painful pleasure—recalling the only night we spent together. I thought about Halimi and what it would be like when he got back. Again, I imagined Nina sneaking into Halimi's hotel room, arriving unannounced, to supervise the interview and the photo shoot, and the angry sex they might have had. I relished that this vision didn't madden or sadden me, not even a little. I imagined her and Halimi in the throes of wild lovemaking, and it turned me on. I got myself off with a tremor and fell asleep.

I awoke with a start, but a quick glance at the clock revealed that I had only slept for twenty minutes. I changed the sheets to Halimi's favorite set—Egyptian cotton in light blue. I put the groceries away, placed the flowers in Simone's blue porcelain vase, and paused once more to muse on the fact that it was just one month earlier that she'd been here and I had gone through *my* narrow passage for the first time. It felt like three lifetimes ago. Still smiling, I stepped into the shower.

The reunion had been joyful. Lily was thrilled to see me in Tel Aviv and did not stop talking about the things she did with Nana Tasha. But when we went to get Halimi at the airport and she first spotted him in the arrival hall, she lost it completely.

She ran at him, and he had to artfully maneuver the suitcase and bags he was holding to be able to catch her in his arms. Several people waiting smiled warmly at our little family, and I blinked to drive the sudden tears from my eyes.

Usually when the three of us were all together, Halimi drove, I sat beside him, and Lily dictated the music from the back. This time, since she was so excited to see him, and he her, I drove, and they sat together in the back. I listened to their conversations ("Daddy, where were you?"— "In Lisbon and in Paris"—"In Miss Bun?!") And the serenity of my past two days was replaced with a fierce happiness, which scared me.

I tried to recall the last time that I felt this happy. I recalled sitting at the window after a wild and satisfying night out, enjoying the mix of warm, homey intimacy and the adventures still in store for me. And then came the text message from Nina, which muddled everything I had believed about myself.

Calm down, I instructed myself in my most assertive inner voice. *Everything is fine now, that's what's important.* Suddenly, I missed my sister. I tried to clear my head of thoughts and focused on driving.

Back home, Lily thundered to her room and, of her own initiative, began to unpack her things and put them away. I went to put on the kettle, and Halimi lit a cigarette at the balcony threshold. It was dark outside, and the balcony light fell on him like a Hopper painting.

"Come here," he said, and we embraced for three straight minutes.

Then, he moved away from me and looked me up and down with that old lewd expression of his—my favorite.

"That Vipassana really did you well," he said with a smile. "You are shining like the sun. Your eyes are green like emeralds." I laughed and wondered who else could utter the word *emeralds* so naturally. "How's the translation coming along?"

"It's coming along all right," I answered. His question surprised me. I thought that he would probe further what exactly had gone on at the Vipassana retreat. Several times, I wondered if I would dare try to tell him about my supernatural experiences.

I wanted to tell him about Jean, I really did. In large part, just to be able to talk to someone about the wonderful, arousing, and liberating feeling of realizing that I was in love with Jean without having stopped intensely loving Halimi. But he would think that I had completely lost my mind. *Maybe one day I could come up with a story that would put Jean into some more realistic context*, I thought. *Maybe then I could talk about it with Halimi.*

"Did you really get started on the translation?" he asked, surprising me. He always enjoyed hearing about my translation process but very rarely took an active interest.

"No, I just nearly finished reading the original," I said and fixed him with a searching look. "Why do you ask?"

"Just curious," said Halimi and let out a puff of smoke. "By the way, you won't believe what Jacques found out about Richard." I hadn't even asked Halimi how his brother was doing. I perked up.

"Yes?" I was ready for any kind of juicy gossip—Richard was a bigamist, or president of the International Monetary Fund, or was once a woman. But Halimi surprised me yet again.

"So, it turns out that this property has been passed down in Richard's family, from generation to generation, for hundreds of years now," he said, enjoying my interest. He tossed the cigarette butt into the empty ashtray on the balcony table and went inside.

"How many hundreds of years?" I asked, trembling. I sat down on the couch beside him. From Lily's room, I heard the sounds of a person making a mess while tidying up.

"I don't know exactly, but from what Jacques discovered, Richard's family has Crusader origins. His ancestors were *in* the Crusades, can you imagine? And apparently, some branch of the family actually settled here. Sometime in the thirteenth century, one of them bought this property here, and it passed from one generation to the next for all those years. It's crazy—the Mamluk sultanate, the Ottomans, the British Mandate, the State of Israel—and the estate kept being passed down within the family. An actual Crusader property in the midst of our respectable Atlit—can you believe it?"

I needed a few seconds to collect myself and speak without giving away my disproportionate enthusiasm.

"Do you have any idea what the family was called?" I permitted myself a voice of healthy curiosity.

"Diblin, de Ibelin, something like that. Their name changed over time, of course; some of the heiresses married new husbands, and none of them even lived on the property most of the time, but they must have had some kind of power of attorney that also got passed down, and the wording in the land registry was preserved and updated. It's crazy, the documents that Jacques found. I took pictures of some of his scans— want to see them?"

"Later," I said, trying to maintain a steady voice. "Let's eat dinner first."

I chopped vegetables and put out cheese, imagining Jean going and buying a property not far from our spring, where he thought my house was. *Maybe he built (or would build?) a little hut there? So that if I came for a visit, we would have some privacy?* The thought both moved me and made me sad. *Could he be sitting there, waiting for me to drop by and visit? Would he continue to come here all his life?* I shook it off and focused on our dinner. There would be time to think about all this.

Lily ate well at dinner, not demanding something else in place of everything I gave her, and just chewed and swallowed and listened to the two of us. We tried not to make a big deal of it so as not to break the magic, but every so often we nudged each other lightly under the table and winked with satisfaction.

After dinner, Halimi gave us our gifts. He spoiled Lily with sweets from duty-free, a bronze statuette of Artemis, and a sheath that precisely fit the sword that Richard had given her the last time. Lily raced to strap on the sword, and the sheath hung funny because the belt was still big on her. I thought that he would bring me a shawl, something beautiful he found in one of the flea markets that he liked to wander around in when he was abroad, but he surprised me once more.

Inside a red rectangular velvet box, very similar to the one in which he gave me the necklace with the Ibelin coin, lay another necklace with a worn, polished coin.

"What is this?" I asked with faint fear. His eyebrows rose.

"It's a Phoenician coin, from right around this area. I found it in some antique coin stall at the market in Paris. I thought of starting you a collection of ancient coins because you loved that Crusader one so much," he said, a little uncertain.

"It's lovely," I replied and kissed him on the forehead. "And a really sweet idea." His face shone, and his old Cheshire cat smile appeared again. I realized I had missed that smile for a long time.

My finger lingered over the quick dial for Libby for a long time, but I did not dare call. I could not forget how she had shunned me when I decided to go back to Halimi. *Still*, I told myself, *there's a limit to how much yearning one person can maintain*. In the end, I sent a text: "Miss you."

The reply came at once: "Why aren't you writing on WhatsApp? What are you, my grandmother?"

I grinned and meant to call, but she beat me to it.

"So, how's exile, Dita?" Libby asked after we both muttered vague apologies. Libby confessed that she missed me like crazy and hinted that she would even suffer Halimi's presence for the sake of a visit to the new place.

"Truth is, it's pretty great here," I said. "If you want an escape from the frenzy of the city, you are always welcome for a weekend of swimming, lounging, smoking, and gossiping."

"Listen," she said, "I can't not see Lily any longer. Does she miss me?" We agreed that she would come the following Friday.

I spent the rest of the morning making phone calls. I also called my mother-in-law—I wanted to thank her for the gift that she sent me from Paris via Halimi. It was a beautiful copy of the *Roman de la Rose*, the romantic bestseller from the Middle Ages, handcrafted by master restorers of the time, which must have cost a lot of money. I did not know how to thank her properly for the magnificent gift, so I laughed and said that if we fell on hard times, I could always sell it to some enchanted collector. Simone giggled and then grew serious.

"So, how are you these days, my dear? Soli isn't driving you too crazy?" she asked quietly.

"No, not at all," I replied, my heart brimming. It's not every mother-in-law who would talk like that about her son. "He's amazing. Brought me another ancient coin from Paris. Phoenician, this time." I said, trying to lighten the conversation.

"Another coin, ah?" Simone said in French.

"Yes, because I so love the coin that you found at the beach. The Ibelin coin," I said meaningfully. "Tell me," I added, my heart pounding. "Who found it that day, you or Saul?"

"I pointed it out to him," said Simone, back to Hebrew. "And I also suggested that he have a piece of jewelry made for you from it." There was quiet for several seconds. And then she said, "I hope that it was worth it, my dear."

I nodded vigorously, then laughed, remembering she could not see me.

"Totally worth it," I said gratefully.

Afterward, I called my sister. I did not tell her, of course, of my supernatural adventures, but I told her that I thought I had an idea for a story, inspired by the mushrooms that I took that time with Halimi. Dina gave me a penetrating look, as much as a look could penetrate through Zoom.

"An idea for a story?" she asked. "About what?"

"I don't know exactly." I smiled at her pixelated image on the screen. "Something about the cyclical nature of life." My sister shook her head skeptically. Eva came into the room. She waved hi to me and exchanged a few words with Dina.

"It's not so much cyclical as it is a spiral," Dina said suddenly, and my gaze returned to the screen. Eva had left, and my sister lit herself a joint. "As in, it moves in circles, and you return to the same point, but on a different level," she added in a kind of reverie. I assumed this wasn't her first joint that morning.

"You always have to be smarter than me," I laughed. She laughed too. "I'll put that in the story," I said.

I looked up from the French manuscript I was translating and peeked at Halimi. He patted his knees; I set the papers down on the table and sat on his lap. He held me to him until I almost stopped breathing.

"Are you okay?" I asked into his chest. He hummed in contentment.

"You know," I kept talking into his chest, "a few days ago, I imagined Nina sneaking into your hotel room in Lisbon."

"Yeah, right," he snorted, but I felt his body tense. And then he hugged me again, hard. "I was a little worried that you might be paranoid with me traveling for *Free to Be*," he said. "But before I left, you were so calm and content."

"I am still calm and content, that's what's funny," I said and pulled away from him so I could look him in the eyes. "I didn't picture it angrily or sadly; it just came into my head with a kind of curiosity, and the thought even turned me on a little."

"You pervert," he said, shaking his head affectionately. Then he added, bringing his head closer to me, almost pleadingly, "But you really are happy now, right?"

"Right," I said, surprising myself. I put my head back on his chest. "That's all that matters," he said.

I sliced cherry tomatoes into two, diced a purple onion and cilantro, and cut into an avocado. I sprinkled some salt onto the salad and looked up at the horizon, at the sun rolling toward the sea. I ran through all the events of the past few months and wondered if I would have the courage to pass through my spring and if I would find Jean again. With a pinch of sorrow, I imagined him sitting beside the spring with his lute, composing melodies and waiting for me to appear. I reflected that the house where I lived stood on land that he bought, possibly for me.

Pigeons and sparrows circled in the sky outside my window, but the flock of flamingos had already left Atlit for their summer migration. Those winged, pink hallucinations continued north, but next year they would return, as they always had.

Since I was very young, I've struggled to rise in the morning. I always had such a hard time separating myself from the bed that at some stage I got into the habit of promising myself I'd return to it soon—for an afternoon or even a short morning nap. I knew that the promise was absurd even as I said it to myself, but still it worked. Sometimes, I was even able to make good on it, but that was not the point. The fact of the promise, this tiny, open channel for the possibility that my soft sheets would soon envelop my body and me in dreams again, gave me the strength to rise and to deal with reality and its incessant demands.

It was in such a mood that I now stared at the sunset, turning the horizon pink. I was happy and did not want some other life. But I knew that sooner or later, my soul would cloud over with something or another. Some problem with Lily, some oppressive translation project, or exurban life. And Halimi . . . that man of habit. Something deep between us had changed for the better, but sooner or later, his usual habits might frustrate me again.

I narrowed my eyes at the golden patches that mottled the ruins of the Atlit fortress, the ruins that still awaited me at the well-guarded base. My spring still awaited me beneath the ancient carob in that magical and narrow passage, that book-sized puddle, and if I only wanted, I could dip in my coin and pass into another time.

The sun set, and the specks of gold dissipated into the shadows. I poured olive oil on the salad, took the bread from the toaster, and went out to the yard. Lily and Halimi were sitting in the fork of the Persian lilac tree, sorting leaves.

"Dinner is ready," I said quietly.

ACKNOWLEDGMENTS

To Dr. Navit Barel, who believed in a partial, unpolished manuscript and carried it all the way to publication in Hebrew.

To Deborah Harris and everyone at the Deborah Harris agency—especially Hadar Makov-Hasson and Rena Bunder Rossner—for their faith, guidance, and generous help.

To my translators, Joanna Chen and Zoe Jordan, for bringing this book to life again in English—with exquisite attention to nuance, and to its wild shifts in register, time, and tone.

To Jessica Kasmer-Jacobs, for her tireless commitment and her loving, meticulous edit.

To the entire team at Union Square & Co.: project editor Alison Skrabek, cover designer Claire Sullivan, interior designer Rich Hazelton, art director Patrick Sullivan, production manager Sandy Noman, and especially executive editor Barbara Berger, for her sharp eye and devoted care.

To Dr. Vardit Ruth Shotten Hallel and Yigal Liverant, for their generous help with the historical research—even when one reads dozens of primary sources and scholarly works, there is nothing like deep conversations with generous scholars who share their vast knowledge with such grace.

To my friends Ruth Rosenthal, Yael Elbaz, and Moshe Gilad, for their good-hearted early readings and their sharp, insightful comments.

To my brother, Ezra Glozman, for his steady support of every choice and endeavor in my life.

To my beloved parents, Vladimir and Irene Glozman—no words can capture all that you have given me. Thank you for nurturing in me a love of the written word, and to my mother in particular, for sparking my fascination with the past—especially with the Middle Ages—and for one unforgettable afternoon at the Aqua Bella ruins near Jerusalem, when she told me of a Crusader princess yearning for her homeland in the Holy Land, and opened my eyes to a new, wider way of seeing the place I call home.

To my children, Talia and Matti, who patiently endured the years when I could talk about nothing but the Kingdom of Jerusalem, while I disappeared for hours at the keyboard and emerged glassy-eyed, unsure what century it was.

And above all, to Yonatan Zur, the love of my life—for endless support, spiritual partnership, inspiration for a kind-hearted Crusader nobleman, and for keeping the fire burning—in the kitchen, and in the heart.

TOPICS AND QUESTIONS FOR DISCUSSION

1. Idit's life oscillates between the rituals of home (motherhood, routine, chores) and the allure of the unknown (love, danger, history, magic). What does the novel suggest about the tension between emotional safety and thrill?

2. The novel sets up a subtle interplay between Idit's realistic, personal memories (especially those tied to Halimi) and the medieval past she enters. How do these two forms of "past" echo, challenge, or reshape each other?

3. Ruins appear throughout the novel—ancient ones and emotional ones. How does the story explore the way memories, personal and historical, become fixed or fossilized over time?

4. What role does fantasy—romantic, erotic, historical, and literary—play in Idit's relationship with Halimi and Jean? How do these forms of longing and imagination interact with one another?

5. Early in the novel, a friend describes Halimi as "momentary fantasy." How does the evolution of Idit's relationship with Halimi reflect the tension between romantic fantasy and the limits of real life?

6. What does Halimi represent in contrast to Jean? How does Idit's magical connection with Jean—shaped by chivalric love ideals—expand or complicate her understanding of desire, love, and responsibility?

7. How does the novel use time travel not only as a plot device but as a way to explore memory, imagination, and human connection?

8. Time travel in the novel creates a kind of extraterritorial space— outside the rules of ordinary time, morality, and belonging. How does this "off-map" space echo the emotional and ethical boundaries that nonmonogamous relationships can open or challenge?

9. Both timelines depict women navigating constraint, desire, and expectation. How do the medieval women and the contemporary women mirror or challenge one another? Where do you see continuity—and where rupture?

10. Both the time-slip and the love stories in the novel unfold in spaces that resist ownership—geographical, temporal, or romantic. What does the novel suggest about freedom and responsibility when love itself becomes a form of border crossing?

ABOUT THE AUTHOR

MASHA ZUR-GLOZMAN is a writer, filmmaker, graphic designer, and journalist based in Tel Aviv. She is the visual editor for Israeli newspaper *Haaretz*'s website, after writing and editing for their cultural supplement for a decade. Zur-Glozman was also a book critic for more than fifteen years for *Haaretz* and various Israeli newspapers. This novel, her debut, won the Israeli Geffen prize of speculative fiction in 2020 and the Ministry of Culture prize for debuts. With her husband, Yonatan, Zur-Glozman produced two documentary films: *Amos Oz: The Nature of Dreams* and *Magia Russica*, which were screened in multiple festivals around the globe and broadcasted internationally.

RAISING READERS
Books Build Bright Futures

Thank you for reading this book and for being a reader of books in general. We are so grateful to share being part of a community of readers with you, and we hope you will join us in passing our love of books on to the next generation of readers.

Did you know that reading for enjoyment is the single biggest predictor of a child's future happiness and success?

More than family circumstances, parents' educational background, or income, reading impacts a child's future academic performance, emotional well-being, communication skills, economic security, ambition, and happiness.

Studies show that kids reading for enjoyment in the US is in rapid decline:

- In 2012, 53% of 9-year-olds read almost every day. Just 10 years later, in 2022, the number had fallen to 39%.
- In 2012, 27% of 13-year-olds read for fun daily. By 2023, that number was just 14%.

Together, we can commit to **Raising Readers** and change this trend. How?

- Read to children in your life daily.
- Model reading as a fun activity.
- Reduce screen time.
- Start a family, school, or community book club.
- Visit bookstores and libraries regularly.
- Listen to audiobooks.
- Read the book before you see the movie.
- Encourage your child to read aloud to a pet or stuffed animal.
- Give books as gifts.
- Donate books to families and communities in need.

BOB1217

Books build bright futures, and **Raising Readers** is our shared responsibility.

For more information, visit **JoinRaisingReaders.com**

Sources: National Endowment for the Arts, National Assessment of Educational Progress, WorldBookDay.com, Nielsen BookData's 2023 "Understanding the Children's Book Consumer"